HARD DROP

B.R. KEID

CHAPTER
ONE

BLOCK CAPTAIN HESPER'S drill cadence pounded off the steep granite cliffs outside, marking time into Kaffy's last few seconds of sleep. Up top, the soft, uneven purr of Sammy's dozing was almost soothing compared to the clamor outside. How the dummy slept through it, she'd never know. He better enjoy it while he could. He'd make his gamma level soon enough, then the posters would talk him into signing up.

Be a real hero, Tellie Strong demanded in bold print, dressed in her CDF-issued white and gray uniform on the fading poster plastered above her. The stormy peak of Mount Dodecoron filled the poster's background. *Mind your parents. Help your neighbors. Join the Youth Block Drill today. For humanity!*

The problem with real heroes was they never came home—not for level exams, not for Founding Day, not even when Mother cried at night.

They didn't get to sleep in either. Little rebellions, Mother called mornings like this.

Hard prints of her and Father kept the poster's curled edges from peeling further. They were old, taken back when she was littler. She looked so happy in them, just a little beta and her proud father. No block drill. No Sammy—not yet, anyway. Mother seemed happier then, too. Before he moved them all to Diacad Cliffs and left home again.

Well, she didn't much like the poster anymore. Nobody mentioned the block captains kept score. Or that enough demerits would get you the lash. But the old prints might tear if she moved them. They were priceless, no matter how angry they sometimes made her. Mostly, they just made her sad. A faraway dream that got harder and harder to remember. She'd rather stay here and forget the world outside. Hear the reassuring sounds of Sammy's snoring. Daydream about growing up strong and pretty, just like Tellie. And to remember the way things used to be.

Ms. Strong's lingering stare annoyed her, but not enough to get up. Block drill had already started, and she was late again. One more mark and it would be her turn for the lash. Duray and Nemor would love to see that. Then she'd have to listen to Hesper and Mother go on about what it means to be a proper Aegian. Again.

The rapid open and close of the hab's front door rattled through the metal floor. For a split-second, Aegia's howling storm winds forced their way inside. At least that meant a good air day. Block drill was hard enough when oxygen levels were in range.

"Momma's home," Sammy whispered, throat rattling.

"Granite's crack, you scared me!"

"Sorry."

She'd missed him waking up. Hard to do with his sleepy little wheezing sounds—sounds that meant he was still breathing. That long ago night he had stopped was burned into her brain. The scary rush to the clinic. The medicine that helped him breathe the mountain air. The first time she saw Mother cry. Really cry. Twelfth, what she wouldn't give for just one more minute with him. One more minute to remember the important stuff. But not today. Not ever. She was growing up.

"It's okay." She pulled a fresh jumpsuit off the wall and crawled inside, the magnetic zipper clicking closed along her midline. A quick swish of mouthwash from the sink and it was time to face Mother.

A narrow hall led to the common room, where Mother waited, fists pressed against hips, her neon orange coveralls stained black and smelling like hot metal. A rebreather dangled from her belt, the visor dotted with condensation.

Mother slammed a fistful of field paste onto the stone counter. "Kaffereine Aiolita Br—"

"I *know*, Mother." Even with her back turned, she could feel Mother's gaze boring into her like a rock beam. The front door slid open when she lingered too close, and Dodecoron greeted her with another gust of storm winds.

"Your father—"

Mother's words disappeared amid the sudden gale. Even Block Captain Hesper's drill cadence faded. It didn't matter what either of them said. She was in big trouble either way. It was like Father told her: your mountains never got any smaller. Up and over was the only way.

The door cycled closed, and Mother's voice came back. "Kaffy? I said your father's coming home today on leave."

Today. The word stuck inside her head. It had been six orbits since he'd been home—half as long as she'd been alive. She was still just a beta when they'd taken those prints, when he'd come home to tell her he'd re-enlisted. Again. *There's bad guys in the Cradle, Kaff,* he'd said, a muscly arm tight around her shoulder as she bawled into his chest. *Gotta stop 'em out there so they can't follow us home.*

The next day, he was gone. She'd sat atop their new hab block roof for hours, the Diacad Cliffs at her back, watching orbital shuttles leave the spaceport through scratchy red eyes. Time seemed to stop after that. In her head, it felt like forever ago. In her heart, she was still sitting up there, waving goodbye.

"Today?" Father… coming home. It didn't seem real.

"That's what I said." Mother's glare softened, but only a little. "My unit's been ordered to muster positions, so I need you to get our lots. And make sure your room is clean before he gets home."

Mind your parents, Tellie Strong sang in the back of her mind, just like on the net feeds in the allotment center, hitching a thumb's up while tossing back her long blue hair. But who cared about lots and chores when Father was finally coming home? She wanted to be there when his boots touched Her mountain, not stuck in some stupid line watching the minutes crawl by.

"When?" There were four transports per hour, six hours round-trip to Aegia Prime. Except the expeds usually docked at Two-Gamma, so maybe just five hours depending on what ship he came in on. "If we could get to Ring Two by thirteen-hundred, we can watch his transport land!"

"Are you listening, girl?" Mother snapped, her voice going thin and scratchy like it always did when she'd been up too long. "I've been called up. It's probably just a muster drill, but Twelfth help me, that means you have to take care of things until I'm relieved."

Stupid Planetary Reserve and their stupid training exercises. "Father's finally coming home, and I'm stuck getting lots?"

"You want your father to eat, don't you?"

"Yes, Mother. Thank you, Mother." Kaffy stiffened, a half-hearted stand-at-attention, smile all teeth and no curl.

She reached into the nook carved into the granite doorway. The little reliquary felt cool, just like the tiny figurine of the Twelfth's likeness inside. Father had said the Twelfth would always bring him home to her. That Marines held a special place in Her heart. It had to be true. He was coming home *today*.

She pocketed the little metal god. "And thank you, Holy Mother."

"Hurry up, Kaffy," Mother called from her bedroom. "It's oh-seven-hundred. That line isn't getting any shorter."

"Aye, ma'am!"

The door opened and a wall of cold air met her, smelling of granite and cliff runoff. Like home. Like Father. She breathed deep. Perfect ranges, definitely a good air day. But Father taught her to always have a rebreather: *If the storm ever clears, even for a minute, it's like breathing rock.* No rain, thank the Twelfth, but plenty of wind and thunder. Familiar storm clouds roiled in the sky above. The gray billowing mass always seemed close enough to touch. It reminded her of boiling water, or mating rock snakes. A wall of gray that hid all of Aegia from the bad guys Father talked about.

The Diacad Cliffs rose for a hundred meters behind the hab block. Carved out of Dodecoron's granite skin, they were four kilometers downslope from the summit where the air was mostly breathable. Any higher, and it was too thin. Below the downslope mines, and it was too thick.

Kaffy turned downslope from the cliffs, away from the sound of Block Captain Hesper's drill call. She smiled at the thought of those idiot boys sweating their brains out, until she remembered the number of marks she had. Hesper's lash would hurt worse than a dozen training circuits. But the thought of disappointing Father stung the most. Maybe she should go back and take her licks. Get it over with before Father even landed. But she was already going to be in line all morning, maybe longer. Sometimes the allotment centers ran out. Get whipped *and* go hungry? No, thank you.

The narrow side street opened onto a wide transit lane joining the settlements of Diacad Cliffs and Corongaet to the capital's industrial rings and busy urban center. More than a kilometer downslope, Vestebrae shone pale amber beneath the storm clouds. Holoprojected traffic signals directed transit cars and heavy cargo sleds along the straight thoroughfare down the mountain.

Retro rocket plumes flashed above the distant spaceport as another shuttle descended through the heavy cloud layer.

Kaffy began to jog, her boots pounding against the granite walkway. Proper Aegians didn't slow down for anything. And Father might be on that very transport, just hours away from thirty days together with her.

The allotment center rose above Diacad's administrative blocks, a thin, blank tower of concrete and steel connected to a massive quonset warehouse. Near the edge of the complex, a white flag whipped atop a long pole. In its center was a stylized black vortex with three silver rings. One for each of the Three Colonies, clustered in the vortex's heart.

A line of colonists snaked from the warehouse's open bay doors, through the center gates, then disappeared around the next street corner. Kaffy let out a sigh. It was going to take all day. She'd do it though, a hundred times over. Father was coming home, and he knew how to cook. The thought of hot, crispy vat rats made her mouth water. Her stomach let out a hopeful gurgle.

She walked along the fence, fingers catching on the metal links as she made her way to the back of the line. The tiny statuette warmed in her grip, her thumb tracing its well-worn edges, filling her heart with more thanks.

Madam Ulwin peeked her wrinkled nose around an off-duty Navy officer. "Lady Kaffereine, is that you?"

She'd always called Kaffy Lady Kaffereine, something about her old-timey name. It was embarrassing, but Father insisted Kaffy mind her elders. *Help your neighbors*, Tellie would say.

"Madam Ulwin." Kaffy's chin dipped toward her chest, eyes fixed on the officer's collar. One, two silver pips—a lieutenant, then. Better look at Madam Ulwin before he noticed her staring.

"Come here, good child." She waved Kaffy closer with thin, knobby fingers. "Keep an old woman company on such a beautiful day."

"Yes, ma'am." She fell in line next to Madam Ulwin, ignoring the angry glares of those still stuck in line behind her. The old boulder probably saved her two, maybe three hours.

"Where's your mother?" Madam Ulwin said.

"She worked a double at the shipyard. Now it's PR muster."

"And here you are, fetching lots. Such a good child." Madam Ulwin's grip on Kaffy's shoulder was surprisingly strong.

"How are you, Madam Ulwin?"

"Hungry and cold." The old woman snorted and tugged at the young officer's elbow. "Trying to talk this fine young man into taking me home."

"Ma'am." The lieutenant smiled bashfully. He nodded at Kaffy. "Little ma'am."

He was handsome. Far too young for Madam Ulwin. Talk about rock snakes. And Kaffy was far too young for him. She was five orbits away from her eps levels, and all the boys her age were idiots anyway. Still, she smiled and nodded as the young officer turned back around. Making eyes at a Navy skeeg. What would Father think about that?

"Any word from your father?" Madam Ulwin asked, her eyes lingering on the lieutenant.

"Oh, yes!" Kaffy caught herself too late, her voice loud in the relative quiet of early morning. "He's coming home today. Thirty days leave!"

"Your father." Madam Ulwin grinned, showing pale yellow teeth. "Now there's a proper Aegian."

Eeew, gross. Father was handsome, she guessed, but only in that fatherly way. Not in the rock snakes way. The old boulder had a one-track mind.

Madam Ulwin nudged Kaffy forward, chuckling softly. "I'm only teasing, good girl. You should see your face. Red as Respitian sand."

"When did you ever see Respitia?"

"Never saw it myself, mind you, but my Trevor had been, several times."

"Really?" She didn't know anyone who'd ever been to the other colonies before. Not even Father. High orbit, of course. The patrol lanes, definitely. But Respitia and Vestia? They always seemed so far away, like they could be make believe.

"He captained a cargo hauler." Madam Ulwin raised a finger skyward.

"I thought ship captains were rich?"

"Most are. Twelfth keep him, my Trevor wasn't a particularly good one. Lost no more."

"Lost no more." Maybe it wasn't being a ship's captain, but Master Ulwin must've been good at something to keep a woman like Madam Ulwin.

"Kaffereine Bresto!"

The deep bass of Block Captain Hesper's voice ripped through the solemn moment. The big man stood there, as tall and wide as Dodecoron, sweat ringing his jumpsuit collar. Duray stood there too, rail thin next to their block captain. He clasped Training Block E-10's guidon firmly against his shoulder, the tiny red flag at its tip trembling in the storm winds. Nemor appeared seconds later, still huffing and puffing from drill practice. Together, they stared at her, grinning their mean disapproval.

"Missed you again today, Bresto," Duray spat.

"Yeah." Nemor held up three fingers. "You know what that means."

"At ease, boys." The coiled leather dangled ominously from Hester's utility belt. "Lots are important, aren't they, Bresto?"

"Yes, sir." She was so dead.

"We'll get the matter of your attendance sorted out tomorrow, won't we?"

"Yes, sir." Really, really dead. Hesper was going to whip her in the morning. Probably in front of Father, who would probably whip her again. Sergeant Ned Bresto might be her father, but Madam Ulwin spoke the truth: he was a proper Aegian.

Tears pricked at her eyes, but she refused to blink. Those idiot boys couldn't stop giggling and shoving each other, making it all a thousand times worse.

A low moan echoed in the sky above them. The sound grew louder, no longer a moan but a sad, lonely wail. The sound stabbed into her ears from the pole-mounted sirens overhead. Kaffy covered her ears, no matter what the boys would say. Stupid alarms. Stupid Planetary Reserve training. Stupid girl skipping her block drills. The Twelfth was probably getting her back for sleeping in the last two days. For not doing her best to be a proper Aegian.

She dropped her hands between blares and wiped the tears from her eyes. She'd show Hesper and those idiot boys. She'd take her licks like a woman, like Tellie Strong, like the Twelfth Herself, like—

Hesper stood motionless, his big dumb mouth open, and the color drained from his face, gawking up at the black and gray sky.

A heavy, distant thump shook the ground.

Then another, like Mount Dodecoron itself was trembling. She whirled, heart racing.

Smoke rose like a pillar above the lights of Vestebrae. More retro rockets burned to life above the spaceport, but they were firing in all directions—too fast and out of control. The transports weren't landing. They were crashing.

The scream that tore from the back of her throat made no sound over the sirens. All she could see, could feel, was Father dying in a fiery crash just hours from being united with his family. With her, his daughter, his Kaff. For thirty priceless days. A prayer formed, silent on her lips, and she pressed two fingers to her heart—*tap tap*—just like Mother taught her. *Please don't let it be him. Please let Father be safe.*

A firm hand caught her wrist. She jumped and pulled away, but it was the lieutenant beside her now—not Hesper. His deep brown eyes bore into her, but his voice barely broke through the sirens. "That's the civil alarm. We need to get to a shelter. Now."

CHAPTER
TWO

THE TACTICAL PLOT above the planning table swelled with red contacts. Sergeant Ned Bresto gripped the arms of his jump seat as the tiny blue dot labeled CDNS *Gauntlet* tried to outrun multiple raider craft pinging its six on the holoprojected display. Around the table, company-grade officers and NCOs sat shoulder to shoulder, white-knuckling their way through the transport's rapid acceleration.

The ops deck wasn't built for this many bodies. Sweat and uniform starch turned the air into a humid mess. It reeked of tension wrapped in crisp white-and-grays. Fresh faces and clean uniforms. None of them looked ready for what was coming.

Except Kull. She sat across from him, blonde hair cut chin-length to a militant edge, spine straight despite the crushing acceleration. Her mouth made a hard line as she tracked the incoming contacts. The gold and silver on her collar marked her as a major, but seeing her next to the others, it was clear: she was cut from different stone. A proper Aegian.

The tactical plot screamed warnings as new contacts streamed from the Identify-Friend-or-Foe tac net feeds. Multiple raider destroyers, their predicted firing solutions tracking the orbital station designated *Three-Alpha*. Dozens of corvettes and strike fighters swarmed the larger ships in undisciplined escort patterns.

Something about this attack felt different. Too many squids in one place. Too organized. Raiders kept to the edges of colonial space, picking off supply flights that strayed too far from the patrol lanes. Never had the sacs for a stand-up fight. A large orb flashed red and blue, just thirty thousand meters from Three-Alpha. The confused IFF feed read CDNS *Gerrund Halsey,* one of only two heavy cruisers in the entire Colonial Defense Forces fleet. But that didn't make sense, since incoming tac net data showed its rail guns hammering the Three-Alpha and any friendly ships that came in range.

He'd seen the ship up close back on the orbital. This wasn't a friendly fire situation, or a repeat of the Golden Age coup. This was much worse. The Concordat, humanity's archenemy, had done something to the *Halsey,* turned it against its own. How, he didn't know. But he'd seen enough to hope, Twelfth willing, there wasn't a single living soul left aboard.

Another large orb, colored a bright red dead, pulsed at the forward edge of the raider swarm. IFF returns flashed *NO KNOWN MATCH,* instead coloring and sizing the ship's icon based on tonnage and threat estimates. Bresto closed his eyes—a Concordat forge ship. There was no icon big enough, no color dangerous enough, to reflect the threat that thing posed. He'd been inside it. Fought the archenemy's terrible machines and barely made it out alive. He'd seen the truth with his own eyes. Ships like that had scoured Dead Earth centuries ago, killing that precious blue world and leaving the remnants of humanity clinging to survival inside the Cradle Nebula. A survival that, until two weeks ago, had seemed basically guaranteed. And its presence here, now, left no question that his last mission was a complete failure.

"Hold! On!" Runt's broken colonial standard rumbled over the ops deck's PA.

A burst of thrust gravity pinned Bresto to his seat. The *Gauntlet's* vector line pitched hard to port on the holoproj, responding to some danger only Runt could see. She was a damn good pilot. If there was a way through, she'd find it. If not, this was going to be a short flight.

Another blue orb winked out—CDNS *Incandescent.* A rapidly expanding white orb replaced it, warning that the blast radius of its reactor death was just seconds away from the their position. The entire ship shuddered. Lights and screens flickered from the electromagnetic interference riding the wave of charged particles. It felt as if the Twelfth Herself had reached out and shook the *Gauntlet* like a child's plaything.

"Shit," Kull said, more of a statement of fact than anything. "Remind me to thank our pilot."

"Runt's the best, ma'am. This damned ship… not so much."

"The lupanthae are bred for the void," she said. "Amazing what natural selection will do when your entire species exists on a few dozen starships."

"Ma'am."

Her eyes moved over the display floating above the table. She reached out a hand, then paused. "May I?"

She was the ranking officer. It wasn't up to him. "It's your ship, ma'am."

"A technicality." The display reacted to her touch, rotating as she flicked the edges of the holoproj's field with her fingers. "Where is Lieutenant Park, anyway?"

He thumbed the nub of his left ring finger through his glove, a nervous tic he'd picked up years back. Details of the mission with Park were classified. Not even an executive officer like Kull would have the red-level clearance needed for them. There'd been a tribunal back aboard Three-Alpha. Lots of flag officers. Even a councilman. And that was before the Concordat followed them home. He had enough trouble to deal with.

"Do you know where your CO is, Sergeant?" she repeated.

"Classified, ma'am." *The Twelfth does not hold in Her hand liars and cheats,* went the old refrain. But he hadn't lied, not really. Just because he didn't know where Park was, didn't mean the lieutenant's location wasn't a secret.

She centered the holoproj on the blue glow of a flat disc labeled *Orbital Two-Gamma.* Dozens more blue orbs, tiny next to the massive orbital, clung to the edges of the disc. One labeled CDNS *Victory* began to flash when she tapped it.

"There she is." Her smile was real and dangerous. She tapped the communicator on her wrist. "Colonel Reede, this is Major Kull."

Silence fell over the ops deck as the tac nets routed Kull's transmission. IFF feeds and ship schematics flickered to life beside the *Victory's* tiny blue avatar. She was an exped, an expeditionary transport, built to ferry six exo-reinforced companies of Marines almost anywhere in the Three Colonies in under three standard days. Except Vestia. That backwater was more than a tenday away even on the fastest light chasers.

The transmission chirped an acknowledgment. *"Reede here. Sitrep, Major."*

"En route from Three-Alpha, sir. ETA is fifteen minutes, if the raiders don't fuck us on the way."

"Copy." Reede's gravelly voice faded between squalls of static. *"What's going on out there? Tac nets are backed up, and what I am getting is a little hard to believe."*

"Believe it, Skipper. We've got a genuine Concordat ship in high orbit, making an end run for Aegia." There was a hint of something primal in Kull's stare, deeper than fear, then gone in a blink. "CDF forces have engaged the Lost at Three-Alpha."

"Holy Mother." The transmission went silent. A few seconds later, *"Solid copy, Major. Any good news?"*

"I liberated your command staff from the O-Club." Another round of forced laughter made its way through the officers around her. "Not to mention some wayward Marines in need of more enemies to kill."

A grizzled first sergeant, according to the mass of black pips on his collar, wrinkled his permanent frown in an approving nod.

"And it's a good thing," Kull went on. "I guarantee we're not the only ones with personnel stuck planetside right now."

"Not for long," Reede said. *"As soon as we clear our moorings, we're burning hard for low orbit."*

"What's the mission, sir?"

"Vestebrae." The word buzzed through the choppy interference. *"We're to reinforce Planetary Reserve efforts to prepare for a possible assault on the capital."*

Heat rose in Bresto's core, like a lava vent ready to explode. His family was down there. Lyra, Sammy, and Kaff. Their home was maybe three clicks from Aegia's capital settlement. Lyra had a commission in the PR, one of many luxuries the reserves gave to former

Marines. If she was being mustered, that meant their children would be with their block captain down in the shelters. He counted—one, two, three, deep breath. The Holy Mother would keep them safe. Just like She had always done for Her people, from Dead Earth to the Cradle. Yes, they'd be safe. Even if his orders took him somewhere else.

"Transmitting mission packet now. Twelfth keep you, Major."

"Don't worry, sir. We'll be there in plenty of time to dress for the ball. Kull out." She pulled a datapad from her shoulder bag and studied it. "I guess the tac nets really are jammed. Shouldn't be possible on quantum data freqs."

Humanity didn't invent any of this tech. They took it from the Concordat and made it their own centuries ago. "They can definitely do that, ma'am."

"Just great. One more thing to add to the list." She sighed, and her datapad chimed again. She swiped it with a lazy finger. "Huh. An alert bulletin from the Autonomous Weapons Division."

Bresto's pulse kicked up a notch. A Division alert could mean anything—new combat drone deployments, tactical updates. But his conscience wasn't exactly clean where the Division was concerned. The memory of breaking Sevvers out of their brig back on Three-Alpha still felt fresh, the alarms still ringing in his ears. He'd known there would be consequences. He'd laid hands on CDF personnel. So had the Marines with him—Myers, Olsom, and the twins. With the Concordat ship bearing down and raiders swarming Aegia Prime, the Division should have bigger problems than one missing specialist and the Marines who'd helped him. Or maybe that's exactly what the alert was about.

Hard to tell which way the hammer would fall in the middle of an invasion. He'd done what he was ordered to do. If Sevvers had been right about what they'd found at Cradle's edge, the CDF needed every veteran they had—even the troublemakers.

A lieutenant two seats down laughed. "Twelfth-damned bot jockeys. Where the hell are they now? So much for the future of colonial defense."

The first sergeant at the edge of the group cleared his throat, somehow looking meaner than before.

"Don't take it personally, First Sergeant," the lieutenant went on. "I'm just saying, the Alexander Lehman is parked in high orbit barely three hundred thousand clicks out and there's not a single drone in the battlespace."

There was something unholy about what it took to be a bot jockey —circuitry in their brains and all. But he'd fought with Sevvers back aboard that forge ship. The kid was a clever skeeg. He'd done the impossible. Bresto hadn't liked leaving him back on Three-Alpha, but Kull outranked him and needed a ride.

Most Marines had no love for the Division. Bresto didn't either, but his perspective had… evolved. "They'll be here."

"You don't say, Sergeant." Kull's tone took on a frosty edge. She slid the datapad across the table.

His own face appeared on the screen, right next to the face of Kerry Sevvers. Large block text scrolled beneath the images in caution yellow.

MASTER SPECIALIST KERRY SEVVERS: WANTED FOR THE UNSANCTIONED USE OF DIVISION COMBAT INTELLIGENCES. SERGEANT NED BRESTO: WANTED IN CONNECTION TO THE ESCAPE OF KERRY SEVVERS FROM DIVISION CUSTODY.

Well, shit.

A dull thunk rattled the table. Kull's hand rested on a CP-6 standard-issue blaster pistol, the matte black barrel angled toward him, finger flat against the trigger guard. "I'm waiting, Sergeant."

He met her glare. This wasn't an empty threat. At least the Division hadn't named the others in their little bulletin. The boots were in the *Gauntlet's* cargo bay with the other Marines, had acted on his orders, and Kull didn't seem above spacing all of them on her way back to the *Victory*.

The lie stuck in his throat, but only for a second. "Classified, ma'am."

"Cridshit." The pistol's capacitor whined as Kull flicked the safety off. "There's a war on, and I don't have time to drag you back to Division HQ."

"Sevvers reports to Lieutenant Park, same as me," Bresto said. "Suggest you take it up with our CO. Ma'am."

Kull's gaze narrowed, her finger reaching for the trigger. "You expect me to believe you had lawful orders to break some skeeg out of a Division brig?"

"I damn well did."

The mouthy lieutenant jerked a pistol from his holster and leveled it unceremoniously at Bresto's face.

"That skeeg's the only reason Park and I are still breathing," Bresto said. There was a nervous energy in the lieutenant's eyes. He wouldn't shoot.

Kull would.

The hint of a smile lifted the corner of her mouth. "That might be the first true thing you've said in the last five minutes, Sergeant—"

Klaxons roared to life, their frantic tone piercing in the small ops deck. Running lights in the bulkheads switched to danger red, pulsing in time with the bleating alarms. The strategic display rotated on its own, tracking the *Gauntlet's* current location. Raider fighters appeared at the edge of the globe, three smaller points of light closing fast, their firing solutions tracking.

A long, melancholy chord erupted over the PA. Runt's warning call. This was going to be close.

"That's wolf-speak for tuck it in," Bresto growled. "You want to finish this now, ma'am?"

"You watch your mouth." The lieutenant motioned with his pistol as if Bresto had forgotten it was there.

Kull lifted a hand and waved for the lieutenant to holster his sidearm. He did so, his angry stare locked as he thumbed the holster strap closed. The major did the same, pausing to safety her weapon. The capacitor discharge sounded almost disappointed.

At least Kull had her priorities straight. "Later, then, after the war, ma'am?"

She leaned back in her chair and tightened her straps. "As you say, Sergeant. Later."

"Aye, ma'am."

More alarms buzzed from the holoproj. The raider fighters' weapons vectors began flashing rapidly.

He brought his wrist comms to his lips. "Myers, you copy?"

The connection was instantaneous. *"Yes, Sarnt?"*

"You tell those trigger pullers back there to buckle up. We've got incoming."

PFC LARKE OLSOM couldn't breathe. The G-forces crushed down and held her there while the *Gauntlet's* engines shrieked to redline, every panel on the old scow ready to shake loose. When the ship's aux grav finally compensated—weak as it was—something deep inside her relaxed its grip, and she could breathe again.

The other Marines from Three-Alpha weren't doing much better, their bodies crushed against fold-out jumpseats that lined the bulkheads. Fresh sweat and blood filled the cargo bay, their victory for retaking Three-Alpha's hangar decks carried in that copper smell. They'd won that fight. Got those crews back to their ships. But winning didn't mean safe. Not out here.

The Rikko twins breathed together beside her, like someone had copied and pasted the same Marine. CDF body mods or not, their spacer-thin frames weren't built for this kind of beating. One standard G turned their faces to wrinkled leather. Made 'em look like someone's grampa. Hard to think of them as Marine material at all, but they'd proven that wrong back on Three-Alpha.

Doc Myers took up the space on her right, muttering into his wrist comms like this was all routine. Lance Corporal, sure, but he'd told her to call him Doc about thirty seconds after they'd met. Thirty-one seconds before he'd tried that smile on her. Founders, it was a good smile. But his charm disappeared when the shooting started, replaced by something far more interesting. Not that she was going to tell him that.

Not four hours ago, they'd helped Sergeant Bresto bust some chip-brained bot jockey out of Division custody with these three watching her back. For once, someone had actually asked for her help instead of just taking what they wanted. Funny how that made her want to prove Bresto right about her.

Some start to her Marine career. Not the kind of stuff they put in the recruiting feeds. But they'd clicked somehow, the four of them. Maybe it was the shared crime, or just the way combat changed things. Not that it mattered now. The Concordat had crashed their little party, and she wasn't going to be choosy about new friends while trying to stay alive.

"Sarnt says we have incoming." Even Doc couldn't make that sound good.

"Ain't that just great," she said.

He pulled a multi-tool from his combat engineer kit and probed a maintenance panel nestled among the duraplate tiles at his feet.

"What're you doing?" she asked.

"Wait one." The panel popped open, revealing rows of fine multi-colored wire joined in the center by a small, flat junction. Doc traded the multi-tool for a field terminal and threaded a cable from the terminal to the junction. "I'm going to peek at whatever's chasing us. Beats just sitting here waiting for something bad to happen."

"I thought combat engineers fixed metal and meat?" she asked. "What the hell do you know about ship systems?"

"A good combat engineer knows his way around any system: mechanical, informational, biological." His datapad filled with red block warnings. "Damn. This ship is old. Last maintenance update was thirty-two standard orbits ago. Might as well be speaking squid."

"Aren't all CDF ships old?"

"Most. Not all," the Rikkos said together in their weird, coordinated way.

"The big ones take decades to build, so they have to last," Doc said. Shapes on the screen assembled like digital building blocks beneath his fingers. "But maintenance updates are an annual thing. Someone dug this boat out of mothball recently."

The last of the building blocks fell into place, and the terminal let out an affirmative two-tone chirp.

"There it is. Bringing up sensors and IFF feeds… now."

A flat, 2D image hovered just above the display, a rough outline of the *Gauntlet* at its center—with its angular, arrow-shaped hull, stub wings, and long tail boom. Three dots glowed red just outside their predicted weapons range.

Doc frowned. "Three bogeys at our one-eight-zero."

"Looks like raider strike craft," she said. Their appearance on the plot sent her pulse rate climbing.

"Not bad for a boot-ass Marine straight off the parade deck. Someone was paying attention during threat ID training."

"Could be worse, right?" Probably not, but maybe Doc felt different.

"It's not good," he grumbled. "Squids may be shit engineers, but they're dangerous in numbers. Besides, boats this small don't have any shields, and squid lasers have bite."

Tlan "Smokes" Rikko did his usual thing, cigarette hanging loose from his lips while he talked. "How long to—"

"—the next orbital?" And there was Vlan, right on cue. Those two took weird to a whole other level, finishing each other's thoughts like that.

Doc swiped the threat feed away and called up the nav plot. "At a hundred KPS relative, about ten minutes, give or take."

Olsom settled back, swallowing the tightness in her throat. That was a long time with raiders on their ass.

The transport's sub-light engines fired again, the brief punch of high-Gs softened by the aux grav seconds later. A series of alarm tones rang from the terminal as the threat feed reappeared.

"Aw, Twelfth! More raider fighters inbound, tracking on two-eight-zero." Doc gripped the terminal under one arm and pulled his harness tight with the other. "Squids caught us in a pincer. They've got—"

Laser impacts drilled fast and sharp against the outer hull plates above. Combat lighting switched from bad to worse, turning everything red dead. Olsom braced hard. Whatever came next was going to hurt. The howl over the PA vibrated in her bones.

"Uh, we've got a problem," Doc said.

"No shit!"

"Not them. I'm seeing thermal warnings in junction 1-6-Bronze-8."

Combat lighting made everything blood-dark, but there was no mistaking that smell. Metal getting hot enough to kill.

Olsom's harness clicked free and she launched from her seat. Every ship carried fire suppression gear, even a rust bucket like this. She'd find it. Had to find it.

"What the hell are you doing?" Doc shouted. "We're still evasive!"

The smell had her now, all memory and teeth. Ma used to say there was a wild thing in her, something that knew when to run and when to fight. That maybe it liked the fight a little too much. Right now, that wild thing was screaming about the smell of hot metal.

"Ain't dying in a fire, Doc." She was already scanning the bulkheads. Somewhere. Had to be somewhere.

"One more grav delay and you're a stain on the bulkhead!"

"Didn't know you cared." Focus, girl. Basic training had drilled ship layout into her head until she dreamed about it. Emergency gear always followed a pattern, if you knew where to look. And there it was, four seats down, red against gray. The extinguisher practically jumped into her hand as she grabbed for it.

Now, to find the fire. Beneath her feet, the aux grav made every step feel like a guess. She only needed one, maybe two minutes, but didn't trust the old ship keep her upright long. Other Marines had left their seats, searching for the source as well. Smoke gathered near the ceiling, a hot, pitch black storm cloud that smelled like the twelve hells.

"Doc, where the hell is junction one-six-whatever?"

"It's here, in the cargo bay. Starboard-side." He pointed to the bulkhead opposite of him. "Look for an open maintenance panel."

She spotted it quick enough, throwing sparks like angry stars. Her boots barely touched the deck as she wove through the cargo locks, extinguisher clutched tight. Then the whole universe tilted. The engines' punch turned everything sideways, leaving her hanging in air that couldn't decide which way to pull. When gravity finally picked a winner, she hit the deck hard. Everything hurt and her stomach was doing backflips, but she still had the extinguisher.

No time to think. Just aim, breathe, and shoot. Retardant gel flowed from the extinguisher's nozzle, clinging to the junction grid in thick, expanding gobs. The panel spit more sparks as the gel did its work, but the smoke began to clear. Maybe they'd make it after all. Maybe Doc had seen her save the day.

"How's that for—"

The cargo bay erupted in a burst of light, heat, and a metal-rending *bang!* Her eyes burned, the long ghost of a laser beam still fading in her vision. The *Gauntlet's* klaxons began their three-tone wail. Rapid decompression. Damn squids had stuck them good.

"Patch kit!" Doc threw off his harness and dove toward the floor where a funnel cloud of smoke whistled through a puncture in the deck plate.

"On it," the Rikkos shouted back.

"Decompression, decompression, decompression!" came the call from the front of the cargo bay. "Rebreathers, now!"

The hazard strips led her right to the emergency station, those endless training drills finally paying off. Standard layout, standard symbols, standard everything.

She thumbed the release. Empty. She blinked. Empty meant dead. Empty meant someone had cleaned this ship out and sent them out anyway.

"I got nothing," shouted another Marine four cells aft.

"No pressure, Doc," she said, "but this boat's flying without vacuum kits."

The Rikkos jogged back toward the breach carrying a flat metal crate between them. Doc pulled the crate beside him, its mag-locks engaging with an electric clack.

"You're wrong, Bugs. Keep looking." He pulled a plasma torch from the crate and cut away the jagged edges of the puncture. "This torch might work in a vacuum, but I don't."

She found another box near the rear of the cargo bay. No vacuum kits. No medkits. But there was something inside this one, half a handprint smudged against the interior lid. In the hazard lighting, it looked redder than red. Like old blood.

Doc let out a ragged cough as he showed the twins where to place the sheet of hull patch. "Where's our masks?"

The bite in his voice made her wince. "I'm telling you, there ain't any!" Not her fault nobody bothered to pack this flying coffin before they launched.

"Okay, okay." White-hot plasma burned from his torch, welding the hull patch to the deck. "Get my terminal. Let me know what else on this piece of shit needs fixed."

The terminal felt heavier in her lap. Bulkier, more rugged than the admin block basic model. She tapped it, and the screen went all buttons and symbols.

"What am I supposed to be—? Doc, none of this makes any sense."

"Shit!" The venting had stopped but something still whistled through a gap where the patch hadn't stuck. Doc was already moving, second patch in hand, torch spitting white fire. "System diagnostics. Upper right. Maybe."

"Maybe?" The menu might as well be written in lupanthaese. *NAV CTRL. COMM CTRL. FTL CTRL.* Half the options were grayed out. The other half might as well have been. "I… I don't see it. Doesn't anything work on this ship?"

"Figure it out," Doc spat.

Olsom slid her finger over the screen, scrolling to reveal more options. *CARGO CTRL. POD CTRL. SYS DIAGS.* There it was. The menu slipped sideways, replaced by another list of building block shapes colored red or green.

"Got it!"

"Alright, let's take it by the numbers," Doc said, hair soaked with sweat. "Remember, green good, red dead."

"Yeah."

"Sub-light engines."

She blew a breath. "Green. Good."

"Holy Twelfth, I could kiss you. Hull integrity."

And damn if she didn't want him to mean it, just a little. "Er, red."

"Yeah, yeah," Doc groaned. The patch's thin edge beaded beneath the torch. "RCS."

"Good."

"Well, at least we can still run. Aux grav."

"Good." The building block labeled *AUX GRAV* flashed twice, then went red. "Wait, no. It's red."

"Shit. Probably power feedback from the junction on one-six." He tossed the torch into the crate. "This is as good as it gets. Any more heat and the patches will tear. Hey, Rikkos, give me a hand."

Together, Doc and the twins hauled the repair crate over the leaky welds and re-magnetized it.

Doc gave the crate a kick. "Good enough for Navy work."

"Floaty," the Rikkos said, giving twin thumbs up.

The background hum of aux grav fields faded away, and there was no force keeping them on the floor. The click of boot magnetics rippled through the cargo bay as the Marines returned to their jump seats. Olsom strapped on her harness, keeping one hand on the bulky field terminal.

A warning flashed on its screen: *IFF UPDATE. NEW CONTACTS.*

"Hold on." She tapped the alert, and the screen flipped back to the threat display. Six red dots zig-zagged behind the *Gauntlet,* their weapon vector lines flashing with incoming fire. Too many of them. They were gonna—

Except, they were dropping back, edging beyond the maximum effective range of their lasers.

Two dots emerged at the opposite edge of the screen. Small and fast moving. IFF returns labeled them *Razor One* and *Razor Two,* colored friendly blue.

"Founders, they're ours!"

"*Gauntlet, this is Razor One,*" the pilot crooned over the PA, calm and cool like the jet jockeys always did in the COLNET feeds. "*Looks like you've got some uninvited guests.*"

"Razor One, Victory Five. You're just in time," the major's voice came next with no hint of concern. "These squids crashed our party and now they're shitting on the floor."

"Just call us the clean-up crew, Victory Five. Victory Actual sends his regards."

The cargo bay went wild, everyone acting like they hadn't just about died.

Doc slapped her shoulder. "Angels sent from the Twelfth Herself."

Even the spacer twins looked alive through their wrinkled faces. Olsom managed something close to a grin, but she felt like old shit, Twelfth or no. The smoke, the heat. Too close. Too real.

On the threat feed, the two blue markers split apart, their movement vector lines stretching as they gained speed. The red dots did the same, their focus switching from the *Gauntlet* to the incoming strike fighters. Razor Flight was outnumbered but not outgunned. Weapons vectors flashed between the passing strike craft, and two red dots faded from the plot.

"Hard dock, two minutes," the wolf growled over the PA.

"Hard dock?" Her stomach already knew she wouldn't like the answer. "That's bad, right?"

"Put it this way—" Doc tucked the terminal away with a too-casual shrug. "Remember all that fun we just had with gravity? That was practice."

Founders, the twins. "You two gonna be—?"

She almost didn't recognize them. Without gravity yanking at their faces, they actually looked their age. Just two eps floating there without a care in the void. Hard to believe these were the same geezers who'd been fighting beside her ten minutes ago. Founders take her, they looked normal.

Smokes nodded. "Our body mods are—"

"—guaranteed within human norms," Vlan said.

"What does that mean?"

"You live, we live," they said through identical, mischievous grins.

The sound of barked orders and clattering gear grew silent. Subtle vibrations buzzed through the deck, and a queasiness in the pit of her stomach said they were maneuvering for a braking burn.

"Here we go. Twelfth save us." Doc's grin faded.

"Whatever you say, Doc," she said.

The engines roared and suddenly she was being crushed from

every direction. Breathing became a fight she was losing. Alert lights started faded to nothing as black crept in from the edges of her vision. Just had to stay alive. One second at a time. Couldn't think about home. Couldn't think about Ma and Pa. Couldn't think about how space was just another fire waiting to take what it wanted.

The noise died except for metal cooling and engines purring. She could see again, could breathe again, could almost believe they'd made it. Then something big reached out and caught them. The stop knocked her teeth together, and suddenly gravity had new opinions about which way was down. Her guts didn't agree. She barely got her harness off and she was retching, bile hitting the deck between her boots.

Her throat still burned when Major Kull's voice came over the PA. "Welcome to the Victory, Marines."

Hands steadied her shoulders—Doc and Vlan, while Smokes hovered nearby. All of them wearing those done-but-not-dead grins. Still breathing. Still together.

Maybe death was waiting around every corner out here in the void. But staying alive was the one thing she knew how to do. The blocks had taught her to fight for herself. The Colonial Defense Marines had taught her something else—how to fight for others. And for the second time, these new squad mates seemed to have her back. They weren't friends. Not really. Not yet. But maybe there was something there worth fighting for.

BRESTO KILLED the klaxons mid-wail as the *Gauntlet* settled inside the *Victory's* launch bay. The combat lighting clicked off, replaced by the stark white of fleet-standard overheads. Something had overheated and blown, and the stink of melted plastics and scorched electronics made his head ache. Could've been a lot worse, if Runt hadn't outflown those squids.

His face still shone next to Sevvers's on the datapad. Nobody moved.

The nervous lieutenant's fingers danced toward the pad. "What do we do with him, Major?"

"I'll handle this. The rest of you, see to your units—and find homes for those grunts in the cargo bay."

"Aye, ma'am." The lieutenant joined the rest Kull's command staff as they filed from the room.

The cockpit hatch cycled open, spilling the sour smell of lupanthae musk into the ops bay. Runt ducked slowly through the hatchway designed for human pilots. She was shorter than most wolves despite standing head and shoulders above Bresto. Picking her call sign had been easy.

She surveyed the room with big, golden eyes, her nose and ears working. "Pack safe?"

Thanks to her. "Solid flying, as usual."

Kull pointed at Runt's familial coat, with its lines of small, colorful patches adorning the chest and sleeves, each part of a story she'd so far refused to tell. "The sergeant is right. I'll see you get a Flying Triad for what you did—a real medal to pin on that coat of yours."

Runt hooted a disgruntled chord, lips curled in a toothy scowl. She was almost too easygoing for a jet jockey, so long as you didn't mess with her ship.

Kull didn't even blink, turning the datapad where Runt could see it. "Did you know anything about this?"

Runt padded closer, her potent smell wrinkling the major's nose. "Kerry. Sevvers. Is safe?"

"As safe as we are," Bresto said before turning to Kull. "Look, Major, Runt didn't know. We didn't get very far before the Concordat attacked."

"Too bad." Kull dismissed the alert from her datapad and tapped her wrist comms. "Flight Ops, Victory Five."

"*Flight Ops here.*" The reply came through loud and clear over the heavy machinery and hydraulics in the background. "*Send your traffic, Victory Five.*"

"I want priority flight status given to the Gauntlet and her crew. They have important business. The secret kind. Let's not keep them waiting."

"*Copy priority status on Bay Two. Be advised, Victory Actual has ordered an azure drop package. All companies. All drop ships.*"

"How long?"

"*Uh, we're looking at approximately sixty minutes, Victory Five.*"

She set the datapad down too hard. "Understood, Flight Ops. Keep me informed."

"*Aye, ma'am. Flight Ops out.*"

Her finger struck the table next to the datapad. "Let me be perfectly clear, Sergeant."

Here it came. What was her next move?

"You will remain on the Gauntlet until Flight Ops clears you for departure. You will not set foot on the Victory."

So, no brig time, no Division handover, just a kind of exile with whatever resources the *Gauntlet* had left. It was a smart play. If he lived, her problem was solved; if he died out there, she'd have a clean conscience. He'd seen officers make worse calls.

"Clear, ma'am."

PFC Olsom peeked around the hatch, with Myers and the twins crowded in behind her. Too bad just being here marked them as targets for Kull, too. Damn boots couldn't read a room.

"Uh, excuse me? Sarnt?" Olsom said.

Kull waved them in. "Come in, Marines, you're just in time. You came in with Sergeant Bresto, right?"

"Yes, ma'am." The word *ma'am* came out as two syllables in Olsom's slow Vestian drawl.

"Have any of you seen Kerry Sevvers?"

Bresto's teeth snapped together. Twelfth keep their damned mouths shut. They'd only followed his orders. He'd take whatever sanction Kull gave—wasn't his first, definitely wouldn't be his last—but there was no need to shit on these young Marines' careers.

Olsom wasn't helping. All those pips must've made her nervous. Even her damn freckles screamed guilt.

"Private Olsom, is it?" Kull asked.

Olsom straightened to attention. "Private First Class, ma'am."

"Of course. A PFC on Three-Alpha. I take it you're a brand-new Marine?" Kull was having fun with this.

"Marched off the parade deck yesterday, ma'am."

"I see. Quite the first day."

"Nothing we couldn't handle, ma'am." There it was, that stubborn certainty, back on Olsom's face.

It's why he'd picked her to help him. But she wasn't Special Ops. Didn't have his connections. Couldn't afford the price of following his orders. "Ma'am, they didn't—"

"I'll ask you again, Private First Class..." There was no smile on Kull's face now. Just danger. "Have you seen Kerry Sevvers?"

Getting out of this was easy if she played it right. Mouth shut. Be the dumb boot. Lying to officers was a thing you had to do sometimes. Twelfth help him, he'd done it enough.

Something shifted on Olsom's face. Not quite a grin but showing a hint of teeth. "Don't know no Sevvers, ma'am."

Runt hooted a concerned note. She'd seen it, too.

Kull chuckled. "Indeed, wolf. There *is* something… savage about the PFC. Let's be glad she's on our side."

The datapad in her hand buzzed with an incoming message. Perfect timing. The Division might have their heads up their autonomous asses, but Kull and the *Victory* had bigger problems. Had a mission. A twinge of envy tightened in his chest. Who knew what Park had planned for him with a Concordat invasion underway.

Kull turned back to Olsom and the others. "I'll make you a deal. Join Victory's defense of Aegia, and all is forgotten. Or…" She hooked a thumb toward Bresto. "Go back with these two and take your chances out there. Personally, I—"

Her wrist comms chirped. *"Major. Colonel Reede."*

"Go ahead, Skipper."

"Report to the command deck, double time. We're drop-ready in one hour."

"Aye, sir." She toggled the connection closed. "You heard the skipper, Marines. We won't wait."

Bresto stood, navigating the ache in his hip. Capital ship gravity felt good on an aching frame, constant and balanced—nothing like a soft low-power field. Too bad the young Marines in front of him only stoked the slow burn in his belly. Kull was gone. They should be, too. He had work to do.

"What in the hell are you still doing here?" he barked.

"We're with you, Sarnt," Olsom said.

Doc didn't look so sure, and the twins didn't look like much of anything at all except maybe a spatial anomaly.

"What're our orders?" she continued.

He laughed. "I'm not your CO, boot. You think that major gives twelve shits about my orders?"

But what *was* he going to do next, now that he was here? He stepped to the control deck and brought up the local tac net feeds on the holoproj.

Aegia Prime was a scramble of blue and red sensor returns. Tactical estimates put the Concordat forge ship at just over four hours from low orbit, but a forward wing of raider corvettes was only sixty minutes away. The race to be the first ones planetside was going to be close, and there was still no sign of a coordinated response from CDF command.

Just seeing the archenemy so close to his homeworld made him furious—that he, Sevvers, and Park might have led them here... He didn't want to think it. Didn't want to give those dark thoughts power. Holy Mother, there was too much at stake to doubt himself now.

"The number one priority is to secure Aegia." He turned the projection, revealing the peak of Mount Dodecoron. Vestebrae. Corongaet. Diacad. Lyra and the kids were right *there*. "You can't let those things loose on the surface. There are people—families—down there."

Doc nodded. "Sarnt's right."

"You say that like you ain't coming," Olsom said.

There was anger—no, resentment, in her eyes. She was a slight thing, even with her wider Vestian shoulders. Sort of reminded him of PFC Dalon, their breacher on Park's little mission to Cradle's edge that started this Twelfth-forsaken mess. Dalon was Vestian too, a good Marine. The longer he looked at Olsom, the more the memory of the boy came flooding back. Damn shame what'd happened to him. Lost no more.

He shook the memory loose. "You heard the major. Runt and I are void-bound the second we get clearance. You all don't want to be here when that happens."

"Why not?"

The slow burn in his gut began to rise. She had a mouth on her—not like Dalon at all. "Not your concern, Private."

"We helped you." She was all teeth now, a little wild thing. Kull was right about her. "Hurt people to break that skeeg out—for you. All due respect, Sarnt, you made it our concern."

Insubordinate little shit. Bresto's jaw clenched as he fought for control. All he could see when she opened her damn mouth was Dalon, locked in combat with that Lost abomination. Dalon, aboard the same forge ship now burning for Aegia.

"Sevvers didn't belong in that cell, Private," he said, "especially now. Can't help we had to smash a few skeeg heads to do the right thing."

Myers took her by the elbow. "Bugs, come on. Drop it."

"Drop it?" She shook Myers loose. "You haven't been straight with us, Sarnt, not once. What out there is more important than saving your home? Why are you leaving us now?"

Each question drove the memory of the daxed's blade deeper into Dalon's hardsuit. The fast-twitch muscles in Bresto's shoulders and arms shivered. The upstart little boot had run her mouth a second too long.

Olsom's eyes widened and she settled back on her heels.

A long, clawed hand closed around his arm.

"No," Runt said. No sad chords, no anger, no judgment. Just *no*.

Olsom didn't even flinch.

The memory of Dalon was mercifully gone.

He'd forgotten to breathe—Holy Mother, keep him from his anger. Faith took root in a quiet heart. So did self-control. He drew a deep breath: two, three, four, in through the nose and hold. Feel the pulse settle. A simple technique all Aegians learned as young betas, but some learned quicker than others. And his heart had always been so stormy.

"Nothing is more important than Aegia," he finally said, "but you heard the major. I'm a liability, so long as the Division is looking for me."

"Don't they have—"

"—bigger problems now?" the twins said.

"You'd think," he replied. "But Sevvers is a magnet for trouble."

"Where will you go, Sarnt?" Myers asked.

He ignored the hitch in his chest. "Wherever my CO sends me."

"Yeah, but what about us?" Olsom's voice low but steady, a flicker of hurt in her eyes that fled as soon as he saw it. "What are we supposed to do?"

"You follow orders, just like me. That's the job. Look, I know you want answers, but right now, defending Aegia is what matters. The Victory gives you the best shot at both."

"Ooh-fucking-rah." Myers pushed past her and extended an open hand. "It's been an honor, Sarnt Bresto."

So ready to prove himself—well, there'd be plenty of chances for that once the Concordat touched down. Bresto jabbed a finger into the serpent-and-piston section patch on Myers's white-and-grays. "Just keep the blood and oil moving, Marine."

Myers took a step back, deflated. "Aye, Sarnt."

The twins followed him out.

Olsom's eyes shimmered, wet with emotion as she turned to go. Whatever her problem was, she needed to get over it. He didn't have time for hurt feelings.

He leaned on the edge of the table, rubbing the nub of his left ring finger through the glove. The room felt cavernous with the others gone. Only the soft hum of electronics and the distant, muffled sounds of the outside hangar deck remained. The harsh overhead lighting cast long shadows across the planning table, and the idling holoproj had gone dark.

Runt loosed a big, keening yawn. "Hmph. Pups."

"No shit." The dull ache knotted tight in his hip. "Looks like you and I are going back out there."

"Will make it." She slapped a hand against the fibrosteel bulkhead. "Is perfect machine."

"Even after that scrap with the raiders?"

"Cargo bay, damaged." She warbled a bright, upbeat chord. "Forward bays, good."

"You're the jet jockey. I just work here." He poked at the control deck with an index finger, hunting for the comms logs. "Any traffic from Lieutenant Park?"

"Much int—interf… Much noise."

He winced. If the Navy and Division didn't take that forge ship out, they'd all be Lost before long.

The endless list of tac net packets relayed through the *Gauntlet's* systems were mostly IFF updates and control handshakes. No direct messages from Park or Sevvers. Planetary Reserve data flowed in from ground stations in Vestebrae. Lyra would be in one of them by now if the PR had their shit together. They were lucky to have a former Marine like her. But even she wasn't ready for what was coming for them. Squids were bad enough. But the bugs? The Lost? He'd been prodding the keys for what felt like a very long time when he noticed Runt's reflection staring back from the flatscreen display.

"What?"

"Pups. Need pack."

He grunted and kept working. Wolves and their pack instincts—way different from Marine unit structure. "They're Victory Marines now. That chain of command will take care of them."

Simple as that. Had to be.

Her disapproving snort filled the ops bay.

"What?" He stabbed at the keys. "Our mission's blown. The Concordat are back. Our one shot at stopping them vanished back there on that forge ship, vanished with Lernus and that... that girl. Park better have a plan worth all this."

Runt's claws clicked across the controls, and Aegia materialized above them, eternal storms masking the threat markers now converging on his home. Her hand thumped his chest. "Bresto's pups. Need pack."

Her touch burned through his uniform, scorching the certainty of duty into something he couldn't control. Not pain or guilt—he could handle those. This was older. Deeper.

The swirling planet above the holoproj called to him. He was born and raised on the Holy Mother's mountain. A granite son of the storms. His family, his own pack, right where he'd left them—all while he helped Park chase ghosts through the Cradle.

Same choice. Same cost.

Every time.

He pushed away her hand. "Stow that shit. I've got orders, and so do you."

The Holy Mother taught that faith required sacrifice. Well, he'd given up enough family moments to know that lesson by heart. One more sacrifice wouldn't break him, not if it meant keeping the Concordat off Her mountain.

The control deck's tactical feeds showed what he really needed to see: enemy positions, vectors of attack, hard data that demanded action.

"I'll find a way to contact Park," he said. "You make sure we're ready to fly."

CHAPTER
FIVE

OLSOM FOLLOWED Doc and the twins down the *Gauntlet's* cargo ramp and into the churning mess that was the CDNS *Victory's* hangar deck. The air was thick with the copper taste of sub-light exhaust and betrayal. It figured that Bresto had thrown her away first chance he got. Folks always did. She'd hoped the Marines would be different. Not family, but somewhere to belong. So much for that.

Hazard stripes outlined the busy transit corridor. A hangar tech blew past with an armful of drop chutes, close enough to feel the static off his coveralls. Another hatch cycled open, landing with a clang against the deck plate. Doc was already several paces ahead, moving easy through the mess like he knew right where he was headed. Sure would be nice to know where the hell that was.

Just like the depot all over again. No, further back than that. The admin blocks, where you learned quick to keep your head down and your mouth shut. Never knowing what was coming next or who'd be gone tomorrow. Hundred days of that at the recruit depot felt like breathing water, and now here she was, gasping all over again. Six more orbits of this shit show, if she made it past today. Though maybe… She stole a glance at Doc, at the twins following quiet behind her. They seemed different. Maybe having folks at her six counted for something this time.

Doc made a crisp about-face, moving backward along the bustling walkway with drill-field precision. "Drop prep's already started. One hard cred says we beat the squids planetside."

Smokes took a drag from his cigarette, pinched the coal between his fingers, and stuck the unused portion in his breast pocket. "I'll take—"

"—that bet." Vlan's eyes flicked to Olsom as he spoke, throwing off that perfect twin-timing just enough to notice. He handed his brother a single, CDF-issued hard credit. Smokes tucked the clear, plexene wafer in the same pocket and padded it thoughtfully.

"You in?" Doc waggled his eyebrows at her, his own cred pinched between two fingers.

Tempting. Back in the blocks, you didn't bet creds. No one had any, or you wouldn't be there. No, you bet meals, shower time, who got to sleep with a wall at their back. Small choices, but they kept you alive, traded away with a smile like they didn't matter. Doc made throwing away hard currency look easy. But she knew better. Who knew what would happen next, or how long they'd stay together. Founders knew she had nothing left to lose but herself.

She looked away, heat rising in her cheeks. "Too rich for my blood."

The hangar deck ceiling towered overhead almost four levels. Not as grand as Three-Alpha's hangar rings, but standing in the *Victory's* hollow core gave a sense of the size of the ship. Several dropships sat in their cradles, all armor plated and hard lines, their noses to the hazard-striped doors running the full length of the bay.

More of the dull green craft emerged from recesses in the exterior bulkheads, pulled by heavy gantries running along tracks in the ceiling. Deck crew in hazard vests and red helmets worked together to ready each ship, one running the gantry, the other directing traffic, all so those ships could plunge into the planet below.

She'd never dropped before. One simulated drop at the depot, that was it. The mechanics of leaving the *Victory*, surviving re-entry, the possibility—no, the certainty—of landing under fire, it was all theoretical.

Theory didn't much suit her. "How do we know which one's ours?"

"Depends on the unit we end up with." Doc spun to face the line of ships. "One platoon per dropship. Three platoons per company. Six companies to an exped."

A Marine emerged through the crush of hangar personnel, decked out in full tactical kit—body armor, load-bearing gear, a CR-11 blaster rifle mag-locked to his chest plate—all of it colored the pixelated white and gray of the Marine Combat Uniform. His unbothered stare and corporal pips said this was not his first ride on the *Victory*. He probably ate drops for morning chow.

"Hey, boots, you the last ones off that scow?" He pointed to the *Gauntlet's* tail boom jutting from the receiving bay behind them.

"Yes, Corporal," Doc and the twins snapped.

"Good. You're with me. Name's Lessig." The corporal turned and waved for them to follow. "You from the depot?"

"Yes," the twins said.

"Wow." Lessig paused, eyeing the twins a second longer than was comfortable. "There a name for your condition?"

"Gravity." The Rikkos shrugged.

"Not many spacers in the Marines."

"They can hold their own," Doc said.

"And you are?"

"Lance Corporal Myers," Doc said. "Just finished combat engineering school."

"Mechanic and medic, good to go."

"We've all seen combat," Doc went on. "Helped take back Three-Alpha's hangar deck. For a while, anyway."

"I heard it's bad out there." Lessig waved them through the armored hatchway, out of the hangar deck and into the *Victory's* starboard arterial. "What about you?"

Just inside the broad passageway, two access lifts lined the interior bulkhead. He slapped the lift control and one door rattled open.

"Hello, Victory to PFC Olsom."

Oh shit, he meant her. "Wh—ah, me?"

The edge of Lessig's mouth lifted slightly as he squinted at her uniform. "You basic and blooded, too?"

"Yeah, er, yes, Corporal."

"Three shiny-ass boots and one brand new doc." Lessig reclined against the wall as the door closed and the lift jerked upward. "Could be worse."

"Where we headed, Corporal?" Myers asked.

"Deck Three, Company Berths. You'll report to Lieutenant Revan and do whatever the hell he says, check?"

"Yes, Corporal."

The lift shuddered to a halt, a chime signaling their arrival. Marines filed past the open door, long busy lines stretching fore and aft. NCOs barked orders and junior Marines complied, filling the charcoal gray corridor with the familiar cadence of task and purpose.

"Come on." Lessig strode into the corridor, the other junior enlisted making room as he passed by. "Designators on the bulkheads tell you where you're at. We're looking for F-3 at the end of the hall."

Company designations flashed by as they hurried down the hall. The large block letters laser-etched into the bulkhead were half as tall as Olsom, painted the same familiar dropship green. The smell of deck wash and rank sweat drifted through open squad bay doors. Inside, rows of neatly made bunks stacked three-high from deck to ceiling.

As promised, the letters F-3 marked the end of the corridor. The office across from the squad bay was small, with barely enough room for the young lieutenant seated at the tiny desk, busily gesturing to his datapad. Lessig knocked at the door frame.

"Enter." The officer waved them in without looking up.

"Got the last of the stragglers from Three-Alpha, sir."

"Good." The lieutenant looked up from his work, his optimism fading as he stared at Olsom and the others through the office window. "Only four?"

"That's all I found, sir."

"Twelfth-dammit, we're still short." The lieutenant frowned at his datapad, drumming his fingers on his desk. "Fine, send them in."

Lessig emerged from the tiny office with another barely there smile. "Go on. I'll come get you when it's our turn in the armory. Fifteen minutes tops, so talk fast."

By the time Doc and the twins pushed their way in behind Olsom, it was standing room only. There wasn't much to the small space: a mass-fabricated desk with built-in flatscreen, a squeaky rolling chair, and nothing on the bulkheads other than power junctions and atmo ducts. Place looked temporary.

There wasn't much to the lieutenant, either. He was trim and fit in his well-pressed white-and-grays, his hair buzzed high and tight, every bit as mass-fabricated as his office. Typical academy polish—healthy skin, perfect teeth—probably from a family with creds to spare. The scant ribbons on his chest said Corporal Lessig had been at this longer than him. The name stenciled on his crisp uniform was REVAN.

"Names, ranks, and MOS, please." He handed the datapad to Doc. "Sign the indoc form, bottom right."

"Lance Corporal Rob Myers, Combat Engineer, sir." Doc pressed his thumb on the pad, then passed it to Smokes.

Doc's service record filled the flatscreen terminal on the desk. Aegian. Made hab block drill guide—whatever the hell that meant—when he was just a gamma. Even his service ident looked handsome, showing off his short, wavy hair and chiseled jaw.

"Welcome aboard, son," Revan said. "You ready to give your heart and your life to the Twelfth in defense of Her mountain and Her people?"

"Yes, sir." Doc straightened, his boots knocking together sharply. He thumped a fist to his chest, pressing his knuckles into his ribs. Not a military salute, but a religious one.

Olsom turned away. Typical Aegians, wearing their faith like armor. She never understood their obsession with the Twelfth, but watching Doc's unwavering conviction, she felt a spike of envy. Must be nice to have that kind of certainty, especially now.

Revan's eyes flicked to the twins.

"Vlan and Tlan Rikko, Private—"

"—First Class, basically trained, sir."

His stare narrowed. "Aren't you two a little old for the Marines?"

"It's the gravity, sir," they said.

"I see." Revan scanned his terminal. "Born in the ERMC. Bet you're both ready for some payback today."

"Yes, sir."

"I see you have skeletal mods. You'll pull a lot of G's in our drop, and Aegia's gravity is a bit over standard. You have your boosters on you?"

They both patted the bulky meds in their pockets and nodded.

Vlan offered her the datapad. She jumped and fumbled for it. Her turn.

The indoc form read like an admin block waiver, lots of legal jargon demanding everything and giving nothing. *Emergency wartime transfer: CDMS Victory, F Company, Third Platoon.* She'd signed a million of these in the last hundred days. One more wouldn't kill her.

"PFC Larke Olsom, sir." The datapad accepted her thumbprint with a haptic buzz before she passed it back. "Basically trained, sir."

"Strong scores on your exo sims." Revan's eyes scanned the display. "Your senior drill instructor says you have an aptitude for close combat drill, particularly hand-to-hand."

"Grew up in an admin block, sir." Just saying it brought back the memories of tight bunks, moldy showers, and sour testosterone. "Had to learn early."

Revan set the pad down and looked at her, his eyes lingering, as if he'd never seen an admin block refugee before.

"I understand Vestia can be a wild place. I'm sorry to hear that, Private."

"Don't be. I'm not." Wild was an understatement. This proper officer wouldn't last one turn in the Tangle. "Sir."

"Very well." Revan rolled back his chair until it knocked against the rear bulkhead. "Welcome to F Company, Third Platoon. I need ten more of you, but we'll make do.

"I'm your platoon commander, Lieutenant Pius Revan. Corporal Lessig is First Squad leader and my acting platoon sergeant. As you'll see, we're very shorthanded. The Concordat caught us mid-rotation and nearly thirty percent of Victory Marines are still on the surface."

The chair creaked as Revan stood, datapad in hand. His fingers danced across the screen, pausing only when he stopped to scrutinize each of them in turn.

"I'm going to need two hundred percent from each one of you to make up the difference. Listen to your NCOs and your fellow non-comms. They know the Victory way. Twelfth-willing, in time, so will you."

"Yes, sir," Olsom snapped, her words blending with Doc's and the twins.

"Good. Tlan, exo operator. You're with Toelke and Mezzior. Squad Three, Fireteam Two."

Smokes didn't react, didn't even blink. Almost like he didn't hear. Or didn't want to.

"Olsom, exo operator. Vlan, breacher. Myers, combat engineer. You're now Squad Three, Fireteam Three."

Something bright and dangerous bloomed in her chest. After Bresto dumped her like spare parts, she'd been sure everything would split apart again. That's how things always went. But here was Revan, putting them all in the same squad. Side by side on the firing line, just like Three-Alpha. Just like it meant something.

And exo operator. No exo school yet, but she was basically qualified. And Founders take her if that wasn't the least important part. Doc and the twins would stay together, right there with her. They'd be—

The noise started low, animal like. Vlan's face twisted up, eyes spilling fat tears while that dying sound kept building in his throat. She looked him up and down, half-expecting some kind of wound. Nothing. This wasn't the hard ass Marine who'd fought beside her on Three-Alpha anymore. His legs gave out, and Smokes caught him, held him while he shook and keened against his brother's chest. Not a twitch, not a word. He just stood there holding his brother. It was the strangest thing. These two had killed raiders together barely two hours ago, moved like they shared the same brain. Now this.

Revan slammed the datapad down on the small desk. "What in twelve hells?"

"I… I don't know, sir." Doc's usual confidence wavered. He turned to her, eyes begging for help.

Vlan remained locked in his trance-like state. This wasn't like them. Always in step, always together. Sitting beside each other when they first met, always within arm's reach even as they fought their way to the *Gauntlet*. Not once had she seen one without the other close by.

"They've never been apart," she murmured, more to herself than anyone else. No wonder Vlan was coming apart. Hell, they probably hadn't been separated since they were whelps.

Her excitement about keeping the squad together turned to ash in her mouth. What good was staying together if they were already broken?

"Calm down, Private, that's an order!" Revan shouted.

Vlan's rhythmic wail grew louder.

"Sir," Olsom began. "You can't—"

"What?"

"You can't separate them."

The line of of F Company Marines coming and going outside Revan's office began to stall. Some whispered, others laughed, all of them staring at Vlan through the office window. Revan's bewildered gaze hung on the brother a second longer before turning to Olsom.

"This isn't a psych ward." He let out a short, humorless laugh. "I need combat ready Marines, not… whatever this is."

"They can fight, sir, I swear. They just—"

"Then get them squared away, Private." Revan slid the chair beneath his desk and moved toward the exit. His face loomed close to hers, cheeks red beneath his angry stare. "Out," he hissed. "All of you. Now."

"Aye, sir."

Olsom took Vlan by the arm and pulled him from Revan's office. He tried to struggle, still keening for his brother, but Doc was right behind them, ushering Smokes through the door. Revan stormed after them, datapad under one arm. The other Marines scattered at his approach. He waved the datapad in the air. "What are you all staring at? Get to the armory, now. We drop in forty!"

Vlan's sobbing mellowed, but he still clung to his brother, who stood near the F-3 squad bay door fumbling for a cigarette with his free hand. Doc reached into his kit and pulled out an auto-doc. He squinted at the little screen, adjusting the machine, the control knob clicking loudly with each turn.

There was no time for this. Olsom stepped in front of him, voice low. "What are you doing?"

"Just a little something for his nerves."

Doc tugged at Vlan's collar. He didn't flinch, just hung on to Smokes, face hidden, while his brother's hand moved mechanically, thumb striking the lighter again and again trying to ignite it.

"What the hell, Doc?" Olsom hissed, her voice lowering as more Marines walked past. "You can't just drug him. We're going back out there!"

Doc threw a nervous head nod to the passing Marines, then leaned closer.

"You heard Revan," he whispered. "You really think he's going to change our billets now because Vlan threw a tantrum?"

She glanced back down the hallway, but the lieutenant was already out of sight. The man refused to see—to fix—the problem he'd caused. He was an officer. He didn't have to. Doc was right. It'd be up to them to figure this out.

"Look, you're the exo operator." Doc's gaze settled on her, heavier than usual. "That makes you fireteam leader. So, this is your call."

"What?" They didn't cover this kind of stuff in basic training. "*You're* the lance corporal. You've got rank, time in service—"

"Don't be such a boot," he smirked, the hint of a flirt in his curled lips. "Billet trumps rank every time. And you'll be the one wearing metal soon enough."

Fireteam leader. Yeah, she'd memorized the field manual on small unit tactics same as any new recruit, but manuals were just words on a screen. Real leading meant real dying if you fucked it up. Bresto knew that when he'd thrown her away. No room for screw ups on his super secret op. Now Vlan was falling apart in front of her and these Marines were supposed to trust her with their lives. She barely trusted herself.

"I... I don't know." She shook her head for what felt like a long time, as if waiting for an answer to appear. "What would you do?"

"It's my job to keep Marines combat effective." He tilted his head toward Vlan. "That is *not* combat effective."

"What would you give him?"

"FL-7, a field-grade anxiolytic." Doc held the device toward her. "Just takes the edge off."

The tiny display blinked steadily: *FL-7—15.0mg standard Dose.*

Advise patient to side effects of mild sedation, disorientation, potential motor skill impairment.

"Will he still be able to fight?"

"Can he still pull a trigger? Yes." Doc's frown didn't make her feel any better. "Though I wouldn't let him handle a brick of plasmex for an hour or two."

"He's our fucking breacher, Doc!" An anxious laugh burst from her lips. "I don't know. This don't feel right."

Smokes stood there, still holding his brother, eyes wide and pleading. His jaw clenched and unclenched, the movement so slight she almost missed it. With a slight turn, he held Vlan closer, neck bared to her like some kind of sacrifice. Only thing was, Smokes didn't show weakness. Not ever. This wasn't about what he wanted; this was about what his brother needed.

She couldn't argue with that. "Okay, Doc. Give it to him."

Doc pressed the auto-doc to Vlan's neck, a flat puff of air the only clue anything had happened. Almost immediately, Vlan's whimpering softened and his breathing began to steady. Even Smokes seemed to relax, like he'd been dosed second-hand.

Olsom let out a breath, but the knot in her gut didn't loosen. Drugging Vlan was just patching a leaky hull. She'd have to figure out a way to get them back together. Until then, this patch job would have to hold.

CHAPTER
SIX

THE OPS BAY bulkheads creaked and groaned as the *Gauntlet's* old, idle bones fought the constant tug of the *Victory's* aux grav. Tinny voices crackled through the control deck's emitters, fragmentary reports of the battle raging in higher orbit. Razor Flight had chased off another wing of raider strike craft, but heavier ships were en route.

Bresto shifted in his seat, trying to appease the dull ache still gnawing at his hip. The console spat out long strings of data, none of it useful, none of it what he needed. The comms relay refreshed again. No sign of Park. If Park was off the nets, he'd need a backup plan. Going after the forge ship on his own was suicide. Maybe go back for Sevvers, or drop with Victory, if Kull didn't put him down.

"You got anything?"

A somber chord hummed back at him from the cockpit. That was a no.

"Any update from Flight Ops?"

"Thirty minutes." Runt whistled a brighter, more optimistic note this time. "Refuel ops commencing."

He hadn't expected that kind of assist, not from Kull. There was an aggressiveness to her that was unusual for a command-level officer. But she must have authorized the refueling op. Maybe she had a softer side after all. Maybe—

A new log entry flashed rapidly on the display. The sound of battle chatter faded into static and a familiar voice erupted over the ops bay PA.

"Gauntlet, Gauntlet, this is Park." The lieutenant's calm, commanding presence hissed through the static soaked relays. About Twelfth-damned time. No holo. No video. He wasn't in-system.

Bresto keyed the mic. "Park, this is Gauntlet. Verify ident and password. Challenge is Obsidian, over."

"Ident is White-Teal-Seven-Niner-Two." The delay was subtle, half a second at most. Wherever Park was, he was near a tac net relay. *"Password is Deadlock, over."*

It was him.

Runt bounded from the cockpit, boots and claws scraping against the metal decking as she slid to a stop at Bresto's side. She kneeled by the control deck, cooing through her big, open-mouthed grin.

"Confirmed. Where are you, sir?" Bresto asked.

"No time." Park's usual polite formality was gone. *"Give me a sitrep, Sergeant. Colonial Intelligence has blocked every tactical feed out of the Aegian node."*

No wonder Park was UA. He didn't know. Bresto pecked at the control deck's keys, bundling the latest tac net data logs and forwarding them along his carrier signal. A progress bar raced to completion.

"Data packet inbound, sir. It's bad. That forge ship we found has woken up somehow. It attacked Aegia Prime with a squadron of raider cap ships. Orbital Three-Alpha is under siege. They caught us completely by surprise."

"What's the status of the Gauntlet and our team? How quickly can you make FTL?"

Park wanted them to jump. To leave. But the Concordat were here, at Aegia. That's where the fight was. That's where they needed to be.

"Did you copy my last, sir? The Concordat have attacked Aegia Prime. Orbital facilities are under sustained assault. They're headed for—"

"Break, break, break. I read you loud and clear, Sergeant. Stand by for incoming data feed."

Another progress bar leaped to the fore. Bresto drummed his fingers against the deck's metal housing, watching the counter climb— ten percent, thirty percent. No way that feed contained anything more critical to the survival of humanity than the defense of its most important colony.

The planning table's holoproj buzzed. Photons coalesced into the shape of the Cradle Nebula, a swirling vortex of highly volatile gasses, lit purple and blue by the young stars within. Three points of light blinked into being near the nebula's calm, stable core: Respitia, Aegia, and Vestia.

"After our mission to the forge ship," Park went on through a hiss of static, *"early warning relays picked up unknown signal spikes on the Cradle's eastern edge."*

Signal blooms erupted like miniature novae along the nebula's right-hand side. Their echoes crisscrossed each other, racing toward the colonies faster than anything natural could move. Most of the signal sources were deep within the nebular wall, trapped inside light years of highly reactive gasses. But a few lingered perilously close to the colonial frontier, some just past the eastern reaches.

Eleven in all. A coincidence. Had to be.

One of the signal blooms began to pulse. Runt moaned a fearful chord that trailed off into a sharp keen.

"That marked signal originated in the same location as the derelict we boarded."

So it wasn't a coincidence. There were more forge ships out there. Lots more. And they were all coming online. "Twelfth save us. Did... did we do this, sir?"

The transmission went clear-comms quiet, punctuated by the throb of background static. Above the planning table, the holoproj replayed the Concordat's surprise attack on Aegia Prime in cold tactical detail. The derelict's signal began its rapid ingress, colliding with the tiny gray speck that was humanity's second colony. Tactical metadata appeared next—enemy numbers increasing, friendly numbers decreasing.

"No, Bresto, we didn't start this." Maybe it was the interference, but Park wasn't convincing. *"We probably hurried their plans along, though.*

Why else attack Aegia with just one ship when there are so many more coming online? But the rest are coming."

Two additional signal blooms flashed on the projection. One near the first derelict's original location, another a few dozen light years to the nebular south.

Cold dread settled in Bresto's gut. If this data was accurate, humanity didn't stand a chance. Aegia was under siege, and Respitia would be soon. The Three Colonies could fall in less than a standard year.

A third location pulsed—deep inside colonial space, west of the reaches, fifteen light years from Respitia. The projection rotated, focusing on the latest signal. It was much smaller, the echoes fading shortly after they began. It was a miracle the relays caught it at all.

They had been hiding among them all along. Waiting. Twelfth save them. "Founders, how did the bugs hide a forge ship inside the patrol lanes?"

"I'm not sure they did." The third pulse replayed again. *"That last signal is weaker than the others and there's a lot more quantum jitter."*

"So, what is it?"

"No idea, but signal analysis indicates the Concordat are looking for it."

What in the hell would the archenemy need from that old rock? They were technologically superior to humanity in every way. It took an actual miracle, the Twelfth Herself, to escape from Dead Earth.

The holoproj traced an FTL flight vector from the first signal bloom toward the third. The dashed line blinked rapidly, reflecting the deck processors' best guess at the intended destination. But it wasn't certain. Respitia was very close by.

"I don't know, sir. Could be headed for Respitia. A second wave, to take out our manufacturing base. Hell, take out the Founding Council. It's what I'd do."

"The timing of the new signal is too coincidental." A blurt of static ripped through Park's transmission, squealing and thrashing like a living thing. *"I believe whatever made that new signal is very important to the Concordat, and we're going to find it before they do."*

Believe. The word didn't sound right. Park was no Aegian. He dealt in facts, not faith. If he was speculating now, it meant he was working with incomplete intel. Dangerous, with so much at stake. The Concordat at their doorstep, and Park wanted to chase ghosts. Something didn't add up. There had to be more to this.

"Say again, sir. You believe?"

"Believe, know… it doesn't matter. Whoever she was, Agent Lernus was looking for something she thought could stop this war before it started."

But it did matter. "As Sevvers told it, Lernus tried to kill us. Sir."

The holographic projection zoomed in on the new signal, past frames full of nebular gas and empty space, to a lonely star fifteen light years from Respitia. There were no planets, just dense bands of asteroids. The view panned closer, highlighting one rock hidden among hundreds of others. Metadata said it was an abandoned mining installation, as old as the *Gauntlet,* maybe older. It had been empty for a long time.

Runt leaned toward the display, ears working like she could hear it. "That is signal source?"

"Consortium records say it's been abandoned for decades." Recon imagery overlaid the asteroid's 3D wireframe, showing docking collars, transfer chutes, and other evidence of human activity. *"It never produced a single ton of ore. Systemic mechanical and network failures from the first day the mine opened. The consortiums shut it down and wrote off the loss."*

"And you really think the Concordat are after one of our old rocks?" It sounded crazier said out loud.

"Something inside it. Maybe whatever Lernus was looking for. Something that can stop the Concordat once and for all."

The rock continued its slow rotation above the planning table, ingress and egress points marked and highlighted in order of tactical value. Recommended team makeup and deployment patterns scrolled next to the asteroid. A full squad up-armored in CDF hardsuits. Division drone support. Park had barely been gone a day, and he'd already planned out their next mission. Almost like he knew this was coming.

"What aren't you telling me, sir?"

Park's signal lights lit up, but the transmission was eerily silent. Bresto could practically hear the man's gears turning across the net. He'd struck a nerve. The lieutenant fucking knew something.

The hologram shifted again, panning to one of the CDF's Orbital Resupply Depots on the nearest patrol lane closest to Park's haunted rock.

"I want you, Sevvers, and his remaining AI en route to ORD Bedrock within the hour. We'll collect the gear we need and review the mission parameters there."

If this was a joke, it wasn't funny. Maybe it was some twisted psyche eval, making sure his head was still screwed on tight after their last mission. It better be, or he was going to put his fist through the control deck's screen. "Me and Sevvers are wanted by the Division. My home is under siege by the Concordat. And you want to chase ghost signals on some old rock?"

"Wanted by the Division?" There was genuine surprise in Park's tone. Not the reaction he expected. *"Why?"*

Runt's low chord morphed into a growl. "Bresto say *Park say to—"*

"I got your message that he'd been locked up, sir," Bresto said. Runt wasn't happy about what they'd done to get Sevvers out, despite her crush on the skeeg. Still wasn't, apparently. "I got him out of there, just like you told me to."

A wave of static ripped through Park's reply. Outbound comms were degrading fast, and he still needed answers.

"Say again, sir?"

"—didn't—nd any message—"

Processor integrity and comm array warnings burst across the display. The smell of hot circuitry wafted through the control deck's cooling grills. Park's signal light went dark.

"Sir?" Bresto struck the side of the deck. The screen jumped and went black. "Twelfth-dammit!"

He swung back to slap the deck again, when Runt's big paw took him by the wrist. Her mouth hung open in a non-threatening way, but there was a sternness in her eyes.

"You not fix." The wolf really loved her ship.

"I know." Bresto slumped in his seat. "Fucking squids and their lucky shot."

"We go?" Runt asked. "See Park?"

The projection of ORD *Bedrock* turned lazily above the planning table. They had their orders. The ship was almost refueled…

Hell no. They'd done enough running for one day. None of this added up—not Park's new mission or his surprise about the Division. Sevvers had been Park's ace on their last mission. His combat drones were the only reason one fireteam of Marines could've done what they did aboard that derelict. Who else but Park would've wanted him out?

Doubt killed. He knew it. Experience said to follow orders, but the doubt inside him was getting louder. Aegia was in clear danger. His family was in clear danger. He didn't give twelve shits about some haunted rock. Had never been one for nuance or complex strategy. Give him a clear enemy, a straight fight.

So that's what he'd do—pick a straight fight. It beat sitting on his ass while his home world burned. Park had some explaining to do. "Wait here. I'll be back."

She padded after him, humming a lupanthaese warning song. "But Kull say—"

"I know what Kull say. I'll just steer clear of the command deck." He drew his blaster rifle from the weapons rack beside the exit hatch. Charge level, full. Fire selector, set to safe. "No one's going to mind some Marine moving through an exped with a little purpose."

"Go. With you," she insisted between discordant notes.

"It's safer for both of us if you stay. Besides, the Concordat will be here soon enough. Best if the Gauntlet is ready to fly before then."

"Where Bresto go?"

"I just need to find a working tac net array," he said. "And I know where they keep dozens of them on this ship."

Runt's pleas faded as he wound through the jump bay and into the cargo hold. The place was empty, hazard lights still flashing, the smell of smoke and welded hull patch still hanging on the air.

A shadow drifted up the open cargo ramp. Human. Male. His hazard vest said he was deck crew. Technician, probably. The hangar tech stopped abruptly, startled. Bresto slung his rifle.

"Apologies, Sergeant," he said with a relieved grin. "Flight Ops wanted to update you, but your comms were showing as down."

"And?"

"Your sub-light cells are topped off." The tech swallowed. "There's a launch window for you in twenty-five minutes when the inbound traffic slows down."

There wasn't any time to waste then. "That enough time for you to check our comms?"

The tech shrugged the tool satchel hanging on his shoulder. "Maybe. Depends on if it's a full buffer or fused silicon."

"What does a full buffer smell like?"

The tech laughed. "It doesn't."

"Better get to it then." Bresto moved to the *Gauntlet's* cargo ramp. Twenty-five minutes. That was his window for answers. He'd find working comms, then decide what to do.

"Where are you going, Sergeant?" the tech asked.

"Nowhere." He scanned the hangar deck for any sign of Kull or her command staff. All clear. He trudged down the ramp into the beating heart of the CDNS *Victory*.

CHAPTER
SEVEN

SQUAD BAY F-3 hummed with pre-drop tension. Marines filled the common area between rows of bunks stacked three high, swapping anxious chatter while they prepped for their mission. Open boxes littered the deck, brimming with foil tubes of field paste and sterile packs of hygiene wipes. Supply crates colored the same Marine green crowded the center aisle.

Olsom urged Vlan onward, searching the pressure-molded benches at the foot of each bunk for an open seat. Doc's drug had worked wonders. Vlan had stopped sobbing, maybe stopped feeling anything. His bright red face drew skeptical stares from the other Marines as they shuffled past.

"Fresh meat," someone called out from a nearby bunk.

"Welcome to the fleet," another smirked.

"Ignore them. They don't know you," Olsom whispered. "They don't know any of us."

"The racks are marked." Doc pointed to the nearest bunk where the numbers *1-2* were stenciled on the metal frame. "First Squad, Second Fireteam."

Easy enough.

She led Myers and the twins to Third Squad's racks at the furthest corner of the bay. The communal head was only a few meters away, and the nearby air smelled of soap and wet feet. The shower doors called to her. What she wouldn't give to stand under hot water, even for a few seconds. Let it wash away the day's horror and violence. But there was no time for that.

3-3's bunks were pristinely made, the sheets crisply folded and tucked beneath the mattress by whoever last occupied them. Ident-triggered padlocks hung from the three connected lockers, a reminder that this space still belonged to someone else. Her and the others were just filling in until Lieutenant Revan could get his people back. Then it would be off to some other bunk on some other ship for the rest of this Twelfth-forsaken war.

Load-bearing tactical vests kitted out with equipment pouches and armor plates lay in a messy pile in the center aisle. She rooted through the heavy gear, hunting for her size. Nothing but mediums, like always.

"Dammit, there's never any smalls." She dropped a tac vest back into its crate.

"They're adjustable." Doc shrugged into his tac vest with practiced ease, clipping it closed and giving the chest plate a reassuring thump.

"Yeah, from medium-ish to medium-er." She offered a vest to Vlan. "Here you go. Time to suit up."

The twin said nothing, still staring at his brother. Smokes didn't seem much better, each movement looking unsure—almost painful— as he pulled a vest from the crate.

"Thank—" Smokes nodded to his twin.

Vlan blinked as if he'd just woken up. "—you."

Olsom slapped Vlan on the shoulder as he took the vest and slowly slipped it on.

"Look alive, new blood!"

She turned in time to spot a packet of field wipes sailing toward her head and caught them with a surprised grunt. A young woman waved to her, weaving through the crowded bay, a spare tac vest hanging off her shoulder.

"You look like a small," the woman said. Her dark complexion and curly black hair stood out among the paler Aegians. She was strong-chinned and thick-bodied like them, with cheekbones to kill for.

"Good eye. Good arm, too."

"It's part of the job." The woman lobbed the spare vest onto the bottom bunk and stuck out a gloved hand. Her grip was firm. "Private Kitrelle, 3-2-2 breacher."

"PFC Olsom, 3-3-3 fireteam leader, I guess."

Kitrelle's eyes were warm and friendly despite her martial features. Olsom hadn't expected a welcoming gesture from their new unit, but damn did she need one.

"Who's your new friend, Bugs?" Doc asked, flashing a grin. "Lance Corporal Myers, Combat Engineer. Please, call me Doc."

"Look at you, all storms and granite." Kitrelle turned and hooked a thumb back at Doc. "He always like this?"

"Pretty much." Olsom let her grin slip. Cheekbones here wasn't half bad. Helped she wasn't interested in Doc.

"They pick you up from Two-Gamma?" Kitrelle sat hard on the bench and fidgeted with the straps on her tac vest, watching the Rikkos stare awkwardly at each other from both sides of the crate.

"Three-Alpha," Olsom said.

"Oh, shit. Is it as bad as they say? The raiders must be insane, attacking us head on like this."

"Not just raiders." She could still remember the look of tired dread on that bot jockey's face when he'd told her. "The Concordat are back. The Lost are… they're real. It's all real."

The words flowed out of her. There were a lot of old myths about Dead Earth. Billions of people—*billions*—taken and "daxed" into mindless, once-human machines. Believed to be lost forever, hence their tragic name.

Everyone knew daxed were real. There were daxed in the colonies. Last census put them at just under a quarter million. But they weren't mindless killing machines like in the stories. Most of them served the CDF. A few didn't. Something about their principles.

Their origin story had been just another myth until that moment on the tram ride to Three-Alpha's hangar deck. The void lit up all around them. Their own ships turned against them. Bresto was an asshole, but he wasn't a liar. No reason to doubt the bot jockey either. The Lost were real, and they were back.

There were fewer than a million humans in the Three Colonies. If there really were billions of Lost coming for them, humanity didn't stand a chance.

"Lost?" Kitrelle coughed out. "As in, *the* Lost?"

"Yeah."

"And you've seen them? With your own eyes?"

"Not exactly, I—"

"It's true." Doc sat beside Kitrelle, leaning a little too close. "Security forces barely held them off while we exfilled to the Victory."

"Yeah." Maybe this Aegian would believe one of her own. Maybe Doc could take a hint.

"I didn't…" Kitrelle began. "Sorry, they never tell us anything."

"That's standard operating procedure," Doc said.

"Archenemy invades? Tell no one. Sounds about right."

"Colony administrators are all the same," Olsom said. "They just don't want a panic."

"Aegia isn't like the other colonies, Vestian," Kitrelle shot back. "We remember where we came from, and who brought us here. If the Lost are out there, then the Twelfth won't be far behind."

The Twelfth. Now there was a Founders' tale. The god that had led humanity from Dead Earth to the Cradle, and who'd managed to save a few daxed along the way, it seemed.

Maybe if she had grown up beneath the safety of Aegia Prime, she would believe in a mythical guardian, too. Or maybe, after today, there'd be no more believers.

A young man strode from the showers into their side of the squad bay, his white-and-grays rolled to his waist revealing a lithe, tone frame that was borderline malnourished. His skin was a deep tan, almost bronze in the pale ship lighting.

He had to be Respitian. A wide scar split his full lips. More old injuries traced unsettling lines around his shaved head. Definitely Respitian.

"Twelfth isn't here," he said. "She not ever coming back."

Doc's jaw tensed. "What do you know, duster?"

"I know a story when I hear one, mountain man." The Respitian rolled his eyes and thumbed the padlock to the first locker on the opposite bunk.

"Don't mind that asshole," Kitrelle said. "Mez wouldn't know the Twelfth if She bit him in the ass."

Mez… Maybe this was Mezzior. The one Revan mentioned before Vlan lost it. Just great.

"She? No." Mez's reflection gazed at them from a mirror inside the locker, his lips curled in a serpentine grin. "You, though? Mez know that for sure."

Kitrelle rose from the bench. "I'm gonna scramjet. Your new squad mate is getting on my last damn nerve."

"Nice meeting you." Doc grinned again. "Save me a seat on the dropship, all right?"

Kitrelle rolled her eyes at Doc's little flirt. "Clean up and suit up, okay, new blood? Those things work better when you wear them."

Yeah, Cheekbones was alright. "Thanks."

Kitrelle moved back across the squad bay, exchanging easy words and more broad smiles with the other Marines of Third Platoon. It felt good to meet a friendly face, even if Kitrelle was a rough-around-the-edges zealot. Looking at the other Marines in their platoon, it seemed that personality was standard operating procedure, too.

Olsom caught a whiff of stale sweat and grimaced. Was that her? She lifted an arm and sniffed. Yep. The urge to feel clean, even for a second, was overwhelming. Wipes in hand, she retreated to the bottom bunk's semi-private confines beneath the shadow of the middle bunk.

"Kitrelle seems good to go," Doc said, glancing back as Olsom unzipped her uniform top. "Definitely a proper Aegian."

"Kitrelle's way out of your orbit." She snorted, heat rising in her cheeks. "Turn around."

He looked away and reclined against the metal bars at the foot of the bed. "You misunderstand me, Bugs. It's important for unit cohesion to get to know the other squads."

"Oh, I read you. Loud and clear."

She peeled the uniform down to her waist. No one seemed to notice. Who was she kidding? The Marine Recruit Depot had gnarled her already wiry frame. Burned away what passed for curves, buffed her already prominent shoulders. Not the kind of body that would turn heads in a room full of barrel-chested mountain folk.

Maybe Doc might try to steal another peek. Maybe she wanted him to. Could be fun. He was pretty for a Marine, with an easy confidence. Maybe in another universe. But here, she was fireteam leader. Wouldn't help things to be another notch on his chest plate. Guy like him probably had more than a few. She could see why.

The sterile wipes felt cool against her skin but did little for the wild smell rising from her underarms. Alcohol bit into cuts and scrapes she didn't remember getting. The fighting on Three-Alpha had happened so fast, she'd been on autopilot the whole time. With any luck, that same adrenaline-fueled focus would get her through whatever hell waited for them planetside. She tossed aside the last wipe, feeling sticky, damp, and irritated. Better than nothing maybe, but she was in no way clean.

A flicker of light drew her eye to the opposite bunk. Mez's reflection leered back at her from the mirror. His laser-like gaze made her skin crawl.

He slammed the locker closed. "Mmm, they grow 'em lean on Vestia, don't they? Mez bets you flex real good."

The words oozed like oil down her spine, a sickly-sweet sound that stung the back of her throat. Some things never changed. There was always some shitass like Mez lurking around. The admin blocks. The recruit depot. And now the CDNS *Victory*. Just another scav looking to bully their way to an easy score, even in the middle of a war. Not today, asshole. Not ever.

She turned her back on him, ignoring the burn of his stare between her shoulder blades as she slipped her arms through her uniform sleeves.

"Watch your fucking mouth, Mezzior," Doc said.

A warm flutter rose in her chest, but she tamped it down. Maybe Doc didn't have a clue, but he cared, in his way, and that was enough. She'd be damned if she was going to let anyone treat her like scraps to be fought over. The admin blocks taught her that.

Better to look out for yourself, lest you owe something in return. "At ease, Doc."

"Aye, PFC." His voice dripped sarcasm.

"At ease, Doc," Mez repeated, the scar through his lips thickened by his smile. "You trained him real well, girl."

Doc launched from his seat and thumped his chest plate with both fists. "Good to go duster! Why don't you say that again to my fucking face?"

"Hey!" Olsom rolled from the bunk and caught the drag handle of Doc's tac vest. A slight turn at her waist and he was off balance, forcing him backwards until his center-of-gravity returned.

"Hey! What the hell, Bugs?"

"I don't want any of us to end up on Revan or Lessig's shit list." She stole a glance down the center of the squad bay. No one cared about their little exchange. Yet. "Besides, I can handle myself, okay?"

A low chuckle came from behind her. "Girl can handle Mez anytime."

Mez's stare felt like a tangible thing trickling down her back. She turned, shoulders squared, fists clenched at her side. His eyes were sticky things that made her itch for more sterile wipes.

His tone deepened as he mimicked her Vestian drawl, eyes lingering on her uniform. "Olsom. O-l-s-o-m. Just one letter shy of wholesome, ain't ya? Bet that's a lie."

"Take my name outta your mouth, Mez."

He edged closer, lips parting, hand reaching for her waist. "You first."

She shifted back a step, the cold snap of fight-or-flight surging through her veins.

Smokes lumbered forward, almost half a meter taller than Mez and just as skinny. His eyes were set hard, the anger plain on his wrinkled face. "Back off, you…"

Vlan didn't seem to notice—half-awake, hands gripping his tac vest collar while he stared at the toes of his boots. Smokes' anger turned to confusion, like he couldn't finish the words on his own.

Mez watched them with a hang-jawed grin.

"Why, looky here," he said, still in his mocking Vestian, "the spacer wants to play hero. Sit down, freak, before Mez bend you harder than gravity."

Instinct took over, a current through a live wire. She gouged Mez's throat with fingers straight as a knife's edge. He fell backward, choking, stumbling, eyes wide with shock. She threw her body weight into him, landing an elbow strike to his face that pinned him to the locker. The feel of his face mashed against the metal door brought a rush of satisfaction. The wild thing in her purred.

His crazy blue eyes found hers, his swelling lip not enough to hide his repulsive grin. The soft click of opening metal sent more electricity through her nerves. Something sharp pressed against her belly. A blade, a knife—something. Electricity turned to icy panic.

"Mez got you, Wholesome." He chuckled, face still smashed between her elbow and the locker. The knife's point slipped through synthweave fabric and bit her skin. "Mez always got you."

She froze, pulse drumming in her ears. Noone else seemed to notice, and those that did looked more entertained than concerned. They couldn't see the knife. Or they didn't care.

She grabbed his wrist, but his arm wouldn't budge. No leverage up close. Whatever Mez was doing, this wasn't Marine training. Gang shit, maybe. Maybe all the stories about Respitian slums were true?

"What's your hurry, girl?" he asked in his oily, urban tone. His eyes raked her up and down again. "We all gonna die soon. You and Mez no different. Might as well go out with a—"

"Quit grab-assing around, you two." Corporal Lessig's booming voice sent a ripple of relief through her core. "There's a fucking war on. Get your asses to the exo bay, now."

The knife vanished from her side, along with Mez's slimy grin. She stepped back, one hand still up in a guard, the other cradling her stomach. No blood. Mez knew his way around a blade.

The rest of Third Platoon began double-timing out of the exit hatch.

Lessig moved through them with a purpose, his scowl somewhere between confusion and annoyance.

"Bad move on your first day." He stopped short, tsk-tsking through bared teeth. "A boot like you ought to know better."

Her first instinct was to run to him. To point out the monster who'd threatened her. But that wasn't how the Colonial Defense Marines operated. Slaying monsters was a part of the job. Her job.

Standard operating procedure. And there were so many monsters just then.

She dropped her hands and stood at attention. "Aye, Corporal."

"And you." Lessig leveled a finger at Mez. "You're on your last fucking life, Mezzior. You got me?"

"Aye, Corporal." Mez straightened, barely, just enough not to get his ass beaten for insubordination. He leered back at her from the corners of his eyes.

This wasn't over. Not by a long shot. But they would have to settle up later. The Concordat were on their way, and it was time to metal up.

CHAPTER
EIGHT

THE EXO BAY doors rolled shut with a heavy bang. Bresto scanned the orderly rows of exo armor standing in formation down the center of the bay.

"Sarnt." The young armory tech hung a right down the gangway along the bulkhead wall. Damn kid didn't even bother to check his idents. Lucky for him. Nothing to see here. Just another Marine sergeant preparing for a fight. Even if it was the wrong one.

Metal umbilicals hung like thick, black rope from the high ceiling, keeping the dormant exo suits connected to the *Victory's* power and data feeds. He knew every square millimeter, every panel and seam on those machines. Had been a fireteam leader a long time. Too long. The smell of armor paint and magneto-hydraulics centered him in a way that was hard to explain. More of a home than Diacad Cliffs ever was. He was proud of that. Sad, too.

Platoons of Marines flowed through the hatchways on the opposite side of the bay. Company A, according to the large block letter etched on the nearby pylon. Armorers distributed tac gear and small arms. Platoon sergeants bellowed for fireteam leaders to "Metal up!"

Twelfth, what he wouldn't give to go with them. Nothing in the Cradle could stop a Marine and his exo. Warrior squids had a good thirty kilos on the average human male. The exos evened the odds and then some. These models might not be top-of-the-line CDF hard suits, but they were more than capable of protecting Aegia.

Exos also had their own tac net relay, able to sync with tactical and strategic feeds on a planetary scale. Exactly what he needed to get comms with Park back. They weren't powerful enough to reach out-system on their own, but he might be able to forward a transmission on the ship's relay while they were still connected to the *Victory's* arrays. A few minutes with an empty suit and its control deck, then he could confirm his orders. Maybe even change Park's mind about this wild crid chase to some haunted rock.

He wouldn't have much time. Victory would be gearing up—by company, by platoon, by squad—preparing for the drop. A, B, C, all the way to F. That gave him fifteen, maybe twenty minutes, if he borrowed one of Company F's exos. That could work.

The armory tech looked up from his bench as Bresto made his way to Company F's staging area. "Need something, Sarnt?"

Bresto shrugged the slung rifle on his shoulder. "No. Brought my own."

"Don't remember seeing you around. You one of the scratch Marines we picked up from the orbitals?"

Twelfth Herself. *Now* the damn tech had questions.

"Yeah."

"Someone already issue your personal?"

Not exactly. He'd lifted it off some unconscious Division guard when he'd gotten Sevvers out of the brig. That wasn't part of the original plan, but the Concordat's sudden arrival required some improvising. Last thing he needed was this tech scanning his rifle. That would set off alarms from here to Respitia after what he'd done to get it.

"Picked it up on Three-Alpha." That was technically true.

"Oh, shit. You've seen some action already. Let me just check it in for you. You know, chain of custody."

Bresto eyed the kid's rank. Time to use his own.

"Look, Lance Corporal, the XO wants me to make sure this metal is good to go. We can take care of the admin shit after the war, check?"

"Say again, Sarnt? The major asked *you* to do exo prep?" The tech didn't buy it. Made sense. This was not standard operating procedure.

"We've been over these suits twice since the attack began. It's all in the logs."

Twelfth save him. At least the kid was trying to do his job now, but his timing sucked.

"How many combat drops have you prepped, Marine?"

The tech swallowed. "None, Sarnt."

"There's your answer. The major wants more experienced eyes on before we drop into the shit storm that's waiting for us." Even as he said it, he wanted it to be true. To go and fight with them. For his family. "And I don't want to give her a reason to add my balls to what is undoubtedly an extensive collection, check?"

The tech snorted. "Yes, Sarnt. Sorry, Sarnt."

Bresto set his jaw. That could have gone all kinds of sideways. He didn't blame the kid for trying to do his job. But on a day like today, no one was checking idents. Their enemies were made of scales and tendrils. Of metal. Chitin. All the admin work could wait.

Company F's exos waited in formation at the aft end of the bay. Each machine stood at attention, their operator cages open and waiting. The MAC-4s weren't vacuum-proof like hard suits. No reactive armor; no thrust vectoring system. No auto-doc, either.

But they were 500 kilos heavier with a Halton reactor to match. Bigger, stronger, meaner. Two primary arms for environment manipulation and close combat. Fleet-standard weapon hardpoints for exoserved weapons and utility platforms. These models were kitted out in the Mark Three, his personal favorite. It added a dedicated secondary reactor and two more control arms equipped with a light railgun and a FAB.

On its own, one MAC-4 Mark Three could do serious damage. An exped full would lay waste to the enemies of humanity. He almost relished the fight. Felt the tang of adrenaline and violence in his blood.

The end of the exo bay was empty. Nobody watching. No prying questions. The corner unit's shoulder plate felt cool against his fingertips. Its unit designator read 3-3-3. Third Platoon, Third Squad, Third Fireteam. Tail-end Copper. Last of the last.

This exo had seen some action. The MAC-4 design was fifty, maybe sixty years old. Most of these units had probably been around that long, and 3-3-3 was no exception. Scratches and gouges in the armor plate had been painted over and over again in Colonial Defense Marine green. Duller than CDF standard green good. A holdover from Dead Earth, someone had told him once.

Inside the cage, the familiar mesh seatback gripped his shoulders and back. 3-3-3's operator terminal flashed ready—a pitch black screen with scrolling amber text. The control stick on the right arm rig clicked with each nudge until the COMMS MAINT option glowed dirty yellow.

No mission tasking. Local net feeds only. Extra-system relay access restricted. Select primary net channel.

Shit. Without relay access, he couldn't reach Park from this or any other exo aboard the *Victory*. Part of him was glad. The rock mission made zero sense. Maybe there was some bigger picture Park had his eye on, but the situation at Aegia was plenty bad and plenty big. Maybe the Aegian feeds…

Access granted.

He thumbed through the local net channels, one by one. If he couldn't reach Park, he was duty-bound to do everything he could to repel the Concordat invasion of his home. And since Kull didn't want him on her ship, that left the Planetary Reserve.

Tiny voices began to play through the exo's emitters.

"—Cargo Ops Azure-12 requesting immediate void support. Raider corvettes inbound on our—"

Not his problem. Nothing he could do. Numbers turned on the terminal screen as he scrolled through the tac net frequencies. Slowly, Aegia's Planetary Reserve net channels clicked into focus. The voices planetside were less panicked, more bored or confused. That checked out.

"This is OP-6, nothing to report."

"—Edmunsson, move your ass, or the CO's going to—"

Fucking Planetary Reserve. They were lucky to have a former Marine like Lyra.

"OP-12 here. I see multiple debris impacts inside Vestebrae. No sign of hostiles—"

Things were still relatively quiet on the surface. Good. Better debris hitting the capitol than raider landing craft. His home was a few kilometers away in Diacad Cliffs. He still had time.

Bresto locked in the PR channel and keyed in their private freq: *484.092.ti.0.* The channel prefix corresponded to the day they'd met. Lyra was a trigger-puller, too, back then—hard as granite and twice as mean. But she gave it all up when Kaff was born. He couldn't do it.

Lyra still loved him. She didn't know any other way. But her love had an edge to it ever since that had only gotten sharper.

The emitters chirped with incoming traffic. Lyra's voice filtered through the tiny emitters, rich and gravelly. *"This is Reserve Lieutenant Lyra Bresto, broadcasting on a dedicated channel—"*

Twelfth, how he'd missed her. "Lyra, it's Ned. Solid copy."

"—for Marine Sergeant Ned Bresto." She kept talking, like she hadn't heard him. The signal strength indicator on the edge of the exo's control terminal read full strength. *"I've mustered to a predetermined staging area. Can't say where, of course. OPSEC protocols are in full effect."*

"I read you, Lyra. What's your status? Where are—"

"There's some kind of attack in high orbit. Reserve Command isn't telling us anything, per usual. You know how staff officers can be. But something has them scared. Rumor underground says they've mustered the entire reserve."

It wasn't her. Just a recording.

He squeezed the push-to-talk until the bulky plastec casing let out a hollow crack, furious that she couldn't hear him. "It's the Concordat. They're back."

"The kids…" For the first time, she sounded afraid. *"I left them home alone when I reported in. Sammy hasn't been feeling well, and Kaffy missed her drills, so I sent her to get our lots."*

The ache in his chest went deeper, swirling in his guts. Sammy was by himself. Kaff was at the allotment center, out in the open. And Lyra was Twelfth-only-knew where, with the forge ship bearing down on them all.

"They're opening up the shelters." Exhaustion crept in between her words. *"I know the block captains will round everyone up, but the kids won't be together. So, I'm worried."*

The rhythmic shuffle of touch static bled through her signal, like she was adjusting her throat mic.

"I know you're close. If you receive this... get down here and find them. Please. You owe me that, Ned."

The signal chirped again, and she faded from his ears. Five seconds later, another chirp, and the message played again. Reserve Lieutenant Lyra Bresto, broadcasting on a dedicated channel. A message loop left just for him, right where she knew he would find it.

He sagged back into the exo's mesh seat. The comm logs said the transmission was an hour old. Sammy and Kaff *should* be safely underground by now. The settlements trained for this. But Lyra seemed worried. She'd mustered in a hurry by the sounds of it, too quick to make sure the kids got where they needed to go.

Maybe Reserve Command knew what they were up against. Or maybe they still had their thumbs up their asses. Typical officers were bad enough, mostly rich brats looking for glory. But those in Reserve Command were different—a special kind of lazy, entitled bootlickers. They couldn't handle what was coming.

Nothing about it made him feel any better about Lyra's safety, or the kids.

The distant rumble of boots on deck plating shook him from his thoughts. A wave of voices grew clearer with each passing second.

"Metal up!" someone shouted, the words bouncing off the steep bulkheads. "Let's go, Company F, double time!"

Out of time. 3-3-3 was someone else's rig. He keyed away the comms maintenance screen when a thick shadow fell across the exo's terminal.

"Comm problems, Sergeant?" The man's voice tripped a switch in Bresto's memory. Deep and refined. A staff officer. The long row of silver pips op his collar marked him as a colonel. Had to be Reede, *Victory's* CO.

"No, sir." Bresto punched the terminal's standby key, and the screen went blank. He stepped out of 3-3-3's cage, made a smart about-face and stood at attention.

The colonel held up a hand and shook his head. "At ease, Marine. Bresto. You're from Three-Alpha."

"Yes, sir."

"Hell of a job you all did back there. Station defenses are holding, barely." Reede's gaze swept the rows of exos behind him. "No rest for the weary, though."

"Sir."

Sounded like Reede didn't know that Kull had ordered him to stay aboard the *Gauntlet*. Didn't matter now. He wasn't about to ask. Reede took a step down the gangway and motioned for him to follow. He kept two respectful paces back, just to the colonel's left.

"Is it true what they say? That thing out there is a Concordat ship?"

"Yes, sir."

"And the Lost?"

"Yes, sir. They were assaulting the hangar ring before we exfilled. Wouldn't have made it without the Daxed Corps backing us up."

"No Found daxed to back us up where we're going. You've seen those things up close. Fought them. What can you tell me about their tactics, their weaknesses?"

Weaknesses—right. "None to speak of, sir. I've seen the big ones take an LEC slug center-mass and stand back up. And the skinny ones..." He grimaced at the thought of the masked gray corpses dancing through the air, their razor-sharp appendages slicing through armor, flesh, and bone. "Charged particles will put them down. If you can hit them."

Reede's face pinched. "And they really are... human?"

"Not anymore, sir. Not in a long time."

"Damn," Reede muttered. "Sounds like we're in for one hell of a fight."

"Sir, if those things get down there, then it's already too late."

Reede stifled a tired laugh. "The Victory is equipped for surface actions—settlement and station defense, not void warfare. Our MAC-4s aren't airtight. I won't send my Marines into a hostile boarding action aboard an alien ship with only emergency rebreathers."

Top of the line hardsuits and Division combat drones were the only way Bresto's reinforced fireteam had escaped the forge ship with only 50% casualties. That, and whatever Lernus was. Reede was right. A direct attack on the forge ship was suicide.

"No, Sergeant, we'll keep the archenemy off the Holy Mother's mountain. And pray that the Autonomous Weapons Division destroys that Concordat ship before it reaches the surface."

"Yes, sir." Six hours in, and there was still no sign of a Division counterassault. Any fucking day, Sevvers. Somebody needed to fight this battle, if he couldn't.

Reede continued onward down the gangway. "Major Kull says you're on a classified run for some Spec Ops lieutenant out of Respitia. Must be important, given what we're facing here. Victory could use an NCO with your experience, especially now."

So, Kull had briefed Reede after all. Reede must've seen things a little differently, since Bresto wasn't being marched to the *Victory's* brig at gun point.

"It is, sir. Important." The colonel's laser-like stare said he wasn't convinced. "We were aboard that thing when it was just a derelict at the edge of the Cradle. Looking for something that could stop the Concordat for good."

Reede came to a stop in the middle of the gangway. Junior Marines jogged past them, drop ready in their tac gear and blaster rifles, shouting "By your leave, sir!"

"You knew this would happen?" There was a hint of danger in Reede's tone. Like he might blame Bresto for everything that had happened that day, and for all the suffering and death to come. Maybe he should.

"No, sir. That ship was dead when we found it." Bresto met Reede's icy stare, straight-backed, arms at his sides. "Colonial Intelligence and Fleet Command kept our mission details under wraps. Didn't want to cause a panic."

"Hmph, Colonial Intelligence indeed." One corner of Reede's lips lifted in a grim smile.

"You don't know the half of it, sir."

Reede studied Bresto a long moment. Like he was searching for something. For the truth, maybe. Whatever he found seemed to satisfy him. His focus shifted to the Marines rushing around them.

Reede clasped Bresto's shoulder in a firm grip. "Well, son, I hope you find what it is you're looking for out there. We'll hold the mountain until you get back."

"Thank you, sir."

The colonel turned to go, then paused. "I'll keep a jump seat open for you. If you change your mind."

Reede disappeared into the crowd, the colonel's words still echoing in Bresto's ears. The exo bay suddenly felt too small, too crowded. Lyra's voice played on a loop inside his head, her message tinged with fear and desperation. Kaff and Sammy, alone in a world on fire. And here he was, caught between duty and family, orders and instinct.

If there really was a way to end the Concordat threat, once and for all, he'd be crazy not to try. But the doubt in him was growing louder, and it sounded just like Lyra. What did it matter if he couldn't save his family when they were *right there*? Yeah, the choice was always shit, but this one felt different. Like it would change everything. For Aegia. For his family. For him.

THE EXO BAY doors parted with a heavy rumble, revealing a forest of matte green steel and barely controlled chaos. Olsom waited at the threshold, tac gear snugged a little too tight around her body. Rows of MAC-4 exo suits gazed back at her through their empty operator cages. Techs in grease-stained overalls darted between them, their shouts lost between bursts of mag-driven tools and whirring servos. The clank of heavy tread on metal deck plate echoed through the bay as other *Victory* companies put their exos through hasty function checks.

"Let's go, boot," Lessig barked, giving a not-so-gentle nudge forward.

The smell of ozone and machine grease hit like a wall. She sniffed again, deeper. So familiar. Something she'd grown up around. Before— No. No time for that.

As they turned down the gangway, Lessig's gruff exterior softened slightly. "First time in an exo bay?"

"Yes, Corporal," she said, still staring at the hulking machines.

"At ease with that. Keep it tight when staff NCOs or the brass are around. Otherwise, it's just Lessig."

"Roger."

"These beauties are about to become your new best friend." He rapped his knuckles against the nearest suit's shin plate. "Just like good hardwine, they only get better with age."

Doc's eyes gleamed with excitement as he pointed to another MAC-4 at the edge of the exo pit. "Check it out. Primary arms for close combat, plus two secondaries—that's your LEC and FAB."

Thank you, Lance Corporal Know-It-All. "I know, Doc."

"You don't know shit until you've seen these things in action." He held out an arm like a long gun and mimed a jerking recoil. "Fwap-boom! Nothing left but loose atoms."

She grinned. "Done a lot of combat drops, have you?"

"Live fire ranges. Range maintenance is part of a combat engineer's OTJ."

On-the-job training. She was about to get a lot of that. They all were.

The twins' unsteady footsteps drew closer. Smokes's face was a mask of concentration. Vlan drifted along at his side, eyes flitting from one machine to the next.

"You two okay?"

"It's the drug," Smokes began.

Vlan let his mouth hang open. "It feels… floaty."

They seemed better. Or maybe that was wishful thinking. The thought of Vlan drugged out of his mind or inconsolable without his brother sat like a tungsten slug in her gut. But Smokes had his own fireteam to lead, and Vlan was her responsibility now. Bet they didn't teach that at exo school.

"But you're good to go?" she repeated.

The twins exchanged a look, then nodded together. "We can fight," they said, Vlan's words slurring a second behind.

"Mez wanna see that." The Respitian sidled up behind them, hands in his pockets, looking more like sand-blown block trash than a Colonial Defense Marine. "Bet those squiddies chew you up and spit you out."

"You first," the twins replied.

"Hmph." Mez paced around the twins, putting himself between them and Olsom.

The familiar spike of adrenaline stung her veins. He wouldn't get the drop on her again. "Back off, Mez."

He spun to face her, hands raised in mock surrender. "Easy, Wholesome. Same team, remember?"

"Hey, Mez," Lessig said.

"Yeah, Corporal?"

"Fuck off."

"Aye, Corporal." Mez flashed a scarred grin and shuffled off into the armory crowd.

Lessig didn't know Mez had threatened to stab her just for sticking up for her friend. She'd had disagreements with other Marines. Some even came to blows. But none had ever threatened to kill her over anything. But ratting Mez out felt petty now, with the Concordat on the verge of winning the first battle in this new war and taking the one of the Three Colonies with it.

"Mez is a dick," Lessig said with no trace of judgment.

She smirked. "Yes, he is."

"But you need to let that shit go." Lessig was taller and three times as wide, which made his firm stare cut right through her. "When you're getting lit up by squid laser fire, it all comes down to the humans to your left and right. Even the dicks."

Yeah. Petty was the right word.

Private Kitrelle waved from the other side of the line, then started towards Olsom with a half-dozen more Marines in tow. They had already drawn the rest of their tac gear: wrist-mounted flexscreens with tac net access, ballistic helmets with charge absorbent weave and integrated comms, and CR-11 blaster rifles with integrated optics and spare charge packs. Everything a Marine needed to fight in atmo. Kitrelle had a line of brick-shaped pouches hanging from the front of her vest. Plasmex charges, standard issue for a breacher. She was wearing enough inert plasma to blow a hole in the *Victory's* fibrosteel skin.

"New blood!" Kitrelle swaggered like a pinup from the recruiting posters. "Why aren't you metalled up yet? We've got archenemy to kill."

"Got held up," Olsom said, but Mez was gone.

A stocky Marine next to the breacher stepped forward, cleft chin beneath a wide face screwed into a skeptical glare. Olsom didn't like it. Bet he didn't look at other mountain folk that way.

"Kitty says you came in hot from Three-Alpha," the Marine said. Prelk. "That right?"

"Yeah, that's us," Doc said.

Something flashed across Prelk's face—embarrassment, maybe, or fear. "She said you said you saw the Lost."

The words were an explosive decompression, silencing the crowd around them. Dozens of eyes were on her in an instant. Curious. Skeptical. Angry. Afraid. Who was this Vestian to tell them their faith had been wrong all along? That humanity's savior had left a few loose ends that threatened to wipe out everything they had left.

"Well, I didn't... *see* them." She cleared her throat. "But it's true. They were there, on Three—"

"Crid shit," someone shouted.

"Twelfth save us," called another.

Fists thudded against chestplates, with more Aegians taking up the display. Kitrelle pressed her knuckles to the brick of plasmex over her heart, beaming with granite pride.

"She is our shield!" Prelk bellowed.

Kitrelle stood straighter. "We are Her sword!"

More Marines picking up the refrain. Even Doc joined in, quietly at first, then louder. "For Her glory. For humanity. For the Lost!"

The drone of voices faded, all eyes still fixed on Olsom like she'd been the target of some religious assault. Mez reappeared at the end of the line, dressed in his breacher's loadout. He threw another gnarled grin, as if to say, *they're all fucking crazy, eh?* The raw solidarity of it turned her stomach.

"Twelfth Herself!" a gravelly voice boomed. "What is this? Crid fuckin', Twelfth-damned prayer hour?"

Hot, sour breath stung the back of Olsom's neck. The crowd of faithful snapped to attention, their religious certainty replaced with the familiar terror only a senior NCO could bring. The look on Doc's face confirmed what she already knew. She turned, slowly, ready for it all to end. Ready to die. To simply cease to exist.

The older man stood just a few centimeters taller than her. He was slim for an Aegian, all gristle and sinew. A scar with a face. He wore no tac gear, the sleeves of his faded white-and-grays rolled halfway up his forearms. The scent of shaving cream and boot polish followed him, his hair so high-and-tight every strand stood at attention. There were more black pips on his collar than she had seconds left to live.

"Who. The fuck. Are you?" First Sergeant Druggan shouted, each word an orbital strike to the face. Flecks of spittle misted her cheek.

"PFC Larke Olsom, First Sarnt!" She snapped to, stiff as the corpse she was about to be.

His narrow, gray eyes scanned the gangway like targeting lasers, taking in the other Marines before snapping back to her. She was done for. Target acquired and locked. Shot over. Vapor. What had Doc said? Oh yeah, loose atoms.

"Are you the Twelfth reborn?" he said, still shouting. "Am I to give my heart and life to you in service to humanity?"

Shame burned behind her eyes. She bit the inside of her lip, hard, to hold back the tears.

"No," she managed, trying not to blink. She couldn't cry. Could. Not. Cry. "No, First Sarnt."

Druggan lifted his chin, gazing at her over his crooked nose. He roared down the gangway: "You hear that, you limp-dicked, greasy-handed fucks? Your attention has been misplaced. So get your shiny asses in gear. We got enemy to kill. Move!"

That last word sent the Marines of Company F down the passageway to their waiting exos. Olsom turned to go. She wanted out of there, to be gone, to disappear.

"Not you." Druggan's voice was a low predator growl.

She froze mid-stride. Doc stared back at her, eyes wide, begging her not to move. The Rikkos stooped in the middle of the gangway, eyebrows raised. She turned back to the first sergeant, uncertainty clamping tight around her throat.

Druggan eyed the ceiling. "Lessig!"

The corporal appeared seconds later, still tightening the straps of his own tac gear. He seemed unbothered by Druggan's outburst. "Yes, First Sarnt?"

"The Twelfth Herself has seen fit to deliver us fresh killers from Orbital Three-Alpha." Druggan's steely eyes betrayed nothing. But there was more to him than his cold, soulless exterior let on. "I want them metalled up yesterday. We've got atmo to burn."

"Aye, First Sarnt." He made a fist, adjusting the fit of his flexscreen. "Come on, this way."

Olsom stood at attention again. "Aye, Corporal. Thank you, First Sarnt."

Druggan loosed a smokey chuckle as he turned to leave. "You want to thank me? Kill more of those fuckers."

———

Olsom lifted the lip of her helmet and tightened the chin strap to keep it in place. Nervous sweat itched her neck and back, her tac gear holding on to the humidity like a walk through the Tangle back home.

The MAC-4 loomed in front of her, part exo suit, part metal monster, its operator cage hinged up and open like a plexene jaw. Its long metal arms hung from raised shoulders, nearly scraping the deck like a Vestian field ape, all shoulders and head with no neck. Like it was locked in permanent, shrugged confusion. The ident 3-3-3 was stenciled in flat black on its shoulder guards.

Doc weaved his fingers together and bent over. "Go on. I'll boost you up."

"I got it." She grabbed the handles on either side of the mesh seat and hauled herself into the cage. Doc's hand found her back, holding her steady while she faced outward and slotted her arms and legs into the control rigs.

Cockpit wasn't the right word. Operators didn't pilot an exo, they wore it. Computers translated their movement into the MAC-4's legs and primary arms. Hat sticks in the arm rigs controlled the weapon systems.

A strap pulled tight around her leg. "Too tight?" Doc asked. She shook her head, and Doc snugged the other leg rig to her thigh. "Put your harness on and I'll button you up."

"Okay." She fumbled with the heavy buckle until the six straps locked into place. The operator cage swung closed, the overhead light dimming slightly through the thick canopy. The greasy smell teasing her memory grew stronger in the confines of the cage.

Doc took a step back and grinned that damn grin. "Looking real metal, Bugs. How does it feel?"

"Heavy." The control rigs kept her legs tight to 3-3-3's, and they wouldn't budge. "It smells like old man sweat in here."

Doc chuckled. "Smells like Victory."

"Oh, Twelfth, was that a pun?" Too cute, Doc.

He banged his knuckles on the canopy, then pointed at the control terminal on her side of the plexene. "Run your pre-starts. You can navigate the menu with your hat triggers."

"I know, I know."

One click of the control hat and the terminal powered on.

MARINE ARMOR, COMBAT, MOD 4.

...Pre-Start Checks: Incomplete.

...Ready Status: Standby Mode.

She tabbed the hat down one, turning the words *PRE-START CHECKS* a pale yellow on the black screen. Miniaturized fusion had been around for a long time, but there was something about having the equivalent of a tiny sun strapped to her back that didn't sit well in the pit of her stomach.

"Pre-starts go."

The powerpack at her back hummed to life. Exhaust fans whirred, followed by the *clicky-clack* sound of fusion magnetics warming up. Hydraulics hissed as start-up logs flashed across the terminal screen.

INITIATING PRE-START CHECKS.

...Operating System: Good.

...Mobility System: Good.

...Comm System: Good.

...Auxiliary Weapons System: Good.

...Fusion Control: Good.

...Cooling System: FAILURE.

Sweet Founders, a startup failure. Even the exo didn't like her. "Uh, Doc?"

"What is it?"

"It says cooling system failure?" She gave the terminal screen a tap.

"On it." Doc vanished behind the exo. A few seconds later, heavy metal bangs vibrated through the exo suit. "Try again!"

Something clicked into place. The sound of spinning fans grew louder, thrumming through the back of her suit. It felt as if she might launch from the deck like some atmospheric transport. The control terminal flashed green.

...Pre-Start Checks: Good.

...Ready Status: Startup Mode.

Well, well—Doc knew his shit after all. She'd never hear the end of it.

"Hey, you good?" he shouted.

Thanks to him. "Yes!"

"Just some debris in the starboard exhaust fan." Doc reappeared, face pressed to the canopy, eyeing the control terminal. "What are you waiting for? Metal up, girl!"

Three clicks right and the reactor start command lit up.

"Clear!" she shouted and keyed the hat. A loud, electric clap emanated from the big machine. Energy levels on the control terminal climbed from red to yellow, then green. 3-3-3 vibrated with power. The plexene canopy lit up with a holographic heads-up display, filling up with blue returns from the IFF feeds. Doc's blue avatar filled the display.

Umbilicals came free with a hiss and a snap. Suddenly, the heavy machine felt limber, almost weightless. She put one foot in front of the other to keep from falling. 3-3-3 responded, servos humming as its thick metal leg mirrored her own. There was the slightest delay, barely half a heartbeat, like stepping in wet mud. The exo's sawtooth tread clanged hard against the deck plate.

"Woah-ho," she said, grinning uncontrollably. She raised her arms in a fighting stance, and the exo did the same.

Doc smiled back at her over the black metal fists.

"How do I look?" she called.

"Like the god of metal and broken hearts." He took a few steps back. "Safeties on?"

Weapon status indicators glowed green good in the corner of the HUD. "Uh, yeah."

"Then show me the goods, girl." He tapped his flexscreen. "Let's start with the LEC, light electromag—."

"Rail gun, got it." She jammed the left control hat forward. Servos hummed as the port-side auxiliary arm swung forward, revealing a thick, gunmetal cannon two meters long. An underslung drum magazine held twenty tungsten slugs, and thick black power cables ran from the rear housing along the arm and to the secondary powerpack on the Mark Three.

"LEC looks good," he said, mostly to himself, still swiping at his flexscreen. "Now show me the FAB, the—"

"Fireteam Automatic Blaster." The right control hat clicked forward, and a fourth arm appeared. The FAB's matte black tri-barrels whirred and locked into place. Separate targeting reticles appeared on the HUD, one for each weapon. She worked both control hats at once, panning the targeting reticules over Doc's head at the nearby bulkhead. The lethal arms whirred, tracking their movements. Firing just one of these weapons must be incredible. But both at the same time? The wild thing in her licked its lips.

"Whoa." He ducked out of the way and stepped beneath the heavy weapons. "Careful where you point those things. You might give a guy ideas."

"In your dreams." She rolled her eyes to hide the flash of warmth crawling up her neck.

"Now, now, let's keep it professional." He aimed a flashlight into the grooves along the railgun's underside, then between the barrels of the FAB. "All good here. You can put these away for now. You know, leave a little to the imagination."

A chirp sounded in her helmet. Lieutenant Revan's ident lit up her HUD. "—*All fireteam leaders, prepare for drop package inload. I say again, unit designation is Fury 3. All fireteam leaders, prepare for drop package inload. We drop in ten. Fury 3 Actual, out.*"

The warning echoed in her head. She'd gone from recruit training to the front lines in the blink of an eye, and now she was expected to lead. 3-3-3's confines suddenly felt alien, oppressive.

Doc held a finger to the side of his helmet, listening. He was… calm, excited even. How? Ten minutes to drop, and he looked like he was confirming a lunch date. Maybe he was just better at faking it. Right now, she'd settle for her hands to stop shaking long enough to work the damn controls.

Colonel Reede's ident appeared next—Commanding Officer, Victory Expeditionary Force. It was happening. This was it.

"Attention Victory personnel. This is Victory Actual. I'll be brief, because time is not on our side. Our archenemy, the Concordat, the killers of Dead Earth, have launched a surprise attack on Aegia Prime."

The channel went clear comms quiet. Marines turned to the observation platform on the starboard side of the bay. Colonel Reede's distant figure gripped the railing, glowing friendly blue through the HUD. Major Kull stood beside him, looking more machine than 3-3-3. First Sergeant Druggan was there, too, along with other senior staff.

"With raider squadrons and captured CDF vessels in support, their forge ship has achieved void superiority in high orbit. Orbital Three-Alpha is under sustained assault, but CDF forces still control the station."

Muted cheers rippled through the Marine formation. Reede lifted a hand, his stern face paled in the HUD's blue glow.

"Their objective is to remove Aegia Prime from the board and take control of Vestebrae and its outlying settlements." He seemed to scan the crowd as if looking for someone, before continuing, *"I have multiple reports that Lost daxed have been sighted among the attacking forces. I don't need to remind any of you of our history. The stakes here are nothing less than the subjugation of our bodies and the annihilation of our spirit. If Aegia falls, the Three Colonies will fall."*

Olsom's grip tightened on the controls. This was never just about Aegia. It was everything. Everyone. Her mind raced to Vestia, to those she'd left behind. If she failed here, they wouldn't stand a chance. Cold clarity settled over her. She wouldn't—*couldn't*—fail. Not while she could still fight. Even if no one back home had ever fought for her.

Colonel Reede eyed the formation beneath him, jaw set firm, his voice loud in the bay. *"There is no surrender. No retreat. Twelfth-willing, there is only Victory."*

First Sergeant Druggan snapped to attention, his gruff voice echoing off tall bulkheads. "Give 'em one, Victory!"

The roar rose like a thunderstorm above the formation of white and gray uniforms and green metal. It stirred something old and primal deep in Olsom's heart. The fear began to fade, replaced with a certainty born of training and faith. Not in some god, but in the Marines at her side and the leaders at her front. A glimmer of something like belonging.

She pumped a metal fist to the ceiling and took up the call. The wild thing in her arched its neck and howled.

"Ooh-rah!" she roared. Again and again, until her throat ran raw.

Colonel Reede made a crisp about face, returned the major's salute, then strode from the observation deck.

Kull took his place at the railing, adjusted her throat mic, and spoke.

"Dismissed, Marines," she bellowed. Her ident flashed in the command net feed. *"All companies to your dropships. Let's go pick a fight."*

Heavy interior partitions, two decks high, rumbled open, revealing a long ramp leading down to the hangar deck. Eighteen dropships waited nose to nose, payload doors down and locked, each ready to receive a platoon and its exos. The thunderous cheers had barely faded when the sound of alert klaxons ripped through the bay. Hazard lights spun along the wall, bathing the fibrosteel plate in danger red.

Her HUD flashed an urgent shipwide broadcast as the exo bay's PA crackled to life. *"All hands, all hands. Multiple raider craft inbound on an intercept course. Security teams report immediately to Engineering, Hangar, and Command decks. Prepare to repel borders. This is not a drill. I repeat, this is not a drill."*

Exos from First Squad began to move, then Second, then Third. She fell in behind Smokes's machine, 3-3-2. Even his exo seemed sluggish. Doc and Vlan kept pace beside her.

"Fury 3, Fury 3, proceed directly to your dropships." Revan's voice crackled through her headset. *"Azure 2 drew the short straw and will provide security for our drop."*

Olsom thumbed her push-to-talk: "Sir, we can help them—"

"Negative, 3-3-3. Your fight's on the ground. Maintain comms discipline, over."

Just like the blocks. Remember your place. "Solid copy, Actual. 3-3-3 out."

She walked the rig down the long ramp toward the dropships below. The hangar deck shook with the drumbeat of incoming weapons fire on the Victory's shields. Security personnel filled the transit lanes, ushering the flight ops crew to the relative safety of the arterials.

Her surge of adrenaline curdled into icy dread. So much for picking a fight. The fight had come for them.

BRESTO TRUDGED up the *Gauntlet's* cargo ramp, boots feeling heavier the higher he climbed. Each step felt like retreating from the battlefield. Admitting defeat. Colonel Reede's expeditionary force was minutes from taking the fight to the enemy—a real fight, not some secret mission to Cradle's edge where the truth would stay hidden, along with the fates of those who would die there. Lost no more.

An emergency kit hung open on the cargo bay wall. He looked around, searching for rebreathers or medkits that would've spilled out. Nothing. The kit closed with a soft click.

His family was down there. Sure, Aegians trained for this. Lyra was a former Marine with a Planetary Reserve commission. She could handle herself. Kaff had been old enough for block drills since she made her gammas. Sammy would keep up, Twelfth save him. They'd all be safe, so long as the CDF could destroy that damn forge ship.

Halfway inside the bay, someone had done a decent patch job on the decking. He tested the fresh sealant glistening along the edges with his boot. Hangar crews must've reinforced it when they docked. A scorched panel marked the ceiling above where a squid's lucky shot nearly cooked them all.

But the measure of a man was in keeping his family safe. He'd re-enlisted twice, shortly before both kids were born, to prove his worth to them and the Holy Mother. He'd spent more than half his life running the patrol lanes, killing raider squids that strayed too close. Important work, but nothing that measured up to the sacrifices he'd made. The time he'd lost with the family he wanted to protect.

Park had promised him that: a secret rescue mission that would ensure the security of the Three Colonies for generations. Bresto had signed the transfer to Special Ops without a moment's hesitation. Lyra was furious.

Bad enough, you being gone, she'd said, the words a splinter in his thoughts. But to Cradle's edge under full OPSEC—transponder dark, no comms home? She'd spat nails. *Sounds like a one-way trip to me.*

Appeasing her wasn't easy, but he had leave stacked up. Lots of it. He'd take it, for once. Make time to sort things out… when he got back. When she and the kids and the whole damn Cradle were safe for generations.

Park had promised him that.

Runt met him at the center of the cargo bay, hunched over in a vain attempt to make herself less intimidating to the technician beside her. But the rows of long teeth in her open-mouth grin were unsettling to the uninitiated. One of her ears swiveled in his direction.

"Bresto," she said, with a trio of cheerful chords. "Ship. Repaired. *We* can launch."

We. She always said that word with pride.

"Good." Bresto turned to the tech. "Comms up?"

"I had to replace some hardware. Two signal processor chips—"

That sounded like a yes. No time to listen to how the skeeg heroically soldered silicon. He made for the rear hatch, the stark white of the jump bay forcing a squint.

Runt offered the tech a warbling apology and padded after him.

"So, radio's working. Any word from Park?" Bresto asked.

"Yes." Runt sounded more curt than usual. Something was up.

Past the jump bay, the galley was empty. No Mace. No Dalon. Sevvers and Park gone. The Concordat at their doorstep. So much for Park's promises.

"Well? What did he say?"

"Same. Message." A melancholy chord whistled through her nose. "Bring. Kerry Sevvers. To Bedrock."

Frustration bubbled over into anger. It had been a few orbits since he'd punched a superior officer. But the itch definitely needed scratched. "Sevvers has to kill that forge ship, full stop. I won't take him away from this fight. I… I can't."

He collapsed into the control deck's seat, fingers centimeters from the comms controls. Park could like it, or kiss his—

Klaxons screamed twelve hells through the *Victory's* hangar deck. Not drop alerts. Proximity warnings. The control deck flashed to life, its own tinny speakers bleating an alarm. The overhead lights went dark, replaced a heartbeat later with the grim red dead of combat lighting.

"All hands, all hands." The *Gauntlet's* PA echoed the *Victory's*. "Multiple raider craft inbound on an intercept course. Security teams report immediately to Engineering, Hangar, and Command decks. Prepare to repel borders. This is not a drill. I repeat, this is not a drill."

The Concordat had reached Two-Gamma. He was out of time. They all were. "Get these engines hot. Now." Bresto rocketed from the chair, rifle pressed into his shoulder as he jogged toward the cargo bay.

Runt stuck her thick neck out of the hatchway behind him. "Where Bresto go?"

Beneath the *Gauntlet's* launch bay, masters-at-arms were waving for hangar techs to leave the area. The armored partitions between the exo and hangar bays trundled open, sickeningly slow. Victory exos stomped down the long boarding ramp one at a time, then two. The dull buzz of point-defense cannons vibrated through the bulkheads.

"I'm going to give the security teams an assist." He paused halfway down the ramp. "We need to cover the Marines until—"

The *Victory* listed violently. Reality shook to the sound of rending metal and hull breach warnings. He struck the deck like a hammer, his vision darkening. The emergency aux grav held him in place through the worst of the impact tremors.

He rolled to one side, clinging to consciousness, focusing on the honking klaxons and the rapid drumbeat of charging exos. Fucking squids. Had to be. They didn't land so much as crash. And only they were dumb enough to board a Marine ship.

The *buzz-crack* of laser fire confirmed it. The raiders loved lasers for their reliability and low power requirements. They couldn't put a dent in fibrosteel, but they could tear up the interior of any ship given enough time.

He found his footing and hugged the launch bay wall. Around the corner, two clutches of raider warriors charged down the open ramp of a stolen transport four bays down. They were big, ugly things in black patchwork armor and bulbous helmets, fronds twitching and curling over their mouths.

The scaley fucks actually thought they could keep Victory from dropping.

The nearest squid glowed red dead in his rifle optics. He jogged the fire selector to burst with his thumb—one click, then another. The CR-11 snapped out three blaster bolts in rapid succession. The first missed by millimeters, but two and three found their marks. The squid's helmet shattered in a flash of red sparks just before a wet, blue mist erupted from between its chest plates.

The other squids kept moving, ignoring their fallen, bounding under covering fire in pairs. Most of them ran for the drop ships. But others peeled off toward the arterial hatchways at the aft end of the deck. They would cut their way through and try to cause havoc on the command deck. Or scrub the reactors in engineering, Division-style.

"Let's move!" he shouted to the masters-at-arms below him. "Before they take the dropships!"

The master-at-arms acknowledged with a hand signal and led his team forward, using the dropship ramps as cover. Bresto lunged from cover, sprinting aft along the tops of the launch ramps. He dove into next launch bay partition, took a knee, and loosed a barrage of covering fire into a pair of squids who'd sighted in on the advancing team.

His wrist comms let out a chirp, signaling an open channel. What he wouldn't give for some field comms. Reflective weave, armor plate, and a bandolier of charge packs would be nice, too.

"Any Victory elements, this is Sarnt Bresto of the CDMS Gauntlet, do you copy?"

"This is Azure 2-3-1," came a young Marine's voice through a crackle of static. *"Tracking your IFF at bay four. What do you see up there, Sarnt?"*

"Squids in the wire. They're going for your dropships, aft end of the bay." With no way to share targeting data, he pointed his rifle toward the enemy, trusting the Marine could see him in his exo's optics. "You've got friendlies advancing along the port side transit. Starboard side's all yours."

"Starboard side, solid copy. I'll spread the word. Race you there, Sarnt."

Challenge accepted. "Roger, Bresto out."

A trio of exos at the bottom of the boarding ramp took off at a heavy jog, hooking left at the line of dropships and thundering down the port side transit. More Marines followed on foot—Azure 2-3's breachers and docs. More exos fell in behind them. It was only a matter of time now. No way thirty-something squids could hold up to a squad of Marines and their exos. But they could still do some damage on their way out.

Bresto vaulted another launch bay partition, his heavy stride picking up speed. Two hulking black shapes emerged around the far wall, a pair of advancing squids who also thought the high ground was a good idea.

Muscle memory kicked in. He dropped and slid, the deck plate burning his thigh through his white-and-grays. His rifle snapped up, spitting charged particles. Smoking blue craters erupted between the lead squid's patchwork armor and it toppled sideways over the railing.

The trailing squid shouldered its laser. A thin beam of cadmium red cooked the air centimeters from Bresto's face. He twisted, firing from prone. The squid's bulbous helmet shattered like rotten hard-fruit, and it fell to the deck, sucking toxic human atmo through its fronds.

"Moarv'esk!" the thing coughed. It pointed at him with a gloved tendril, its green scales glistening in spinning cones of hazard light. More scratchy squid speak crackled from its comms. "Moarv—"

Its head disfigured in a cloud of blue blood. Bresto hugged the deck, sighting over his scope for any other squids that might rush the high ground. Three seconds passed. Seven. Forward.

The hangar deck's aft bulkhead loomed ahead of him. He moved at a crouch, keeping the next partition between him and the incoming fire. Staccato vibrations shook the bay, an unholy zipping sound—Fuck yes. Marine metal. Exo-served weapons. FABs.

Below him, Azure 2-3 laid into the onrushing squids. Long streams of blaster bolts ripped through loose gear carts and equipment crates they used for cover. The three exos advanced at leftward angles—move, shoot, move, shoot—trying to flank the squids that had taken up positions in and around the lead dropship. Laser beams lashed against the suits' fibrosteel plate, but the exos kept pushing forward.

The Marines had the dropships handled. That left the squids trying to breach the arterials. He raced down the launch ramp into the transit corridor, laser fire chasing after him, and dove behind a dropship skid, startling a master-at-arms.

"Twelfth Herself! Thought you were one of them, Sarnt!"

"We need to secure those hatches," Bresto barked, pointing toward the aft bulkhead.

"That place is crawling with squids!"

"We just gotta keep their heads down so they don't breach the doors." He eyed the exos advancing on the opposite side of the deck, only their thick legs visible beneath the bellies of the dropships between them. "The Marines will be there in five minutes, tops. Think you can handle it until then?"

"Yeah, Sarnt, we can do it."

"All right, I move, you shoot, check?" Hopefully, the Navy skeegs knew something about Marine tactics. "Then it's your turn."

"Come on, you heard the man!" The security detail laid down covering fire, sending waves of charged particles sparking and banging against the arterial hatches.

Bresto cut around behind them, then ducked forward beneath the dropships, keeping their skids and ramps between him and the enemy. Ten meters, twenty.

Too far. The hiss of laser on metal forced him down. Four squids lumbered toward him at a slow crawl. They were hard to miss, barely able to crouch beneath the dropships given their size. His return fire was quick and lethal, and they were close enough to hear their last, frothy breaths.

He signaled the masters-at-arms forward. "Move up! Go! Go!"

The aft hatchways were forty meters out. Squid warriors laid down covering fire while the smaller, pink scaled workers assembled some kind of plasma cutter or mining drill. It didn't take a breacher to know they'd make quick work of the hatches. He sighted in, dropping one worker with his first shot. The others took cover behind their machine as the warriors' laser rifles scorched the surrounding air.

"Here, Sarnt," the young master-at-arms said, breathless.

"Good." Bresto sighted through his optics. "Find cover and shoot where I shoot."

A warrior fell next; its thick, trunk-like leg severed at the torso.

Bresto's rifle buzzed a warning tone, its charge indicator pulsing at 50%. "Aim for the little ones and those machines. Don't let them into the arterials!"

The security team kept up their fire, keeping the squids pinned down. Bresto worked his blaster rifle methodically, sending single shots into easy targets, center mass. Slowly, the crackle of laser fire grew less frequent, surrendering to the Victory Marines' momentum.

"Let's go, Marines, wake up and smell the glory!" a voice called from behind. It was the first sergeant from their escape from Three-Alpha. He was moving from dropship to dropship, shoving Marines and exos alike up the ramps. "The Twelfth and the skipper wait for no one!"

Flash traffic ripped through Bresto's comms, a blood-curdling scream that strained the wrist badge's emitters. A loud boom rang through the hangar deck. He winced—exo down. He knew the sound by heart.

"This is Azure 2-3-1." Nervous tension strangled the Marine's transmission. *"We are taking effective fire near the vicinity of the breach, over. 2-3-3 is down. I say again, Hartmann is down."*

Bresto swung his rifle toward the damaged launch bay, his optics not showing any threats through the smoke and debris. But something had changed. Squids didn't have the gear or the egg sacs to take down an exo on their own. The clack of mandibles answered him, echoing from the stolen transport, followed by the *thwap* of outgoing plasma bursts. Pulsing green balls of ionized gas spat from the smoke-filled launch bay into Azure 2-3's position.

Bugs. Here. The squids had brought their Concordat masters with them.

———

Bugs changed the threat assessment. Plasma fires could easily destroy their dropships. Even burn through to the arterials, eventually. If Reede was going to drop, he had to do it now.

"Colonel Reed, Sarnt Bresto." No response. "Colonel Reed, this is Sarnt Bresto, over."

"The colonel's busy, Sergeant," Kull responded through a wave of static. *"I thought I told you to get off my ship."*

"This isn't just some squid raid, ma'am. Victory needs to drop. Now."

Kull's grim laughter sounded mechanical through the emitters. *"We have multiple raider attack corvettes closing on our position. If we drop now, we'll lose half our ships before they hit atmo."*

"You're going to lose them all if you—" The channel chirped closed.

Kull wasn't listening. She didn't know how dangerous this new enemy was. They didn't have time to reach lower orbit or wait for backup to clear the void. Those bugs would tear through the *Victory* like she was made of plastec. He could almost feel the heat, smell the acrid fumes of melting metal. And wherever the bugs went, the Lost were never far behind.

He turned to the master-at-arms. "New objective. We're going to push up and support the exos at the rear of the bay."

"Aye, Sarnt."

"Now." He ducked around the landing skid and hurled himself forward. The hangar deck became a burning, bouncing blur. "Move, move, move!"

The smell of smoke and burned squid choked the aft hangar deck.

Alien corpses were strewn about in messy chunks around the lead dropship, evidence of the gruesome effectiveness of exo-served weapons. But the Marines weren't invincible. An exo lay crumpled near the lead dropship's cockpit, green flames melting its fibrosteel plate like hot wax. The two remaining exos took halting steps backwards, their FABs punishing the damaged transport jutting through the breached launch bay.

His hip socket protested as he accelerated around them. "Azure 2-3-1, Sarnt Bresto. We're coming in hot at your forty-five."

Long, spindly shadows stretched from the ruined transport's open side hatch. The first bugs scuttled out between a lull in the assault, their bronze staves spitting hot plasma at the retreating exos.

They were ugly things. Tall and thin, with broad, flat heads and large compound eyes. Rust brown uniforms covered their black, chitinous exoskeletons. Their six segmented limbs seemed to operate as arms or legs depending on their orientation and surroundings.

"What the hell are those things?" Azure 2-3-1 signaled back.

"That's the archenemy. Those things killed Earth." Bresto's targeting reticule flashed red dead. "You packing tungsten?"

"Affirmative, Sarnt."

"Then kill them back."

"Stand by, Sarnt. Azure 2 Actual, this is 2-3-1. Requesting weapons free on the LEC. We're taking effective fire from… from Concordat forces in the vicinity of the breached launch bay, over."

"Negative, 2-3-1. You'll decompress the hangar, over."

Bresto snarled. Idiot officer needed to trust his Marines.

"Break, break! Azure 2-3-1, this is Victory Actual." Reede's voice echoed over the din of small arms fire. The man was close. *"You have my authorization to light those bastards up. Give 'em a proper Colonial Defense Marine welcome."*

Sounded like Reede knew how to win a war. Good. Twelfth save him.

Azure 2-3's remaining exos swung their railgun arms forward. A high-pitched whine cut through the bedlam, their long barrels smoldering with charge heat. Twenty more seconds, and those bugs would be vapor.

"Decompression, decompression, decompression!" Kull shouted over the nets. *"All Victory elements, ready your magnetics and rebreathers."*

The atmo fields would hold. Otherwise, they'd have to trip the blast doors. Bresto triggered his boot magnetics. Better safe than sorry.

Incoming plasma licked at Azure 2-3's treads, but the exos kept working their FABs over the bugs' position. More of the things chittered and shrieked, bounding from the transport and covering behind debris.

"Azure 2-3-1, firing."

The first outgoing round screamed into the transport. A solid tungsten slug ripped through tortured hull plate in a flash of light and smoke. The impact rocked the ship back, its hull ringing like a struck bell. Beyond the launch bay door, the atmo field flickered as the transport's bulk displaced the energy keeping breathable air inside the hangar.

"Azure 2-3-2, firing."

The next round cut the ruined transport in two. Secondary explosions erupted deep inside it, sending the dead ship hurtling into the void in bulky chunks.

The atmo field shimmered but held. Another squad of Marines and their exos joined the first and together began pushing the remaining enemy toward the now vacant launch bay.

"Good kill, Azure 2-3." Reede appeared at Bresto's side, a deep scowl wrinkling his gentlemanly features. Like the presence of the enemy aboard his ship offended him. "Well done covering our flank, Sergeant. See what you're going to miss?"

"Yes, sir." The charge level on his rifle read 15%. "Got any spare charge packs?"

"Yeah. Right next to that seat I saved you." Reede chuckled. "Now that we've got a little breathing room, the supply techs at S-4 will get you squared away. Anything you need."

"Thank you, sir."

Major Kull waited for them at the rear of the lead dropship. She looked unfazed by the surprise attack on their ship, even had a little carbon residue on her cheek from blaster rifle discharge. Her eyes narrowed at him. Still hung up on that Division bulletin, despite what he'd done to help her Marines.

"What's our status, Major?" Reede asked.

"Everyone's drop ready except Fury and Azure." She glanced down the drop line toward the open exo bay partitions. "Fury's boarding now while Azure mops up."

"I want you to drop with Fury 3. I know Revan's shorthanded, but he needs to kick their asses in gear. You'll see to it."

"Aye, sir." She threw Bresto one last frown then jogged away.

Reede watched Azure 2 advanced on the smoldering launch bay. "Well, Sergeant," he clapped Bresto on the shoulder, "I guess this is where we part ways. Whatever mission you're on, I hope it's worth it." He extended a gloved hand, and Bresto shook it. "Twelfth save you, son."

"Thank you, sir."

More hard clacking echoed through the hangar. Six-limbed forms dropped from the ceiling onto the lead dropship, their plasma staves glowing white hot. There were three of them, just standing there, weapons primed and ready. Why weren't they firing?

"Get down!" Bresto aimed and fired at the closest bug. Chunks of chitin fell from its body on clear streams of yellow fluid. The bug shrieked back at him, clutching its staff like a walking stick, but did not return fire.

Through his optics, the air around the bugs shimmered with heat. Like their staves might—

Something barreled into him, knocking him to the ground. As he fell, the air above him turned to green-white fire.

———

Bresto sat up with a start, tasting the scorched air between racking coughs. Black smoke curled around him, backlit by green flames guttering across the remains of the lead dropship. He found his rifle on the deck beside him. A quick function check said it was good to go.

"Sir?" He came to his feet, shouting through the smoke. "Colonel Reede!"

Something moved on the deck just a few meters away. He sighted in on it, smoke stinging his eyes, index finger tensing on the trigger. Warnings flashed in his optics, but the reticle finally turned blue.

The colonel lay on his side, his tac gear and white-and-grays scorched black. Blood pooled on the duraplate beneath him.

"You still here?" the colonel rasped.

"Hold on, sir." Bresto's wrist comms buzzed back no connection. "Rail fire fragged my comms."

"No matter." Reede slipped a sidearm from its holster and sat up, the other hand cradling his stomach. "Those damn things got the jump on us. Help me up."

He took Reede by the forearm and pulled him to his feet. The man looked whole, but his face was turning white. A ragged red stain seeped beneath his tac vest.

"You need a doc, sir."

"I need a Twelfth-damned status report. I don't hear outgoing fire." Reede squinted through the smoke, fumbling for his comms. "Victory Actual to Azure 2-3. Azure 2-3, do you copy?"

"Anything?" Bresto asked.

"No. We've got to help them."

A shrill, hollow scream rose above the crackling flames. The sound dragged on for endless seconds, echoing off the fibrosteel bulkheads until it seemed to come from every direction. It clawed at his ears, crawled up his spine—just like on the forge ship and Three-Alpha. The unmistakable sound of a tortured, soulless thing driven to kill those that still had one.

"What in the name of the Holy Mother?" Reede mumbled.

Bresto took him by the shoulders. Kull may not have listened, but he would make Reede hear him.

"Sir, there are Lost aboard your ship." Another once-human scream joined their chorus of agony. "Drop now before you lose the whole damn expeditionary force."

"Lost." Reede gripped his push-to-talk. "Victory Actual to Flight Ops. Initiate pre-drop sequence and prepare to scuttle the ship."

Drop klaxons blasted their tri-tone warning in defiance of the Lost's screams. Mechanisms vibrated through the heavy deck plate. Reede took a step forward, almost doubling over with a grunt.

"Come on, sir," Bresto said, propping him up. "Let's get you to a dropship."

"I don't think so." Reede slipped a hand beneath his armored vest. His fingers reappeared covered in blood. "I won't survive the drop. Wouldn't be any good if I did."

"Sir, those things will—"

"I know. No need to get yourself killed lugging a dead man around. Get out of here, Marine, that's an order."

A loud knock reverberated through the deck as the drop bay doors began to open. Up and down the transit corridors, spinning lights turned the black smoke a pulsing amber brown.

Bresto's whole world became that moment, that choice. Park's mission suddenly felt so distant and abstract. The Victory was lost. Aegia waited below, storm-wrapped and vulnerable. Twenty years of service. Twenty years of putting the duty first. And what did he have to show for it? A half-finger where his ring should be and two kids who barely knew him.

Reede coughed. "You're going to miss your ride, Sergeant."

The weight of home felt so much heavier. Kaffy and Sammy were down there somewhere. Everything he'd done, all the days gone, the missions run, had been for them. And for what? *You owe me that*, Lyra had said. He did. Maybe this was how he finally paid that debt.

Behind him, dropship ramps cycled closed. Mission parameters had changed. The objective was clear now. Not some haunted rock out in the void, but right there beneath those storm clouds. The mission was home. Had always been home.

Protect his colony. Find his family. Let Park chase ghosts.

"Aye, sir." Bresto took a step back, thumb going to the nub of his ring finger. "Twelfth save you, sir."

He turned and charged through the billowing smoke, the hazard lights guiding him down the flight line. Six dropships left. Five. Four. The ramps closed as soon he reached them, bulky drop cradles lifting the craft nose down over the widening doors. The void stared back at him through the thin sheet of atmospheric shielding, Aegia's storm-wrapped surface filling the view. Three ships left. Two. No chance he'd make those. The last dropship waited like a beacon in the madness, ramp still down and locked. Last chance.

"Bresto!" Runt's transmission crackled through his wrist comms. "Respond!"

"I'm here, Runt," he said through labored breaths.

"Great danger," she howled. "Must go now!"

"Change of plans." He was only seconds away now. The *Gauntlet's* tail boom loomed overhead, vanishing behind him as he sprinted past. "You're leaving without me. I'm dropping with Victory."

"But, Park—"

"Go to Bedrock." His volume rose with his anger. "Tell Park if he wants to save humanity to get his ass back to Aegia!"

There. It felt good to say it, but the pinpricks of relief quickly faded. For a heartbeat, doubt stabbed at him. Park would call this dereliction. A court martial offense. His career torched in one more reckless decision. But none of that mattered when the Concordat were tearing through your homeworld. When families—his family—were in the line of fire.

He arrived at the last dropship, its ramp still down and locked. More screams echoed behind him, followed by the crisp snap of blaster fire.

He stumbled up and into the crew bay. The familiar tang of exo grease and recycled atmo hit him first, an old friend he hadn't realized he'd missed. The weight on his shoulders shifted—different now, but no lighter. He'd traded Park's secret mission for a drop into hell with Marines he barely knew. But they were heading where he needed to go. Toward Aegia. Toward Lyra and the kids. Toward something that mattered.

Exos filled the center aisle, clamped down and ready for drop. Marines seated around them looked at him with grim confusion— another stray picked up in the chaos. He didn't care what they thought. For the first time in years, his choice aligned with his heart. This was the fight that counted.

He slapped the ramp controls closed and thumbed the pilot comms. "Ramp closing, we're drop ready."

"Drop ready, aye," came the reply over the PA.

The ship's interior swallowed him up, the sudden quiet a stark contrast to the chaos outside. Hushed conversations faded as he hunted for an open seat. His hip ached. He had no tac gear, no exo, but he'd make do. This was where he belonged.

"That you, Sarnt?" Myers. One of the Rikkos sat beside him, staring blankly ahead. No sign of the girl or the chain-smoking twin. "Welcome to Fury 3."

Bresto slumped into the last open seat just as the dropship lifted into position. The craft's nose tilted downward, *Victory's* aux grav pulling him and everyone else toward the cockpit and the open drop doors below.

Major Kull and the nervous lieutenant occupied the command seats near the cockpit hatch. Kull's icy stare said she knew Reede wasn't coming. That maybe she blamed him for it somehow. Lucky for him, there were more dangerous things to shoot at.

"Victory Actual to all Victory elements!" Reede's voice boomed over the dropship's PA. Static-filled shrieks ripped through the transmission, but the man's voice never wavered. *"Emergency launch procedures authorized. I say again: drop, drop, drop! For your families, for your colony, for humanity, drop!"*

CHAPTER
ELEVEN

KAFFY CLUNG to Madam Ulwin's cold, gnarled hand as the alert sirens wailed overhead. All around them, proper Aegians cowered together like scared children, desperate for the safety of Diacad Cliff's Civil Defense Shelter Sienna-2. The shelter looked like a flat, gray box someone had smooshed down, all blocky and serious against the stormy sky. Like it, too, wanted to hide from whatever terrible thing was happening above the storms.

She tried not to worry about where Father, Mother, or Sammy might be. But that only made her worry more. The fear hardened in her stomach like week-old crid.

The line had barely moved since they arrived, sending frantic whispers through the line that the shelter was full. Hesper and the kind lieutenant had gone to see if there was any room. The lieutenant said they wouldn't be long, but it had been almost thirty minutes. Too long.

"How are you faring, Lady Kaffereine?" Madam Ulwin said, giving Kaffy's hand a squeeze.

Sad. Hungry. Cold. Scared. "I'm okay."

"Of course you are, dear." Another distant boom rippled across the sky, sending gasps and screams through the lines of waiting colonists. Madam Ulwin's grip tightened again. "Don't you worry your pretty head. Your family is, too. I know it."

"How?"

"The Holy Mother looks after all Her children, dear. Every day since Dead Earth." Madam Ulwin pointed to a statue at the corner of the medical clinic across the lane. It was giant, as tall as the clinic. A cloaked figure with broad shoulders, its face hidden behind a blank mask. In both hands, it gripped a huge sword blade-down toward the rock. Centuries of storms had weathered the granite features smooth, just like the tiny figurine in Kaffy's pocket.

"Yeah." Kaffy forced a smile. "You're right."

Madam Ulwin didn't know, she *believed*. That was different. Father and Mother would say they were the same thing, but Kaffy wasn't so sure. She believed in the Twelfth, of course. Everyone did, as sure as the storms. But the granite statue's solemn presence didn't make her feel any better as they waited outside the shelter's big, fibrosteel doors.

A shadow flitted against the statue's base. There was a person there, but it looked… wrong. Like a big doll someone had left in the rain. The way it seemed to sway gave her the creeps. Back and forth, up and down, over and over, like in some scary trance.

She squeezed Madam Ulwin's hand tighter. "Who is that?"

"Who is who, Lady Kaffereine?" Madam Ulwin squinted at the thing, wrinkling her old nose. "Don't you bother with that, dear."

"What? What is it?"

"That's a daxed. Not Lost, but not quite Found. An outsider." Madam Ulwin stooped a little, her mouth next to Kaffy's ear. "Best to leave it alone."

Yeah, she'd heard of those. Even saw one once—sort of, not up close —at their old allotment center in Corongaet. Outsiders seemed to keep to themselves, usually near the colony's outskirts. Weird that one would be here, now, near all these people and the alarms blaring overhead.

Block Captain Hesper's voice carried from the front of the line. "But surely someone needs to stay with the civilians, Lieutenant. For their protection."

The lieutenant emerged from the rows of people, Hesper and the boys close behind. "Good news, Madam Ulwin. They should have you and the children inside in ten minutes."

"You're not coming with us?"

"No, ma'am. When you all are safe," the lieutenant threw Hesper a stern look, "we'll report to the nearest muster point."

"Very good, you brave young man. You see there, dear?" Madam Ulwin grinned, one finger pointed skyward. "The Twelfth keeps us always."

"Yes, ma'am." Kaffy liked the lieutenant. He was all right, for a skeeg. Nothing like Hesper.

"Yes, ma'am," Duray mimed with a snort.

"Shut up." Stupid boy.

He puffed out his chest. "Make me, Bresto."

"Enough, you vile young man," Madam Ulwin crowed. The pitch of her voice made Kaffy giggle. "What would your parents say?"

Duray folded his arms, his red face twisted in a sneer, but he didn't talk back.

"Duray, perhaps you should stay close to me." Hesper cleared his throat, eyes darting between the Planetary Reserve guards lining up along the shelter's outer walls.

Of all the people to be stuck in a shelter with. Even Sammy would be better than Hesper and his little brown-nosers. The thought of Sammy made her heart ache. Twelfth keep him. Mother probably made sure of that before she left. Yeah. He would be okay.

The line crawled forward, the minutes dragging on. Her feet ached, and it felt like her stomach was eating itself. She stood on her toes, searching the guards for any sign of Mother, but saw none.

The outsider was closer now, still swaying beneath the statue in the howling storm winds. It lifted a hand in a slow flourish, long fingers stained a bright, piercing blue, and began smudging them against the heavy gray stone at the statue's base. Only then did she see the whirlpool of color beneath its fingers. Reds faded into orange, then melted into blues, forming a hypnotic spiral that seemed to stare right back at her. Beckoning her closer. The daxed wasn't swaying; it was painting. Faster than her eyes could follow.

"Lady Kaffereine? Where are you going?"

The daxed wore a shawl of patchwork rags stained in dried, weathered paint. Blooms of dry black soiled the rainbow of colors. The smell of spoiled rations lingered in the air.

Up close, the painting took on mesmerizing detail, more like a blueprint than art. Where the blue and red met formed bands of deep purple. Pinpricks of ruby and gold dotted the swirling colors like tiny stars. Aegia was a gray, dull place. The splash of color amidst the sirens and storms felt like its own little rebellion.

"Lady Kaffereine," the daxed said with the slightest hint of awe. The dry, mechanical voice froze Kaffy in place. Its head turned slightly, still hidden beneath the shawl. "Is that your name, gamma?"

"Who, me?"

Soft clicks emanated from beneath the shawl. A *scritch-scratching* sound like metal on bone.

It daubed a finger in a vial of blue paint embedded in its forearm and resumed its work. All of it—fingers, arms, every bone in its once-human body—seemed stretched beyond physical limits. Even seated on the ground, it was centimeters taller than her.

A sudden chill cut her to the bone. "It's… just Kaffy."

"Just Kaffy," it repeated.

"How… how do you know I'm a gamma?"

"Height: 146.35 centimeters. Weight: 43.4 kilograms." Its hand trembled mid-stroke. "Bone density: 1.167 grams per cubic centimeter. Cranial sutures: 76—no, 77 percent fused. All well within the upper bounds of the gamma designation. Your heart rate is elevated, and your cortisol levels are above baseline. Are you afraid, Just Kaffy?"

It felt like the daxed had opened her up and peeked inside without even looking. "N-No. How do you know all that stuff?"

"Passive millimeter-wave scanning and quantum tunneling spectroscopy allow for the non-invasive analysis of your molecular composition and structural integrity." The daxed canted its head at an impossible angle, still staring at the drying paint. "Your biosignature is quite distinct, Just Kaffy."

"No, my name—it's not Just Kaffy. It's just. Kaffy."

The daxed stopped its work, dipped its long thumb in a dollop of ruby, and scrawled the words *JUST KAFFY* in perfect block print above the swirling mass of colors. Its movements were inhumanly quick, shoulders dancing as it worked.

"Like this?" In one fluid motion, it whirled to face her.

Kaffy stumbled back, a scream catching in her throat. She thought daxed were people. Used to be… people, but—

A taut, ashen face looked down at her from beneath the shawl. Black, lidless eyes glared, wide and all-seeing. Thin lips peeled back in a painful grimace, revealing pale, almost translucent teeth. Glinting circuitry crisscrossed the meat of its sockets and gums like the stitches in its tattered clothing.

Its right hand was stained every color imaginable. An opening in its left forearm held a dozen little vials of fresh paint just above the bone. Cables, synthetic guts, and shriveled entrails spilled from its ruined torso. It wasn't sitting. It had no legs.

Once-human, Father had called them a long time ago. She didn't understand it then, but the meaning was painfully obvious now. This thing was not human. Not anymore. Not in a long, long time.

"Your pulse is climbing. Do not be alarmed." The daxed retreated inside its shawl, the words seeming to come from deep inside its throat. Like its mouth no longer made the sounds. The metal clicks came again. Louder. "My appearance is unsettling, but I mean you no harm. You may stay or go as you wish."

The daxed spun on one hand and resumed its rapid smudging of paint on stone. But something kept her rooted in that spot. It was scary, but… fascinating, too. The Twelfth Herself had saved this poor broken thing, and many more like it, a really long time ago. In a weird way, it was living proof of the faith she'd known her whole life. She squeezed the little figurine in her pocket, feeling a sudden, desperate need to stay near.

"What are you painting?"

"A memory."

"Of what?"

"I… cannot remember."

"What? How do you not remember the memory that you're painting?"

"It is impolite to discuss such things." It glanced back, one black eye gleaming from beneath the shawl.

"I'm sorry."

Its teeth glowed in the storm light. "You meant no harm."

A distant boom sent another wave of panic through the lines of colonists. The daxed didn't seem to mind, fast but delicate strokes from its long fingers bringing the tiny painting to life in stark detail. So many colors. So many stars. It was the Cradle Nebula. Had to be.

"Do…" It didn't make sense, but she asked anyway. "Do you know what's happening up there?"

The daxed didn't answer, its head craned skyward for what felt like a long while. Maybe it was scanning the storms with its wave quantum thingies. But the longer it stared, the more it seemed to focus on the statue.

A third explosion vibrated beneath her boots and up into her stomach. It felt different, stronger. Closer.

The daxed dipped its fingers into a ragged tear in the crook of its left arm. It didn't look like the little bulbs of color nestled in its forearm, more like a wound. String of oily black fluid dripped from its fingers as they came free.

Slowly, it placed a tiny black smudge at the edge of the little painted Cradle. Messier, not like the intricate detail of color. Then another, and another, until the right-hand side was covered in oily shadow. The rotten smell grew stronger.

The darkness terrified her. Blacker than black. "What is that?"

Nothing. Then, with a quick jerk, it traced thick black lines from the smudges right into the Cradle's heart. Right where she knew the Three Colonies would be.

"What're you doing, Bresto?" Duray stepped next to her, their block troop's guidon broken down and tucked under his arm. His nose wrinkled in disgust. "Gross. What is that smell?"

Duray's whine cut through her fear like a mining drill. She needed the distraction, thank the Twelfth, even if it was just a stupid boy.

"Aren't you supposed to stay with Hesper?"

"Someone's got to keep you out of trouble." Duray threw a smug grin. "Can't leave you alone with this thing."

"Can't mind your own business, more like."

"Keep it up. I bet you get a mark for this, too." Duray chuckled. "That's two lashings."

"You really are stupid, aren't you?" She gave Duray a shove. "We're in serious trouble, and all you can talk about is getting someone else whipped."

Duray tugged at the cuff of his sleeve, his right hand forming into a fist. "I'll show you—"

"You are both right." The daxed abruptly straightened, so fast it made Kaffy's breath catch. Duray staggered back, his eyes wide and unblinking. "You must go with your own kind. It is not safe here."

"Come with us then," Kaffy said. If this… *painter* was good enough to be saved by the Twelfth, it was good enough to be saved now.

Voices rose behind her, colonists crowded around Sienna-2's heavy doors, demanding to be let inside. PR troopers pushed back, shouting for calm. Hesper and Nemor pressed toward the entrance, while the lieutenant and Madam Ulwin waved for her and Duray to come back, their voices shrinking beneath the sirens.

"I cannot accompany you inside the shelter." The painter's skull-like grimace stretched into the ghost of a smile. "But you are a most thoughtful gamma, Just Kaffy."

Another sound ripped the air, close and loud. Long cones of fire burned through the dark clouds as a hulking shape punched through the stormy haze. It looked like a metal animal, an ugly, scaly thing with huge fins billowing in the wind. Not a colony transport. Not a freighter. Something worse. The ship plummeted, engines screaming. No time to—

It crashed behind a nearby building in a spray of light and granite. A wall of heat and sound slammed into her, lifting her off her feet.

Something reached out and caught her—long, thin fingers smelling of paint and spoiled food. She and the painter tumbled together through the chaos of smoke and gravel. She only noticed it had Duray, too, when they hit the ground and he let out a shout.

For a moment, everything was quiet, muffled. Slowly, sound returned. The crackle of flames, the cries of the injured, the hiss of heavy pneumatics. Kaffy sat up with a start, still blinking away stars. The shelter door was closing. They were going to get left behind.

"Duray, get up." She grabbed his arm and shook.

He moaned. "Wha—?"

"They're closing the shelter." The painter didn't move. She grabbed its paint-stained hand and pulled. "Come on, get up!"

"What?" Duray repeated, fully awake now. He stood, wobbling slightly. "Leave that thing. We gotta go!"

"No!" Kaffy pulled hard, but even without legs, the painter was so heavy. "It saved us!"

"Are you crazy?" Duray tugged at her shoulder. "That thing's not even human. It's probably dead!"

"But—"

"Time's up, Bresto!" Duray wrapped both arms around her and yanked, but she refused to let go. Together, they fell in a pile beside the motionless daxed.

Through the smoke and dust, Kaffy spotted Hesper and Nemor barging toward the shelter's doors. The block captain was practically dragging Nemor by the arm. "Make way!" he shouted, voice cracking. "Reserve personnel coming through!"

Duray stumbled forward, still dazed from his fall. "Wait! Don't leave me!"

Hesper's panic spread like a sickness. The reservists could do little to stop the avalanche of people from piling into the shelter. Hesper and Nemor slipped inside, disappearing into its granite depths without so much as a look back.

One guard officer raised his gun to the sky and fired. "Stand back! Sienna-2 is at capacity. I say again, Sienna-2 is full!" The door sealed shut with a heavy thud. "There are shelters near the Corongaet drop that still have room. Proceed downslope immediately."

Kaffy's pulse hammered in her throat. They were locked out. Hesper had just left them there to save his own stupid neck. A voice in her head that sounded a lot like Father's kept saying, *Coward, coward, coward!*

More soft clicks emanated from the painter's head, like gears falling into place. Its fingers twitched, leaving smears of color on the granite walkway. It was enough to push the sudden anger back for the moment.

"Thoughtful gamma," it said again, hollow and raspy. The painter rose on its ruined torso that curved unnaturally into a seated position. "Your lack of self-preservation is unusual."

Madam Ulwin emerged through the smoke, the young lieutenant at her side holding her up. A trickle of blood ran from her dust-stained cheek. "Lady Kaffereine? Thank the Holy Mother, you're alive!"

The lieutenant stormed closer. "You, boy. And you, little ma'am. Come away from there. To me."

"No, it's okay." Kaffy took a step back toward the painter. "It's not dangerous. It saved us."

The lieutenant stopped, the hard edge in his gaze softening just a little. "Is that true? Did you help these children?"

The painter threw back its hood, revealing a bald head covered in taut gray skin sutured closed at the back. Black veins wound beneath its scalp, thick and pulsing.

"It is, CDF." Its peeled back grin took on a defiant edge.

"Can you move?"

"I can."

"Then come with us. It seems little ma'am won't go without you, and we can't stay here. That was a raider transport. This place will be crawling with squids soon."

"Raiders?" Madam Ulwin pressed a hand to her chest. "No, it can't be. Not here. Not on Dodec—"

"Cephalonids. Warrior caste." The skin around the painter's eyes wrinkled into a lidless frown. "Thirty-three individuals. They are coming this way."

"What do they want?" Kaffy asked.

The daxed's eyes unfocused, as if it was looking right through her. "Everything."

"Then you have to come!"

"As you say, Just… Lady Kaffereine." The legless daxed dipped in a low bow, then hobbled forward on its hands to her side.

"We should stay away from crowds." The lieutenant waved them toward a quiet side street behind the shelter. "They'll draw the squids in first."

The daxed gave Kaffy a sideways glance. "He is correct."

Madam Ulwin hobbled down the side street, leaning on the lieutenant for support. The daxed scuttled after them, leaving a faint trail of colorful smears on the gray granite. Kaffy began to follow, then noticed Duray wasn't moving.

"Duray, come on!"

"They left us," he mumbled, eyes fixed on the shelter door. "I can't believe they just left us."

"Yeah, well…" Kaffy took a deep breath. One. Two. Three—just like Father taught her. Duray didn't look so stupid just then. Just scared, like her. She gripped the little figurine tight in her pocket. "We're not alone. We'll be okay."

CHAPTER
TWELVE

FURY 3'S DROPSHIP plunged through the drop bay doors, shrugging off the *Victory's* aux grav field. Proximity alarms whooped inside the troop deck. Combat lighting flicked on, turning the rows of Marines and exos a grim red dead.

The PA clicked. "We got incoming. Hold on to your chow."

Bresto felt the punch of rapid acceleration hit hard in an explosion of sound and vibration. Two G's, maybe three, and climbing. The Marines around him barked back against the thrust gravity with strained *ooh-rahs*. They didn't understand the reality of what they were facing, but he wouldn't stifle their courage. They'd need it. Besides, he'd be right there with them, a few rank pips and more than a few years back.

He might be on another doomed ship, fighting to stay conscious while outrunning squids. But this time, he was moving toward the fight. Toward his family. And it felt damn good, whatever the danger.

Major Kull's mouth moved silently against the roar of the engines, a hand on her push-to-talk. Trying to reach Colonel Reede, maybe, or coordinate with the other dropships. The thrust wrinkled her stern, martial features, made her look ancient. She could've been the Rikkos mother just then.

The twins. Vlan Rikko sat nearby, pinned to his seat like a broken toy. "He okay?"

"Yeah, he got a booster in before we dropped." Myers sucked in a labored breath. "He'll live."

It seemed crazy, growing up in little to no aux grav only to join the Marines. But he'd learned not everyone lived like Aegians did. They did what they had to, to make it. Still, there were other divisions of the CDF less abusive.

Hard impacts drummed the dropship's thick armor plate. Light fire, probably squid strike craft. But those little things had no range, which meant their bigger ships wouldn't be far behind. He eyed the ceiling, found the pair of legs dangling from the turret mount.

"What're you waiting for, Marine? Get those guns talking!" he growled. Working the turret would be a bitch in high G, but they needed to shoot back.

"Bad angle," the Marine shouted back. "They're keeping the other dropships between us and them!"

Smart. Too smart for squids. Maybe they'd been playing dumb all along. Maybe it was the presence of the Concordat and their so-called gods. A kind of insane zealotry that focused them. He'd seen it first-hand, back aboard the forge ship. Maybe they thought now was their time for righteous vengeance.

Cridshit. Whatever gods the bugs and squids prayed to hadn't been enough to stop him. He'd seen other things aboard the derelict, too. Undeniable proof that the Twelfth was with him, with humanity. A woman with incredible power. A dead girl brought back to life. Not so simple, though, if—

A tone buzzed through Bresto's wrist comms. Not a tac comms acknowledgment, but some kind of signal override. No one spoke.

"Send it."

"Bresto, it's Sevvers." Master Specialist Kerry Sevvers' voice ripped from the tiny device with his typical mix of fear and panic.

Bresto laughed out loud. Thank the Twelfth, the damned skeeg was still alive. "What do you want? I'm busy."

"Where's Cylla?" Sevvers asked, his desperation morphing into a

shaky courage. The bot jockey was still combat effective, even without a Marine escort. *"Where's the Gauntlet?"*

If anyone could've gotten away before the *Victory* blew, it was her. She could fly that ship through anything.

But the truth was he didn't know. He'd just ran like hell to the last drop ship. "I have no fucking idea."

More laser fire beat against the outer hull. Then another, heavier force shook the ship. A blast wave, danger close. They'd lost a drop-ship, maybe more than one.

"Getting hot down here, skeeg," he said. "Sure could use some close-void support."

"Oh, Twelfth, no." Kull looked up. "Marines! Brace for—"

The whole universe shook, turning the dropship interior into a blur of lines and color. Another blast wave, a big one, the hand of an angry god. Bresto knew what that meant—this was the end. Of the ride, of his life, of everything.

The *Victory* was gone.

Waves of fusion radiation sailed past, all that was left of the ship that had taken them in after the flight from Aegia Prime. But the end didn't come, not for Fury 3. Reede was gone, and so were the monsters that tried to stop them. Lights flickered, and the engines fell silent, lifting the invisible weight from Bresto's chest. Someone puked a few seats down, filling the air with the stink of bile and soured field paste.

"Holy Twelfth, what was that?" Myers asked.

Bresto swabbed the sweat from his eyes. What had begun the day for these young Marines as legends and parables taught in Basics School had turned crushingly real in a few hours. Now they'd just paid a terrible price for humanity's lack of preparedness.

"The Victory has been destroyed." Kull tucked the datapad into her tac vest. "Colonel Reede ordered the ship to be scuttled to prevent it from falling into enemy hands."

The lieutenant next to her abruptly straightened. "Lost no more!"

"Lost no more!" the Marines of Fury 3 chorused.

"You okay, Doc?" Olsom's Vestian drawl rang out from the line of exos.

"Still breathing," Myers replied.

"Got eyes on Vlan?"

"He's okay. Oh, yeah." Myers' tone brightened. "Sarnt Bresto's dropping with us."

That shut her up. Still bitter about being told off. Oh, well. That was the job. Standard operating procedure. At least the "pups" were all here, as Runt had called them. She'd be glad they were together, wherever she was.

"Hey, Sarnt," Myers started.

"What?"

"We've got squids on our six. Shouldn't we be accelerating?"

"That blast wave probably nudged us over the max drop speed." The momentary weightlessness felt good.

"What's our max drop speed?"

"A lot. But if we hit atmo too fast, we bounce off, break up, or make a new crater at terminal velocity."

"Those sound almost as bad as getting holed by a bunch of squids."

"That's the job, Marine."

"Embrace the suck. Aye, S—"

"Uh, I got something weird here," the turret gunner said. "IFF is glitching on me or something."

"Specifics, Marine," Bresto grunted back. Fury 3 was damn green.

"Right." The gunner hesitated. "IFF feed says there are more friendlies inbound."

"That's good."

"But there's too many," the gunner insisted. "I'm tracking hundreds of returns. We don't have that many ships, do we?"

"No, we do not." A cool satisfaction pushed back against the malaise of the *Victory's* destruction. That skeeg Sevvers had finally done it.

"Not Navy," Kull called out from her command seat. "Autonomous Weapons Division. The Alexander Lehman finally got her drones off. ETA ninety seconds."

A collective groan rippled through the troop deck. To any hardcore trigger-puller, there was nothing worse than being rescued by the Division. They called themselves the future of colonial defense, an opinion most Marines took issue with. Bresto knew better. So would they, after today.

"Guess your skeeg found his bots, eh, Sarnt?" Myers asked.

"Never a doubt."

"I don't think I—"

"Hey, what the fuck?" The gunner slapped the targeting console. "I'm locked out of my controls!"

"I'm very sorry." The voice emanating from the console was feminine, but with a cold preciseness that gave away its true nature. *"But my targeting algorithms are more accurate than your manual controls by a factor of seven-point-two."*

One of Sevvers' bots. The illegal one. "That you, Six?"

"In the code chains, Sergeant." Six's voice detached from the turret console and moved to his wrist comms. It sounded so human—too human. *"I'm very glad you are safe."*

More incoming fire struck the dropship. "Are we?"

Six giggled back. *"Momentarily."*

The point-defense cannons in the turret buzzed to life, sending pulses of tight vibrations through the bulkheads with each burst of high-velocity rounds. The dropship shook seconds later. Multiple blast waves.

"Splash four," Six said.

The bot had skills. "Good kill, Six. Save some for us."

The AI took a breath, another creepy human-like affect. *"I'm afraid there are plenty left to go around. My swarm sensors show raider transports on multiple approach vectors to the colony."*

"Where, Six? Where specifically?"

"I am tracking multiple touchdowns in the vicinity of Vestebrae, Corongaet..." The bot went on, ticking off district names like lines on a maintenance checklist. *"And Diacad Cliffs."*

The squids were going to beat them to the surface. To his home.

"Oh, man," Myers mumbled.

"What about the Lost?" Bresto asked, not wanting to know the answer. "Have the Lost made planetfall?"

"I... I don't know." The regret in the bot's voice was real. *"Their*

capsules are hard to track under optimal conditions, and multiple ship kills have polluted my sensor streams."

"They were on the Victory."

"Then they are penetrating deeper into the battlespace, and it is only a matter of time. I'm very sorry, Sergeant." The motherly concern in Six's tone faded. *"You must evacuate as many colonists from the surface as you can. Otherwise, they will—"*

"I know." He didn't need to hear the rest. He'd seen what the Concordat were capable of. How they turned colonists into daxed. To think what they might do to Lyra and the kids... He pushed the thought away. "You kill that forge ship, Six, you understand me? Leave the colony to us."

"I do, Sergeant. I will."

"Oh, and keep that skeeg of yours in one piece. The only one that gets to hurt him is me, check?"

Another surprised breath whispered from his comms. *"Yes, er, aye, Sergeant."* Six—she, it, *whatever*—sounded close to tears. *"I swear it."*

"Good to go. Bresto out." He closed the connection. Now the forge ship was Sevvers' problem. And Six's. Six and Sevvers. He laughed at that. Olsom had been right. It was a weird name for a bot.

Myers blinked. "That voice on your comms."

"What about it?"

"Was that—"

"The future? Maybe." But the future wasn't here yet. There weren't enough Division bots around to save his home. No, this fight would take meat and metal. The old-fashioned way.

Static crackled through the dropship's PA. "Fury 3, I've got good news and bad. Good news is scopes are clean. The Division's cleared a path." More groans from the Marines. "Bad news is, we picked up some extra delta-v in the fight. And you know what that means."

Myers waited. "No, I don't. What does that mean?"

"Bounce off. Break up. Crater." Bresto snugged the harness straps tight across his chest. "Like I said, boot, it's gonna be a hard drop."

CHAPTER
THIRTEEN

ANOTHER POCKET of turbulence set Olsom's teeth rattling, her vision blurring despite the stabilizers in 3-3-3's cage. The troop deck stank of sweat and vomit, but the acrid bite of hot ablative plating was starting to overpower everything else. Her stomach lurched with each new wave. Worse than the *Gauntlet,* worse than any sim in basic. She needed to throw up, needed that moment of relief, but her body wouldn't cooperate. Just dry heaves and bitter thoughts. And now Bresto had appeared, some twisted answer to a prayer she hadn't meant to make.

Her fireteam's vitals flickered steady blue on the terminal—Doc and Vlan's life signs threading through the intense vibration. Doc's heart rate was strong and steady, while hers read like a trawler motor about to throw a thruster coil. Even falling out of the sky, he was probably wearing that damn grin. The same one he'd flashed when they'd first met. The one that made her want to punch him sometimes. The one that made her less afraid right now.

Dodecoron appeared in stark relief on the strategic overlay, a massive granite sentinel that dominated the digital horizon. Even through the tactical filter, the mountain was something alive. Not like the forest-wrapped valleys and rivers back home that seemed to breathe with the seasons. This thing had grown straight through Aegia's skin, almost touching the void. All granite pride and defiance, just like the people who lived on it. It really was a crown upon that rocky world. Dodecoron. The Twelfth's crown. Growing up near the peak of something like that, of course you believed in gods.

"Victory 5 to all Victory companies." Major Kull's voice lit up broadcast comms, barely audible above the roar of re-entry. *"With the Victory off the board, expeditionary intel is offline. We're trying to link up with CDF command elements still operating at Aegia Prime, but until then, we're on our own."*

The death of the CDNS *Victory* still didn't seem real, though she'd felt it hard enough. It didn't seem possible that the metal corridors she just walked through no longer existed. That they were headed to the surface to stop an invasion all on their own.

The strategic overlay shifted on the screen, zooming in on a large city break a few kilometers beneath the mountain peak, just below the storms. Vestebrae. It was laid out in overlapping concentric circles, just like back home, filled with tightly packed structures stitched together by transit lanes and mag-lev rail. But it was big. Made Vestia's tiny capital of Foundwell look like a sapling next to one of the Tangle's old mothers. Back home, settlements grew organic through the forest breaks. Here, they'd carved their home straight from the mountain's bones at the top of the world.

"Thanks to our friends on the Alexander Lehman," Kull went on, a little stink on the word friends, *"we've confirmed several raider incursions across every Vestebrae district. Forward elements touched down fifteen minutes ago, and a larger force is mirroring our drop."*

Red dots bloomed across the city diagram. It looked all scattershot with no clear focus. No strategy. Just chaos.

"Our primary objective is to secure evacuation routes from the outer settlements." More dots appeared, cutting mean red lines through the city diagram. Twelfth, there were a lot of them. *"Planetary Reserve has activated their emergency protocols, but civilian shelters are at capacity. We need to establish safe corridors to move these people deeper into the urban core."* A new overlay highlighted potential evac routes in pale blue

veins pulsing with desperate humanity. *"Azure, Battle, Cyclone, and Dragon elements will push downslope toward Corongaet. Easy and Fury elements will deploy along the Diacad transit to cover our six."*

Victory's landing zones painted Diacad Cliffs Colonial-Defense blue. But where that blue bled into danger red, it turned to bruised purple.

She thumbed her push-to-talk. "You hear that, Doc? We got our objective. Our first mission!"

"In the rear with the gear," Doc groaned. "Vanguard units have all the fun."

"What's your hurry? You know someone at Corongaet?"

Doc didn't answer, but his vitals ticked up a notch. Stupid girl. Too obsessed with his lady-killer smile to bother asking where he was from.

Kull's ident lit up again. *"This doesn't look like a typical raider smash and grab. We've confirmed multiple company-sized elements. And with the forge ship maneuvering for low orbit, I think they plan to stay."* The monitor panned to the settlement capitol of Vestebrae, highlighting the primary spaceport at the center. *"We will deny them that opportunity. Once we have secured evacuation routes for the civilians, we will retake and hold the spaceport to allow for rapid deployment of reinforcements that are en route. The Concordat are back to finish what they've started. Colonel Reede and the crew of the Victory sacrificed themselves for this one chance to save our home. Don't let them down."*

Secure the evac routes. Move the civvies. Hold the spaceport. Keep the supply lines open. Kull made it sound so simple. Olsom wanted to believe her. After all, she was wearing two tons of Marine fibrosteel, armed with enough firepower to clear-cut through anything the raiders brought groundside. But this was starting to feel more like Three-Alpha. Back home, it was the easy-looking paths that usually got you eaten.

Her platoon comms clicked over in her ear. *"Fury 3, this is 3 Actual,"* Lieutenant Revan said, his voice so strained it almost cracked. *"Prepare for touchdown. I want you unloaded in standard dispersal patterns the second that ramp drops. Exos, provide cover for your fireteams. And for Twelfth's sake, keep eyes on your IFF. We don't know who or what is waiting for us down there."*

The drop timer counted down toward zero. Nothing about this felt standard. Her first time on another colony just to fight house-to-house on a mountain fortress. The tactical display showed clean vector lines and defensive positions, but she knew better. Three-Alpha had been packed with admin personnel and other non-combatants, but the Concordat rolled them up like stampeding ankrin. Civvies would be way worse.

The dropship engines roared, pushing back against Aegia's heavier gravity. Metal screamed, and the craft shook, setting down bone-jarringly hard on its skids. Mag locks reversed, throwing the drop ramp wide open. A cold wind ripped through the troop deck, howling like something from a childhood nightmare.

"Move, move, move!" Lessig bellowed.

The line of exos tromped down the ramp to the sound of heavy tread. Olsom found the lock release and keyed it open, her exo free and swaying slightly in the wind. She followed Smokes's exo down the ramp.

The roiling storm clouds looked alive—endless, crisscrossing rivers of charcoal gray moving fast as a combat shuttle. The wind seemed to pull the very air from her lungs. This storm had teeth.

"Come on, 3-3-3, get in formation."

She tore herself from the wild sky. "Roger. Moving."

Her scopes showed clear. Nothing—IFF feeds blank beside the friendly returns from Fury 3. Row after row of squat gray buildings shone through her tactical overlays—lines of wind-polished stonework with heavy doors and very few windows. Distant fires twinkled above the roof lines; a hint of smoke carried on the wind. The place called Diacad Cliffs looked military, not civilian, just bunkers in shades of gray carved from the mountainside. She took another deep breath, trying to choke back her beating heart, but her pulse kept climbing, black spots dancing at the edge of her vision. Combat nerves, had to be.

"Hey, Bugs." Doc. He sounded far away. "You okay?"

"I'm fine." Each word pulled the air out of her. Panic sweat itched a path down her forehead. She sucked in another lungful, needles of fear stitching up her spine. Something was… the mountain air—too thin. She couldn't breathe.

"Don't sound fine." 3-3-3's cage hissed open and Doc was there, rebreather in hand. He placed it gently over her face, threading the straps over her helmet. "The air's real thin up here. You'll adjust. Mostly. Always keep one of these close."

"You…" She gasped for air so fast it hurt. The mask's re-oxygenated mix sent a wave of relief and euphoria through her. Her head swam, the whole granite world suddenly dreamlike and strange. "You don't need it?"

His grin didn't quite reach his eyes. "Grew up a click or so downs-lope from here. This is a good air day."

Everything felt suddenly brighter, sharper, like breaking surface after river diving too long. She caught herself giggling—actually giggling—as she stared blankly at his casually heroic smile. Part of her wanted to accept it was real. That he'd really be there for her when it mattered. The wild thing in her hissed it was all a lie. But the warmth in her chest kept spreading with each lungful, and that wounded part of her drifted further and further away.

"Thanks." It felt natural, him watching her six like that. Natural as breathing.

He palmed the exo's cage release closed. "That's my job. To keep you and this rig going."

She believed him.

Movement flickered across the tactical display. Fuzzy white ghosts flitted between the line-drawn buildings on the display. Unknown contacts. She shook off the sloppy warm feelings, thumb on the FAB's control hat.

"I've got something. Get behind me, Doc." The big machine turned to face the line of buildings, FAB kicking out and forward in a whir of servos and charging capacitors. "3-1-1, this is 3-3-3. Possible contacts at our zero-four-five."

"Hostile?" Lessig asked.

"IFF can't make 'em out." She edged 3-3-3 forward, hoping for a better scan.

"How many?"

Still nothing. "I don't know—"

"What do *you know, Private?"* Lieutenant Revan cut in.

"Confirmed, unknown contacts," another Marine called out on the net. *"Twenty. Maybe thirty. They're headed this way. Two minutes out."*

"Now that I can work with." Revan again. Smug bastard.

New orders flashed across her screen. Standard exo line. Support elements covering behind. Fire coordination between squads, just like the sims.

"Fury 3, line up and prepare to engage," Revan said. *"Let's give these squids a Victory welcome."*

Warnings bleated from the terminal display. 3-3-3 was in the line of fire. She needed to back up, but Doc was still behind her.

"Doc, you clear?"

"Hang on."

The white ghosts on her screen flitted closer. There were more than thirty of them. A lot more.

"No time—" Then she heard it, the soft whimpering beneath Doc's voice. Vlan. "Vlan, sound off. You okay?"

The noise coming from Vlan's comms was the keening sound of a person cut in two—raw and animal and absolutely the last thing she needed right now.

"He is definitely not okay," Doc said. *"I could dose him again, but it sounds like we're about to be in it."*

A bright red beam flashed overhead, sparking against a nearby stone wall with an angry buzz. She tried to duck, but the best 3-3-3 could manage was a slight bend in the knees. Exos didn't really take cover. They were cover.

"Hold fire, Fury 3. Let them get close." There was an anxious tension in Revan's voice that vanished when he cut over to direct comms. *"Get in line, 3-3-3."*

"We gotta go, Doc." She panned the FAB until the targeting reticle rested over the narrow alley the shot had come from.

"Okay, okay, moving." Doc and Vlan's signal locators drifted away from the exo in a slow, straight line. *"You're clear!"*

She took one step back when the IFF feed pinged again with the bright chirp of friendly contacts. A smudge of blue flashed on the screen, then faded back to white. Another beam snapped by, closer, but still no threat. Another flash of blue.

"3 Actual, 3-3-3." Olsom's finger hovered just above the FAB's trigger. "I'm not sure, but I'm seeing friendly returns on the IFF."

"Friendlies my ass," Revan snapped. *"We've got laser fire incoming and thirty plus contacts closing fast. You've got five seconds to get on line or I'll have your pip."*

Another contact resolved, this one fighting to show colonial blue through the interference. The returns kept shifting between white and blue, as uncertain as she was.

"Sir, please, just let me confirm—"

"Three seconds."

"They might be civvies," she pressed, her voice cracking. "Or CDF. Something's screwing with the feeds."

"Time's up." Static crackled as Revan switched to all-squad. *"Fury 3, weapons free in five, four—"*

"Belay that order!" Bresto leaned his big round head into the operator cage. "What do you see, boot?"

The cage suddenly felt small. Bastard had abandoned her aboard the *Victory*, and now here he was, like nothing had changed.

"3-3-3!" Revan barked. *"What the hell are you doing? You're in the line of fire!"*

"What did you see?" There was desperation beneath Bresto's parade deck bark, like he was searching for something specific.

But he *was* here now. He needed her help. Whatever it was, she could help him. Just like Three-Alpha. Another blue blip appeared, more solid than the others. Moving with purpose.

"There!" She stabbed a finger at the display.

He pulled his head from the cage. "Fury 3 Actual, Sarnt Bresto. There are friendlies converging on your position, over."

"Sergeant Bresto, 3 Actual. This channel is for Victory assets only. Clear the nets or I'll—"

A flash of movement pulled her attention from the argument, something quick and desperate in the alley's murk. Her arm found 3-3-3's control rig by instinct as Revan and Bresto's voices faded to background noise. The FAB tracked smooth across the granite faces, its targeting overlays cutting through the gloom as the wild thing screamed *danger coming.*

"Hold!" Bresto raised a closed fist, blaster rifle tight in his shoulder.

Then a voice cut through it all, high and thin and terrified. "Help us!"

A young girl emerged through the FAB's high-res optics. She couldn't have been more than a gamma. Blood matted her hair where it ran down her face, turning her gray jumpsuit black around the collar. She was half-carrying, half-dragging a smaller child. They looked so young in the harsh light of 3-3-3's weapons feeds.

"Doc." Olsom almost couldn't get the word out. All that training, all those combat sims, and all she could see was her own abandonment and pain. "You gotta help her."

"On it." His response was instant, professional. He was past her in a heartbeat, moving the children toward the relative shelter of the high block walls. The autodoc's soft diagnostic tone seemed obscene against the whine of charged weapons.

They kept coming from the shadows. Not raiders. Colonists. Some sprinting, others limping. These weren't the proper Aegians Doc bragged about. These were prey animals, running blind from monsters in the dark.

The enemy's laser strike came surgical and precise, cutting through the crowd like target practice. Bodies fell tangled together.

Her rage crystallized into something cold and sharp. The squids had used these people as bait, and when the Marines didn't take it, they'd decided to do the killing themselves. IFF resolved the raiders' positions one by one. This was an ambush, and they'd walked right into it.

"*Contact front!*" Lessig's voice cut through her realization. "*Full raider clutch straight ahead at our zero-zero-zero!*"

"They were waiting for us." Bresto's tone went flat. "Doc, get those kids behind us. Olsom, on me. Get your rig up now. Give these people some cover."

She swung 3-3-3 forward. The FAB's targeting system painted heat signatures across her display, raiders flowing between buildings like predators closing for the kill. No more hiding. No more testing. They were coming.

"Orders?" someone asked through the static.

"We assault through." Bresto checked his weapon with mechanical precision. "Time to metal up."

CHAPTER
FOURTEEN

THERE WERE TOO MANY PEOPLE. Families. Mothers, young children. Bresto thought he recognized some of them, their pale faces tugging at the edges of his memory. It had been so long since he'd been home. The smell of cooked air and laser discharge was more familiar than the block ID numbers stenciled on the thick stone walls.

Too many people, and no clear shot. The raider's silhouette rose at the far edge of the alley: big, armored, and ugly, its red laser beams cutting through the waves of fleeing colonists.

Bresto's rifle optics flashed friendly fire warnings as human faces obscured his target. "Go, go, go!"

A young man sprinted past, panic on his dust covered face. The kid couldn't have been a few turns older than Kaffy. His block captain should've evacuated him already. All these people should be underground, not running scared. His kids might be doing the same damn thing. They could be right here, right—no. Focus, Marine.

PFC Olsom was a few meters behind, the old MAC-4 plodding along as she took her Twelfth-damned time coming up to meet him. She was a boot. Didn't trust the metal yet. Didn't believe the Twelfth and eight centimeters of fibrosteel plate would keep her safe. But the exo could take it. She needed to have faith.

And these people needed cover. Now.

"Move up!" he bellowed. "Right here! Now!"

"Moving," she said with a false calm, more machine than her rig. Fear did that to people. "I—"

"You're not moving fast enough!"

"Sarnt, I don't have a clear shot!"

Damn boot didn't understand what he needed. FABs could vaporize unarmored targets. "Hold your fire. Just put yourself between them and the squids and keep. Pushing. Forward."

Two more exos came up the alleyway behind her. The blank stare of Smokes Rikko caught him as the lanky spacer brought 3-3-2 to a halt. The other kid he didn't know, 3-3-1. Both as green as Olsom. A crowd of civilians moved past before 3-3-1 lurched forward.

"Rikko, what's the holdup?"

No answer. Just the low whine of idle reactors and incoming laser fire.

"It's his brother, Sarnt," Doc Myers responded instead.

"Don't care. Rikko, get on line now!"

3-3-2 lifted one leg and set it right back down. The twin spacers were beyond weird, but they weren't cowards.

"Myers. What do you mean, his brother?"

"The lieutenant split them up, and Vlan hasn't been right since. Neither of them, really."

Twelfth Herself, the twins really were inseparable. Both combat ineffective without the other. He could fix this, but not until they secured the alley.

"Smokes." Bresto waved down 3-3-2 until the twin looked up. "You want to help your brother? You get that rig on line right now. We have to hold this lane to break the assault."

Smokes said nothing, but 3-3-2 lumbered forward, the exo going from a long stride to a heavy jog. Third Squad's exos came together, a fibrosteel wall nine meters wide the fleeing colonists began funneling around. They'd pushed into the assault. That was a start.

"What in the hell are you doing, Third Squad?" Fury 3 Actual sounded small on wrist comms. *"Fall back to the transit before you're cut off!"*

Too bad the lieutenant was as green as his platoon. That was two bad orders in so many minutes.

"Negative, negative," Bresto cut in. "They're almost at the next junction. Push First and Second Squads forward up the parallel lanes so we can get more guns on the squids' positions."

"I have my orders, Sergeant. The transit corridor is our—" the lieutenant's voice caught as another wave of civilians stumbled past Third Squad's position. *"We can't abandon our primary objective for every refugee we encounter."*

"Then what are we doing here, sir, if not to save these people?"

For three endless seconds, only static filled the channel. Then: *"First and Second Squads, take the secondary and tertiary junctions."*

Interference couldn't mask the tremor in the lieutenant's voice when he switched to private comms. *"Understand something, Sergeant. When this clusterfuck is over, you're going to learn exactly why officers don't take tactical advice from every NCO with a service stripe."*

Junior officers were all the same. This one would learn a thing or two, assuming he survived the day.

"Sarnt!" Olsom shouted. "I have a shot!"

The laugh escaped before he could stop it. Finally, something was going right.

"What do you want, a parade?" He braced against the violence that was coming. Twelfth, he'd give anything to be pulling that trigger. "Weapons free, Third Squad. Burn 'em up."

The alleyway erupted in a storm of charged particles, their FABs' tri-barrels spinning. Blaster bolts screamed through the narrow alley in tight, overlapping lines, forcing the raiders to scramble for cover that wasn't there. Stone melted. Metal hissed. Scaled meat turned to steam.

The sound was overwhelming, like being inside an industrial crusher, but Bresto couldn't stop grinning. *This* was Marine power, six tons of Colonial Defense metal proving why humanity had survived this long. The initiative turned; the raider clutch that had been hunting them seconds before now fled in panic, their laser fire ineffective against the advancing wall of fibrosteel and fury.

They'd taken the initiative. Time to press it. "Third Squad support, move up!"

Doc Myers appeared through the smoke, half-carrying the other twin. He caught the combat engineer by his sleeve.

"He serviceable?" Bresto scanned Vlan's tac gear, hunting for blood or burns.

Vlan stared forward, his eyes focused on the exos at the end of the alley. Focused on his brother.

"Negative, Sarnt. Not without his brother."

"Let him go." Bresto took Vlan by the shoulders and gave him a brisk shake. "Hey, Rikko, listen up!"

Vlan only whimpered. The killing edge Bresto had seen back on Three-Alpha was gone.

"You want to fight with your brother?"

Something flickered in Vlan's empty stare before he managed a single, sharp nod.

"Good. Form up with his fireteam and stay there. If I catch you further than three meters from your brother, I'll kick your skinny ass back to whatever rock made you. Understood?"

The change was immediate and total. Vlan's thousand-yard stare snapped into focus, his tall frame straightening to its full height. Then he was moving, closing the distance to his brother's exo at a dead sprint. He stumbled between the advancing line of Marines, long legs eating up ground like he'd been shot from a railgun. He reached 3-3-2 in seconds, falling into step beside the war machine as if he'd never left.

The kid could move when properly motivated.

Doc's relief was palpable. "I didn't know what else to do with him, Sarnt."

"Yeah?" He gave Doc a shove. "Try doing your job next time."

Myer's face crumpled. "But I—"

"But nothing, Marine." Bresto leveled a finger at him. "Whatever it takes to keep 'em in the fight. You under—"

"*3 Actual, 3-1-1,*" Fury 3's First squad leader tacked out. "*I've got squids breaking contact in my sector. Requesting permission to pursue. We can turn them into field paste if we move now.*"

Fury 3 Actual sounded almost giddy. "*Permission granted, 3-1-1. Good hunting.*"

Myers's OTJ would have to wait. That was another bad call from the lieutenant. Raiders were dumb animals—all muscle and momentum until you put them down. But these squids moved with purpose, their retreat too practiced to be panic. Twenty years of combat experience screamed trap, and that junction was the trigger. Had to be. The man was about to learn that lesson the hard way.

"Hold position, 3-1-1." Bresto winced. He could almost *feel* the ambush. It didn't help that he was practically blind to the situation—no flexscreen for tactical feeds, no proper comms, not even a damn chest rig and armor plate. "These squids haven't committed their heavy weapons, and we've got no eyes on what is waiting for us beyond the junction. Keep up your fire with Second and Third squads. Make them come to you, over."

"Negative on hold, unknown station." 3-1-1's reply dripped with arrogance and adrenaline. *"I have direction from my platoon commander. Maybe check your comms authorization before countermanding orders again, over."*

The Twelfth-damned lieutenant wasn't done proving his command presence, either. *"Second and Third Squads, push forward into the junction. Pursue and destroy all raider forces in the immediate vicinity."*

That idiot was going to get them all killed. Bresto pushed through the wall of heat coming off Third Squad's guns. He needed eyes on the junction. The alley opened onto a service transit he knew too well—block maintenance, emergency vehicles, the lane where he'd caught Kaffy trying to catch a stray kinlin the day they moved in. Six orbits felt like six hundred just then. The block numbers stenciled in the granite made his throat tight. E-07. Three units down was home, assuming it was still standing. The rage nearly choked him. Fucking squids, prowling through his settlement like they owned it. He'd spent half his life keeping them at arm's length from the colonies, and now they were close enough to spit on his front door.

He keyed his wrist comms. "Third Squad, listen up. Maintain your spacing and watch your sectors. These squids know exactly what they're doing. The second you clear that junction, expect company from above."

Third Squad's metal lined up along the transit, better than most boots. The thunder of their FABs had settled into something more deliberate—single bursts, controlled pairs, operators picking their shots. But the squids' war-speech filtering through the stonework made his skin crawl. He'd heard their death-screams enough times to know the difference. They weren't running scared.

The transit grew still, and for a moment, there was nothing but the whisper of storm winds. Something else cut through, not quite sound, more like the ghost of industrial equipment warming up, humming in the meat of his jaw.

He glanced at the nearest Marine, a Respitian whose face looked like a grid of old knife wounds. "Tell me you hear that."

"Mez know that sound." The Marine's scarred face split into an ugly grin. "Heard it in the loading docks all the time growing up, right when the cargo lifts fail. Right before everything comes crashing down. But this…" He licked his lips. "This gonna hurt more."

Some kind of power-on sequence. Twelfth save them all. Bresto scanned the sheer granite walls, hunting shadows that didn't belong. The familiar stink of an ambush was already in his nose, like molten rock and ozone. The squids had something big nearby. Had to. But where?

Doc Myer's voice cut through the growing vibration: "Holy Mother, the wall!"

The face of the housing block lit up from within, veins of magma burning through the granite. Stone softened and began to sag, dripping molten gobs into the transit below. A concentrated shaft of green-white death punched through the melting stone like it wasn't there, smashing into one of Second Squad's exos.

The Marine inside never had a chance. Their final moments transmitted through the machine itself, the massive exo jerking like a broken puppet until the beam finally burned through the backup systems and power relays.

The hair on the back of Bresto's neck lifted. The squids hadn't built that on their own. That was Concordat tech.

All his experience came down to this, keeping Marines alive five seconds at a time. "Metal up! Cross those arms! Protect your cages! Now get some fire on that position!"

The remaining exos moved as one, their primary arms forming fibrosteel shields while their FABs lit up the melting stone.

Red bolts sparked and scattered against some kind of energy screen, lighting up the interior of the melting hab block. The barrier shimmered with each impact, revealing the pink-scaled workers scrambling behind. Their weapon looked like something straight out of the forge ship, all tendrils and burning light. And they were about to fire it again.

"Third Squad, keep those FABs talkin'!" Bresto worked his way down the line, picking his hunters. Two breachers, two combat engineers, all trigger pullers. Just enough teeth for what he had in mind. Each Marine fell in behind him without question. That plasma cannon wouldn't expect visitors from the flank. "All of you. On me, let's move."

He led them to the far end of Third Platoon's line, keeping them tight to the corners of the large hab block. Above and behind them, charged particles against the squids' shield formed a constant light-show. Between the noise and the FABs keeping their heads down, they might have just enough diversion to work with. Might even live through this.

"Orders, Sarnt?" The breacher checked her demo loadout. Black curls escaped her helmet as she worked, her storm-dark features focused entirely on the plasmex blocks beneath her fingers.

"What's your name, Marine?"

"PFC Kitrelle. Ready to make an entrance, Sarnt."

"You've got the breach." He turned. The scarred Respitian was still there. "Name?"

"Mez, Sarnt."

"You're her backup."

"Aye, Sarnt," Mez chorused.

Bresto fixed the combat engineers and let his hard stare demand their names.

"Toelke, Sarnt."

"Rosch, Sarnt."

Bresto kept his voice low. "I've got point. Rosch, you're my shadow. Kitrelle, you're next. Toelke, stick to Mez. When that breach goes, every squid's gonna try for better cover. Keep your sectors clear and find that weapon crew. They die first."

"Ooh-rah," came their reply, low, subtle, but filled with grit and purpose.

The hab's upslope exterior was still mostly solid, but heat bled through Bresto's gloves as he pressed forward. Above them, the stone groaned and shifted, fighting to maintain its shape. No sign of sentries on the roofline. Nothing. Not so smart after all. Bresto pressed two fingers against the wall, signaling for his team to stack up.

Kitrelle tapped the wall twice, finding the hollow space between support struts that every hab block shared, the weak point in otherwise solid granite. She worked quickly, molding the gray-green plasmex into a rough cone shape before pressing the magnetic detonator deep into its center. The rest of the team fell into position behind her, shoulders pressed to granite, nothing but cold focus in their eyes.

Kitrelle threw him a nod. Ready. The squid weapon fired again, its heavy plasma whine making Bresto's teeth ache. Time to end this.

"Breach, breach, breach!"

The plasmex detonated with a sharp crack that Bresto felt in his bones. Superheated gas carved through the granite wall in precisely engineered violence, the shaped blast forcing debris inward instead of out. The pressure differential tried to suck Bresto off his feet as he crossed the threshold, but combat instinct kept him moving. Through the smoke and stone dust, he could see the squids' shield flickering. Their ugly, shocked faces made perfect targets.

His rifle found the first pink-scale at the shield generator, three well-placed blaster bolts cooking through its thin armor. The warrior manning the cannon swung its bulk around, but Rosch's blaster fire caught it in the throat. The rest tried to flee deeper into the hab, but the docs were thorough. Someone—Kitrelle or Mez—cooked the cannon's power source with a small charge.

Eight seconds, and then it was over. Bresto scanned the ruined hab through his scope.

"Clear." It was as much a question as a statement.

"Clear!" Kitrelle barked, then Rosch a second later.

Outside, the hammer of FAB bolts slowed, then stopped. Victory echoed in the sudden quiet—the whir of exo servos advancing up the transit, the practiced calls of "clear" from fireteam to fireteam. Even the constant storm winds seemed to pause, as if the Twelfth Herself approved of their work.

"Cease fire, cease fire, targets destroyed," came the net call. The young lieutenant sounded relieved. Humbled. *"Good work. All of you."*

Bresto shouldered past the celebrating Marines, through the hab and into the block hall. Three units down. Someone said something, a congratulations, maybe, but he couldn't hear it. Three units down. His home. The rage that had carried him through the fight twisted into something colder as he crossed the threshold. The hall was empty, the walls still warm from the raiders' weapon. No bodies. No signs of life. Three units down. Then two. Hab Block E-10.

Carbon scoring marred the door to his home. Deep scratches crisscrossed over the duraplate panels. Someone had opened the access control, exposing the wiring inside—raiders trying to get in, or emergency crews breaking people out. No way to tell.

The depth of his failure engulfed him. Holy Mother, forgive him. He felt hollow—soulless—as he brought the rifle to his shoulder and waved the door open.

THE DOOR CYCLED open with a soft hiss, revealing a space so familiar it hurt. Bresto swept his rifle left to right, clearing the cramped entryway more from decades of muscle memory than tactical necessity. Dust motes drifted through shafts of amber light from the overhead panels, stirred by the door's pneumatics.

He edged forward, carving the room into segments with his rifle—high to low, near to far. Nothing looked familiar through the harsh light of his optics. Their worn couch to his right. The corner desk where Kaff did her studies, its tiny flat screen dark and silent. All of it mass-fabricated and still too expensive to replace.

The air tasted like metal and burned stone, but beneath it all was home—uniform starch, a hint of crid fat, that persistent smell of damp from the block's aging atmo recyclers. The smells were so familiar; it was as if he'd never left.

He moved into the living room, rifle muzzle tracking over the stone bar that separated the small space from the even smaller kitchen. The hab felt preserved, like a museum of their lives together. Nothing broken or ransacked. Kaff's level certificates hung in order on the wall: alpha, beta, gamma. He'd missed all of them. Sammy's, too, though his newest beta cert looked strange next to Bresto's memories of the tiny alpha whose cries filled these halls.

Nothing was wrong. That's what was wrong. No signs of struggle, no evidence the raiders made their way inside, or took anything if they did. Just the quiet aftermath of a family's morning routine interrupted.

Only the empty bar looked off. Too clean. Then he remembered. The family hard print was brand new when he'd placed it there the day they'd moved in—him, Lyra and her pregnant belly, and little Kaff at the spaceport's observation deck. The thin Vestian pine frame had cost a fortune. Two months' deployment pay. Lyra was furious, but the picture was special. It deserved better than cheap heat-molded plastec. And now it was gone.

The raiders wouldn't have taken it. No technical value. But Lyra? She'd been so angry when he left home the second time. Said she didn't want to keep raising the kids on her own, like he was choosing the CDF over them again. Maybe she'd taken it down. Traded the frame for something more valuable than memories. Maybe she'd gotten tired of living with his ghost.

A foil tube of field paste lay beside the sink in the kitchen. Planetary Reserve issue, squeezed from the middle like Lyra always did. She never was a homemaker, left the cooking to him whenever he was around. Old habits died hard. But the half-eaten meal meant she'd been there just hours before. Closer than ever and still so far away.

There was no evidence of breakfast cleanup, no morning dishes in the sink. They'd called her up before she could feed the kids. And Kaff—Twelfth save him, she'd sent Kaff out for their lots. She'd never made it back. His little girl was somewhere in this mess, alone. And if Lyra was gone, and Kaff was gone, that left only Sammy. Here.

The kids' room door gave with a sharp crack. Bresto swept left, then right, but the room was empty. Unmade bunks rose on the far wall. The sink dripped slow and steady near the door, droplets striking a half-full cup of mouthwash.

"Sammy?"

The word was loud in the empty room. No one answered. He searched the top bunk anyway, but found only tangled sheets and a Pulmanex inhaler. Twelfth, he didn't know. Six orbits gone, and Lyra hadn't mentioned it. For some, the mountain's thin air proved too much. He couldn't remember Kaff ever needing to wear a rebreather. She was born for this altitude.

Rifle low, he eased into their bedroom. Lyra's bedroom, really. Her scent lingered—colony soap and shipyard grease—but she was long gone. The closet hung open; her Reserve white-and-grays missing from their hangar, field kit gone from the wall rack. Their Aegian gray jumpsuits hung together side-by-side beside her shipyard coveralls, empty like the room.

He moved to the bed and sat. The hab was clear. Nothing moved in the shadows. Nothing waited to kill him. No one to rescue. Just the hollow feeling of coming home too late.

The thin Vestian pine frame lay face-down on the nightstand. He reached for it, half-afraid of what else she might have changed. But the carved wood was smooth beneath his touch, the print still pristine after all these years. She'd moved it, yes, but kept it close. Kept him close.

He yanked the print free, ignoring the frame's flimsy metal clasps, and studied it. Kaff grinned ear-to-ear, hand tight to his. Lyra cradled her belly, her gaze warm but unsettled. A distant cargo transport rose behind them on fusion drive plumes. He slid the photo carefully from its frame to his breast pocket, patted it closed, and stalked back into the kitchen.

The wall locker yielded just one packet of colony rations, still sealed, its expiry date too far in the future to ever worry about. Not much to show for his NCO pay and her double shifts. It was this place. Diacad Cliffs wasn't cheap. But Vestebrae's urban core was far beyond their means, and they had outgrown their old place in Corongaet. Besides, Kaff and Sammy deserved the best opportunities they could afford.

Not that any of it mattered anymore. All that mattered now was finding the kids and keeping them safe. His rifle's charge level blinked sixty percent. Could be worse, depending on how many squids stood between them. Kaff was easy—the allotment center, maybe the nearby shelter. But the meds meant Sammy couldn't breathe in this thin air, not for long. Their block captain should've gotten him out, but the number of colonists left behind said he couldn't count on that.

Rage came back like an old friend. Six orbits away, fighting humanity's enemies, and the colony had failed him. His finger found the trigger guard, tapping an angry rhythm. Some cowardly block captain had abandoned his children. PR command had mustered Lyra too soon, or too late. The whole Twelfth-damned system left his children exposed when the enemy came. They would all—

Boot steps echoed through the open door. Bresto spun, weapon up, finger tensing on the trigger. The nervous lieutenant—the one from the *Gauntlet*, Fury 3's platoon commander—peered back at him through the rifle's optics.

"Lower your weapon, Sergeant."

Bresto did so, but slowly. The man *had* threatened to shoot him once, after all.

"Well, if it isn't Fury 3 Actual. Sir."

"I'm Lieutenant Revan. And you're Sergeant Bresto. We need to talk."

Now wasn't the time. Bresto slung his rifle, snatched the tube of field paste off the counter and squeezed a plug into his mouth. "So talk. Sir."

"I run a disciplined platoon, Sergeant." The man's tone was all spite and nerves—typical urban core, officer academy cridshit. He said the word sergeant like he'd been practicing in a mirror. "Insubordination won't be tolerated. We can't have confusion in the ranks. Not today."

"Lucky for you, I'm not *in* your ranks. Sir."

Revan seethed. "Your actions aboard Three-Alpha were highly suspect. With the Concordat coming down around us, the major was well within her right to shoot you."

"Is that what you're here to do, sir? Shoot me?"

Revan's gaze faltered, moving from the rifle on Bresto's shoulder to somewhere on the floor.

He didn't have time for this. "Good to go, sir. I'll just be on my way."

"Wait." Revan sidestepped, putting himself between Bresto and the door.

He stopped centimeters from Revan. Maybe the man had a sack after all. Still, not a smart move.

"I'm no fool," Revan said.

Doubtful.

"However." Revan shifted his weight back, the academy polish cracking. "My initial assessment of the situation at the junction was incorrect. Your actions saved lives. I won't forget that."

"Good. Your platoon sergeant fu—"

"Acting platoon sergeant. Corporal Lessig lacks the combat and leadership experience the situation requires."

Corporal? Platoon sergeant was a staff NCO billet. So, it was desperation behind the sudden bravery. No wonder Revan had screwed up so badly.

"The Victory was conducting troop rotations when the attack started," Revan went on. "Lots of our senior fireteam leaders and NCOs were cycling through—taking leave, being discharged. We were days... weeks away from full strength."

"Well, you don't want me, sir." What was it Park had said about him? Oh, yeah. "I'm difficult."

"I know your type." The venom in Revan's voice slid back. "Five service stripes and still just a sergeant."

Just a sergeant. If Revan kept this up, it would be Private Bresto soon, assuming he survived this war. "Like I said."

"It doesn't have to be that way. Fight for me, and I'll see that you get your pips back. Staff Sergeant. *Gunnery* Sergeant, even."

The rage died in his throat, replaced with sour disgust. Colonel Reede's death had created a vacuum, and this academy-polished turd was already climbing. Tactical experience plus a seasoned NCO would make him stand out to whoever took command. And that was almost certainly Major Kull.

"Appreciate the offer, sir, but I've got more pressing concerns."

Revan matched him step-for-step back toward the door. As much as Bresto wanted to hit the son-of-a-bitch, he didn't need the Concordat *and* the Marines hunting him.

Revan held his hands up, palms out, urging him to stop. "Bresto. This is your home, isn't it?"

Pressure built behind Bresto's temples. He wanted to bury this sorry excuse for an officer beneath ninety kilos of pissed-off husband and father.

"They aren't here, are they?" The apprehension in Revan's eyes was unmistakable, but he had committed. "What's your plan? You going to find them all by yourself?"

"I ain't your man," Bresto hissed. "Now get out of my way. Sir."

Revan didn't move. "I can help you. F-Find them."

Find them. He breathed deep, trying to calm the storm raging inside him. One. Two. Stop. Think things through. If the man really could help him—wanted to help—he needed to know.

"How?"

"As my platoon sergeant."

So, Revan *was* climbing.

Revan's scheme tumbled out. "You'll have priority access to planetary nets. Couple that with intel feeds from Aegia Prime on the flexscreen I'll issue you, and you'll have more intelligence at your fingertips than that wrist comms of yours can muster."

The little comms on Bresto's wrist was meant for fleet duty, or garrison, not frontline missions like this. With a flexscreen and enough time, he'd be able to patch into Lyra's comms directly. Maybe even tap the shelter feeds and get eyes on the kids. The possibilities kept growing. Secure some tac gear. Frags. More charge packs.

Was he actually considering this?

"A platoon of Marines gives you better odds than going alone," Revan continued. "And our mission takes us straight down the main transit, all the way to Vestebrae proper."

"What if they aren't on the main transit?"

"Well, if they aren't near the main transit by now, Sergeant, they're already… lost."

The word was a shape charge in his brain. He threw Revan against the wall and held him there, staring at the small man wriggling beneath his grip. He wasn't mad at Revan. Not directly. He just hated that, after all that, Revan was right. And the growing calm on the man's face said he knew it, too.

"Fine, I'll do it."

"Good." Revan keyed his comms when Bresto let go. "3-1-1, 3 Actual."

"Go for 3-1-1."

"Dismount and proceed directly to my pos, break. Bring a full set of tac gear, size large, break. Our new platoon sergeant has just arrived, over."

"Say again, sir? Platoon serg—"

"Now, Lessig."

"Aye, sir. En route."

"Excellent." Revan's smile was back. "Now we can—"

"One thing, sir." Bresto stepped closer. "Out there, when the air's hot, you listen to me. No more academy shit against the archenemy. Sir."

"Naturally." Revan's politician smile never wavered. "Though I'm sure you understand the *attention* that comes with your new position. Every decision noted. Every result scrutinized. And not just by me."

The arrangement left a bad taste in Bresto's mouth. He needed to spit, to wash the ambition out, but he wouldn't. Not in his own home. Lyra would kill him. "Naturally."

"Take a moment. But make it quick. We've got a war to win."

The stink of ambition followed Revan out of the hab. Bresto took another look around the hab. Not his last, though. Tactical assessments were changing, but for the better. He had a platoon again. He had reach. A way forward.

But that meant he had two missions now. His family, and the thousands of others struggling to survive the Concordat assault. Twelfth save him if he had to pick one over the other.

At the door, he reached inside the reliquary. There was only smooth stone where the Twelfth's statuette should be. Kaff had taken it, just like he'd taught her. Faith and family, together.

He'd find them both.

CHAPTER
SIXTEEN

STATIC CRACKLED across 3-3-3's tactical display as Olsom tracked another phantom contact, some piece of burning debris the optics couldn't quite resolve. Her heart was still racing, but in a good way—the best way—like she could fight forever. The squids had brought their fancy tech, their plasma cannons and energy shields, and Third Platoon had taken it all apart. It felt like being drunk, but better. Faster. Cleaner. She flexed 3-3-3's primary arms, watching the thick limbs mirror her movements. The whole fucking universe made sense when you were wrapped in Marine metal.

The screams of the FABs still buzzed in her ears, and holy shit what a sound. Her heart kicked into overdrive remembering how the raiders simply disappeared beneath her sights. No dramatic death screams or whatever squids did when they died. Just metal and grit painting the stone raider blue. Her rebreather was starting to fog just thinking about it.

Funny how an hour ago she'd been ready to piss herself coming off that dropship. Now? Bring on the whole damn forge ship. Now she was invincible.

She watched the junction through two sets of eyes. 3-3-3's combat feeds painted tactical data across her ops terminal. Above that, the canopy's HUD gave an unfiltered view of her overwatch sector. The transit lane cut deep into the mountain's granite face, highlighted in soft blue vectors that tracked its path downslope. Vestebrae glowed electric orange in the distance, its skyline notched by distant fires. Lightning ripped across the flowing gray-black clouds. The thunder shook through her metal frame. Glimpses of black specs burned the sky on needles of flame—raider ships touching down like terrible shooting stars.

She couldn't stop replaying it. One second, they were getting lit up by that plasma beam, their FABs useless against the squid's barrier. Then Bresto had gone and pulled that crazy flanking maneuver. A thunderclap of breaching charges, and the whole hab just collapsed inward. The rest of the firefight lasted maybe ten seconds. When the smoke cleared, Third Platoon owned the junction, and she'd seen it all through her combat optics like some kind of beautiful training sim. Except the dead squids were real. The victory was real. And damn, did it feel good.

"Time to dismount." Doc's voice cut through her replay. "Need to run some maintenance checks."

"Get your own metal." She took a fighter's stance, putting her fists between them. The exo did the same, mimicking the playful motion. "I'm on a winning streak. I'm gonna—"

"Going to what? Win harder?"

"Damn straight." She threw a punch in slow motion, the metal fist stopping centimeters from his nose. He didn't move.

"Bugs." His voice went soft, almost gentle. "Do I need to explain the benefits of preventative maintenance?"

3-3-3's powerpack whined down to idle, and she had to force herself out of the cage. Doc was in before her boots hit stone. He worked the terminal like he was mad at it without so much as a word to her.

"What crawled up your ass and died?" The words came out almost sing-song. She bounced anxiously on her toes, still riding the wave.

He didn't look up. "Nothing. Just doing my job for once."

"Oh please, Lance Corporal Professional. Next you'll be telling me how to polish my boots and make my bunk."

His silence ate at her combat high. The electricity coursing through her veins dimmed as the wild thing inside her screamed to retreat, warning what would come next was too close. Too real. But something else won out. Her hand found his wrist, and the contact seemed to crack something in him.

He looked at her then, really looked at her.

The ache in her chest came sharp and quick. "You okay?"

"He just…" A muscle worked in his jaw.

"He who? What happened, Doc?"

"Sarnt Bresto happened, that's what."

Bresto—so she wasn't the only one. What an overbearing son-of-a—

"He takes one look at Vlan and knows exactly what to do. 'Stay within three meters of your brother.' That simple. Meanwhile, I'm the one who had to watch him fall apart. I'm the one that dragged him through that mess."

So that was all. Olsom bit back a grin. Seeing Doc's soft underbelly felt good. He was human, not granite, after all. But the hurt in his voice was real.

"And then he tells me to do my job?" He stabbed a finger at the terminal. "Like I hadn't tried everything else first? Like I wanted to pump Vlan full of anxios?"

"Hey," she began, giving his wrist a squeeze. "I okayed the drugs. What were we supposed to do? Tell the lieutenant to pound waves?"

"Right?" Doc finally cracked a smile. A warm thing, pretty as ever. He leaned back in the restraints and sighed. "Sarnt Bresto, man. Fuck that guy."

She grinned back. "Yeah. Fuck that guy."

The silence that followed felt electric, her post-combat rush transforming into a different kind of heat. Her hand was still on his wrist. She laughed, suddenly nervous, and pulled away.

Doc's cocky grin returned full force. "Careful there, Bugs. You're gonna run hot." He tapped a finger at the screen. "See? Your primary cooling matrix is in the yellow. Like to ride this rig hard, I see."

"In your dreams, Doc," she shot back, her cheeks turning warm. It was good to have him back. "Now shut up and fix my damn rig."

The Rikkos appeared from nowhere, their wrinkled faces split in identical grins. "What did—"

"—we miss?"

Olsom's heart leaped at the sight of them. She threw her arms around them both. The twins even hugged her back in perfect sync, their long arms gentle despite their strength. A little awkward, maybe —fuck it, this felt too good. Another win for the good guys.

"You're back," she said into Vlan's shoulder. "Like, really back."

"Weren't ever—"

"—really gone."

Doc's laugh was genuine, if a little forced. "Guess all they needed was each other."

"Tell me about 3-3-2," she said to Smokes. "How'd it handle?"

"Like precision machinery," the twins answered together.

"You should've seen them working the firing line," Doc said, still tapping away the screen. 3-3-3's dorsal cooling vents whined open and jetted hot exhaust. It stank of spent reactor coolant and grease, like some kind of metallic fart. She had to try not to snort.

Smokes brought a cigarette to his lips, hand shielding his lighter from the wind. "They tried to break through—"

"—when the sarnt rushed 'em." Vlan breathed deep, eyes moving like he was still seeing it.

"Turned them all to blue paste," Doc said, wiping his hands together. "Smokes, who's got your rig?"

"Doc Toelke," they said.

"He seems good."

"You hear what he's saying?" the twins went on. Smokes took a long drag of his cigarette before they spoke again. "Says the sarnt charged right through their shield. Took out a warrior in hand-to-hand."

"That right?" Olsom said.

"Bet he did." Another burst of steam vented from 3-3-3's back, yanking Doc's attention back to the terminal. "Come on, you piece of shit."

"Problem?" she asked sweetly.

"Heat vents are locked. Need my kit." He paused, mouth open. "Which I may have left back at the hab."

"The great Doc Myers, unprepared?" Moving her real legs would do some good. "I'll get it. Since apparently, I'm the only professional around here."

"Just because you're all metal now doesn't make you an engineer."

Her grin stretched from ear to ear. "No, but at least I know where my tools are!"

The primary junction opened up before her as she jogged past the other fireteams' positions. Marines from other squads had already set up blocking positions—one exo, sometimes two, and their support. She didn't know them yet, but a few threw casual nods her way. Hours ago, she was an outsider. But after today…

The fighting had left its mark on the granite thoroughfare. Scoring from weapons' fire, deep gouges from the plasma beam, the acrid stink of melted stone filtering through her rebreather. The half-collapsed hab block above caught her attention. The air around the hole the squids had made still shimmered with heat, the second hole where Bresto had breached visible through it. Hard to imagine hand-to-hand combat up there, but the results spoke for themselves.

A wet, animal sound stopped her cold. Just off the transit, a line of casualties had been arranged at the base of the hab. What the hell? Didn't remember any injuries, but—

The destroyed exo stood guard over them, its operator cage peeled open like a metal flower, edges still glowing dull red where the beam had cut through. Three bodies were lined up beside it, draped in emergency blankets that did little to hide the damage beneath. One was more pieces than person.

The victory high crashed, replaced by a creeping shame. She'd practically danced through the junction, high on her own survival, while these Marines… while they…

Wait—of course, people had died. This was war. But she'd felt so immortal in her metal, she'd forgotten what it really cost.

"Hey, new blood." Kitrelle materialized from the shadows of the blown-out hab. "You need something?"

"Uh, yeah." Olsom made herself focus. "Doc's kit."

"Myers? Think I saw him inside earlier. Fair warning though—place is still hot. Literally and figuratively."

They picked their way through the debris-strewn ground level, below the path Bresto's team had carved through the squids' emplacement. Whole sections of ceiling were open to the level above, cracked stone and power cabling dangling from the openings. Emergency lighting flickered, giving everything a surreal quality. There was a warm, organic stink to the place, eerily close to fresh-killed crid.

The fighting inside must've been hell. "Did you see it go down?"

"I was there." Kitrelle made a fist and pressed her thumb to it. "Boom."

"Wow."

Kitrelle ducked under a hanging cable, then held it up for Olsom. "It was poetry in plasmex. But your sarnt's got some moves. For an old guy."

"He's not my—"

She stopped short, the wild thing hissing danger. A raider slumped against the wall ahead, a warrior, its helmet split open to reveal rows of feeding tendrils. The thing was enormous, a hundred kilos easy. Maybe one-thirty.

It took another heartbeat to realize it was dead. Blaster impacts marred its black armor plate, blue blood seeping from the open wounds. Still, Olsom ached for her rig. For the blaster rifle she'd left strapped in its cage. That was a mistake she wouldn't make again.

"Big bastard, right?" Kitrelle said. "They're different up close. Not like on your targeting feeds."

Mez came around from behind, dropping to a crouch beside the corpse. His scarred fingers worked the seals beneath its chin. "Time for show and tell. Come see what Mez got."

Kitrelle turned and spat. "You're sick. And you're full of shit about taking this one down."

"Oh?" His hands came away a slick blue. "Who put those holes in it then? Not you."

The helmet came free with a wet hiss, releasing a wave of salt-copper stink. Its head was a bulge of predatory angles—razor-sharp tendrils framing pointed teeth. Green scales caught the light as its head lolled forward, but its big, black eyes seemed to drink in the gloom. Olsom had seen pictures in basic—autopsies, weapon test results—but those technical docs hadn't captured the raw alienness of the thing.

"Tell me, friend. Who killed you?" Mez gripped the dead warrior's jaw, working the tendrils like puppet strings. Then he gurgled, as if underwater, "Mez did! Mez did!"

"You're sick, duster."

"Aw, don't be like that, Wholesome." Blue blood dripped from his fingers as he waggled its tendrils. "Too much warrior for you? Mez can be gentler."

Sick freak. "Just try it."

"You can't handle Mez."

"Bet I can." Kitrelle drove a boot into Mez's back. He fell sideways, chuckling, and lay back on the stone floor with that ugly smile, motioning for her to join him.

"Maybe so."

"Eew, get up." Kitrelle unshouldered her rifle started toward the block hall. "Lessig's making the rounds. You want to explain this to him?"

"Mez don't explain nothin'." He rose, wiping the squid blood on his camouflaged trousers.

"Third Platoon!"

The call echoed down the corridor, and suddenly everyone was moving. Mez's slouch disappeared as he snapped to, while Kitrelle somehow managed to look like she'd been at parade rest the whole time.

Lieutenant Revan strode in, hand wrapped around his push-to-talk. "Negative, we are oscar mike. Have them hold that facility. Do you understand me?"

Corporal Lessig was right behind him, looking like he had the wind knocked out of him. Sergeant Bresto appeared next, damn near like a raider in full tac gear. His fingers moved rapidly over his flexscreen, so busy he didn't seem to notice where he was.

"Sir," Kitrelle blurted, "we were just—"

"Save it." Revan's eyes swept the room. "We've got a PR unit pinned down at the Diacad Memorial Clinic. A hundred-plus civilians inside. Another full raider clutch is on their way."

Another mission. Perfect. More squids to kill, more colonists to save. She was ready.

Bresto looked up from his screen and started toward Mez, took him by the arm. Mez took a step back, eyes wide, but Bresto had him. Together, they rounded the corner, past the dead squid and straight for Olsom.

"Changes to the roster." Bresto's voice was pure granite. "Vlan Rikko's been moved to 3-3-2."

"Yes, Sarnt, I—" Oh, shit. No. No, no, no! She knew—holy shit, she *knew* what was coming.

"Mezzior's your new breacher." He looked at Mez. "Olsom's your new fireteam leader. Effective immediately. Don't embarrass me."

Mez stumbled closer when Bresto let him go.

Bresto muscled past without a word, his tac gear scraping on stone. Olsom stepped back to miss him, but her boot caught something solid. She fell back, the warm stone floor bruising her tailbone. A combat engineer's pack lay beneath her feet, the name MYERS stenciled large and proud on the handle.

A twisted shadow stood over her. "Relax, Wholesome." Mez offered a hand, teeth bared in a predatory grin. "Mez got you."

CHAPTER
SEVENTEEN

"MOVE LIKE YOU MEAN IT, MARINES!"

Bresto's voice carried over the drum of boots and metal, Third Platoon double-timing down Diacad's main transportation artery. The transit was built for heavy cargo sleds and bulk personnel transports, six lanes stretching thirty meters wide, designed to channel cargo and personnel between Vestebrae's upslope settlements and its central urban core. Today, it carried Marines. Fury. Hope.

Their formation was textbook: three columns pushing forward at a steady clip, with MAC-4s providing mobile cover and overwatch on the flanks. Lessig was out front in 3-1-1, doing the same for Bresto and Revan while also setting pace. Humans tired quicker than metal, so he maintained a low trot as they wound past abandoned transports and building debris.

Bresto kept up despite the dull ache in his hip, scrolling through the tac net feeds on his flexscreen between breaths. The PR feeds were bleak. More raiders were setting down every hour, each landing zone kilometers from the last. Almost like their strategy was to have no strategy, to keep the CDF guessing.

The orbital feeds, glitchy as they were, painted a darker picture. Occasional bursts of data showed Division drones engaging the Concordat fleet, but Sevvers' bots were spread too thin. Another rogue CDF ship had attacked the *Alexander Lehman* head on, danger close, letting the forge ship cut a path to low orbit uncontested. CDF reinforcements were inbound, still twenty-plus hours away, even at emergency speeds. That was a long time for the Victory Marines to hold back the archenemy on their own.

Distant weapons' fire echoed off the high block walls—the static buzz of lasers, the bright snap of charged particles. His feeds confirmed the squids had initiated contact with the PR unit holding the clinic. They were fifteen minutes out at current pace. Too slow. Kaff and Sammy might be among the hundred or so civilians packed into the clinic, or of the thousand huddled behind the fibrosteel doors of Shelter Sienna-2. And if the clinic fell, the shelter was only a matter of time.

"Fury 3, Victory 5." Kull's voice crackled over the command net. *"Sitrep, over."*

"En route to Diacad Memorial," Revan said. The man wasn't even breathing hard, despite their steady pace. Being young and dumb had its advantages. "ETA is fourteen mikes, over."

"I need that location secured, Fury 3. The squids are hitting our evac columns hard, and my forward elements can't push through Corongaet with our rear exposed."

"Copy that." Revan's jaw worked silently. "Though with all due respect, ma'am, my platoon could be of more use—"

"Hold what I tell you to hold, Lieutenant. Victory 5, out."

Revan killed the connection with an angry jab. He had that look again, as if the next rung to his career had just moved on him.

"Options, Sergeant."

"Depends how they're deployed." Bresto pulled up the clinic's schematics on his flexscreen and flicked them toward Revan. "If they're hitting the main entrance, we split the squads and flank through this maintenance access. If they've got the whole perimeter, we form a wedge with the exos and punch straight through." He zoomed in on the loading dock. "Either way, those civilians need an exit that isn't full of squid."

"What about risks?"

Bresto laughed. Of course there were risks. Revan's academy polish really was starting to show.

"I don't see the humor here," Revan snapped. "While we babysit this facility, the real war is happening downslope."

"You want risks?" He expanded the tactical display. "Split squads leaves us exposed. Wedge formation puts all our exos in one place." He zoomed out, showing the growing number of unknown contacts appearing throughout Diacad. "But our biggest risk is taking too long. Whatever's out there, we don't want it reaching those civilians first."

After everything that had happened—the Concordat's orbital assault, the destruction of the *Victory*—Revan must've seen this as a way to pad his resume. Like this was some kind of game, and not a war for their survival. Well, unlike Revan, he knew how to pick his battles. His flexscreen vibrated, the display flashing with incoming tightbeam comms.

"Hey, Sarnt." Lessig's signal was low and even inside his helmet. *"The lieutenant isn't wrong, you know. Just in terms of numbers, we'd do more good at the Gaet."*

The Gaet. The easy way Lessig said it, like someone born there. No wonder he saw it Revan's way—his people were down there, same as Bresto's were up here.

"Which block?" he asked.

"Sarnt?"

"In the Gaet." Bresto cleared his throat, the cold, thin air not satisfying like it should. He'd been breathing ship atmo too long. "Which block you from?"

"Block D-23. We just called it Dead Drop."

"Dead Drop. With that cliff face behind the scrap yard?" Rough place. Good people.

"The one and only. Had a transport chit for home today. Guess the Concordat had other plans."

"We're all doing good today, Corporal. We'll get to Corongaet when the Holy Mother needs us there."

"Yes, Sarnt." The transmission clicked over to all-squad comms as 3-1-1 began to slow. *"I've got something. Junction ahead. Looks like an admin block."*

The granite lanes stretched before them as the transit opened into Diacad's administrative district. The allotment center rose through curtains of smoke, its warehouse wing cratered by heavy weapons fire. Kaff had been here, waiting. And there was nothing left.

Whatever hit the quonset's roof had punched right through, buckling the entire structure. The loading doors lay flat against the dock, blasted off their tracks. Electrical fires burned inside, feeding columns of black smoke into the storm winds. The admin tower—what was left of it—blocked half the transit. Bodies lay dead among the rubble. Human bodies. So many dead.

The sight hollowed him from the inside out. Not just dead. Obliterated. Images of his baby girl trapped beneath tons of burning metal, or shot and left for dead in the street, refused to leave him, stoking the rage in his belly. Fucking squids, they'd—

"Sarnt?" Lessig.

One, two, three, four. Focus. The job wasn't done, and this place was still dangerous.

"Hold." Bresto barely got the word out through the tightness in his chest. "Third Squad, I want scans of that building. Could be civilians in there. Could be squids, so heads on a swivel."

Revan leaned close. "Why are we stopping? A bit early for personal errands, isn't it?"

"Quiet." The air burned Bresto's lungs as he took a steadying breath, pushing the anger down where it belonged—until he needed it.

Incoming IFF data buzzed his flexscreen. Too much dull blue—civilians and PR, all dead. None of the idents stuck out to him. Some dull red, too, though not as many. The fight hadn't ended well, but at least there was one.

The warehouse interior flashed with environmental hazard warnings. Fire, smoke, unexploded ordnance. There was something else, a gap in the data, like a hole in reality, right in the center of it all.

"Sant Bresto," Smokes Rikko's transmission crackled to life with a slight echo. Probably Vlan. *"You copy?"*

"Go for Sarnt Bresto."

"Got eyes on something." Another delay, a subtle change in tone. *"Sensors can't make it out."*

"I see it. What is it?"

Olsom's signal lit up. *"No idea, Sarnt. Whatever it is, it ain't ours."*

"Wait one." He turned to the other squads and motioned them to spread out. They were going to be around a little longer, so overwatch was critical. And he needed the hell away from Revan. "I'm on my way."

Third Squad had cut through the facility's outer security, past the exterior fence and between empty cargo containers. Their signal markers led to a side entrance near the loading bay, its access panel still sparking from forced entry. His boots scraped against spent charge packs—the stamps on them PR issue. They'd tried to hold this facility. Hadn't worked out.

Toelke was waiting for him. "This way, Sarnt."

They pushed deeper into the warehouse, through curtains of smoke lit by damaged power relays. Toelke kept them moving, following routes Third Squad had already cleared. Storage racks lined the main corridor, most toppled over, all of them stripped clean.

Bresto strained through the haze, searching every shadow and corner for signs of survivors. Every step felt like betrayal. Like he was leaving Kaff behind again.

The rest of Third Squad's position markers clustered in the central staging area, the exos parting as he neared. A Concordat forge capsule dominated the space beneath the cratered roof, the surrounding fires glinting in its bone white hull. The pill-shaped thing was massive— squad-sized at least—and covered in circuitous markings that made his eyes hurt. He'd seen hundreds of them aboard the derelict, but this one was different. Active. Black fluid dripped from a hairline crack in its surface, pooling on the deck beneath it like spent coolant. But coolant didn't crawl across the floor like it was searching for something.

"Fall back."

Olsom. "Sarnt?"

"Back up." He leveled his rifle at the thing. "Ten meters. Now!"

Third Squad obeyed. The exos tracked backwards, their FABs now trained on the terrible machine. The others fanned out, searching for cover.

The black liquid oozed closer, filling his scope with signal noise and unknown contact warnings. He needed to know what, if anything, was inside. If the Lost had come to Aegia, this was now a very different war.

He edged forward, keeping his distance from the ooze. The air felt thicker the closer he got, a sickly-sweet odor cloying at the back of his throat. Five meters away and his eyes began to water. It smelled worse than death.

A crack spread across the capsule's surface to the sound of breaking glass. The gap widened, and the capsule opened, revealing a pool of black liquid that didn't move, didn't ripple, didn't follow any rules that made sense.

He took two measured steps back, finger tight on the trigger. The capsule looked empty.

The black liquid surged and disgorged something onto the deck. A human form curled tight in the fetal position. It wore colony gray coveralls soaked through with dark fluid. Its skin looked burned, covered in a wet film that glowed in the flames. Its head turned, too smooth, too misshapen, and Bresto's blood ran cold. A thin mask blurred its face, shifting and flowing like mercury.

It screamed. Too loud, too long, to still be human.

This capsule hadn't brought the Lost to Aegia. It was here to make them.

The Lost daxed reached out, long, thin fingers trembling in the heat. Bresto's trigger work was pure instinct. Two bolts reflected off the unfinished mask while the third smashed through its ribs. Frothy pink and black gore bubbled out of its chest, trailing bits of organic circuitry. Its scream faded to a death rattle, a long, slow exhale. A free soul. Lost no more.

Something touched his boot—ice cold through the leather, tendrils of black liquid hunting for gaps in the material. Bresto lurched backward and kicked the boot free. It spun away, still trailing the black ooze, and fell beside the fallen daxed. The liquid surged inside like it could smell what had worn it.

"Railguns up!" He half-crawled back away from the capsule, eyes locked on the black mass that was his boot. Someone was on him a second later, dragging him behind the exo line. "Three rounds each. Center mass. Nothing but atoms."

FABs stowed and railguns deployed in a clatter of metal and servos. The weapons cycled on, capacitors humming. Bresto wanted to look, to watch the terrible machine die, but this was as danger close as it got. He ducked in behind 3-3-3's right leg, his back toward the coming fury. The Marine who'd pulled him out fell in beside him— Doc Myers. Kid had done good. A proper Aegian.

Adrenaline bubbled into laughter. This was going to be fucking metal.

The first shot lasted a microsecond—nothing but the high-pitched whine of slug discharge and acoustic trauma. The aftermath felt eternal. Pressure and heat slammed into him, nearly throwing him from cover as debris filled the air. 3-3-3's railgun cycled up again, a rising tremor through its armor plate. More vibrations, this time in his ringing ears. Someone was shouting over comms.

The sound of the second shot punched through his skull and into his jaw. The warehouse air crackled with discharge, tasting of ozone and something vaguely organic. His flexscreen display turned to static. Heat poured off 3-3-3's frame when the third shot hit without warning. Too soon. His whole body burned as the air cooked around him. He was shouting now—*cease fire, cease fire!*—but heard nothing. No more waiting, he had to know. If tungsten slugs couldn't crack that capsule, they were already dead. They just didn't know it yet.

Moving hurt, but he forced himself upright. The warehouse was more smoke than air, thick clouds being dragged away by Aegia's endless storms. Third Squad reappeared through the haze. Three exos, rails still hot. Five support Marines, no, six as Mezzior emerged from cover. Everyone breathing. Everyone standing. He shifted his weight off his bad hip and felt the odd sensation of warm duraplate through his left sock. His Twelfth-damned boot. He hadn't dreamed that.

The capsule was all but gone, its pale alloy twisted into perfect rings by immense kinetic force. What remained of the black liquid looked crystallized, burnt gristle at the bottom of a pan. The daxed was mostly vapor—bundles of wire filament and other cyborg parts he didn't want to understand. But something caught his eye. Deeper in the wreckage, partially hidden by scorched metal. More bodies, or what was left. At least three, curled tight, never to be born.

Bresto moved closer, his gait off slightly. He had to be sure. Couldn't let the bugs turn his home into a Twelfth-forsaken forge. The black, crystalline flakes didn't move. Didn't react at all. He almost kicked the daxed remains with his other boot, then thought better of it. So, they *could* kill these capsules, even if it took nine tungsten slugs to do it. His fingers brushed against his chest plate, two taps. Thank the Holy Mother.

"Sarnt." Corporal Lessig stood there, dismounted from 3-1-1, the rest of Third Platoon assembled beyond the staging area, railguns up. The promise of tungsten and violence had brought them running. Revan stood, arms crossed on the loading dock, a different kind of murder in his eyes.

Bresto's flexscreen pulsed with fresh data as the electro-mag noise cleared. The raiders had the clinic boxed in, and the PR signals were fading. A debrief would have to wait. The capsule was gone and a lot of civilians needed rescuing.

Besides, Kaff wasn't here. She couldn't be. The Holy Mother wouldn't allow it. Not after all he'd sacrificed in Her service. His daughter was out there somewhere—alive, surviving, fighting maybe—and until he found a body that proved otherwise, faith would carry him forward. One battle at a time.

"Third Platoon, we're moving!" His throat burned. "Exos, form a wedge. Time to make a hole."

CHAPTER
EIGHTEEN

IFF RETURNS PAINTED Olsom's tactical display in harsh red and blue strokes, the squids' positions surrounding Diacad Memorial like a noose. Flashes of laser fire lit up the clinic's upper level through her canopy. Blaster bolts snapped back, down into the raiders' hasty positions.

Adrenaline sang in her blood. A hundred civilians trapped in there. Maybe more. Reservists pinned down, their numbers probably dwindling by the minute. Not that the squids would get much further—not with Third Platoon on scene now. Not with her metal ready to crack this siege wide open.

Shooting the FAB was incredible, but the railgun… holy shit. That capsule thing had been terrifying. It was all wrong in ways that made her skin crawl, but it had died just the same. She flexed 3-3-3's primary arms, feeling the connection between body and machine. Nothing could stand against this. Against her.

"Tighten it up, 3-3-3." Lessig's voice crackled through her helmet comms. *"You're drifting right."*

"Copy that."

"Someone please tell the feral what a wedge is," came another voice. The ident flashed: Prelk, 3-2-2's operator. The big bastard from the exo

bay. A round of muffled laughter and acknowledgment pings lit up her terminal.

Let 'em laugh. Like the wild girl from the Three Colonies' least civilized world could grasp the finer points of exo warfare. It didn't bother her. 3-3-3 didn't give a shit where she came from, and she didn't either. Not in a long time.

"*Lock it up,*" Lessig growled. "*Wedge is simple. Point of the blade. We drive deep, then split their line wide open to make room for support. It's all knuckles and tread until your sectors are clear, then let 'em have it with the FAB.*"

Fresh contacts bloomed red across her tactical display. The first laser strikes came quick and precise—flash, spark, gone—faster than the eye could track, but 3-3-3 barely registered the impacts. Lessig's rig picked up speed, and she followed, muscle memory taking over.

"*Contact, ninety seconds.*" Lessig sounded cold as vacuum, his jog turning into a run. "*Let's do this. For Victory.*"

The words stirred something primal in her. An instinct from darker days, except now she wasn't prey anymore. She was the apex predator. And it was time to hunt.

Sharp pops erupted in a wave of sound that sent dust and rock fragments spinning into the open transit. Something tall and large at the clinic's upslope edge began to lean. A statue of a masked warrior in heavy robes, sword pointed toward the mountain, worn smooth by centuries of storms. Then physics took over.

The Twelfth's likeness fell with awful grace, throwing up clouds of pulverized rock as it slammed into the transit, blocking their advance. Her tactical feed refreshed, showing the squids repositioning. They'd turned the holy symbol into a barrier.

Third Platoon's charge died thirty meters from the statue's base. Lessig keyed his comms, hesitated, then went silent.

Someone else filled the void: "*Holy Mother, have mercy.*"

Two FABs crackled to life, hosing down the squids' new position. Stray bolts arced off the statue's granite skin, throwing weird shadows as they ripped through the dust and into the storm.

"*Stand down!*" came a thick shout over comms. "*Show some fucking respect!*"

One gun went quiet, but the other kept talking. Olsom knew this kind of fear. Felt it herself, a long time ago. Right now, these Aegians weren't just Marines. They were Her *children*. And statue or not, their Holy Mother had just fallen.

A laser strike found her canopy, the flash sending her heart into her throat. For a split second, she was that scared kid again, too, hunting for shadows to hide in. To survive.

"First and Second squads!" Bresto's familiar voice boomed over the incoming fire, not on the nets, but among them. "Flank left and assault through! Funnel them between the block wall and the statue!"

He appeared in front of her, slapping her canopy with a gloved fist.

"Third Squad!" He was yelling so loud. "Breach the perimeter! Get inside and clear those grounds!"

He was gone a second later. New waypoints flashed onto her screen, drawing a path to the clinic's security gate. Most of the red had clustered behind the statue, but a few returns showed the squids had scaled the walls and were inside the grounds. It all made sense. First and Second Squads would keep the raiders' heads down while Third Squad cleaned up inside.

"3-3-1, 3-3-2, form up." The order came naturally, her voice surprisingly steady. The other exos responded instantly, their heavy treads crunching granite as they took position on her flanks. Together, they pushed past the statue's smoldering base toward their new objective.

Visibility was bad in the smoke and rock dust. A building loomed in front of her, but it looked wrong. All short and squat, with heavy doors three meters square and looking just as thick. The tactical display read *CIVIL DEFENSE SHELTER SIENNA-2*, outlining it in thin blue lines and reading hundreds of civilian contacts deep inside.

Bodies of reservist and raider both were stacked like cargo skids near the entrance. The thick fibrosteel doors looked untouched. Someone had held this ground. Hard.

"To the CDF forces in the vicinity of Diacad Memorial." A new signal cut across the nets. A woman. Young. Scared. *"This is Reserve Platoon 182, Squad J. We've lost contact with Command. There's just six of us left. The squids… they've made it onto the grounds. We're—"*

The waypoint markers led her to the clinic's high stone walls. Mark

Three combat optics pierced the dust and smoke, revealing three raiders scaling the thick metal gate. The FAB spun up with its familiar whine.

"Sending station, sending station, this is Fury 3-3-3." She held the trigger down, watching the squids come apart in sprays of blue. No response on the nets. "Squad J, Squad J, do you copy?"

Proximity alarms warbled on her left side. She jabbed the triple barrels into the charging squid's chest. A heartbeat later and it was mist on the canopy, filling the cage with that fresh crid smell. More blaster bolts snapped overhead.

"Getting lit up from both sides here," the twins said.

First and Second Squads had gone to work. Time to get inside.

More raiders appeared at the gate. The FAB made quick work of them, but the heavy weapons fire was taking its toll. The gate's duraplate frame had begun to buckle and warp. A shrill tone cut through her satisfaction as heat advisory warnings burned across her terminal in bright red dead. A quick tap silenced it. Too close to stop now.

She approached the gate at full stride, FAB cycling up and out of the way. The primary control arms found purchase in the warped duraplate. Making a bigger hole was risky; the squids were opportunistic bastards. But exos couldn't exactly vault a two-meter wall. Two tons of Marine metal needed a proper door.

Black armor flashed in the smoke. The raider appeared in the widening gap, gleaming wet through the canopy.

No time to think. Just react.

3-3-3's fist came down clumsy and hard on the squid's back, the only real feedback the crunch of metal as its body pressed against the ruined gate. For a horrible second, she imagined every cracking bone, every rupturing organ. It looked so fragile.

The raider slipped from the gate and began writhing at her feet. Up close, clumsy would have to do. She lifted 3-3-3's right leg, setting the massive tread down on the raider's helmet. There was a moment of resistance—composite and bone fighting hydraulics and fibrosteel—before everything gave way against the granite with a wet crack.

Beyond the crushed gate, the path to the clinic lay open.

Inside the grounds, everything felt different. The block walls dampened the sounds of storm and battle outside, leaving an eerie quiet. Strange plants rose from beds of crushed stone, woody things grown into sharp shapes that wouldn't make it one turn in the Tangle. More corpses broke up the strange geometry, staining the gravel red and blue.

"Squad J, this is Fury 3-3-3." Her FAB tracked another target scrambling for cover. "We're inside the grounds. What's your position?"

Only static answered as she put the raider down.

"Squad J, mark your position… Does anyone copy?"

"Tracking movement on the second floor," 3-3-1 called out. Patrim per his net ident.

"Friendly?"

"Unknown. Signal's real squish—" A raider flew apart amid bright red lines from 3-3-1's FAB.

"Real what?" The twins' voices carried a grin.

"Squishy," Patrim finished, sounding embarrassed. *"The signal's squishy, alright? It's a technical term."*

"Whatever you say… Squishy," Olsom said. The callsign basically declared itself. Even the twins chuckled over comms.

"Oh, come on," Patrim groaned.

"Smokes, are you getting anything?"

The long pause made her stomach tight. *"IFF returns looking heavy. Nothing on comms—"*

Proximity alerts screamed as fresh contacts poured through the breach they'd made. The squids had found their door.

"Gate! 3-3-1, 3-3-2, guns on the gate!"

Their FABs opened up together, turning the breach into a killing field. Her finger stayed locked on the trigger, fear making her tight bursts sloppy and long. Squids died in waves of bolt fire, their bodies piling up in the entrance. Sweat ran beneath her rebreather as a cunty voice shrieked at her from the terminal: *HEAT WARNING, HEAT WARNING!*

Let the fucking thing cook. She wasn't done yet.

The FAB's rhythm changed, its rapid thunder becoming uneven.

New warnings flashed. One barrel down, too hot. The others would follow if she kept this up.

"Doc, I need you," she called. "Barrel change, now!"

"Negative, Bugs." The stress in his voice made her heart sting. *"We're pinned down near the statue. First and Second's metal are pushing through—"*

"I know! They're pushing them right to us!" She was shouting now, screw comms discipline. What was left of the gate finally collapsed as more raiders piled through. One nearly slipped past until 3-3-2 took it apart.

"Listen, your cooling system was—" More alarms cut him off, screaming through her cage. *"—with the vents, remember?"*

The operator cage felt like an oven, her controls fighting back against every movement. *HEAT WARNING, HEAT WARNING,* the bitch inside the terminal shrieked.

The display flickered. Her FAB clicked once, twice, then died. Two tiny stars strapped to her back, and the fucking cooling system picked right then to stop working. 3-3-3 ground to a stop, the constant whine of fusion power suddenly gone.

SHUTDOWN, SHUTDOWN, that fucking exo monitor bitch declared, *REACTOR TEMPS CRITICAL!*

A dozen more raiders slipped toward their line. Too many. 3-3-1 and 3-3-2 couldn't track them all. Something tore loose inside her chest —a scream clawing its way up her throat like a trapped animal finally breaking free. The primal sound ripped from her lungs, but 3-3-3 stayed dead silent, its systems dark and unresponsive. Metal groaned behind her as the dorsal vents finally gave way, a low, pained sound. Hot exhaust erupted from 3-3-3's back.

Movement flashed through the haze—a raider, turning toward the sound. It pulled something dark and sharp from its belt.

Her own fucking machine had just given her away.

The alien stalked toward her with arms spread wide. The knife was crude—fat and black—but that point would open her up just fine.

"Ga, t'iisa, ga." It clicked and moaned at her, each harsh syllable a phlegmy gurgle.

Her body turned liquid with fear. Muscles, breathing, nothing worked. She couldn't even manage a scream. Out. She needed out.

"Dleshlelm'ovlik." The alien raised its blade, gurgle rising to a wet scream. "Dleshlelm'olvlen!"

It slammed into the cage as she yanked her arms inside. The blade found the elbow joint of her right control rig with a metallic shriek, missing skin by centimeters. The raider pressed closer, nearly matching 3-3-3's height and bulk. She watched it strain against the stuck blade, her hands fumbling for her rifle mount. Those black eyes found her through the plexene, and suddenly she was prey again.

"T'iisa, t'iisa," it clicked. Oil ran from the exo's right elbow joint as the squid jerked again, the blade edging out by centimeters.

She flipped the fire selector to full auto, propping the barrel against the flickering terminal right at the thing's chest. The cage was too cramped for proper aim. Opening it would make her vulnerable. But staying inside was just a slower death.

The release threw her canopy wide, knocking the raider off balance. Its blade tore free as her rifle chattered, walking bolts up its chest. Blue blood sprayed across her uniform—she didn't even remember pulling the trigger.

Through the gore, she caught two more raiders advancing. Laser light and impact sparks flashed beside her head. Shoulder, sight, squeeze. They fell together.

She slapped her harness release and dismounted, already tracking her next target. This wasn't control. It was something else. Training. Instinct. She just needed fucking out.

Her feet hit the ground and time went all elastic. Like sinking beneath the river after a long day on the trawler. Her rifle seemed to float in her hands as she drifted between targets. Sight picture, trigger squeeze, blue mist. Again and again. Someone was trying to reach her on comms—tinny voices scratching above the surface of consciousness. No time. Too deep. The nightmare in the cage had revealed a deeper truth. She wasn't invulnerable. Wasn't some god of war. Just a presence, one of dozens, carried along on this bloody tide.

"Look out!"

The frantic cry snapped the world back into focus. The raider was right there, bleeding but still coming. Her rifle came up—too late. The squid batted it away like a toy, sending shooting pain through her wrists. Gloved tendrils found her throat, and a heartbeat later, her boots were scraping air.

She clawed for breath. Even through the blinding panic, she could feel the raider's stare. One dying creature studying another. Her neck stiffened, pushing back against its grip, when it drew a ragged gasp through its helmet.

"Morith'len v'ga t'iisa." A wet pause. Pained. "Sheshk'olvna. Sheshk—"

A blast erupted with light and percussion and wet heat. She hit the granite, hard, the taste of live wire and chlorine in her mouth. The raider's broken skull leaked blue matter beside her, its empty black eyes staring.

Someone grabbed her, hauled her to sitting.

"Holy Twelfth, you're alive!" The woman's hands trembled against her shoulders, as if they both might float away. "I thought… I mean, I didn't think…"

The woman was Olsom's age, barely in her eps levels, though the odd-looking rank pips on her collar might mean NCO. Corporal maybe, if the count was the same. The gray mountain etched prominently on her unit patch was no surprise, but the words *RESERVE PLATOON 182* were.

"Squad J?" Her throat burned.

The woman's eyes went wide, filling with tears. She threw her arms around Olsom, faces pressed together. "You saved us. Twelfth keep you, you saved us."

Olsom squeezed back, humanity rushing in like breaching the waves. She found herself gasping—alive, if not quite whole.

"Bugs!" The shout came with running footsteps. Someone shoved the woman aside. "Move. Move!"

Suddenly Doc was there. His hands found her throat, feeling for damage, then her pulse. The flashlight came next, its bright beam needling her eyes beneath the storm's gray gloom. His field triage was brutally efficient, but there was something comforting in his urgency, in knowing someone needed her to be okay. He jerked the autodoc from his kit and twisted the control knob.

She caught his wrist. "Doc. I'm okay."

"Told you to watch those vents." He pressed the autodoc against her neck anyway, its metal cold on her bruised skin. There was a soft puff of air as the meds hit her bloodstream. "Anti-inflammatories, plus something for the pain."

Relief spread like warm sap through her, taking the bite off the sting in her throat. Doc's hands were steady as he helped her up, the young reservist hovering nearby. The world tilted for a moment before finding its level.

The worried creases around his eyes finally smoothed away. That handsome grin never looked so good. "You're right. Still serviceable."

The clinic grounds had gone quiet. Dead raiders lay scattered across the gravel gardens, their blue blood turning the crushed stone purple. Third Platoon filtered in through the breach, Marines taking positions along the block walls and around the clinic proper. 3-3-1 and 3-3-2 approached on clanking treads, their FABs glowing and stinking of ozone. Mez waited in their shadow, his narrow eyes locked on her. The look had a different edge—something personal, betrayal almost. Fuck him.

"You." Revan strode in amongst them, with Bresto in tow. "Report."

The reservist straightened. "Reserve Sergeant Neleth Vestron, sir. Squad J. Six of us left. We've got one hundred and five colonists still inside. Without Fury 3-3-3's help, we wouldn't have made it."

"Where's your CO?"

"KIA, sir." Her voice caught. "I'm senior."

"Very well." He nodded. "Take me to your CP. I want everything you have on raider activities in the vicinity."

"Aye, sir." She led Revan to the clinic's reinforced doors and followed him inside.

Bresto jerked his chin toward the wall. "Mezzior, Toelke, Ollins, you're on overwatch with the others. Rest of Third Squad, inside. Eat something. Rest if you can. We won't stay long."

"Go on," Doc said, already walking back toward 3-3-3. "I've got to resurrect your metal."

"I could help," she said.

"And deny me my moment of glory?" That damn smile again. "Not a chance."

The clinic beckoned—the promise of a place to sit, a change of socks, thicker atmo—but something nagged at her. The rifle. She'd forgotten her rifle.

It lay near the high stone wall, polymer housing scratched but intact. A quick capacitor cycle confirmed it was good to go. The fallen statue lay beyond the gate, cracks in its granite skin. The Twelfth's blank face stared back at her, its eternal gaze holding her there. Like it knew things she didn't. About herself. About everything.

A cold wind cut through her, and the moment passed. She shouldered her rifle and headed inside.

CHAPTER
NINETEEN

CONCORDAT SHIPS WERE STILL COMING DOWN. Bresto counted five more contacts burning through the dense storm layer. Some lit their fusion drives, cutting lines of fire across the darkening sky. Some didn't, decelerating in other, more alien ways. Each one disappeared into Vestebrae's urban core, vanishing among the concentric rings of lights, granite, and duraplate. The clinic's rooftop was a perfect observation post to see every new arrival added to the forces set against them.

Aegia's star was setting fast, a dim white orb near the horizon, barely visible through the blackening storm. The air had gone sharp and cold, heavy with the smell of rain. Behind him, Revan and Reserve Platoon 182's acting senior spoke in low voices, but Bresto kept his eyes on the horizon. They assumed these were all raider landing craft. But they could be forge capsules, each one carrying that black poison that could turn more of humanity into Lost.

It didn't matter what the lieutenant or the reservist thought. He knew what was coming. He needed to make sure Kull did, too.

The whine of sub-light drives cut through the storm winds. Another contact dropped below the clouds—clean lines, dropship green. It came in fast and precise, riding the clinic's landing beacons.

The ship's weight hit the pad with practiced violence, hydraulics screaming.

Major Kull was on the ramp before it finished cycling, her command staff close behind. She looked different, harder. Ready for the fight that was coming.

"Welcome, Major," Revan began, "if you'll just follow—"

But Kull was already three steps ahead of him. Revan hustled to catch up, waving over Bresto and the reservist. First Sergeant Druggan appeared at Bresto's shoulder as they hurried through the rooftop entrance.

"Brief me," was all Kull said. He knew what that meant: convince me this is worth my time. Good to go. He had plenty to show her.

They descended the stairwell in a rush, Revan struggling to explain the warehouse fight between breaths. "The capsule was unlike anything—I mean, when Sergeant Bresto discovered—"

Medical staff scattered as Kull powered through the hallway. She threw the CP door open, startling a reservist hunched over the planning table's tactical display. The reserve sergeant accompanying them called the room to attention.

"As you were." Kull sank into the seat at the head of the table, helmet in her lap. "Tell me what you found, Sergeant. All of it."

"Net access." Bresto flicked the combat footage from his flexscreen toward the planning table. The tech routed power to the holoproj, and suddenly they were all back there. Third Squad moving through smoke and fire until the capsule appeared. Its pristine hull seemed to drink in the light, those circuit-like patterns shifting and flowing across its surface. Bresto's thumb found the knuckle of his half-finger automatically.

"That's Concordat tech." Everything he was about to say was red-level classified. Need to know. But Kull damn sure needed to know this. "My team encountered these aboard that forge ship sixteen turns ago."

"*You?* Were aboard that thing?" Revan took a step back.

Kull didn't flinch. Just stared at him through the holofeed.

"The ship had entire decks for what they called the Forge." Flashes of black and red corridors invaded his thoughts. "That's where we found out the truth. The Concordat weren't just keeping the Lost from Dead Earth in stasis. They were still taking people. Making more of those things."

The footage played on, showing the capsule crack open. The reserve sergeant's gasp cut through the CP as the newly made Lost spilled onto the deck, its mask still forming. PFC Olsom let out a curse on the recording just as Bresto put the Lost down.

He had to make them understand. "Don't you see? They've brought the Forge to us. They don't need to land that ship anymore. Just scatter these things across the colony. One capsule did this in a few hours. Think about what dozens could do. Hundreds. I've seen worse than that crawl out of those pods."

Myers appeared in the display, dragging Bresto away from the capsule. Then Third Squad's railguns opened up, turning the feed to static and leaving the CP in eerie silence.

Kull leaned back in her chair. "What do we do, Sergeant?"

Hope surged through him. Maybe she'd seen enough to listen. To do something about it. "Dedicate at least two companies to hunting these things down. Full sweeps of every district, building to building if we—"

"With all due respect, Sergeant," Revan said, "you spent two hundred kilos of tungsten on a single capsule. Even if we located more, we don't have the ordnance to handle them all."

"The garrison fleet does," Bresto shot back. "We mark targets. Let the skeegs handle the rest."

Revan went quiet. Druggan's grunt of approval filled the silence.

Something changed in Kull's expression. He'd lost her. That moment of connection, of understanding, gone cold like a dead star.

"Two things." She swiped the combat footage away, replacing it with a strategic overlay of Aegia Prime. Red contacts swarmed the orbital approaches, the forge ship at their center. "First, the fleet has other problems." Another flick revealed a tactical feed of Vestebrae. Her hand swept across the Corongaet access toward the urban core. "Second, I've got thirty thousand colonists exposed out there. The upslope shelters are full, and the security situation is tenuous.

"I don't disagree with you, Sergeant. But this goes above my pay grade. Marine Command wants our civilians secure. And for the next eighteen hours, we're the only ones that can do that job."

"Eighteen hours is a long time to be wrong, ma'am." The words came out harder than he meant, desperation bleeding through into anger. He'd forgotten to count.

"And I can't start ordering orbital strikes on my own colony—not with a third of its population exposed—without command approval."

"Then get it!" He brought his fist down on the planning table with a bang. "General Strumman, he's on Three-Alpha now—"

"At ease, Marine." Druggan said, only to him.

"Control your man, Lieutenant," Kull sneered.

"You're dismissed, Sergeant." Revan didn't hesitate, suddenly brave and serious and still green as shit. "Outside. Now."

Bresto stormed into the hall, rage burning behind his eyes. The door hissed again and he spun, ready to unleash on whichever officer had followed, but found First Sergeant Druggan and the young reservist standing there instead.

"Let's go." Druggan jerked his chin down the hall, his voice pure gravel, and started down the hall at a measured pace.

Combat damage decorated the clinic hall—broken admin terminals, carbon burns scarring the clinic's bright walls. Clinic personnel were returning to work now that the immediate threat had passed.

Druggan glanced at the reservist and she got the message, falling back to give them space.

"Sweet Twelfth's tits, son." Druggan's low chuckle scraped against the walls. "You really know how to piss on a parade."

"First Sarnt, the major—"

"Stow it. Kull's following orders. Good orders." He paused near a shattered display, his reflection fractured in the broken screen. "But that's not what this is about. The colonel's dead. Victory's gone."

"Lost no more." Bresto's throat went tight. The thought of Reede standing his ground flooded back—one Marine against an army of Lost. In his final moments, Reede had understood the threat. Had sacrificed himself to fight it. Which made Kull's hesitation even harder to swallow. Thirty thousand lives wouldn't mean shit if the Concordat turned them all into once-human machines.

"Kull just made Skipper the hard way, and now she's got four hundred Marines and thirty thousand civilians depending on her." Druggan shook his head. "Last thing she needs is some hot-headed sergeant telling her how to run her war."

"Aye, First Sarnt." The words felt hollow in his mouth. "Won't happen again."

"Right." Druggan sighed. "You got family?"

Icy cold stabbed behind his ribs. "Yes, First Sarnt."

"Here?"

He nodded. "You?"

"Married to the Marines since I made eps." The first sergeant grunted. "Had a brief thing with the Division. Teaching bot jockeys the proper way to kill."

"No shit?"

"Wasn't for me. They're too cerebral for my taste."

A blurry-eyed junior clerk in clinic whites tapped updates into a flatscreen. A hot pot of tea steamed on the counter.

"May I?" Druggan asked the clerk.

"Of course, First Sergeant."

Druggan poured himself a cup. His sip was loud in the relative quiet of the hallway, prompting a quick glance from the clerk.

"Take thirty, Marine." It was an order, not a suggestion. "Maybe someone around here can tell you something about your family." His gaze dropped to Bresto's exposed sock. "And see to your uniform. You're severely out of reg."

Druggan turned back toward the CP, tea in hand. The reservist lingered until the first sergeant was out of sight.

"Sergeant Bresto." She was young for an NCO, reserve or not.

"Sarnt."

She approached the counter. "Excuse me. Can you help this Marine find his family?"

"I can try. COLNET's been glitchy all day." The clerk's fingers hovered over the terminal. "What are their names?"

His mouth went dry. Knowing nothing was almost better than knowing the wrong thing. "Bresto. Kaffereine and Sammiel Bresto."

The reserve sergeant smiled. "Kaffereine. Pretty name."

"My daughter."

The clerk tapped out their names on the glowing plexene, paging through lists of names and status reports.

His answer came too quickly. "They're not patients here."

Hope warred with experience in Bresto's gut. Not here didn't mean they weren't hurt. It just meant they weren't here.

The clerk pulled up the shelter feeds, another long feed of scrolling names. His pause said everything. "No record in the shelter network either, I'm afraid."

"Most shelters are way over capacity." The reservist's voice was gentle. "They might not have logged everyone yet."

He knew better. PR and the Security Administration had practiced for scenarios like this. His children should be on a list somewhere, if they were still alive.

"… with me," she was saying.

"What?"

She led him to a nearby stairwell. "We've got a hundred and five people in the sub-level beneath the clinic. They're not registered anywhere. We took them in when Sienna-2 filled up."

They hammered down the steps together, two at a time. Pain shot through Bresto's hip with each step, his sock sliding on the cold metal steps. He ignored it, taking the stairs faster.

"I saw children with the last group," she panted as they descended. "From all over Diacad."

The sub-level door crashed open. Colonists lined the halls, passing around field paste and water.

"We couldn't turn them away," she said, moving through the crowd. "Not after the shelter closed. We just kept making room until the raiders hit us."

None of the faces in the hallway were familiar. His chest went tight as they reached the door. He went to shoulder through, to see his children behind it, but the reservist put a hand on the latch.

"Easy now," she said quietly. "These people have been through a lot."

The door creaked opened on worn hinges. The smell of sweat and fear and too many bodies filled the room. What looked like medical equipment storage was filled wall to wall with people. Some slept sitting up against the walls, others huddled in small groups. A young beta looked up at him with Kaff's eyes, but it wasn't her. None of them were.

He held the door, one step inside. "Kaff—" The word broke apart in his mouth again. He forced a scowl to mask the pain, made himself continue. "Kaffereine? Sammiel?"

The words echoed in the crowded space. A few colonists exchanged glances, and a low murmur passed through the room. But no one answered. No one came forward. His stomach turned as the silence stretched.

The door clicked closed behind him. He'd told himself not to hope, that finding them here was unlikely. But that didn't stop the icy certainty spreading through his chest.

They weren't home. They weren't in the shelters. They weren't here.

"I'm so sorry, Sergeant. Maybe—"

He left her at the door, stalking to the stairwell, then up at a jog. He pushed through the clinic's main level, past rows of exam rooms, between admin stations, through hallways thick with Marines who stank of combat and stale socks. He had to get out. Had to escape the suffocating weight of his failure before he did something he'd regret.

The main doors barely had time to cycle before he squeezed through into the evening air. He kept going, past the ruined gate and into the transit. The fallen statue lay there, the broken god offering no comfort as he leaned against its base.

One, two, three. Deep breath. Four. Fi—fuck it.

He couldn't stay still and began pacing circles near the statue's base. The words poured out of him like poison. He'd done everything She asked. The prayers, every night since he was a beta. He'd climbed to the top of Her mountain. Spent two decades fighting in Her name.

"I was there!" He drove a finger at the broken stone. "Watching good Marines die. Fighting *Your* archenemy. I chose service over family because that's what *You* demanded of me. So where the..." He almost couldn't say it. "Where the fuck are You now?"

The inscription carved into the stone base screamed back at him:

SALVATION THROUGH FAITH. FAITH THROUGH SERVICE. SERVICE THROUGH SACRIFICE. The ancient words were barely legible amid the blast damage. Salvation. Sacrifice. The straight line between those words was a path he'd followed unquestioningly his whole life. Now, it felt like a cruel joke.

A shock of color beneath the debris grabbed his eye. Paint, maybe, out of place on the cracked gray stone. He wiped the dust clear, revealing swirls of color. It was the Cradle, rendered in brilliant detail, marked through with strange black lines. Then, in bright red above the nebula, stenciled in crisp block letters: *JUST KAFFY.*

His stomach lurched. He read it again and again.

Just. Kaffy.

The paint was fresh, rock dust sticking to it in places. There weren't many Kaffereines in Vestebrae. Lyra had picked the name—strong and noble, she'd said, perfect for their little warrior. For a heartbeat, it felt like she was right there with him. The far away sound of her laughter drifted through his mind. He wanted so badly to snatch her up from wherever she was and hold her tight. To tell her everything would be all right. That she had nothing to fear.

The night sky erupted, brightening the storm like daybreak. A new star burned high above, turning clouds from storm-black to mid-day gray, casting harsh shadows across the transit.

Hope dissipated into the searing light. Something massive had just died in orbit. The *Alexander Lehman* maybe, or one of the orbitals. He looked down at those two words—Just Kaffy. Maybe he'd found this trace of her just in time to watch everything they'd fought for burn away. The Twelfth's answer to his doubt, written in fire across Her sky.

The shelter's massive doors ground open with a hydraulic whine. People filed out—reservists in white-and-grays, a well-dressed young man who didn't belong in Diacad, more security personnel in hazard vests. It was a lot of people. Maybe the reservist was right. Maybe his kids were somewhere inside.

He shouldered through the crowd. "Kaff? Sammy?"

Another reservist caught his arm, explained these were volunteers. With the raiders gone, they wanted to help. To serve. Like proper Aegians.

Bresto swiped sweat and dust from his eyes. Proper Aegians. Proper Aegians would've made sure the blocks were clear. Would've triple-fucking-checked the census logs.

A big man in block drill uniform stepped through the door, bags under his eyes. His uniform sleeve was badged with a block number. E-10.

The nametape stenciled on the man's uniform was like a combat marker in Bresto's brain. Target acquired. Bresto grabbed the block captain by the shoulders, spinning him around.

"My kids. Where are they, Hesper? Where the fuck are my kids?"

"I… I don't…" The color drained from Hesper's face. "Wait. Bresto?"

The headbutt was just muscle memory. Hesper's nose gave with the satisfying crack of a mission accomplished. Bresto found the block captain's collar before he could drop, slamming him back against the shelter's stone wall.

"Kaffereine Bresto!" His rage burned hotter than the orbital detonation. "Sammiel Bresto!"

Blood poured from Hesper's nose, and his words came out garbled. "I don't know" and "I'm sorry."

Wrong answer. Bresto ripped the disciplinary whip from Hesper's duty belt. Voices rose around him, hands grabbing at his uniform, but he ignored them all. The synthweave sang as the first blow laid a red line across Hesper's cheek.

"Coward!" The word tore from his throat. The second strike drew blood. "COWARD!"

Someone caught his arm as he wound up for another blow. He turned and drove his elbow into the man's chest, feeling bone give beneath the strike.

The man fell away gasping for air, but more hands grabbed at Bresto. He lashed out blind, his one boot finding purchase in someone's leg. He surged forward, trying to hit Hesper again as two reservists dragged him away. White light exploded inside his skull as something solid connected with the back of his head. The ground rushed up to meet him.

The familiar whine of a CR-11 hummed above him.

"Stay down." Someone he should know.

Bresto rolled onto his back, vision swimming.

Rosch stood over him. "What in twelve hells? Sarnt?"

Lessig was beside him, apparently enjoying himself. "You got a funny way of celebrating, Sarnt."

"Cel—?" Bresto blinked away the pain. "Celebrating?"

"You don't know? That forge ship of yours? The fleet just took it out."

CHAPTER
TWENTY

OLSOM COULDN'T REMEMBER SITTING down. One moment she was walking, the next her ass hit cold granite near the office doorway. The room looked like how her brain felt—shattered flatscreen, ceiling panels dangling. An office chair lay on its side like a dead thing, wheels still spinning lazily. Her body ached in places she didn't know could ache, her throat tasting of scorched metal.

Kitrelle dug through her pack, the rustle of fabric and gear almost soothing. On the office desk, Werner—pretty sure that was her name—worked a brush over her CR-11's focusing rod. Olsom's eyelids grew heavy, but each time she got close, that wild thing in her would snap awake, hissing: *not safe.*

Her stomach growled, the sound almost lost beneath Werner's maintenance and the bootsteps in the hall. When was her last real meal? Before the drop? Before Three-Alpha? Yeah, crid and rats with Doc and the twins, before Bresto and the Concordat showed up and ruined everything. Her hands found the field paste tube on autopilot. The paste rolled across her tongue—like eating river sludge—and she forced it down. Not even close to the same.

"Shot, over," Kitrelle announced, emerging victorious from her pack. She tossed a tube of field paste to Werner.

"How do they expect us to eat this shit?" Werner asked, tearing the seal with her teeth.

"Like this." Kitrelle squeezed a fat rope of paste into her mouth. "And now we'll be shitting granite for weeks."

A hint of ozone drifted into the room and Olsom's mind went back to the clinic grounds. To that dying raider that almost killed her. Those words that weren't quite words. Utterly alien, but still somehow vaguely familiar.

"Awful quiet over there, new blood." Kitrelle slid down the wall next to her, their shoulders touching. The contact should have made Olsom flinch but didn't. "You okay?"

"Yeah."

"Uh huh." Kitrelle's laugh was gentle. "You have to get it out, you know? Otherwise, it gets stuck up here, bouncing around until you go crazy. Trust me on that one."

Nothing about Kitrelle added up. No haunted admin block look; no scarred edges or hollow places like Olsom saw in the mirror every day. Marine recruit training made everyone harder, meaner—that was the whole point. But here was Kitrelle, wearing softness like armor. People only kept that kind of certainty when they'd had choices. Real ones.

"Wasn't so bad," she said.

"The hell it wasn't," Werner said. "You pushed straight through their line. Killed so hard your metal gave out."

"3-3-3's a good rig."

It felt like a lie. The exo had let her down when she needed it most. But it was just a machine, one she wouldn't be alive without. It couldn't abandon her any more than a rifle with an empty charge pack. Not like—

"Sure." Kitrelle's smile had an edge now. "All those squids didn't just die on their own. So how was it? Really?"

"Really fucking scary." Olsom's laugh cracked halfway through, and she had to look away. She swallowed, waited, until she could trust her voice again. "Felt like a dream. Not real."

Werner swooned. "Ooh, a dream."

Kitrelle laughed again, hard, and it felt like permission to breathe.

"One of the squids spoke to me before it died."

The alien words echoed in the quiet inside her head. Time seemed to stop, the stillness broken only by distant voices in the clinic halls. Kitrelle's hand settled on Olsom's knee, urging her on. Her nose wrinkled and she pulled her hand back—something about the room, maybe, that combat stink that permeated everything.

"Well?" Werner blurted. "What'd it say?"

Olsom's tongue worked against her teeth, trying to shape the alien syllables. "Morf… morith-len? Fuck, I can't—" The wet sounds died in her throat as those alien eyes filled her mind again. Not angry or afraid, but something else entirely. "It just looked… sad. Right at the end."

Werner doubled over. "A sad squid!" She wiped tears from her eyes. "You're poetic as hell, Vestian, I'll give you that."

"Come on," Kitrelle chided, but she was smiling too.

A hollow feeling spread in Olsom's chest as she struggled to form even the ghost of a smile. All she could see were those eyes. Not afraid, not angry, just something that felt too familiar from something so alien.

"Bugs!" Doc filled the doorway, white-and-grays dark with sweat and oil, sleeves rolled to show forearms vanishing under black grease. One of 3-3-3's vent assembly dangled from his grip, green paint scarred and bubbled. "Found you."

That smile was pure heart fuel.

"Hey." She felt suddenly younger, like some ditsy delta, watching him drop down next to her. Shoulder to shoulder. The smell of her rig clung to him—carbon scoring and fusion wash—marking him as much 3-3-3's as she was. A weird warmth filled the void insider her at that thought.

"Problem was right here." He dumped the twisted metal across her knees, finger tracing the edge of the assembly. "Vent kept sticking, made the others freeze up. Can't fix that in the field, so I pulled it. Rest of the vents are good to go, though. Running smooth."

Kitrelle leaned against her other side. Werner wasn't even pretending to clean her weapon anymore, just watching with a crooked grin.

Olsom felt her face go hot. The wild thing in her chittered for more space, the sudden closeness squeezing her like a trap.

"Barrels," she blurted. So much for PFC Professional. "The FAB, I mean. Is it—"

"Bugs." The way he said it made her stomach flip, even with that cocked eyebrow like she'd grown gills. "Do I look like some boot-ass spanner skeeg?"

A snorting laugh burst from her throat, warm and unexpected.

"Unbelievable. After I changed your barrels? Restocked your spares?" His wounded act crumbled beneath that damn smile. "No faith. None at all."

He pushed off the wall but left the vent assembly in her lap. "You good, though? Any pain? Seeing spots?"

The sudden care in his voice hit harder than any squid. "I'm good."

"All right. I'm going to see if Toelke or Thannick need a hand. Tac if you need me." He gave Kitrelle and Werner a passing nod. "Ladies."

And then he was gone, leaving an empty doorway and too many feelings.

"Wow," Werner said, deadpanned and staring. "Just. Wow."

"Shut up." Olsom's voice cracked on the words, heat rushing to her face.

Kitrelle's voice was gentle, almost sisterly. "Why does he call you Bugs?"

"Back on Three-Alpha, before all this." The memory was twenty hours old and felt like it belonged to someone else now. "He was such an ass at first. Took one look and said, 'you're Vestian.' Guessed what my folks did, just like that."

"Which is?"

Strange how old wounds mattered less after watching people get atomized. Admin blocks, family drama, all ancient history now.

"They ran a co-op trawler," she began. Just saying the words out loud took her back to the warm belly of the old ship in mid-season. The sound of pa's music blaring through the lard room. Crid calls like dry reeds on the wind. "Out in the Tangle. Hunting crid, rendering their fat for colony rations."

"Yummy," Werner said.

"So you grew up cooking bugs."

"Almost." It did sound kind of funny, put that way.

"You like him."

Werner thrust her rifle's lower receiver rhythmically between her legs, rattling the desk as she undulated back and forth. "*Someone* needs a dose of that autodoc—a little bit of that bedside manner."

"Stop," Olsom snapped. It wasn't like that, not exactly. Problem was, it was hard to say exactly what that something was.

Feelings for Myers. Yeah, no point denying that. They were there, in some weird space between attraction and… something else. Something that made her light up when he smiled.

"Don't get mad." Kitrelle nudged her shoulder. "The heart wants, you know?"

Olsom didn't know what to say. What did she want from Kitrelle—permission? Understanding? Some field manual explaining the knots in her guts?

"Besides," Kitrelle went on, "your boy's got it bad, too. A hard-charger like that sees you've pissed yourself and doesn't say a word? Just keeps right on smiling? That's Marine-grade special."

Ice flooded her guts. The damp patch down her trouser leg, that ammonia bite she'd missed while riding that kill-drunk high. Somewhere in that firefight, that primal struggle for life and death, her bladder had gone UA without orders. *Fuck.*

"No shame, given the day you've had," Kitrelle added quickly. "Not like you could smell it with that rebreather on anyway."

Werner kept quiet, just nodded like she'd been there, done that, too.

Kitrelle shrugged, like it was no big deal. This woman, this proper Aegian, had been nothing but kind. No one ever helped admin block trash without wanting something in return. Except Kitrelle just did. Again.

"My uniforms," Olsom swallowed hard, "they're all back on Three-Alpha."

"Founders, new blood." Kitrelle dug a rolled-up uniform and sterile wipes from her pack. "Should fit you. Pack smarter next time, okay?"

Olsom rose unsteadily, eyes on the door. If she could just find a head before the lieutenant or Bresto spotted her. She took two steps, then stopped cold.

"Why are you being so nice to me?"

Kitrelle was still looking at her, waiting. "Same team, that's all." But there was something more, something that said she understood what it meant to need help and actually get it.

Outside the room, the hall was empty. Signs pointed to a head two doors down. Olsom ghosted through the door, her movements pure admin block instinct. No one behind the door. No feet visible under the stalls. Still, she checked each one anyway, that wild thing in her hissing to make sure. The last door creaked open to reveal more blessed nothing.

The stall clanged shut behind her. She collapsed onto the toilet, her hands shaking as she stripped her tac gear and hung it from a steel peg on the wall. The sweaty uniform peeled away like dead skin. Skivvies, too, slick with animal fear and human shame. She kicked the whole mess into the corner. Someone else's problem now.

The sterile wipes left her skin tingling, almost burning. Not shower clean, but it felt better, and that was something. She let the cool air do its work, then pulled on Kitrelle's spare uniform, a hint of something floral in the fabric. It hung loose around her hips but otherwise fit fine. Her tac gear went back on last, the straps heavy on her shoulders, and immediately the sweat and carbon started seeping in. Like dirty was part of the uniform.

Metal screamed as the door to the head slammed. Olsom was moving before she could think, boots tucked up on the toilet lid, breath held, heart hammering. She almost didn't fit. A man's voice boomed through the stalls: "Everyone outside, now!"

The fear ebbed as more boots thundered past, voices rising in excitement, not panic. As the door banged shut, her flexscreen began vibrating with alerts. Squad updates, platoon feeds—something big was happening.

The hall was alive with the sound of boots and conversation. She pushed through clusters of celebrating Marines, trying to catch fragments of conversation over the growing noise. Her flexscreen offered no answers, just routine updates about watch rotations and equipment checks. Nothing that explained why everyone was running for the exits like they'd won the damn war.

Something knocked against her leg. Olsom stumbled and caught herself. A small boy looked up at her. Beta, probably, with a head too big for his thin frame, skin pale even by Aegian standards.

She knelt beside him as more Marines thundered past. "You okay?"

He seemed fine. Tough little thing, didn't even cry. Just held onto his rebreather with both hands like his life depended on it. Maybe it did. She knew the feeling.

"Yes." His voice was so tiny, too small for his big green eyes.

There was something about the boy. Maybe his lost look, that alone-in-a-crowd stillness. Too familiar. No way to just walk past that, even if she wanted to.

"My name's Ol—Larke. My name is Larke."

"Larke." The way he said it made her smile despite everything. Kid was going to be trouble when he got older.

"Bugs!" Doc's boots squeaked against the floor as he pulled up short. "What are you—never mind, just come on!"

"Hold on." She batted his reaching hands away.

The twins appeared through the rush of Marines, Toelke bringing up the rear.

"Those skeegs did it," Smokes said.

Vlan's grin matched his brother's. "We're going to see!"

Something about the boy kept nagging at her brain. That stubborn little chin, that round head buzzed regulation-short. The way he took everything in stride, like chaos was just normal. She *knew* that face.

"What's happening, Doc?" She looked up. The raw joy on his face made her heart do that stupid flutter thing again.

"That forge ship—the fleet just turned it to atoms. It's gone, Bugs. Fucking gone!"

Her jaw went slack, eyes stinging with phantom tears. They'd done it. They'd actually done it. She had lived through this nightmare. Maybe things would be back to normal soon. No more war, no more Mez, no more Twelfth-damned Sergeant Bres—

Bresto. *Bresto.* She twisted back to the boy—yeah, it was all over his face. She couldn't unsee it now. "Hey, what's your name?"

"Sammiel."

"Sammiel what?"

"Sammiel Bresto, Larke ma'am. Mother calls me Sammy. Sissy, too."

The revelation was almost too much. She felt drunk on it. Bresto might be a top-shelf asshole, but he deserved to know his son was still alive.

"Woah," the twins said.

Doc whispered a curse. "Wait, is that—"

"What's your pa call you, Sammy?" Olsom asked.

His nose wrinkled. "Pa?"

"Sorry, your father." She couldn't stop smiling. "What does your father call you?"

The boy seemed to fold in on himself, eyes finding the floor. His tiny shrug hit her somewhere deep.

She took his hand in hers, squeezing gently until he looked up. "Come on. Let's go find out."

THE WORLD FELL AWAY beneath Kaffy's boots, a dizzy tumble of metal and stone that made her heart skip. The drop station's massive lift tracks stretched all the way down to Corongaet, so far that even the heavy sleds resembled pebbles at the bottom. Storm winds rushed up the cliff, making her feel every bit of that distance. She squeezed the Twelfth's statuette in her palm until the worn edges bit into her skin.

"Protect your servants—Mother and Father—wherever they are. Sammy, too." Another gust pressed on her boots, and for a split second, it felt like she could go up and over the railing. "And maybe You could keep an eye on me too? Since we're kind of stuck up here and all."

A string of spit sailed beneath her, followed by Duray's cackling laugh. He was balanced on the railing like some wild kinlin, taking aim at another of the leather-winged animals nesting on the cliff face. The shot found its mark, and the animal beat its wings against the stone, sending up a cloud of dust.

Kaffy rolled her eyes toward the storm, two fingers, two taps above her heart. "And I guess Father would want me to ask You to look after idiots like Duray too. Even if he is being extra stupid right now."

"Stupid?" Duray swung around the railing post, boots scraping metal. "You're the stupid one. That's not how you pray at all."

She clutched the statuette closer. "I'm not—I mean, I was just—"

"Holy Mother." His knuckles thumped against his chest as if he wanted to smash through the bone. "Please save this lost little girl. Show her the error of her blasphemous ways." His grin stretched wider. "Set her on a path to Your salvation."

Her face burned with shame and anger. Father had taught her those prayers. Just like talking, he'd said. And now Duray was making fun of her like they meant nothing. She shook the little silver figure at his face.

"Don't judge, don't judge!" Her voice pitched higher. "The tenets say you shouldn't judge!"

His eyes fixed on the silver. "Is that… let me see."

"No!" But he was already moving, hands grasping as she tried to pull away. Their scuffle sent tremors through the metal platform.

"I just—" he grunted, trying to pry her fingers open "—wanna see!"

Kaffy jerked back, the force sending her onto the platform floor. The statuette flew from her hand, spinning lazily through the storm-charged air before it dropped toward the empty space beyond the platform. It caught in the metal grating with a soft ping and stuck there. She scrambled forward on hands and knees, but Duray dove past her, snatching it up with a triumphant laugh.

"Give it!" Rage carried her across the platform and she fell on the boy hard. Her fists found his chest, his shoulders, anywhere she could reach.

"Ow—ha—ow!" He twisted away and shoved, sending her backside into the railing.

It gave just a little, enough to send a dizzy panic through her whole body. She dropped to the floor, head against a metal rail. The statuette gleamed in Duray's grasp. "That's mine!"

"I just want to look," he said between breaths, the precious figurine clasped between his fingers. "Where'd you get it?"

The control room door's hydraulics cut through her anger. Madam Ulwin appeared through the glow of flatscreens, one hand on the hatchway's steel-blue metal, the other white-knuckling a handkerchief to her lips.

"Children!" She barely got the word out through a racking cough. "Have you lost your minds? It's a two-hundred-meter drop to Corongaet, and you're about to take the shortcut!"

Duray made a face at the old woman, then resumed his examination of the Twelfth's statuette. "Ever wonder why She wears a mask? Maybe She's too ugly to look at."

"Madam Ulwin!" She didn't care that she was whining. Duray was bigger, meaner, than her. "Duray took my figurine!"

Madam Ulwin's fingers traced the wall as she edged forward, as if she didn't quite trust her feet on the platform's serrated grate. "Duray, return that to Lady Kaffereine this instant."

Duray slumped. "Yes, ma'am."

"And both of you, inside." Madam Ulwin's pale blue stare forced Kaffy to rise. "The lieutenant was quite clear about staying quiet, though you seem determined to bring every raider in Vestebrae down on us." She let go of the wall just long enough to wave them toward the door. "Inside. Now."

Duray marched over and smacked the precious figure into her palm. "I'm not scared of any raiders."

Kaffy followed him to the door, eyes moving across the towering lift mechanisms, the maze of catwalks and service platforms that connected them, storm-weathered metal stretching out over the cliff's edge. The Diacad drop station wasn't the biggest on the mountain but the emptiness of it made her feel so small.

The control room door hissed shut behind them, cutting off the howling wind. Madam Ulwin found Kaffy's shoulder, gave it a tired squeeze as she passed. Inside, the room smelled funny, the same when the flatscreen at home overheated. The painter perched atop one of the control decks, dabbing colors onto the observation windows in perfect circles and lines.

"PR Command, be advised I have civilians in need of immediate evac." The lieutenant spoke carefully into the little plate on his cuff. He looked tired, like every word pulled something out of him. "We're at the Corongaet drop, Control Station Zero Seven."

"*—egative copy, sending station. We—*" Static swallowed the rest.

"PR Command, say again." Nothing but an endless hiss. He looked up at the painter. "I don't suppose you have any suggestions?"

"I do not." The daxed never stopped working, its shoulders bobbing up and down with each new color or shape.

"So much for faith through service," the lieutenant growled under his breath.

The painter stopped mid-stroke and turned its thin face completely around with sickening ease. "Very well. I might *suggest* you stop broadcasting our location to every sentient within range. That static? The enemy are here, CDF. They will be listening."

"It's just interference," the lieutenant said.

Its lidless eyes studied him.

"Something detonated up there," he continued, "and now everything's covered in electromagnetic—well, it doesn't matter."

Soft clicking emanated from inside its skull. "It does matter, CDF," it said. "Their cathedral is destroyed. I felt it die."

The lieutenant straightened. "Whose cathedral? What are you talking about?"

"Their... forge ship." The painter seemed to struggle with each word, still staring blankly through the observation windows. "The womb of the Makers. The conduit of the Eleven—"

"Wait, you're saying we destroyed it? The raider ship?" The lieutenant's face brightened. A smile tugged at the corner of his mouth. "That's... that's great news. That means we're—"

The painter remained frozen in place. "Not raiders..."

The clicking in its skull changed, settling into an eerie back and forth rhythm—back and forth, back and forth. The swaying sound seemed to fill the small control room, counting down every second until—

"... the Concordat."

Kaffy's breath caught. The Concordat. They... they were just stories to make children mind their parents. Dead Earth. The Exodus. The Reckoning. Hundreds of years ago. No. The Twelfth... She defeated them. The Concordat were gone forever. Father told her so. Mother, too. Everyone! They... they wouldn't lie. Not about this.

"You're wrong," she said, the words stuck in her throat.

The painter's head snapped to face her and the clicking fell silent. Only then did she see the black streaks through the painter's latest work. Black as pure nothingness. They seemed to drink in the light from the overhead lamps.

"Thoughtful gamma," it said. "The Concordat are here. I feel them."

Madam Ulwin's hand went to her chest. "Twelfth keep us," she coughed.

"So what if they are?" The lieutenant made a stiff shrug. "You said we destroyed their ship. Whatever they were planning, it's over."

"The vessel has served its purpose," the painter said, turning back to the window. Its fingers traced one of the black streaks in the paint. "The Eleven's light is cast. And it is blinding."

"That's enough." The lieutenant's voice rang loud in the sudden quiet. "Whatever's happening up there, we still need to get down this mountain. Thats what matters right now."

The painter shrugged and turned back to its work, adding swirls of deep purple to the cloudy plexene.

The lieutenant circled the control table and pulled out a chair. "Please, Madam Ulwin, Little Ma'am, sit. There's nothing to fear. I only need to find us a safe route down. It won't take long."

Something in the way he wouldn't look at them made her uneasy. But her back still smarted from the scuffle, so she hopped into the closest seat.

Duray shuffled past her. "They're just stories. This is stupid." He rolled his eyes and stalked back to the window.

She wanted to believe him. But the painter had been there, so long ago. Maybe it could still *feel* the truth, even if it couldn't remember.

"Thank you, Lieutenant. Such a proper young man." Madam Ulwin's steps were small and careful as she made her way to the chair. The movement seemed to knock something loose, and she was doubled over coughing again. Each bark came harder than the last until she had to grip the chair back to stay upright.

"Water." Her handkerchief came away darker than before. "Sweet Holy Mother, just a drink of water."

The old woman had never looked so frail. So scared.

"Duray." The lieutenant's voice took a deeper tone just then, kind of like Father's. "Emergency kits on the walls, marked with red. Find some water."

"Yes, sir!" Duray started a slow circuit of the room, fingers tracing the wall panels.

The lieutenant jabbed at the control table's flatscreen, cycling through screen after screen of stuff Kaffy didn't understand. The interface looked nothing like the basic school terminal—all sharp angles and blinking markers instead of neat columns. Every few seconds he'd pause, then swipe to the next display with a frustrated grunt. Even the grownups didn't know what they were doing.

"Twelfth-damned—"

"What're you looking for?" She scooted to the edge of her seat for a better look.

He let out a sigh. "You'd think a tac officer would know his way around these systems."

"Tac?" The word reminded her of the sound Mother's boots made on the hab block stairs.

"Tactical networks. They run all military systems and communications." He waved at the screen like it explained itself. "Most colony infrastructure runs on the same protocols."

"Oh." She nodded seriously, but really just wanted to know which button would take them down.

He pointed at one of the shapes. "The drop's in lockdown."

Whatever that meant. She had no clue, and he could tell.

"To keep the raiders from using it. But CDF personnel like me still have maintenance access." He hunched over the screen. "Problem is a place this big has a *lot* of maintenance nodes. It could take hours to—"

"I can help!" She leaned forward eagerly, tapping the flatscreen display in front of her. "Two would be faster."

"Maybe you're right." He leaned closer and pressed his thumb against her terminal. The screen lit up with fresh symbols. "Here."

He flipped through menus faster than she could follow, then stopped. His finger traced the block script. "Look for anything to do with personnel transit or crew transport. Think you can do that?"

"Yes, sir!" It did feel good to help. Better than thinking about light and wombs and other scary stuff.

"If you find something, don't touch it. Tell me, and I'll check."

"Okay." But she was already looking. *Drop Lift 1. Generator 09-C. Mag-Break Cells 4-13.* All gibberish.

Nobody spoke while they worked. Madam Ulwin's breathing had settled into a low wheeze that almost matched the rhythm of their screen taps. A loose cable whipped against the tower in a heavy gust, rattling the whole structure.

Kaffy's eyes stung from the screen glare. The symbols made no sense—colonial standard should be readable. *Main Mag-Break Drivers 1-8. Tertiary Grid Access. Auxiliary Tensioners 15-20.* Any button looked as likely to shoot them into orbit as get them down to Corongaet.

"What're you doing?" Duray asked, suddenly looming behind her.

Kaffy jumped in her seat. "Granite's crack! You scared me!" She drove her fist into Duray's shoulder, but he laughed it off. "I'm helping. Unlike *somebody*."

"Hey! I found the emergency kits." He kicked at the floor. "But someone took all the water."

"Wait—maintenance ladderwell zero-three," she read aloud. "That's stairs, right?"

"Founders, no, child." Madam Ulwin cleared her throat with a phlegmy rattle. "Stairs. I can't."

"We may have no other option." The lieutenant spoke softly. "We've been here too long already."

"I can help you with the stairs," Kaffy offered. The fear was creeping back in, making her wish they were already moving. Anywhere was better than waiting.

"Look!" Duray's finger left a smudge on the screen. "Right there—"

"Don't!" Kaffy swatted his hand away, but it was too late. *CREW TRANSFER LIFT 03* flashed across her screen in bright yellow. The node expanded to fill the screen, sprouting more nodes connected by pulsing lines. *AUX LIGHTING. AUX ACCESS. PRIMARY WINCH CONTROLS. BRAKE LOCK CHARGE.* Through the observation windows, amber warning lights blinked to life on a small platform at the far end of the drop.

The painter froze mid-stroke, its head craning toward the ceiling. More strange clicks emanated from inside its head.

"They are coming."

The lieutenant rounded the table in three quick steps. Madam Ulwin squeaked as he lifted her over his shoulder. "Daxed, get the children to the lift!"

The painter was already at the hatch, paint-stained fingers dancing across the controls. It slid open and then they were running, down the tower steps and into storm winds that tried to tear them from the platform.

Kaffy ran harder than she'd ever run, chasing Duray's back as they raced toward the distant lift. The painter glided past them easily, its ruined body moving with scary smoothness across the grating. The crew lift appeared through the haze: a cage of dull metal, plexene, and safety mesh, ancient warning lights strobing yellow-red-yellow across its frame.

Then the storm's howl changed pitch, air currents reversing. Not the wind. The deep thrum of ship engines, descending. A dark shape punched through the clouds on jets of fire, coming in way too fast. The heat of it washed over her.

The crew lift still seemed far away. Twelfth save them, they weren't going to make it.

Blue streaks cut through the storm, ringing against the ship's side like thunder on metal. More shots hammered up from the transit corridor, each impact leaving craters of fire across the hull. Smoke poured from the wounds as the ship's engines sputtered and failed. The burning ship lurched sideways, growing larger with each passing second.

Through the smoke, the painter waited in the lift cage, waving them inside. Cables snapped bright and loud overhead. She lunged through the door and against the wall, heart hammering.

The lift's cloudy plexene windows showed her everything—the ship hitting the platform in a crash of metal and fire, the lieutenant still running with Madam Ulwin over his shoulder. Then smoke swallowed them both. It swallowed everything.

Heat and wind and darkness crashed into the lift cage. Acrid black stung her eyes as debris clattered against the metal walls. The lift shuddered and swayed, screaming to tear free from its tracks. Time stretched like heated metal.

Kaffy squeezed her eyes shut and pressed the statuette to her chest, fingers tap-tap-tapping above her heart. Everything was ending and she wasn't ready. Mother. Father. She needed Father.

The lift cage shuddered again, and suddenly the lieutenant was there, setting Madam Ulwin against the far wall. Their clothes were scorched, faces black with smoke, but the lieutenant wore the biggest smile she'd ever seen between heavy breaths.

"What is it?" Kaffy asked. "What happened?"

His grin just got bigger. "The Marines happened."

Marines. Hope bloomed in her chest, warm and fragile. Just like that, across all the years, Father felt so close it *hurt*. His massive arms around her, the smell of starch on his uniform, that voice that could shake mountains but always went soft for her. He could keep the monsters away.

The smoke swirled beyond the plexene like an old memory. She blinked through the coming tears, waiting for his larger-than-life presence to emerge from the nightmare. To sweep her up and carry her home.

Green, vaguely human-shaped machines appeared through the clearing smoke, marching down the transit toward the wreckage. Their guns filled the air with painful red lines that sliced through everything they touched. Dark figures tried to escape the burning ship, but the machines found them all. One by one they fell, each death pulling another cheer from deep inside her. These were the raiders who'd hurt Madam Ulwin, who'd chased them here. Who'd taken her family away.

"Down, little ma'am." The lieutenant's hands were already pulling her away from the window.

"No—I need to see!" She struggled against his grip. Father could be right there, so close. "Father won't hurt me!"

"No, he wouldn't. But combat is dangerous for everyone nearby, even family." Another explosion rocked the platform. "We need to leave. Now."

Hope turned to pain as the painter glided to the lift controls, its face cold and soulless. One button press and the door rattled shut.

"No!" She slammed against the door, tears hot on her face. "Father's there! He'll save us, I promise! Just wait. Please!"

The lift jerked downward, and her legs went weak. She slid to her knees, still clinging to the door, screaming for Father as the lift descended through layers of metalwork. The painter wasn't her friend anymore—maybe never was. She hated it; wished they'd never met.

"You are not safe here, Lady Kaffereine." The painter's hollow gaze fixed on the drop station's rim, where flashes of light lit the dark clouds. "That is not a rescue. That is war."

CHAPTER
TWENTY-TWO

THE SURGICAL THEATER stank of blood and antiseptic. Bresto shifted against the observation deck's rear wall, the flex cuffs catching against the rail as he tried to get comfortable. Below him, the Daxed Corps surgeon never blinked as it worked, its metal-laced hands a blur inside some poor woman's chest cavity. Two more gurneys appeared through those doors, then another. Colony standards said one trauma per surgical team. He counted four now, waiting their turn. The daxed might work fast, but time was still time. Someone was going to die down there.

Maybe that was why they'd put him where they did. To remind him of the price innocent people were paying for each block the Concordat took.

A spray of arterial blood painted the daxed's chest. Its cybernetic hands never stopped moving, never trembled, as it clamped the severed vessel. The rest of the surgical team looked exhausted. Human.

Across the observation deck, someone cleared their throat. Revan. He was still here. Still talking, apparently, talking to him.

"—for assaulting your own daughter's block captain. A man chosen by colony administration to safeguard our children. Your children. It's inexcusable."

Bresto's hands tensed, the flex cuffs biting deeper. Kaff… Hesper hadn't protected anyone. He'd abandoned her and who knows how many others out there while the Concordat lit the world on fire.

"The major's considering your immediate relief," Revan went on. "The local advocate may demand charges once we've secured the settlement."

"Charges?" Bresto almost laughed. A gurney squeaked through the theater doors below, bringing another broken body for the Found daxed to put back together. "Tell me, Lieutenant. What's the punishment for a block captain who abandons his post? Who leaves children to die to save himself?"

"Hesper was responsible for dozens of families," Revan said. "Maybe a hundred children. We can't beat our own people bloody because some get left behind. This is war, Sergeant."

Bresto surged to his feet. Left behind? The observation rail creaked as he stepped toward Revan.

"These people are all we have." There weren't quite a million souls in the Three Colonies. Less now. Every single one of them precious beyond measure. His children most of all. "How many of them died because that rock snake was hiding inside the mountain? The families of my block deserved better."

"*You* deserve better, you mean," Revan spat. "That's what this is really about. You're selfish, Sergeant. Assaulting a colonist, compromising our operational readiness, using CDF resources for your own private rescue." His mouth twisted into something ugly. "Only the Holy Mother weighs the measure of our service. Or did you forget that tenet along with the rest of our values?"

Bresto backed against the observation rail. Revan was wrong about a lot of things, but not this. He *had* judged Hesper—harshly—but damn, it had felt good.

Below, the daxed's hands moved with mechanical precision, already closing another patient.

"I told you, sir." He let out a tired laugh, eyes searching the ceiling like he was speaking directly to Her. "I'm difficult."

"And not worth the trouble, clearly. You're a talented NCO, that much is obvious, but—"

The door slid open. First Sergeant Druggan filled the frame, moving straight for Revan without ceremony or salute. His permanent scowl had somehow deepened.

"This is a private meeting, First Sergeant." Revan drew himself up. "I don't recall—"

"The major sent me, sir." The last word seemed to pain Druggan physically.

"Oh." Satisfaction crossed Revan's face. He gestured toward the door. "This way then."

"This pertains to the sergeant as well. The major has considered your request for disciplinary action, and is postponing any formal judgments at this time."

"The major should have told me herself."

"She's telling you now, sir." Druggan shot Bresto a look before fixing on the lieutenant. "The major—the *skipper*—has other concerns. Thirty thousand of them, to be exact."

"Then what would she have me do?"

Druggan's fingers moved across his flexscreen. Revan blinked at the sudden buzz of his datapad.

"All rearguard elements are to proceed directly to the Vestebrae drop station," Druggan said. "Easy got into contact at the Corongaet drop, really messed the place up, so we're dropshipping Easy and Fury directly to the urban core transit."

"What about Diacad?" Bresto couldn't keep the edge from his voice. "Who's covering our six?"

Revan opened his mouth, but Druggan was faster. "PR's holding this ground. Fleet owns the void now that forge ship's gone, so naval support is inbound."

Fleet support. That was something, at least. Though his mind kept going back to that forge capsule. The kind of orbital fire needed to crack those things would level half of Diacad, and put more colonists in the line of fire. There had to be a better way. "What about the Division, can't they—"

"Quiet, Sergeant," Revan said.

"The Alexander Lehman's combat ineffective," Druggan said. "Some kind of… technical difficulty. Guess they blew their wad on that forge ship. We'll get whatever tungsten and strike fighters the regular Navy can spare."

"That's enough!" Revan spat. "First Sergeant—"

"You've got your orders, Lieutenant." Druggan didn't even look at him. "The sergeant and I need the room."

Revan's face went red. He stared at Druggan's rank pips like he was counting them, mouth working, then turned and stormed out.

"Sacred Mother take a piss." Druggan ran a hand over his face. "What a grickex nest, all of it."

Bresto waited, studying the hard-edged first sergeant. Druggan had Kull's ear. Could mean freedom, could mean a blaster bolt to the back of the head. Kull seemed practical enough for either.

"You do not disappoint, Bresto." Druggan moved closer, boots squeaking against the sterile floor. "Took quite a break. Several, from what I hear. That man's going to need reconstructive surgery."

Bresto turned to the theater below, searching the faces of the wounded. No sign of Hesper, but the thought of the block captain bleeding on one of those gurneys brought a satisfaction he didn't try to hide.

Druggan moved closer. His gaze had gone cold, raising the hairs on Bresto's neck. Kull could've already leveled an *unofficial* judgment. Maybe Druggan was here to carry it out personally.

"You're good, Sergeant. Damn good. There's no way in twelve hells that proper piece of shit took back this clinic." Druggan jerked his chin toward the door Revan had used. "That was your work. You talk metal."

The rail bit into Bresto's spine. Druggan was close enough to strike.

"You're a weapon," Druggan went on. "And the skipper needs every weapon she can get her hands on. But a weapon that can't be controlled is just a liability. She needs assurance this cridshit stops here. So, which are you? A weapon, or a liability?"

The Twelfth doesn't hold in Her hand liars and cheats. Bresto didn't hesitate. Druggan would know. "If Hesper abandons my children again, I'll kill him."

Someone rapped at the door.

Druggan pulled a knife—black steel stamped with markings too worn to read, its sawtooth spine catching the surgical theater's light. The blade whipped past Bresto's torso, severing the flex cuffs in one clean stroke.

"Bastard deserved every break," Druggan muttered as the knife slipped back into its carrier. The knock repeated. "For fuck's sake, enter!"

The door opened, and Corporal Lessig stepped inside. PFC Olsom lingered in the doorway, her eyes finding Bresto immediately. She knew what he'd done to Hesper. But there was something else in her expression. Something urgent.

Lessig's words were too low to catch, but they snapped Druggan's focus back to Bresto.

"No shit?" Druggan's frown lifted slightly. More hushed words from Lessig. "Where is he?"

Lessig finally looked at Bresto. "Kitchen."

"Move out, son." Druggan's palm pressed against Bresto's back, steering him forward. That careful touch made his skin crawl. First sergeants didn't do careful.

Then they were moving, past the ladderwell, past the command post, straight for the door at the end of the hall. Olsom watched him with her crooked half-grin. She knew something.

"Olsom," he said, "what's going—"

"Ned!" someone shouted. "Ned Bresto! Wait!"

A young man approached at a half-jog, datapad in hand, a small broadcast drone trailing like an eager pet. His clothes were pure urban core, expensive ferroweave cut to emphasize his slim frame, not a hint of debris on its pristine surface. The kid had probably never been this far upslope in his life.

"The fuck are you?" Druggan snapped.

The drone answered instead, a soft blue light pulsing through its polymer shell.

"This is Drew Storm—" the kid's transformation was instant: wealth and privilege morphing into manufactured gravitas "—casting live from Diacad Memorial, where one of Aegia's finest has turned on his own." He thrust himself into Bresto's space as a hologram of Hesper's battered face shimmered between them. "Tell us why you did it, Ned. What made a decorated Marine assault a block captain?"

The drone darted into Bresto's face before he could process what was happening. He swiped at it, but the little bot was too quick.

Lessig grabbed the kid by his expensive sleeve. "Twelfth-damned wannabe net star. Who do you think you are, Tellie Strong?"

"Let go!" Storm's protest barely masked his excitement as the drone swung to capture the performance. "Is this how the Marines silence the truth? More violence against innocent civilians? What are they hiding in Diacad?"

Lessig hauled Storm toward the ladderwell.

The kid's perfect teeth flashed. "There's a *Storm* brewing in Vestebrae!"

Then it was over. A second of absurdity before he had to face whatever was on the other side of that door. Bad news, maybe. Or worse.

"Twelfth Herself," Druggan said. "Ashamed to share atmo with a rich little prick like that."

Bresto couldn't look away from the door. "What's in there, First Sarnt?"

"Not what, son." Druggan barely cracked a grin. "Who. Go on."

The kitchen was just that, more of a break room than a mess hall. A short counter with a worn ice box and industrial sink, metal dulled by years of harsh cleaners. The sanitizer's indicator light blinked amber, out of solution. Empty tubes of field paste littered the counter.

Bresto stepped inside, confusion building as he scanned the space. A small boy sat at the corner table, hands wrapped around a steaming cup.

The door sealed shut with a soft click.

The boy looked up, and every nerve in Bresto's body came alive, like the Holy Mother had reached down and touched him. He knew this boy. In his marrow. That oversized head on those thin shoulders— he'd looked exactly the same as a beta. But those eyes, green as emerald, those were all Lyra.

"Sammy?" The word caught in his throat. "Sammiel?"

"Yes, sir." So quiet he almost missed it.

The uncertainty in those words gutted him, washing away that surge of recognition. Shame and regret flooded in like storm water. He'd abandoned this boy as an infant, left him with nothing but stories and pictures. Now his own son cowered from him like a stranger, almost lost in an alien invasion of their home.

"Do you—" He winced at how loud he sounded in the small space. "Do you know me?"

Sammy lifted his shoulders in a tiny shrug.

"I looked for you. At the hab. Here. Where were you?"

"In the sub-level." Sammy's voice grew steadier. "I heard someone calling, but there were lots of people. Then Larke ma'am found me, and she got the core-per-ral, and they brought me here."

"Larke?" He didn't recognize that name.

He found the hard print in his pocket and drew it out carefully. Each step toward the table felt measured, deliberate. Didn't want to scare the boy. He placed the print on the table's edge and pushed it toward him.

The boy's eyes moved from the folded image to Bresto's face.

"Take it," Bresto said.

Slowly, carefully, Sammy unfolded the print. His face lit up. "Mother! Sissy!" Then the boy went quiet, those Lyra-green eyes finding him again. Really *saw* him. The recognition tore straight through his father's heart.

"Are you my Father?" The question was equal parts hope and doubt.

Bresto drew himself up, arms crossed like armor. He tried to answer—*yes*—but couldn't find his voice. He was losing this position fast. Had to move, do something, anything, before he was completely overwhelmed.

Instinct took over as he retreated to the counter. The relief of turning away was instant, and the shame of that ate at him.

"Are you hungry?" he asked the cabinets, then stole a glance back. The boy's enthusiastic nod made his heart jump.

He dug out a portable cooktop and fry pan from the bottom

drawer. The ration packet from his pocket made a satisfying thump on the counter. He tore into it, emptying its contents beside the cooktop: a compressed block of vat-grown protein, tube of crid fat, salt crystals in foil. The pan settled onto the cooktop with a soft click. He flipped the power switch. Nothing. No indicator light, no heat. No wonder someone had shoved it away.

"Do you know how to cook?" The doubt in Sammy's tone brought a smile to Bresto's face.

"Usually." He turned the cooktop over and studied it, then nodded at the drawer. "Pretty sure I saw a multi-tool in there. Want to check for me?"

"Yes, sir." Finally, a hint of confidence. Sammy climbed down from his chair and approached the counter, sorting through the drawer with tiny, gentle fingers. A moment later, he held up the multi-tool triumphantly.

The maintenance panel popped free with a sharp crack. Bresto's fingers barely fit, but the power leads eventually came free from the tiny cell inside.

"What're you doing?" Sammy asked, reaching for one of the wires.

"Careful. It's cold now. Most aren't." Bresto took a charge pack from his tac vest, studying the terminals before setting it on the counter. Fifty shots should translate to a few minutes of good heat. The roll of repair tape was in his waist pouch where it was supposed to be. Someone had packed right.

"Cold?" Sammy asked.

The second lead threw a spark when Bresto fixed it to the pack.

"Not anymore." He grinned. So did Sammy.

The cooktop's indicator light blinked to life, followed by the low drone of induction heat. Bresto tore into the protein pouch, labeled simply, *RATS*, releasing that familiar tang that smelled slightly of beer and blood.

He passed the silver tube to Sammy. "Think you can open that? Need all of it in the pan."

Sammy gripped the tube hard but couldn't break the seal.

"See that notch?" He guided the boy's tiny finger to the edge. "Right there."

Sammy grunted with effort, squeezing thick green-white chunks of fat into the hot pan. "It's really hard," he said between clenched teeth.

"That's because it's cold."

The first pieces start to melt, turning clear as water. A grin split Sammy's face. "Not anymore!"

Something in Bresto's chest loosened at that smile, the ice of six orbits away thawing like fat in a pan. He'd missed so much—every developmental milestone, every laugh, every struggle. Yet here was his son, still capable of joy despite everything. Despite him.

Sammy's eyes drifted down, his head tilting slightly. "Where's your other boot?"

He glanced down at his sock-covered foot, wiggling his toes against the cold floor. "Lost it fighting some bad guys."

"Mother says gear adrift is a gift," Sammy said with the simple certainty of a child repeating something he'd heard many times.

"Does she now?" The memory of Lyra's exasperated sighs echoed over years of separation. Still, he couldn't help but smile.

The protein slab hit hot fat with a satisfying hiss. That familiar aroma filled the small space, the sweet fat mixing with the meaty tang, the scents wrapping around each other. Crid and rats. Two meals, every day. Three if you were lucky. It got old if you didn't know how to cook them right.

Sammy wrinkled his nose at the cooking brick. "It's always mushy when Mother makes it."

"Too low and slow. Moves it around too much." Bresto turned the heat up, making the pan sputter and pop. He pulled two plates from the cabinet. "Take these. Table needs setting."

"Yes, sir!" Sammy squared the plates to the table's corners like he was performing a drill, tongue caught between his teeth in concentration. Bresto pretended to study the cooking protein, but he couldn't stop stealing glances. Couldn't quite swallow past whatever was trying to close his throat.

Sammy returned to the counter, practically glowing. "Is it ready?"

"Almost."

"When?"

"Here's the trick." With a practiced twist of the pan, he turned the brick over, showing off the golden-brown crust beneath. "Just one flip."

Sammy bounded to his seat, breathing in deep. "That smells good."

Bresto watch the brick simmer until it was ready. When it loosened against the pan, that's how you knew. A lone knife from the drawer made quick work of the brick. He plated each half, letting the rendered fat run across the surface.

Sammy looked at his plate, then around the table. "No forks?"

"Didn't see any in the drawer." He shrugged, then lifted the seared ration to his mouth with his fingers, savoring the juicy crunch. Beat field paste by a light year.

Sammy copied him with a nervous laugh, then dug in earnestly. Bresto stole glances at him between bites. His appetite was strong. He wouldn't be small for long.

The longer they ate, the more distant the war grew, like something happening in another life. Right now, it was just him and his son, sharing a meal like they should have been doing all along.

He thought the words over and over again. *His son.*

A small burp escaped Sammy, followed by an embarrassed giggle. "'scuse me."

"Amateur hour." Bresto let loose a ripping fart.

Sammy leaned back, cackling.

At ease, boys. Lyra's voice was so clear he could almost see her there, shaking her head at their antics. For a heartbeat, he was home again. That tiny hab they'd scraped to afford, all of them together. Him teaching Sammy good and bad habits. Lyra pretending to be mad. And Kaff—

A knock at the door almost startled him. He'd known it was coming, had felt the countdown in his bones even as he tried to stretch these precious minutes with his son. Like trying to hold on to water.

"Sarnt?" Corporal Lessig's voice carried through the metal.

"Come in."

Lessig entered the kitchen, quiet and efficient, somehow managing to fill less space than a man his size should.

"Core-per-ral!" Sammy pointed excitedly.

"Close enough, little man." Lessig moved to the table, nostrils flaring as he caught the smell. "Damn, Sarnt. You make that?"

"What is it, Lessig?"

"Lieutenant says ten minutes. Dropships inbound." His eyes moved from the counter to their plates, then to Bresto. "Hey, you got any more?"

"Never enough to go around, is there?" Bresto looked at Sammy, who covered another giggle. He offered his plate to Lessig.

"That's a fact." Lessig inhaled what was left in one big bite, then wiped the grease on the plate into his mouth. He set the plate down and burped. His hand found the back of an empty chair, fingers drumming an anxious rhythm.

"You get enough, Sammy?" Bresto asked.

"Yes, sir. Father."

That word moved something inside him. Not the title—he hadn't earned that yet—but the way Sammy said it, like he was trying it out for the first time. Like he wanted it to fit. Bresto had missed so much, but maybe it wasn't too late. Maybe they could build something from here, when the work at hand was done.

"Look, I hate this, Sarnt, but we've got to move," Lessig said with a half-grimace. "Lieutenant's already pissed, and I really don't need him any further up my ass than he is." He looked at Sammy with a shrug. "Sorry."

Standing took more effort than it should have. Bresto's hip screamed at him for moving too fast. Sammy remained perfectly still, watching him with a calmness that defied the chaos he'd been through. The boy would be okay, so long as he was somewhere safe. "I'll handle Revan. But I need you to get my son into that shelter. They won't let me near that place, but you—"

"Sure," Lessig said.

"Whatever it takes." He put his hand on Lessig's shoulder. Lessig had to understand. "He's my son."

Lessig gave a firm nod. "Solid copy, Sarnt. I'll get it done."

Without a word, Sammy rose and came to him. His thin arms barely made it halfway around Bresto's waist. "Be careful."

Sammy's simple buzz cut felt rough beneath his palm, but he

couldn't bring himself to return the hug. If he held the boy now, he wouldn't let go. And the war that waited for him was no place for his son.

"Come on, kid." Lessig's voice was surprisingly gentle. "Ever see a dropship land before?"

They were already moving toward the door.

"No," Sammy said, tiny next to the corporal's bulk. His last glance back was calm as it was devastating.

Lessig caught Bresto's eye and nodded as they disappeared into the hall. "You're gonna love it."

CHAPTER
TWENTY-THREE

THICK HARNESS STRAPS pressed Olsom tight against the mesh seat as turbulence rocked the dropship. Something clicked deep in 3-3-3's frame between jolts. Probably something settling from Doc's repair. He said it might do that, but her hand moved to the terminal anyway.

Reactor temps: normal.

Hydraulic pressure: normal.

Primary and auxiliary systems, all green good. She forced her fingers away from the controls, only to find them drifting back seconds later when the exo's frame gave another soft groan.

Hard to believe they'd actually won. The Concordat forge ship turned to atoms, raiders scrambling to retreat. But that didn't make the mountain's weather any less lethal. Wouldn't that be the cosmic joke? Survive the war just to die from turbulence on a crid run to Vestebrae.

Thunder boomed outside like it had been reading her mind the whole time, sending another tremor through the dropship. In front of her, Smokes's rig shifted slightly, its bulk barely masking Vlan where he dozed in the jumpseat beside it. More Marines lined the walls, some checking weapons, others lost in thought. The new whine from her rig gnawed at her confidence. Doc would know if it meant anything, but he'd already told her to relax. Twice.

She brought up the fireteam feed on her terminal. Doc's vitals scrolled past first, with their typical calm alertness: *ba-bump, ba-bump, ba-bump.* Even if she couldn't see him, something about the rhythm calmed her. Mez's feed pushed its way into view, his pulse racing wild and uneven: *bumpity-bumpity, bumpity-bumpity.* An animal in a trap.

She closed the feed, and the strategic display came up on its own. Corongaet's industrial district spread beneath Fury 3's position marker in neat blue and gray lines—a dense network of processing plants and storage facilities that fed Aegia's shipyards. The settlement sprawled upslope from some place labeled *DROP STATION,* its main transit alive with civilian IFF returns. Cyclone and Dragon companies had formed a cordon along the evac route, their positions tagged in friendly blue. Raider contacts retreated before their advance, red icons winking out as they broke contact.

The command net flashed: *"Fury 3, Victory Actual."*

So, Kull was CO now. Guess that made it official.

Lieutenant Revan's voice came next. *"This is 3 Actual, send it."*

"We've cleared all the way to Vestebrae, but we've got a bottleneck."

Olsom's tactical feed centered on another drop station at Corongaet's lowest point. The facility filled the screen; lift mechanisms and loading platforms stretched hundreds of meters across, all of it grafted onto the mountain's granite face like some ancient machine.

"Twelve hundred colonists per hour," Kull said. *"That's all the Vestebrae drop can handle. One choke point, thirty thousand refugees. The Concordat will see the same tactical weakness we do. That facility will be their primary target when they counterattack."*

"Say again, Victory Actual," Revan tac'd back. *"Counterattack? We've destroyed their forge ship. Their forces are in retreat."*

"Negative, Lieutenant. Raiders don't break contact unless they're regrouping. I've got multiple reports of Concordat forces massing west of your position. They might've lost, but they don't know it yet."

The tactical feed panned westward, leaving the drop station behind. Landing zones appeared among a tangle of metalworks, storage silos and processing plants. Nav markers painted clear lines of advance through the industrial terrain.

"Your drop zones are marked," Kull continued. *"Fury 3 will shadow Fury 1 and 2's push through the metallurgy block. You cannot—I say again—*

cannot allow enemy forces to flank that drop station." She paused. *"Twelfth keep you, Fury 3. Victory Actual, out."*

So, the forge ship was gone, but the Concordat weren't finished. Another tremor ran through the dropship's frame. The diagnostic check was pure reflex now: power levels good, coolant pressure—

A dry chuckle crackled through fireteam comms. *"Anyone else feel like celebrating?"* Mez's voice dripped with something darker than usual. *"Squids're running scared. Makes Mez want to party."*

"Stow that shit," Doc snapped. *"Or did you forget we're not done yet, duster?"*

"Better grit than grease, Doc." Mez's clenched teeth made static over comms. *"You no last one day in the trades."*

"Save your street cred for someone who cares. I'm here to serve. What are you here for?"

"Oh, Mez serve," he said. *"Mez serve you up piece by piece. Show you what real combat look like."*

"Shut up, Mez." The command in Olsom's voice came from nowhere, like the drill instructors back at the depot. *"Keep talking and you'll be breaching with your teeth."*

"Whatever you say, boss lady." His tone went silky smooth. *"Mez always like bossy girls."*

Doc's tac lit up. *"Keep fucking talking—"*

She cut the fireteam feed and switched to tightbeam. Part of her melted at Doc wanting to defend her. The rest of her knew better. *"Don't."* She had to force the words. *"I mean it."*

"Bugs, someone's got to put him in his place."

"Yeah. Me."

"Copy that." His casual tone came back. *"I'm at your disposal, PFC Professional. A barrel change, pressure checks, a serious ass kicking, whatever you need."*

"Just the rig, Doc." But she couldn't stop her smile. *"The rest is my problem."*

The dropship lurched hard to port. Something hammered against the hull plates beneath her feet. Red emergency lighting flooded the troop deck. Alert klaxons drowned out the sound of straining mag-locks. Fresh contacts lit up the terminal, all of them hostile.

Olsom felt the familiar sting of adrenaline. Guess Kull was right. The squids didn't know when to quit.

"Incoming fire from the block," the pilot said through the PA. "Looks like raiders pressing the LZ."

"First Squad, straight up the middle soon as the ramp's down," Bresto ordered. *"Second and Third, roll up their flanks. Let's paint these fuckers blue."*

"Ooh-rah!" Fury 3's response roared through her helmet. Metal screamed against metal as the dropship spiraled downward. The deck lurched up to meet them.

Impact. Her magnetics released with a sudden snap, and the ramp crashed open in a storm of laser fire. Red beams sparked off the bulkheads, filling the troop deck with their ozone stink.

"Go, go, go!" Lessig yelled. First Squad was already moving.

She pushed 3-3-3 forward, following Smokes's rig into chaos. Laser fire crisscrossed overhead as more dropships thundered through the smoke. IFF returns crowded her terminal. Too many friendlies, too much movement. A raider warrior appeared in her sights, but two exos from Fury 2 stepped between them before she could squeeze the trigger.

"What's the play?" Doc called out, tracking targets through his scope.

"I—" 3-3-3's terminal offered no answers, just a crowded mess of IFF markers and movement vectors. Their dropship lifted away behind them, its engine heat a reminder they couldn't stay.

"Third Platoon, advance!" Revan charged past them, Bresto at his shoulder. The lieutenant's order faded beneath the rattle of weapons fire, but Bresto's voice carried clear as he pointed to a loading ramp that climbed the receiving facility.

"High ground! Get your metal up there!"

"Moving!"

3-3-3's treads bit into the ramp as she pushed upward. At the top, the receiving dock was all duraplate and concrete marked with faded traffic lines and caution stripes. Heavy cargo sleds waited silently at their moorings; their beds stacked with sheets of hull plating destined for shipyards in orbit. A waist-high retaining wall ran the length of the platform. Perfect cover.

"I see you." Smokes's ident lit up, then Vlan's. *"Want some company?"*

"Definitely." She marked her position and pinged the rest of Third Squad.

3-3-3 settled against the wall as she took in the combat zone. The foundry complex sprawled across the transit, smelters arranged around a central cooling tower that rose like a metal cone toward the storm. First Squad pushed through its outer gates while Second worked through the maze of storage tanks on their left. The distinctive *rrrrrip-crack* of FABs echoed from deeper in the complex where Fury 1 and 2 were already trading fire with raiders beyond the ore processing center.

Doc took position on her right, his rifle on the wall's edge. Mez slouched against the barrier to her left.

"Get on line," she snapped.

"Seems like they got enough guns down there, boss lady," he said with that mocking drawl.

She brought 3-3-3's metal fist over his head. "Now."

He muttered something but raised his rifle. "Hold up." That oily tone was gone, replaced by something sharper. "Mez see something. By the steam thing, that big dick tower."

His scope feed pinged her terminal. Four raiders, wrestling with what looked like another heavy weapon, rounded the base of the cooling tower. Her finger tensed on the FAB's trigger. She should've seen them first.

Something else stepped into view. It didn't move like the squids, too angular and rigid. The bug emerged from behind the raiders like a nightmare, all compound eyes and black chitin.

"Bugs!" she cried, but fireteam comms was still selected. She spat a curse and flipped to platoon. "3-3-3 to 3-1-1, you've got bugs at your ninety. We're engaging. Keep your heads down!"

She marked targets with quick taps, then flipped back to squad comms. "Fire!"

Third Squad engaged, lighting up the wall with muzzle flashes. She kept her bursts controlled, watching 3-3-3's heat levels between trigger pulls. The constant hiss of steam from the open vent assembly made her skin crawl, but temperature readings held steady.

Raiders scattered in all directions, leaving their heavy weapon behind. The bug rose to its full height, plasma staff raised high, but Third Squad's combined fire tore it apart joint by joint, spraying yellow gore across the cooling tower's base.

"Good kill, 3-3-3," Lessig transmitted. *"Now take that ground. We've got you covered."*

"Third Squad, moving. 3-3-1, uh, Squishy, take point."

"Wait." 3-3-1's net ident lit up. *"Why am I Squishy?"*

"You started it, remember? We'll argue about your callsign later. Right now, Lessig wants us on the roof."

"Copy that." Squishy's exo pushed away from the retaining wall toward a ramp that curved down the dock's western edge. She followed, the twins close behind, their metal thundering across the dock's duraplated panels. They crossed the transit at a run, dodging abandoned heavy sleds, then charged up the foundry's access ramp.

The ramp ended at a broad transfer station, a maze of conveyors and hoists disappearing into the foundry's metal skin. Steam billowed overhead where the cooling tower met the storm.

"Now what?" Mez said. "Mez ain't growing wings."

"Those service rails." Squishy's exo pointed where heavy tracks ran up the foundry's exterior. *"MAC-4s can handle that incline."*

"And snap them right off the wall." Toelke crouched beside the rail mounting, running his fingers along the bracket welds. *"That's ore cart gear, not—"*

"Hold up." Doc took a step forward, studying the rails. "See those reinforcement plates? They're building this place to expand. Those tracks are overengineered. We go one at a time, keep the weight centered, it'll work."

No one moved. Even Squishy's exo seemed to lean back.

"Oh, come on." Doc sounded almost hurt. "When have I been wrong?"

"I trust you." Olsom walked 3-3-3 toward the wall. "Watch my back."

"Always. Remember, spread those arms wide. Distribute the weight better."

3-3-3's metal fingers closed on the plates. The complete absence of feedback was terrifying. No way to know if the grip was solid until she committed her full weight. Or if the plates were going to slip from the damn wall.

Her right leg felt like dead weight as she hunted for a step. The tread found the rail, biting into the duraplate with a dull click. Everything in her screamed to stop, but she forced herself to shift 3-3-3's weight. A mechanical groan rippled through the operator cage as she pulled and stepped simultaneously.

The foundry wall creaked, but the rails held. Then she was airborne, suspended half a meter up, left leg swaying beneath her.

"Mez bet a hard cred Wholesome fall." His laugh turned ugly. "Any takers?"

"I'll take that bet, duster," Doc said.

"Just like zero-g training," Smokes began. Vlan added, *"But not so floaty."*

Step. Pull. Each movement sent a trickle of sweat down her back. Scaling an industrial wall in a MAC-4 was *not* standard operating procedure. 3-3-3's servos screamed against the strain, temperature feeds on the terminal creeping steadily toward yellow. Another step brought the roofline within reach. Metal fingers opened, reaching, then her leg slipped.

White-hot panic hit like a power surge. One endless second ticked by. Founders, she was going to fa—

Her tread struck metal. 3-3-2 stood beneath her, its primary arms raised, holding her up.

"Got you," the twins said. Smokes grimaced inside the operator cage, his own rigged arms reaching out for her. Vlan stood beside his brother's exo, arms up, too, like he had willed it to happen.

Metal groaned as 3-3-2 pushed her upward. Her hands found the edge, and she pulled 3-3-3 onto the roof with one final surge of magneto-hydraulics. Hot steam washed over her, venting from a mess of pipes feeding the central tower. The cold storm winds seemed to weigh the steam down like a fog, dragging it in curling ribbons over the foundry complex and into a nearby supply depot.

Red beams cut through the gray dusk. She triggered her FAB in controlled bursts, answering the squids with sweeping fire across the roofline. The raiders dove for cover as her shots sparked against metal, leaving black rings on the bright duraplate.

"Multiple contacts!" She swung her FAB left as a raider emerged from cover. Her burst caught him in the face. "Down one!"

The rest of Third Squad materialized through the industrial haze, the other exos taking position on her flanks. Doc found cover behind an intake manifold, his precise shots dropping another raider.

His tightbeam signal clicked on. *"Can't let you have all the fun, Bugs."*

"Under the circumstances," she laughed, "I need a new callsign."

"Wholesome?"

"Fuck. Right. Off."

The growl started as distant thunder, then grew into the bone-deep roar of retro rockets. A transport punched through the clouds, its bronze hull gleaming wet between flashes of lightning. This wasn't some suicide drop. The ungainly craft held steady on pillars of fire as it hovered above the complex. Metal hatches screamed open along its flanks.

The bugs hit the roof, their black and brown frames absorbing the impact. Three of them, each one tall as an exo, staves already charged and glowing green. Her targeting systems struggled to track as they scuttled between ventilation stacks. For a split second, she was back at the Diacad hab block, watching green fire turn stone and metal and bodies into slag.

"Metal up!" She pulled 3-3-3's fibrosteel-plated arms tight across her operator cage, the world shrinking to her operator terminal. Combat feeds drew ghostly outlines of machinery and enemies through the industrial steam.

The targeting alert came too late. A bug's signature flashed red on her display, its plasma staff already leveled. The shot connected before she could move.

Sickly green light filled her cage as superheated gas splashed over 3-3-3's crossed arms. The sound was pure nightmare, metal cooking and warping as layers of fibrosteel turned molten. Heat was everywhere, worse than the clinic, strangling her inside the cage. Temperature warnings crowded her terminal. 3-3-3 wasn't even moving, and the gauges were climbing. Doc's repairs weren't enough, not for this. She could hear the other FABs chattering but couldn't find a target. The screen flickered, feeds jumping and tearing.

A flash of movement caught her eye—something angular and twisted. Her finger found the trigger. The FAB's rhythm was off again, each burst sounding sluggish and wrong.

Her attacker revealed itself in a surge of green energy, its weapon charging behind an industrial exchanger. She fired burst after burst, but the bolts banged off the thick duraplate between them.

Terror clawed up her throat. No way she would die like her parents, burned alive trapped in a metal box. 3-3-3's railgun cycled up smoothly, still humming with charge from the capsule fight. She put the crosshairs on the growing plasma sphere and pressed the trigger.

Even through the exo's crossed arms, the *whip-fwap!* of the railgun was deafening. The terminal flashed supernova bright. As the feeds returned, she saw storm light through the neat hole the slug had carved through equipment, bug, and rooftop alike.

The metal tang of rail discharge was heavy in the air as more bug signatures appeared in her HUD. Threat warnings buzzed in her ear.

Her thumb hovered over the comms, that wild thing in her already knowing what came next. Sometimes you had to choose between proper procedure and keeping your people alive. Easy choice.

"Rails free," she choked, tasting sweat on her lips. "Burn the motherfuckers."

CHAPTER
TWENTY-FOUR

FUSION WASH from the raider transport turned the foundry complex molten orange, its engines straining to hold position in Aegia's storms. Bresto crouched behind a cargo sled at the complex's eastern approach, flexscreen buzzing with tactical updates. Second Squad pushed through the volatile storage sector, pressing the ship's flank. Third Squad was making their way onto the foundry roof to provide enfilade fire.

He advanced with First Squad beneath the transport's hovering bulk, their exos keeping tight intervals across the granite floor. Black shapes landed in front of them, clacking hard against the stone. Whatever they were, they made the ten-meter drop look effortless.

No matter, he had three squads converging on the target from different vectors, catching the enemy in a coordinated kill zone.

"Getting real coordinated for squids," Lessig said.

"Not squids," Bresto tac'd back. Just bugs. He could handle bugs.

"Contact at my three-three-zero," Second Squad's leader transmitted. *"Two more squids down."*

"Keep pushing."

The transport couldn't hold more than a dozen bugs, not with a full complement of squids. Maybe two dozen if they really packed them in. Sometimes the Holy Mother made it easy. It all came down to momentum now. Keep moving, keep killing, and the bugs couldn't dig in.

The whine of charging plasma cut through the industrial noise. Bresto brought his rifle up, targeting the bug behind the cargo loader. Its staff burned electric-green, already aimed. Two quick bursts grazed its torso. Yellow mist erupted from its carapace as it stumbled back into cover.

"3-1-1, contact right," he transmitted. "Guns up."

"*Affirmative.*" First Squad's FABs opened up together, their sustained fire turning granite walls into gravel sprays. Something dark and organic flew apart in the barrage.

The bugs broke from the attack, but not in retreat. They climbed everything—walls, tanks, equipment—turning the foundry complex into a three-dimensional maze.

A plasma burst caught 3-1-1's shoulder, the metal glowing red dead.

"*Fuck!*" Lessig metaled up as another shot barely missed.

The shooter chittered from its perch on a storage tank. Bresto's bolt caught it right between its massive eyes, dropping it into the yard.

"Push through!" Revan was beside him now, adding his fire. "Keep moving, Fury 3!" Maybe the lieutenant had been paying attention after—

The world exploded in blue-white heat. A cyclone of kinetic and electromagnetic energy tore the air meters above him. Thunder followed a heartbeat later. His flexscreen dissolved into static, comms cutting out in a wash of electromag interference. A railgun slug had gone hypersonic through the foundry complex. Had to be Third Squad. Some asshole just shot their load danger close.

For a moment, nothing moved. Even the bugs seemed stunned by the violence of it. The exos recovered first, their combat systems hardened against that kind of interference. But comms were still down.

"Fury 3-3, acknowledge." He needed to stop them before—

A second shot thundered. Then a third, electromagnetic discharge so intense it made his teeth sing. Metal screamed as one corner of the processing center collapsed, crushing a bug beneath tons of infrastructure. Debris peppered a nearby exo, forcing it back.

"Cease fire, cease fire!" But comms were down. No way anyone could hear him.

A fourth shot went wide, disappearing into the industrial haze. No telling what it would hit.

He sprinted toward the foundry, grabbing the first rail. He had to reach the roof before Third Squad did any more damage. Fury 1 and 2 were on the other side of the facility, and those slugs could go through a lot of granite. Twelfth help them all.

The rails vibrated beneath his hands as he climbed higher into the static-charged air. His comms spat white noise with each pull upward. Almost there.

He crested the roofline. "Third Squad, stand down!"

One bug stood alone amid loops and rings of pulverized metal, its staff wreathed in green plasma. Third Squad's exos moved toward it, all metal, railguns charging.

He waved them down. "Stop!"

Reality crackled around him. The kinetic wake hit dead on; flung him from the wall like he was nothing. Metal and stone debris followed him through the air, past the foundry wall and the nearby storage tanks, beneath the alien transport.

Then pain. Then darkness.

Then Lyra. *On your feet, Marine.*

The first breath tasted like lightning, like rain-soaked stone, and the memory of Lyra vanished. Someone was dragging him across the broken granite, each movement sending fire through his hip. Combat flickered through the smoke and steam—red streaks of charged particles, the sick green glow of plasma fire. The war hadn't waited.

A bug clattered after him, staff raised. He felt his rifle through the pain haze. The world kept sliding left, but he put the bug down anyway. Two bolts center mass, one in its big ugly head.

"Found him!" Rosch called out as he dragged Bresto behind cover.

Another Marine materialized through the steam, autodoc already humming. Her fingers pressed against his pulse.

"Doc Chella here, Sarnt," she said. "I got you."

"What is it?" he managed.

"Nanite trauma protocol for—"

"No." He grabbed her arm. "Just drugs. I can still fight."

Chella's expression hardened. "That's not how this works—"

"I mean it, Marine."

"Aye, Sarnt." She gave the autodoc's dial two angry turns and forced the applicator to his throat.

His nervous system lit up as the drugs took hold. Not the razorblade burn of medical nanites, just the icy focus of morphase and milspec stims. Standard combat cocktail. Doc Mace had tried to explain it once. The memory of her daxed dead eyes jolted him upright.

The fight for the complex had gone to shit. First Squad bled ground with each passing second. Second was trapped, their exos pressed flat against storage tanks as plasma fire kept them pinned. Third Squad's railguns had gone quiet, but too late. The bugs had the momentum now.

His flexscreen rebooted to an empty tactical display. No friendlies, no targets, just blank space where data should be.

"How's comms?"

"Shitty." Rosch maintained steady fire from cover. "Third Squad really fucked us."

"3 Actual, Bresto." Nothing but static hiss. "Revan! We need to shift left, break Second loose, and push through to the facility!"

The channel crackled uselessly. Looked like he'd have to do this face to face. The blank display showed no sign of the lieutenant's marker.

"Where's Revan?"

"He was headed to the foundry when you went flying." Rosch shrugged. "Could be anywhere by now."

The plasma fire slackened, that telltale pause as the bugs recharged their weapons.

"Copy that." Bresto pushed off the debris and ran. Something jagged bit into his socked foot and he stumbled, but momentum carried him forward. The foundry's access ramp stretched ahead, impossibly long. He hit the personnel entrance at full sprint, shoulder first. The door gave with a hollow bang. The wet gurgle of squid-speech—that distinctive mix of clicking teeth and fluid-filled growls—stopped him cold.

Blaster fire echoed through the hallway. He followed the sound, rifle tracking. He found Revan backed against industrial piping, a dead warrior at his feet. Its black armor was scorched where Revan's shots had punched through.

Revan stared at the corpse, transfixed, like he was trying to memorize every detail.

"Sir?" The corridor stretched empty in both directions. When Revan didn't respond, Bresto shook him. "Sir."

Revan's eyes finally focused on him, pupils still blown wide with adrenaline. "I…" His voice sounded distant, hollow. "I was trying to reach the roof."

"It's a good kill, sir, but we got more to do." Bresto guided him toward the exit, one hand locked on his shoulder. "First Squad's falling back and Second Squad's pinned down."

"And Third?" The lieutenant's voice cracked.

The foundry ceiling shook with the impact of heavy metal. Through the windows, Bresto tracked Third Squad's exos as they dropped from the roof to the transit-side dock. The impacts left craters in the granite and duraplate. Their railguns were stowed, thank the Twelfth.

"They're forming up," he said, swallowing the anger at how thoroughly fucked this assault had become.

Third Squad's support element dropped after their machines, Doc Myers last among them. The combat engineer caught his eye through the plexene. Pure terror in that look. So, Olsom had ordered those shots. Danger close with friendlies all over the complex.

Static ripped through his comms. "3-1-1, *falling back!*" Lessig sounded robotic through the interference. "*Need immediate support!*"

Third Squad's exos pivoted toward the storage tanks, their FABs lighting up the industrial haze. The thunder of their guns almost drowned out the bugs' return fire.

"*Hold—*" Sounded like Olsom. "*—ird Squad is en route.*"

"Ready, sir?" Bresto grabbed Revan's shoulder, forcing eye contact. Revan swallowed hard, but his rifle came up steady.

One sharp nod. "Ready."

Bresto took the door latch, motioning Revan into position. "Three, two—" He mouthed *one* and pushed through.

They sprinted for the dock wall together, rifles tracking. First Squad was caught in a brutal melee near the foundry's main access. Bugs weaved between exos, their plasma staves clashing against metal arms. Third Squad pushed closer, their FABs cutting down reinforcements still jumping from the transport.

3-1-2 staggered backwards, its leg armor glowing where a bug's bronze staff had carved through. Bresto's shots caught the thing center mass, but not before plasma turned the Marine inside to vapor and ash.

Fresh data flooded his flexscreen as IFF returns came back online. Wounded markers everywhere, including his own. One dead. Then the storage tanks exploded, and another marker went from blue to dull gray.

Second Squad emerged from the inferno.

"3-2-1—" 3-2-2's transmission broke apart. *"He's down!"*

These bugs knew exactly what they were doing. Pin them against the foundry while more troops kept dropping in. No way out but through, and that door was nearly closed.

"All stations, Fury 3." Revan's calm was razor thin. "Heavy contact at the metallurgical block. Multiple casualties. Request immediate support."

Nothing but white noise answered.

"All Victory stations, this is—"

Two booms from overhead drowned Revan's transmission. Too precise for thunder. More like the crack of strike fighters breaking atmo. Bresto's eyes went skyward, the prayer on his lips automatic: Twelfth save us.

"Fury 3, this is Razor Flight." The pilot's voice cut through static, cool as vacuum. *"Got bored sitting up here watching you have all the fun, over."*

Bresto keyed his comms before Revan could respond. "Kill that transport, Razor Flight."

"Already locked. Stand by."

"All squads, metal up!" he shouted into squad comms. "Angels coming in hot!"

The storm erupted in streaks of red hate. FABs were impressive weapons, but Navy strike fighters carried real pain. Man-sized bolts hammered into the transport's flank, shredding hull plating and internal bracing. Secondary explosions chained through its guts as the ship listed sideways and began to drift.

Cheers broke from Third Platoon's lines as two gunmetal strike fighters screamed overhead, their turrets still pummeling the transport. The shift in momentum was physical; he could taste it in the air. Everyone, even the bugs, stood transfixed as that bronze monstrosity died in flames.

Bresto sprinted to Lessig's position at the center of their line, dropping two bugs that broke cover—their deaths almost an afterthought. "Push forward!" he shouted to each fireteam he passed, pumping a fist toward the processing facility. "Push the fuck forward!"

Fury 3's weapons sparked across the facility as the bugs fell back. Third Squad advanced first, the least they could do after what they'd done. Second Squad was coming on line to the left, finding their momentum.

Lessig looked like hell, his rig's canopy half-melted. Chella worked half-inside the ruined cage, trauma wrap in her hands.

"Sarnt," Lessig slurred through the pain.

Twelfth save him. "Status."

Chella's face said she didn't appreciate the interruption. "He's serviceable, Sarnt."

"Good to go, Sarnt." Lessig grinned through blood and bruises. "Just getting started."

Kid was tough. Learning the hard way but learning all the same.

"Drive them inside," he said, "but do not enter the facility."

"Why not?" Lessig's face twisted in disappointment.

Bresto pointed skyward. "Let those skeegs earn their pay."

His blackened eyes turned bright with understanding. "Aye, Sarnt. First Squad, on me! Push these fuckers back!"

Bresto marked the processing facility on his combat feed. "Razor Flight, this is Fury 3."

"Go for Razor Flight."

"Bugs going to ground in marked building, over."

"Solid copy, Fury 3. Standing by."

Third Platoon advanced steadily across the complex, laying heavy fire into the retreating enemy. Despite Third Squad's clusterfuck with the railguns, they'd survived. They'd won.

The bugs retreated, finding cover in broken machinery as they fell back. The last of them vanished inside the facility, probably thinking the walls would protect them. Bugspeak rattled from the ruined building. Did they pray in moments like this? Did their gods listen?

It didn't matter.

"Weapons free, Razor Flight."

"Guns, guns, guns."

The strike fighters carved lazy circles overhead, their cannons turning dusk to red day. The facility came apart under sustained fire, whole sections collapsing inward beneath anvils of smoke and flame. Soon nothing remained but burning wreckage.

Bresto waved the support Marines forward, directing them to form a firing line with their exos. They'd need security positions set up before anyone could think about repairs and resupply. Assuming the Navy could spare the resources.

Myers tried to slip past with the others. Time for a little OTJ with Third Squad.

"Myers!"

He stopped cold. "Uh, yeah, Sarnt?"

"Cut the shit." Bresto grabbed a hold of his vest, pulling him in. "Find Olsom and get her down here. Right fucking now."

THE FOUNDRY CORRIDORS stank of plasma discharge and victory. Olsom's fingers kept finding the burns on her white-and-grays where 3-3-3's vent assembly had leaked, but she couldn't stop grinning. Raiders dead, bugs atomized, strike fighters screaming overhead to finish what they'd started. Pure apex predator stuff. Smokes and Vlan stood stock still beside her. Squishy kept shifting around like he needed to piss.

Sergeant Bresto banged through the main entrance into the hall, and her throat went tight. The uneven sound of his steps drew her eye downward. One standard-issue boot, the other foot wrapped in a makeshift bandage, bloody at the edges. He carried a replacement boot in one hand. That determined limp, that hard stare… she knew it from the parade deck, right before your drill instructors *corrected* you.

He stopped at a fallen support beam, set down the boot, and lowered himself with a grimace, working his injured foot into it, all the while studying their little formation.

Bresto's stare found her and her hands locked together behind her back, parade rest perfect, fighting the urge to protect her face. She tried to remember how she'd gotten here—Doc's voice calling her down, the long walk from her rig—but it was all combat haze. Now there was just the growing knot in her stomach and the cold certainty that somehow she'd fucked up bad.

He stood up, wincing as he pressed his foot into the boot. "What happened on the roof?"

He was calm. Measured. Somehow that made it worse. Her mouth worked but nothing came out. They'd kicked ass is what happened. They'd won. Hadn't they?

She could feel the twins' synchronized stare. Squishy wouldn't even look at her, eyes on the deck.

Color rose in Bresto's cheeks, his neck flushed fever red. "What the fuck happened up there?" His voice bounced off the walls, hitting her again and again.

"I—" Nothing would come, then everything all at once. "I, er, we, um…" She forced herself to breathe. Facts. Just say what happened. "Third Squad took the roof after the squids went down. Lessig said to, so we did. Then—" The words stuck again. "Then those fucking bugs dropped in."

She could still feel that heat, that certainty she was about to burn alive. She wanted him to know that fact, too. But his eyes were cold. Dead. Don't cry. "Well, they wouldn't come out, so we went rails free—"

Something shifted in her mind, and the victory she'd felt vanished. The electromagnetic interference that had killed their comms, their combat feeds, even their exos' hardened systems blinking in and out. The foundry roof torn to shreds. Random shots tearing through the complex, through who knew what. Or who. Tears welled in her eyes. She refused to blink, but they fell anyway.

Bresto eyed their little formation. "We?"

"I told them—" She had to look away. "I told them to fire."

"Are you authorized to give that order, Private?"

The rank stung like a slap. "No, Sarnt."

"Explain why."

"Because…" She choked back a sob. All of them were looking at her.

"What's the electromag output of an exo-served railgun?" he asked everyone.

She knew it was massive, but—

"Eight-point-four decibel kilovolts per meter at discharge, Sarnt." Squishy's answer was textbook, straight out of the field manuals.

"Eight-point-four," Bresto repeated. "Your metal can take it. Mostly. Our tac gear can't." He struck his flickering flexscreen for emphasis. "Now, what's its muzzle velocity?"

"Three thousand meters per second, Sarnt." She spat out the numbers, desperate to show she wasn't completely useless.

"Three thousand." His voice went flat, eyes holing her like one of those tungsten slugs. "Takes a hell of a lot of coordination to keep from blinding or killing ourselves with weapons like that. Wouldn't you agree, Private?"

She found her boots again. "Yes, Sarnt."

"That's why those calls come from me or Actual. Period. Full stop. Am I clear?"

"Yes, Sarnt!" they barked together, Olsom choking back another sob.

"Dismissed," Bresto said through his teeth.

She started to turn, already mapping her escape.

"Not you, Private."

The gravity of the order held her in place. The twins drifted past, pity and concern on their wrinkled faces. Squishy didn't bother looking back at all. The foundry door banged shut, leaving just the two of them in the empty metal corridor.

Bresto's transformation was instant. From stern NCO to something dangerous. Primal. "You fucked up real bad, boot."

He moved toward her, and she had to fight not to step back. Twelfth, he was big. But his control was scarier than any rage, the way his anger just waited there, patient as a pred.

"Your fuck up almost cost us the facility." His voice never rose. Low. Even. Like a growl. "You handed the bugs an opening when you killed our comms. And you're Twelfth-damned lucky none of those slugs holed any friendlies."

"I'm sorry, I—"

"Marines died out there." He bent down suddenly, reaching for the boot he just put on, lacing it like he was mad at it. "That maybe didn't have to."

Only then did she realize one boot didn't match the other. Worn different. Whoever had that boot first didn't need it anymore. Her blood went cold, each breath coming shorter. Did she—

"Under different circumstances, you'd never see the inside of an exo again. Be pushing papers for the supply jockeys on some ORD somewhere."

He really meant it. She'd… she'd gotten people killed.

"But circumstances ain't exactly normal right now."

Founders, what had she done?

"Thing is, you've been running Third Squad 'til now. That's over."

The tears came again when she finally blinked. She hadn't asked for any of it, being dumped in the admin blocks, joining the CDF—the fucking Marines of all things—or this nightmare of a war. All she'd done was try to survive. One day at a time. And she still messed it up. Stupid girl.

She straightened to attention. "Aye, Sarnt."

He cocked his head to the door. "Out."

She burst through the door and into the Aegian night. Lightning split the sky, blinding in the dark. Anger burned in her chest, at herself, at Bresto, at the whole Twelfth-damned enemy that had brought them here.

Wind whipped through the air, carrying needles of freezing rain that felt nothing like the fat, warm drops back home. She hadn't thought about Vestia since basic training. Truth was, she'd been glad to be out of the admin blocks, even if it meant a one-way trip to the recruit depot. But now all she wanted was to be in that river again, a scrawny beta drifting in the current without a care in the Cradle.

A Marine on overwatch turned as she passed, eyes sliding off her like she was something dirty. She forced herself toward the line of exos where she'd left Third Squad to find more machines had joined them. It looked like every platoon in F Company had their metal out here now, waiting for whatever came next.

A horn blast nearly stopped her heart. She spun into the glare of high beams as a heavy transport lurched to a halt meters away. The

Planetary Reserve symbol shone above its grill and for one stupid second she thought it might be Vestron, but the unit number wasn't right. A dark shape leaned through the driver window.

"Clear the road, you dumb bitch!"

"Kiss my ass!" she shouted into the lights.

The driver leaned on the horn again and she practically fell out of the way. The vehicle's motor screamed as it accelerated past, spraying her with gritty runoff from its massive wheels.

Down in the muck, she wanted to disappear. It was like everyone knew what she'd done. Like Bresto's had transmitted her dressing down through every tac net on this rock. She dragged herself upright, trying to brush the slate-colored mud from her uniform.

"Hey, Vestian!" The sharp, angry voice startled her. Heavy footsteps splashed toward her through puddles. The Marine kept shouting, not slowing as he closed the distance. "Where do you think you're going?"

The stocky figure was just a blur through her rain-streaked rebreather. Prelk. He'd come at her hard on the *Victory*, all questions about the Lost like she owed him something. Then he'd run his mouth over comms before they hit the clinic. Now here he was, wanting to make her pay for what she did. Maybe he had been crying—his eyes said as much—but that didn't matter. She'd seen his kind before. Give them a centimeter and they'd own you.

His palm struck her shoulder, not hard, but enough to coil that wild part of her. "Yohansson's dead because of what you did. Your fuck-up got my friend killed."

"I didn't kill your friend," she tried to say, her voice garbled through the rebreather's wet emitter.

"Get that shit off your face when you talk to me, feral!" Another push, harder this time, but the old slur stung worse than his hands.

Fine. If nobody gave a shit whether she lived or died anymore, what difference did breathing make? The helmet tabs clicked free and she let it dangle from her gear as she pulled the rebreather away. Her first breath came easier than she expected. There was something different here.

The cold rain felt good against her tear-stained cheeks as she breathed in again. She scrubbed her face with her sleeve, sniffed once, and spat. "I didn't kill your friend."

"You killed our fucking comms!" he snarled.

More Marines approached through the rain. The rest of Second Squad. What was left of them.

"He was trying to warn us." Another push, harder this time. Prelk's voice went thick. "We couldn't hear him. I couldn't hear him."

No more beatings today. "Get your hands off me."

"Easy, new blood." Kitrelle appeared at Prelk's shoulder. Something was different about her, harder than before. Maybe it was just the rain, but she looked like she'd been crying. Just the possibility made everything hurt worse somehow. "Come on, Prelk." Her voice went gentle. "Same team."

"Same team?" Prelk's hands locked onto Olsom's shoulder straps, yanking her close enough to smell the metal on his breath. "Fuck that, Kitty. Your little feral here isn't on any team I know."

Olsom's body triggered before her brain. Arms up through his grip, elbows striking down on the nerve clusters beneath his biceps. He let go with a growl, chin dropping—another mistake. Her left connected with his nose as her right was already coming across. It wasn't enough. The punch barely rocked him.

But big boys like him all had the same weakness. Her boot found his groin and Prelk dropped, hands cupped between his legs. Blood dripped from his nose into the mud.

"Twelfth, Olsom!" Kitrelle rammed a shoulder into her, driving her back.

Olsom clenched her fist as the rest of Second Squad stepped forward, but Kitrelle put herself between them. The other Marines actually took a step back.

Kitrelle glanced back, refusing to look her in the eye. "You need to go."

"Kitrelle, I—"

"Now."

Fine. Fuck her perfect cheekbones and fake friendship. Olsom jerked around and walked away, fumbling her helmet back into place.

Kitrelle had picked a side, and it wasn't hers. Just like everyone else when it came down to it.

Nearer the facility, Third Squad's position had shifted. Marines she didn't know worked the ruins while their exos stood back from the line. 3-3-3 looked abandoned, no sign of Doc or Mez anywhere. Maybe Doc had asked for a transfer. No. She bit back a sob. He wouldn't. He couldn't just leave, not without orders. They wouldn't do that in the middle of a war, but that didn't stop her heart from racing anyway.

Rainwater streamed across the terminal as she settled into 3-3-3's cage. Her synthweave uniform shed the worst of it, but she still shivered against the mesh seat. She ran through her checks mechanically. If only to think about anything else. Power nominal. Heat levels steady. At least something was going right. 3-3-3 still had her back. Her throat got tight at the thought, but she swallowed it down hard. No more crying today either.

More checks: FAB barrels still good. Railgun showed fifteen rounds in the drum, though those could stay there and rust for all the trouble they caused her. Leg and arm joints reading mostly green good. Comms clean, no interference.

"Two-zero-one Actual to Reserve Command." The woman's voice crackled through her headset. Strange. Two-zero-one was a Planetary Reserve ident. PR ran their own nets, way outside Marine tactical bands. The transmission repeated, some kind of signal echo. Add it to the list of things Doc needed to check, assuming he was still around to do it.

Mez emerged from the processing facility's ruins, the rock dust on his uniform turning to gray mud in the rain. Something was different about his walk, and he had a weird gleam in his eyes.

"Why so glum, Whole-some?" His fake drawl cut through the rumbling storm.

She wanted to tell him to eat shit and die, maybe help him with the dying part, but she was too damn tired. Too damn sad. Too damn lonely. "Not now, Mez."

"Aw, what's wrong, boss lady?" He lurched closer, propping himself against 3-3-3's FAB mount. His hand slipped on the thick barrels and he had to catch himself. He looked back at the facility with his scarred grin. "New sarnt no like how you run things, eh?"

"What do *you* know?" Olsom muted the PR officer's ghost comms and looked up from the screen. Something in the breacher's leering grin only added to the sour churn in her stomach.

"Mez don't need no academy levels to see. All this piss over nothing." He leaned back on the FAB mount with a smirk. "We won, didn't we?"

"No shit," she blurted, then caught herself. Agreeing with Mez. Now that was scary.

"Mez find something for times like this." He dropped his pack onto the granite and produced a dented brass container that looked like it was beaten into shape with a rock. The liquid inside sloshed as he gave it a shake, then held it out to her.

"What is it?"

"Mez don't know." His leer widened. "Found it back in that hab block. Taste bad. Feels good."

The hinged cork came free with a soft pop. The smell hit her—sour as her churning guts—followed by a boozy bite that made her eyes water. He chuckled at her.

"Well?" His mocking drawl was gone, that oily tone almost friendly. "What you say, boss lady? Drink to victory?"

CHAPTER
TWENTY-SIX

THE PR TRANSPORT rumbled over broken granite, each turn revealing more refugees trudging downslope through sheets of rain from the open canvas back. Bresto shifted against the metal seat while two lieutenants from Easy traded stories across from him.

Inside the transport, a dozen platoon commanders and their senior NCOs occupied seats meant for three times that many, but here they were, racing to another briefing while smoke still rose from the foundry complex. Kull had summoned Victory's command elements to a briefing, him and Revan included. That left Lessig in charge of Third Platoon back at the complex.

"Watch this," one of the officers said, thumbing his flexscreen. Bug speak crackled through the cabin. The bone-cracking chitter sent a shot of adrenaline through Bresto until blaster fire cut it short.

"Ugly fuckers aren't they?" the other asked.

Maybe they hadn't lost Marines like Third Platoon had. Or maybe they didn't care. His exhaustion barely left room for anger anymore. Revan, at least, seemed to share his distaste, watching the endless stream of civilians instead of the recording.

Two seats down, a staff sergeant nodded slightly. Another platoon sergeant who knew better, not that either of them could blame the young officers. Commissions required academy levels, and that meant having the right family name, the right connections. The right cred balance. Youth and ambition to spare. That's how things worked in the Three Colonies, and there wasn't enough to go around.

The transport lurched to a stop, horn blaring.

"Twelfth Herself, what now?" the first officer asked, still cradling his flexscreen.

"Probably all these colonists," the other groaned. "I don't know why they aren't using the rail system."

"We shut it down," Revan said absently, still watching the crowds outside. "So the archenemy can't use our infrastructure against us."

Revan was finally learning. Amazing what a little violence could do to turn all that academy polish into something useful.

A fist banged on the cab wall.

"Why aren't we moving?" one of the NCOs called.

"Something's got the evacuees all jammed up," the driver shouted back. "They're blocking the transit."

Bresto heaved himself up with a groan. Finally, a reason to stretch his legs. He swung over the gate into the downpour. The staff sergeant dropped down beside him. Someone else needing a break from all the brass. They rounded the transport, boots splashing past synthetic tires that reached his shoulders. Shifting his rifle to his chest plate was pure muscle memory, but he knew he wouldn't need it.

The transport's high beams cut white cones through the rain, illuminating a cluster of colonists huddled in the middle of the transit.

"Make a hole," he called, shouldering through the crowd.

"Please, she needs help!" someone cried out.

A woman stood between two colonists, both arms cradling her pregnant belly. She breathed slow and deliberate, the way Lyra had all those years before. His thumb found the nub of his ring finger. This was the wrong place, the wrong time for something so precious. He gestured the supporters away, sliding in to brace her weight.

"How far apart, ma'am?" He knew just enough to know how little he knew.

"Eight minutes," she said, blinking away the rain clinging to her lashes.

Bresto glanced at the staff sergeant. "Still got time. We'll get you to the drop, ma'am, see about getting you priority transit into Vestebrae."

"Twelfth save you, Sergeant."

She knew his rank. Marine wife, maybe, or Navy. But it was the Holy Mother's strength in her young eyes. No sense wondering if her husband was still alive—couldn't fix that. But this, this he could do. If not for his own family, then for hers.

They walked her back to the transport, the cab's brake lights casting harsh red shadows. The officers' laughter died mid-joke. Revan was already at the gate, metal clicking as he dropped it down.

"Ready?" Bresto asked.

The staff sergeant kneeled beside her. "Ready."

"And… lift," Revan ordered, arms hooked under her shoulders. Her weight shifted smoothly between them as they raised her inside.

They climbed in after her, careful not to jostle their precious cargo. The lieutenant with the flexscreen was already requesting medical support meet them at the drop. Revan stayed close, speaking to her with a gentleness that suggested family somewhere. A sister. Maybe kids of his own. The wheels caught traction, and her cold fingers found Bresto's hand.

"You're going to be fine, ma'am." He made it sound as if he knew the future. Hope was the last thing he could offer.

The transport wound its way through Corongaet's industrial maze as ore intake warehouses gave way to the drop station's sprawling superstructure. Control towers and crisscrossing gantries rose through sheets of rain above abandoned mag lev lines, their amber lights painting wet metal and stone.

The vehicle slowed between parked dropships and PR transports lined up along the closed rail system. They lurched to another stop, horn blaring. Her grip tightened. Panic or pain, he wasn't sure, but it passed quickly, and they were moving again. The transport rolled on a moment longer, rocked side to side one last time, then the brakes caught hard. Through the canvas, he caught the bright pulse of emergency lights reflecting off the granite sheen.

Marines and medical personnel crowded around before the wheels stopped turning. The rear gate dropped but everyone held position, letting red and white vested techs take charge. They knew the drill: vital signs, stretcher prep, stabilization protocols. Mother and child were too important for anything less.

Her grip stayed firm until they lifted her away, then the storm and darkness swallowed her. He felt a hitch of regret in his chest. He hadn't even asked her name. Nothing left but to trust the Twelfth and those techs now.

The Marines climbed down after into the storm. The atmo was thick now, almost to fleet levels, brought surging upslope by the storm's low-pressure system. A lightning strike connected with a nearby tower's grounding rod, crackling bright enough to leave veiny arcs in Bresto's vision.

They huddled beneath the control platform where their lift waited, its floor already ankle-deep in storm runoff. Once inside, the lift jerked upwards, revealing as it rose an endless stream of colonists winding their way toward the drop station from the darkness of Corongaet. The bulkheads shuddered as more strike fighters screamed past. Their atmospheric engines left bright fire lines beneath the clouds.

So many people looking for shelter. Kull's thirty-thousand souls to save. He'd seen the reports. Fury and Easy had given the enemy hell. The PR were taking over security. Rumor was they were going to declare Corongaet and Diacad clear of Concordat forces. The fleet had void superiority. Why the hell march these people downslope through the rain and Twelfth-knows-what-else?

"Anyone wonder why we're sending these people to Vestebrae?" he asked.

The silence felt pointed, like he'd missed something obvious.

"Skipper says Command still wants them in shelters," someone said.

"Vestebrae shelters still have room," one of the lieutenants added.

Revan caught his eye and shrugged, clearly just as confused but smart enough not to voice it. Hopefully, Kull would give them the full picture soon enough.

The lift opened onto organized chaos. Drop station personnel crowded every terminal and holoproj in the control center. Their displays all showed the same thing: drop capacity at one hundred percent. Through the observation windows, massive lifts made for industrial sleds and mass transit ferried hundreds of refugees at a time down the steep slope toward Vestebrae's urban core.

Major Kull had commandeered a nearby conference room for her command post. A holoproj sputtered overhead, constantly updating with fresh tactical feeds. Handwritten notes covered the plexene walls, detailing logistic counts and unit casualties. The Victory's entire command structure packed the space shoulder-to-shoulder, waiting to hear what came next.

Bresto followed Revan into the crowded room. Kull fixed him with a stare that dared him to cause another scene. But the tension had drained from her shoulders, and the dark circles under her eyes couldn't hide a hint of satisfaction.

"Marines…" She stopped, drawing in a steadying breath.

"Give her one," Druggan said, parade-rest perfect beside her.

The response rippled through the packed room like a wave—a low, measured "Ooh-rah, Skipper"—each voice layering onto the others until the sound filled the cramped space.

Not the wild battle cry of Marines charging into combat, but something deeper. More formal. The kind of acknowledgment reserved for moments when the chain of command shifted under fire.

An emergency drop. Losing their exped and commanding officer. All of that and she still managed to keep the archenemy at bay. Whatever Bresto thought of her, Kull had earned this. "'rah, Skipper."

The sound held for three heartbeats, then faded to silence. Kull's throat worked once before she found her voice again.

"Not me." She stabbed a finger on the tabletop. Her voice found its edge. "Aegia stands because of your sacrifices today. This victory is yours."

Tactical feeds bloomed above the holoproj in sharp blue lines, showing Aegia's orbital approaches. Six blue markers appeared— Aegia Prime's orbitals—followed by swarms of red contacts as the battle replayed in fast time.

"At twenty-nine-thirty local, Navy and Division assets executed a highly coordinated alpha strike on the Concordat forge ship." The fat red marker winked out, and Kull's mouth twitched upward. "As of fifteen minutes ago, all remaining raider ships have fled the system. We've got six destroyers and pickets maintaining void superiority while what's left of the garrison fleet pursues. The CDNS Umbra is on station for orbital fire support."

The room erupted in whoops and shoulder slaps before she finished speaking. Even Druggan's granite face cracked at the edges.

She gave them their moment before continuing. "The patrol fleets are coming home. All of them. Marine, Navy, Division. I told Command that fashionably late doesn't work on mountain time."

That brought genuine laughter to the packed space.

The holoproj shifted under her hand, showing lists of inbound ships. Marine expeds and Navy destroyers filled the display, followed by Division-converted drone carriers. The kind of fleet that could start wars. And end them.

"In twenty hours, the CDF is going to turn the Three Colonies into a fortress." She switched views again. The familiar trail of blue leading from Corongaet to the urban core hovered above the table. "Command isn't taking chances, and neither are we. We don't know if this is the end, or just the start. Until we're relieved, our mission is to get every one of those civilians underground. Is that clear?"

No, this didn't make any sense. He'd watched those Concordat ships plunging into Vestebrae from the clinic rooftop. How could it possibly be safer there than here?

"What's the enemy disposition on the ground, ma'am?" he asked.

Kull nodded, almost friendly. "PR Command reports sporadic contact with raiders at the settlement edges." Red dots appeared clustered around Vestebrae's outer ring, while the central corridor stayed pure blue. "They've concentrated most of their reserve forces in the urban core, not like upslope. Should be smooth sailing from here."

"Fucking PR," one of the officers muttered.

Kull's stare went pure tungsten. "Something to add, Lieutenant?"

"No, ma'am."

"What about the Lost?" Bresto asked. The room went dead quiet. No one breathed. "Any reports matching that forge capsule I showed you?"

A low murmur filled the silence.

"No, Sergeant. Nothing from PR matches your telemetry. Captain Guinn." A sharp-looking officer turned at her call. "Your Marines are watching the Corongaet rise. Seen anything unusual?"

"No, ma'am." Pure granite in his voice, and he at least sounded like he had a brain between his ears. "Azure's been downslope in Vestebrae two hours. Some squids, those bug things—but no, no Lost."

"Looks like you found our only capsule, Sergeant," Kull said. "But we've got plenty of tungsten in orbit if more show up."

"We Twelfth-damned better. Ma'am."

Her stare lasted just long enough to make her point before she swiped away the display. "Company and platoon commanders, on me. The rest of you," she fixed Bresto with another warning look, "there's hot chow and tea one deck down. Get warm. Long night ahead."

Revan leaned in close. "I suggest you take her up on that, Sergeant."

"Sir."

Bresto pushed through the door into the busy control center. Station personnel moved between terminals, coordinating drop activities and tracking evacuation numbers. Civilian movements flashed on the large screens facing the drop.

He slowed near a window, straining to see the crowd through the storm. Kaff could be down there somewhere in that flood of humanity. Maybe that wouldn't be so bad, if Kull was right. But he couldn't shake the feeling that she wasn't. None of them were taking the Lost threat seriously. If they really were winning, now was the time to press their initiative.

He passed the lift, finding stairs to the observation deck. There, a handful of personnel watched from a hundred meters up as great slabs of duraplate and fibrosteel ferried refugees into the shining lights of Vestebrae below. The railing felt slick as he leaned over the edge and took in the view.

Far below him, the crowds were visible in the orange glow. Great masses of people moving steadily downslope. Moving to safety. Holy

Mother, keep them all. Keep them close to your heart. Kaff and Lyra, too. Please. Two fingers moved to his chest. Tap, tap.

A flash of ferroweave and drone light hit his senses. "Ned Bresto!"

He knew that voice. Storm. The very last person he wanted to see right now.

The broadcast drone lamp flicked on and bobbed into view. "Ready to comment on accusations of Marine misconduct against upslope colonists?"

"Turn that fucking thing off."

Storm pressed closer, drone right there with him. "Why'd you do it, Sergeant?"

Bad move. Bresto's hands shot out, one snatching the drone from the air, the other fisted in Storm's fancy collar. The machine whined in protest, tiny aux grav emitters fighting his grip. The urban core runt was practically weightless. One quick jerk and gravity would take care of his pest problem.

"Let me go!" Storm squirmed. "Do you—*nnng*—know what that drone costs?"

Bresto studied the machine's housing. Definitely high-end. Something you'd never find outside the core. "What, a thousand creds?"

"Try five thousand," Storm said, a nervous pride in his eyes.

"Five thousand?" He laughed. That was more than him and Lyra earned in a single orbit. He gave the kid a hard shake. "There's not enough shelter space outside the core, and you think I'm the problem?"

"I don't beat people bloody."

"True." Bresto released him. "Your kind just kill more slowly."

"My family pays their tithes. Every quarter." Storm straightened the front of his expensive clothes. "Vestebrae's generosity built those shelters."

One. Two. Deep breath. No sense in proving the kid's point. "That why you're out here? Your generous spirit?"

"The people need to know what's happening." Storm's perfect smile returned. "They deserve the truth."

A bitter smile touched Bresto's lips. Storm wasn't wrong, just aiming at the wrong target. The people needed truth all right. About failed shelters, about block captains who ran. About the Lost, and the end they'd bring if someone didn't stop them.

Well, shit. If Kull wouldn't listen, maybe Vestebrae would. Maybe fear and truth could do what the chain of command couldn't. The Concordat had already shown what happened when the old warnings were ignored.

Kull had her protocols. He had his own. And right now, a fancy civvie with a broadcast drone might be more useful than an entire expeditionary force following the wrong orders.

"How many views you get, average?"

"Few thousand," Storm admitted, his swagger fading.

"Yeah, you're no Tellie Strong." He smirked. "All core types like you?"

"Similar demo."

This kid wasn't talking about plasmex. "Demo?"

"Demographics."

His thumb found his ring finger again. The combat footage would terrify Storm's wealthy viewers. Maybe enough to force Command's hand. Get the right people screaming and Kull would have to respond. Like railguns danger close. Risky, but sometimes necessary.

It wasn't so different from what Olsom had done. Seeing a threat and using the biggest weapon available. He hadn't been wrong to discipline her, but he understood her impulse a little better now.

He straightened, decision made. Felt the weight of it settle across his shoulders like armor plate. Marines adapted. Overcame. Found ways to complete the mission, no matter what. So would he. He couldn't afford to lose this fight.

Still, no way Kull would be so understanding.

"Why?" Storm asked.

"Got a different story for you."

Hunger flashed in the kid's eyes.

"Not your usual rage bait. Something that actually matters."

"Depends on the source." Storm shrugged, trying not to care. He wasn't fooling anyone.

"You're looking at him."

He cocked an eyebrow. "Why should I trust you?"

Bresto snatched his collar again and gave him a firm shake. "Because I'm out here trying to save these people, you little shit. Now, are you Aegian enough to make a difference, or just another core parasite?"

"Okay, okay!" He fumbled a datapad from his fancy jumpsuit. "What've you got?"

A few flicks from his flexscreen and Storm's pad chirped. The blood left Storm's face as combat sounds filled the air between them—the scream of the Lost, the snap of blasters, before the railgun barrage burned the signal away.

Shot, over. No going back now.

His pulse hammered in his temples as the reality of what he'd just done crashed over him. Breach of operational security. Sharing classified combat footage with a civilian. Career suicide at minimum—firing squad at worst—with a few taps on a flexscreen.

But none of that mattered if they were all dead tomorrow. If the Lost were out there, no amount of following protocol would save them. He'd risk his own neck to save others. The mountain. The colony. His family. Wasn't the first time. Wouldn't be the last. That's what made a Marine, when you stripped away all the polish and parade-ground cridshit.

Kull would understand that, even as she tried to destroy him for it. In her position, he might have done the same. Command meant seeing the bigger picture, making the hard calls. But down here in the mud with everyone else, he had to act on what he knew. Now he just needed Storm to understand what they were dealing with.

"What…" Storm swallowed hard. "What was that?"

"The Lost."

Storm's mouth worked silently. No time for the kid to revel in how much shit they were all in.

"Yes, they're real. Yes, they're worse than the bedtime stories your wet nurse tells you. You going to help or not?"

Storm ran the footage again. "Tell me what you need."

He shrugged. This battlefield was different, but he needed to win it like anything else. "Just get the word out. Maximum effect. Whatever it is you do, do it like it fucking matters."

"Got it, chief. Can I have the drone back?"

Bresto let go. The machine zipped to Storm while he worked the datapad with both thumbs.

After a minute, Storm chuckled grimly. "Oh, this is too good."

"Fine. Good."

"Right!" Storm leaned forward, hands going to Bresto's gear.

Bresto swatted him away. "The hell are you doing?"

"Wardrobe's not ideal, but we can work with it. You look the part."

"What part?"

The drone buzzed around, the lamp burning his eyes. "Time to tell your story, chief."

"What? No. Not happening." Bresto reached for the machine, but it darted away.

"You wanted maximum effect." Storm's grin had an edge now. "This is how we get it. You've seen these things. Fought them. The core can't ignore that, no matter how badly they want to keep pretending."

"Fine," Bresto said. "One shot. Make it count."

"Always do." Storm's public persona clicked into place. "This is Drew Storm with breaking news from the Vestebrae drop. With me is Sergeant Ned Bresto of the Victory Expeditionary Force, and what he's about to share will change everything you think you know about this invasion."

The drone's recording indicator flashed red dead. All or nothing now. Fire for effect.

TWENTY-SEVEN

RAIN HAMMERED against the drop platform's hydraulics as it shuddered to a stop. Kaffy gripped the slick railing, staring at the storm through emergency lamps that painted the nearby buildings in flashes of yellow and red. The platform they rode on felt impossibly huge, bigger than her hab block, but that didn't stop people from cramming together. Mostly upslope families like them, pressed shoulder to shoulder, pretending the water on their faces was just rain.

They'd been traveling for hours. First the terrifying descent from Diacad, then the chaotic transfer through Corongaet's packed drop station where emergency crews herded them onto the next platform down. Each stop brought more refugees, more fear, more questions no one could answer.

But no more monsters. Maybe Duray was right. Maybe the Concordat *were* just stories now.

"This is *definitely* bigger than the Diacad drop!" Duray said for the hundredth time. "There has to be one—no, two thousand people on here with us."

She really didn't care how many people were on the platform, so long as it got them downslope safely.

She was still angry. They'd seen Marines two different times today, but that stupid painter or the emergency workers kept dragging them away. The lieutenant promised there'd be room in the Vestebrae shelters, that they were almost done running, but all she could think about was how many times they'd walked away from help.

The platform's horn made her jump, and suddenly everyone was moving. Panic squeezed her chest as bodies pressed in around her. She couldn't see the lieutenant or Madam Ulwin. They'd been there, just a second ago.

Madam Ulwin's racking cough broke above the noise. Thank the Twelfth. She appeared through gaps in the crowd, the lieutenant half-carrying her forward. Kaffy almost smiled at how people made way for his uniform until she realized they were actually shrinking from the painter drifting along behind them. None of them wanted close to that. She couldn't blame them. Not after it had taken her from Father.

"Duray, take Kaffereine's hand!" The lieutenant's voice carried over the crowd. "We have to stay together!"

"Come on." Duray groped for her fingers through the rain.

She slapped his hand away. "I'm not a beta." She'd had enough of people dragging her places today.

The crowd shuffled forward, pressed tight against the lift's safety rails. Emergency crews in bright vests waved them on, their hand lights cutting through the rain.

"Careful now, mind the tracks!" a voice called from ahead. Two vested men guided people over the gap near their corner of the massive lift. "Easy does it, big step down."

One reached for her hand but she ignored him, sliding down on her belly until her boots found the transit floor. Duray jumped down after her, arms wheeling as he stumbled forward. She laughed.

His face went all pouty. "Made it faster than you."

The mass of people flowed outward, filling the transit's wide lanes. Vestebrae proper opened up before them, nothing like she remembered from when she was little. The towers seemed to float on light, their plexene walls glowing through the rain. Flatscreens bigger than her bedroom hung just above the ground floor shops and offices, detailing their evacuation route and shelter closings in brilliant color. Their windows were full of things she'd only seen in net feeds. Nothing like the gray boxes of Diacad Cliffs.

Barriers had sprung up along the transit, sharp edges of plastec and metal that looked out of place against the bright lights. PR troops seemed to be everywhere, their uniforms cleaner than the refugees shuffling past. One of those huge Marine machines—exos, that was it —stood guard near an intersection, its guns pointed to the clouds. Maybe Mother and Father were here somewhere.

"Young lady." The reservist noticed her sizing him up and gave a fancy nod. But she knew upslope when she saw it. Those callused hands, that thick Corongaet accent.

"My mother's in the PR," she said. "Have you seen her?"

"What's her name?"

"Lieutenant Lyra Bresto."

"Hmm." He shook his head. "Don't know her. My lieutenant's a real hard case. Not sweet like your mother I bet."

"Not that sweet," she said, choking on a laugh that wanted to be a sob. She'd take all the lashes Hesper could give just to have her there now, showing everyone exactly how sweet she wasn't.

Concern flickered across the reservist's face. "Are you alone, miss?"

"Uh…" She spun around and saw only strangers' faces pressing past. No lieutenant, no Madam Ulwin. Her stomach dropped. "I mean, no, I'm with—"

"Are you sure?" He took a step closer. "Maybe you should come with me. It'll be safer if—"

"No, thank you!" She forced a smile and backed away. "I see them now. Thanks!"

She didn't see anyone.

"Duray?"

Nothing.

"Duray!"

The cafe door hung partially open, a SHELTER NOTICE sign slapped lopsided against the plexene. Duray was inside, behind the counter, like this was some game of sneak thief. Just perfect. While everyone else was running for their lives, he was hunting for treats. Stupid boy.

She stormed inside and the smell hit her. Warm crid fat and something sweet she couldn't name. Neat rows of little puffs lay beneath perfect crystal glass, all flaky and colorful, too perfect to be food. It belonged here, all dreamy among all the plexene and bright light. Her stomach growled, loud in the empty space. Duray turned at the sound, arm already through the display case's sliding door.

"What're you doing?" she hissed.

"Getting dinner." Duray barely looked up, fingers already wrapped around one of the flakey orbs. "Or breakfast. Whatever. Come on, there's more. Not like these core dummies are gonna miss them."

She hurried behind the display, fingers wrapped around the little statue in her pocket like it might save her from temptation. The smell was overwhelming now. Sweet and rich and dreamy.

"Ever had one of these before?"

"Nuh uh."

He took a slow bite, savoring it. Whatever self-control he had vanished, and he shoved the rest in his mouth, beaming through stuffed cheeks.

"It's so good!" He snatched up several more, pressing one into her palm. "Try it!"

It felt weird in her hands, light and sticky and not at all real. She knew she shouldn't. Father would be so angry. But her mouth was watering, and this wasn't just food, it was like something from a story. Perfect and delicate and probably worth a whole month's lots.

The first melty bite changed everything. Sweet and soft and gone too fast. She knocked Duray sideways with her shoulder, diving into the display case with both hands.

"Hey!" he protested through a mouthful. But she was already stuffing another in her mouth, fingers grasping for more.

"Stop!" Duray whined. "You're taking all of them!"

"You've had plenty." She glared at him, cheeks full. He lunged for her armful of treats. She twisted away, but her boots caught the display case with a loud bang. The treats scattered across the polished granite floor. "No!"

Duray dove after them, crawling right over her.

A scratchy voice cut through their scramble. "What in the name of the Holy Mother?"

A round-faced woman appeared in the backroom doorway; her

smock dusted with pale yellow powder. She let out a gasp. "What is
—? What are you—? Why, you thieving little upslope snakes!"

She darted back into the kitchen and returned with a long metal
push broom, brandishing it at them like a weapon. "Do you have any
idea what you've done?" Her eyes kept moving to the scattered
pastries, face twisted in pain. "They're made of kiff root flour. From
Vestia! *Vestia!*" She jabbed the bristled edge toward Kaffy's face. "Each
kilo costs more than your parents see in a whole orbit!"

Kaffy pushed Duray off and stumbled to her feet. Her face burned
at the site of their muddy bootprints all over the pristine floor. They'd
ruined everything. "Please. We were just so hungry. I can put them
back—"

"You've done quite enough!" The woman forced them toward the
door with more quick jabs. "Out! Out!"

The door wouldn't open fast enough. Kaffy yanked the handle
again, then nearly fell backward as the reservist appeared on the other
side.

"Found you," he began, his eyes moving to the old woman.

"You there!" The woman's shriek made her jump. "These vermin
ruined six hundred creds of cloudspun! A priceless special order!" She
waved the broom at their bootprints. "They've destroyed Mr. Torvahl's
shop!"

"Ma'am, please. The evacuation—"

"What?" She shook her head violently. "Leave my shop to you
upslope savages? I won't!"

"All right, enough." He gestured for Kaffy and Duray to follow.
"Let's go, you two."

"Please don't tell our block captain!" Duray's voice cracked. "I'll
get the lash for sure!"

"Block captain?" The reservist laughed, but it sounded forced.
"Kid, I've got bigger problems than some rich drone's fancy cakes."

That made Kaffy smile. Core drones and their precious Vestian
flour. Maybe this reservist wasn't so bad.

"But you can't be wandering around alone. Where's your
family?"

"We're not alone." Kaffy scanned the crowd again. "Our neighbor

Madam Ulwin is here somewhere. And the lieutenant." But she couldn't spot either of them.

"A lieutenant? You mean your mother?"

"No, I—I don't know his name."

"Let's see if we can make room in this block's shelter." The reservist unclipped his comms unit. "One-Nine-Two Actual, it's Cremmel. One-Nine-Two Actual, do you copy?"

Static filled the air between them until the radio crackled back.

"Private Cremmel, this is PR Command." The voice came through slow and noisy, like talking through broken glass. *"Proceed immediately to shelter designated Sapphire-6 and stand down. Acknowledge."*

"Stand down?" Cremmel frowned at his radio. "What about Ruby-4, Command? Is there any room there?"

The response came instantly, mechanical and cold. *"Proceed directly to shelter designated Sapphire-6 and stand down."*

"Well. Guess that's where they want—"

Thunder cracked overhead, except it wasn't thunder. The screens lining the transit corridor flickered, then filled with a young man's face, the rain beating down on his expensive clothes. Some net streamer she'd never heard of.

"This is Drew Storm with breaking news from the Vestebrae drop." His perfect teeth flashed. "With me is Sergeant Ned Bresto of the Victory Expeditionary—"

Father! Her hand went into her pocket on instinct, found the little figurine of the Holy Mother. Gripped it hard.

"—will change everything you think you know about this invasion."

The screen changed again, and there he was. Father, soaked to the bone in his military uniform. Tired, but alive. She moved toward the screen like he might reach down and pull her through. Everything else disappeared: the painter, the reservist, even Duray. Nothing existed except that screen and Father's image floating above the transit.

He looked so big up there, big as the Twelfth Herself. The camera circled his head, and he watched it carefully, like it might bite. When he cleared his throat, the sound echoed across the transit, louder than the storm.

"Is it on?" Father squinted at something off-screen. "Is it ready?"

"Yes, get on with it!" the streamer hissed from behind the camera.

Father nodded once and squared his shoulders. "Right. This is a warning to all citizens of Aegia. Tonight's attack is more than just a squid raid. The Concordat have returned."

The word seemed to echo through the transit like thunder. Everyone stopped moving at once, faces turned upward. Her chest felt tight, like old nightmares were clawing their way out. The painter was right. The old stories weren't just stories anymore. They were here.

Father said so.

His face twisted. "And the Lost are with them."

A gasp rippled through the crowd. Something changed in the air when he said it, like lightning about to strike.

Cold fingers found her shoulders. "Lady Kaffereine." The painter's voice shook. "We must go—"

"Get off!" She knocked its hand away. It wouldn't take her from Father again. She wouldn't let it.

But the crowd's fear was spreading like fire. Someone screamed "Twelfth save us!" while others backed away.

"Is it one of them?" A woman pointed at the painter. "One of the Lost?"

Everyone was staring now, and the painter's black eyes seemed bigger than she'd ever seen them. The reservist's hands found his gun, lifting it slowly. Then the lieutenant appeared from nowhere, reaching for the barrel. They were shouting at each other; their voices lost in the noise as the crowd pressed back.

She turned back to the screen. To Father. His voice cut through everything else: "The Concordat brought their forge technology to the surface. They're..." His jaw worked. He looked so nervous. "They want to make more of them. More Lost."

She stared at the painter, its too-long limbs, its lidless eyes. Had it been someone's daughter once? Someone's father? Was it afraid when they changed it? Had it really forgotten? The questions made her feel sick, but they kept coming.

The image cut away from Father. "No, wait!"

The new footage stole her voice. A strange machine appeared

through smoke and flame, its white metal skin hard to look at. Something spilled out of it. It looked… like a colonist, then it screamed, and she knew it wasn't. Not anymore.

More terror erupted through the crowd.

"Victory has secured the upslope settlements." Father was back, a hint of pride in his voice even as people pushed and shoved around her. "Diacad and Corongaet are safe. I know Reserve Command wants everyone still seeking shelter to move downslope, but…" The pain returned to his face. "I believe more of these things are out there. If you see them, do not approach. Report them to the nearest CDF forces. We can stop them. We will stop them."

The little figurine felt warm in her palm. Every word he said rang true inside her. She wanted so badly to be there with him, fighting these monsters. To be a proper Aegian, just like him. Whenever he spoke, she wasn't afraid anymore.

He looked at someone off screen. "That's it." A tired shrug. "That's all I've got."

"Whole colony's watching, chief." The well-dressed man again. "Want to say anything to your family?"

Father took a deep breath, and she found herself doing the same. The panicked crowd seemed to fade away until it was just her and him.

"Lyra. Kaff," he began, "don't worry. Sammy's safe upslope."

Suddenly her heart felt too big for her chest. Sammy. Safe. That beautiful dummy. Then something changed in Father's stance. Shouting erupted off-screen.

"I'll find you," he said quickly. "No matter what, I'll find you."

The camera jerked sideways. More Marines were there, weapons raised. *At Father.* Her head went all cloudy, hands forming into fists. The Marines grabbed the young man as he struggled. "What are you doing? People need to know the truth!"

Another Marine stepped into frame, an officer, her face cold as frosted stone. The gun looked tiny in her hand as she aimed it. The screen went black.

"Father?" Her voice cracked. "FATHER!"

Something changed in the crowd. People weren't moving forward anymore. They were flowing back toward the drop station's lifts. Emergency crews waved their light batons, trying to hold them back as empty platforms began rising upslope.

"The lifts are not safe!" someone shouted over a bullhorn. "Proceed to your designated shelter!"

"Take us back!" The cry spread through the crowd. "We won't go further!"

But their desperate cries faded. Her eyes stayed locked on the dark screen. Twelfth, bring Father back. Show her he was okay. So he could tell her what to do.

Light erupted down the transit corridor. A sharp crack shook the drop station's massive spines and made the tower windows rattle in their frames. Like the mountain itself was breaking.

The crowd broke apart. A shoulder caught her hard, spinning her. Another impact knocked her legs out from under her. She hit the ground, palms stinging against wet stone while feet thundered around her.

"Help!" Her voice was lost in the chaos.

Bodies pressed closer, boots splashing centimeters from her face. She needed to move, to get up, but there were too many feet, too many legs, all of them getting closer.

Something cold gripped her wrist, pulling her up and forward through the press of bodies. She tried to look back, to see who—or what—had her, but the crowd was a blur of motion and fear. Another flash lit the transit white-hot, and suddenly she was moving too fast to see anything at all.

CHAPTER
TWENTY-EIGHT

THUNDER RATTLED what was left of the processing facility's walls, but Olsom barely noticed. The hardwine had turned everything soft and distant. Even the dead bug sprawled a few meters away, stinking guts splattered against the stone. Rain hammered the broken granite and duraplate around their hiding spot, but Mez had picked a good one; this corner stayed mostly dry, mostly hidden. Outside, PR transports rolled past, their lights blurring together in the rain, going somewhere important while she did…what exactly?

Mez passed the metal jug back around. She took another pull, letting the burn chase away the chill of failure.

She started to pass the bottle back, then yanked it away with a smirk. Mez watched with laser focus. Even half-cocked, he looked all coiled spring. She took another glug, the booze having lost its sour bite several glugs ago.

His voice was quieter than usual, missing that mocking edge. "Not so wholesome after all."

"Nah." She snorted, then giggled at the strange sound.

When she finally offered the bottle for real, he grabbed it and drank deep. For such a rail-thin bastard, he could really put it away.

His finger jabbed toward movement beyond the facility's broken wall. Marines huddled together, heads bowed, and fists pressed to hearts. More prayer circles. More proper Aegians.

"Mez think they not so proper no more." He laughed, but his eyes held that dead-flat look she'd seen plenty in the mirror. Some hurt that ran too deep, even for booze to touch. "About time they feel the raiders' sting."

"Fuckin' Holy Mother," she slurred. "Did you see 'em? When that statue came down? Lessig and the other mountain folk just balk like it's game fucking over."

"Mez saw. Mez saw."

"Least Bresto acts like he wants to win this war and go home."

Mez offered the bottle back, but the trick was plain on his face. She snatched it before he could change his mind. Nice try, asshole.

"Ah ah ah." Her grin felt sloppy.

He leaned his head back, helmet resting on the rock wall. "So, Wholesome like the sarnt again?"

She took another drink. "Fuuuuck no. Bastard probably slid out of his momma's box at perfect parade rest. No idea what life is like for—" The old hurt rose up and she shoved it back down. Not now. She wouldn't show her belly like that here. Not to Mez.

Something electric filled their dry little space, and the buzz made it hard to tell how much was coming from him and how much from her. Not like Doc. Nothing like Doc. A different kind of tension. Dangerous.

"Raiders' sting. What'd you mean by that?"

He stretched his hand into the rain, watching drops hammer his palm. "What you mean, what Mez mean? Everybody know the story. We think we aaaall alone in the Cradle, then one day raiders come to Respitia and they take and take and take." His voice dropped lower. "Take from everyone."

"Take from you?"

The question hit deep, and that look sent electricity down her spine. The wild thing inside her reared back.

He laughed, batting at the air like swatting bugs. "Mez just a baby alpha, don't remember none of that."

But she'd felt it, that surge of danger when she'd stepped on something raw. She offered the bottle straight up. No tricks. "Back in the squad bay. Why come at me with the knife?"

He took the bottle and gave an exaggerated shrug. "You come at Mez with your fists. Damn quick, too." A hint of respect crept into his voice. "Wholesome start it. Mez finish it."

"What?" The wild thing in her was talking now, all teeth and claws. "I fucking started it? You ran that mouth like you had me figured. Like you knew one fucking thing about—"

"Mez just teasing, girl."

The bottle was halfway to his lips when thunder split the sky. He flinched hard, shoulder crashing into hers, the boozy drink going everywhere. Their closeness made her want to shrink back, to make space, but it all happened slow and sticky through the sour haze.

"Damn, sorry." He got real still and wouldn't look at her. Nothing like the cocky bastard who'd tried to gut her. Maybe he wasn't quite the mon—

"Bugs?" Doc's voice bounced between broken walls, cutting through engine whine and drumming rain.

Shit. Shit shit *shit*. Anyone but Doc. Not now, not like this. She stuffed the bottle into Mez's lap and scrambled to get up, hands sliding on wet stone, the ground tilting more than it should.

Doc appeared in the doorway just as she found her balance, his automatic smile fading as he took in the scene. "There you… are?"

"Hey." She ran fingers through her soaked hair and fumbled her helmet back on, unable to look him in the eye. "Hey."

"Hey, back. I was gonna…" He gestured at the rebreather dangling from her belt. "Rain brings the good air upslope. Looks like you worked that out."

She forced a grin and took careful steps toward him. The tension in the air went sideways with Doc there. A different kind of danger. Made her all clumsy.

Fuck it, play the part. "Status?"

"Huh?"

"What's our, um, status?"

"Status?" He leaned in close, sniffed, then choked back a laugh. "Twelfth Herself, Bugs, are you pissed?"

Her face went plasma hot before she realized he meant drunk, and then everything just kept getting hotter because TWELFTH HERSELF what kind of idiot gets plastered in a combat zone with someone who tried to gut her like a crid just because Bresto hurt her feelings about the railgun thing which okay maybe she deserved but that didn't mean she had to prove him right by drinking with the one person in the unit more screwed up than her while the only person she actually trusted—maybe even weirdly loved a little bit and not just for his bedside manner—watched her fall apart.

"What? No piss here." She tried to purse her lips, but they felt fuzzy, more like a pout. Very professional. Very serious. "Where've you been?"

"Doing my job, PFC." His tone had an edge she wasn't sure was him or the booze. "Third Squad's in pretty good shape. The others, not so much. Me, Toelke, and Thannick were making rounds, trying to help out."

"Great." The word fell flat. Stupid. This was all her fault. Third Platoon bled because of her. "Good."

"You sure you're okay?" He leaned past her, studying Mez in the corner. "It's been a day."

Her heart hammered so hard; no way he didn't feel it. She breathed him in—maintenance scrub and fresh sweat, that sharp scent of someone who'd been working hard. Their helmets clicked together, and her hand found his waist before she could stop herself. Her eyes drifted closed.

"How you doing, Bugs?" His grin pressed against her cheek.

"Could be better." Her fingers pressed into his white-and-grays, trying to say what she couldn't.

"I bet." He pulled away with a laugh that stung. "Let's get you back to on line before you do something else you'll regret."

Shame erupted in her belly, crawled up her throat like acid, then turned all white-hot savage. "So that's how it is."

"What?"

"Too proper for a feral?"

"Fuck off, you're drunk."

"Sure am." Her laugh was all edges. "What did you say, back in the brig? I'm no Tellie Strong?"

Pain flashed across his face, but she was too far gone to care. "Hang on, that's not—"

"Are you two actually doing this right now?" Kitrelle stood in the entrance like she owned the place, dark curls rain-plastered to her perfect cheekbones. Great. Time for round two. "What the actual fuck, Mez? Hardwine? *Really?*"

She bent and snatched the flask from his hands, then tipped it back and drained the rest in one long pull. The empty flask bounced off Mez's shoulder and clanked against the cracked stone floor.

"Damn. That's pretty good." Kitrelle came closer, arms crossed. "You're something else, new blood."

Bad enough Doc had seen her like this. Now Kitrelle. "Guess you're still pissed at me."

"Of course I'm fucking pissed." She thumped Olsom's chest plate. "You really screwed up, and bad things happened."

Olsom finally looked up. There was nothing soft in Kitrelle's storm-dark eyes. "Same team?"

"Not much choice. There's a war on, remember?" Kitrelle's voice hadn't lost its edge. "But you really screwed up back there."

"Yeah, well." Olsom swayed slightly, one hand finding the wall for balance. "Join the fucking club."

Kitrelle stepped closer, close enough to smell the chemical bite of plasmex. "You think this is funny? People died because—"

"Because I fucked up. Not because I'm some f—" She couldn't say the word. "Not because of where I'm from."

For a moment they just stared at each other, the rumble of thunder and strike craft echoing beneath the storm. Then Kitrelle's expression shifted, not quite softening but losing some of its sharp edge.

"The hardwine's got her feeling things," Doc said from somewhere.

"Fuck off, Doc," Olsom said, eyes still locked on Kitrelle.

"Read the room, Myers." Kitrelle stepped back toward the door. Her voice went flat, professional. "Let's get you squared away. We've got a war to fight, and I'm not covering for you if Lessig comes looking."

They wound their way out of the broken facility. The air felt thick as river water, but the rain's cold bite felt good against her burning face. Lightning cracked overhead, painting 3-3-3 in stark lines against the dark. The exo waited, cage open and hungry, rain streaming off the canopy.

Doc appeared as Kitrelle helped her into the cage. His hands reached for her harness straps, but Olsom batted them away. She shot him a warning glance before clicking the buckles herself.

With an exaggerated sigh, he fished his datapad from its kit and fed the interface cable into 3-3-3's ops terminal. "Any complaints?"

"Yeah," she said, "you're a dick."

"About the rig, Bugs."

"Oh." Her snort turned into a belch. "Comms are doing this ghosty thing."

"Ghosty comms. Sure, I deal with that all the time."

"Here, listen." Her fingers found the emitter volume and cranked it hard right.

Nothing came at first. Then the pop and hiss of lightning strikes, the usual back-and-forth of Fury elements watching their sectors. Standard war noises, far as wars went.

"I don't hear anything strange," Kitrelle said.

"But it's there!" Olsom's voice went high. "I swear it's there!"

"You know," Doc grinned, "hardwine's famous for—"

"Shut up," both women cut him off.

The squeal of feedback made them jump. Harsh pulses cut through the static before a woman's voice materialized like smoke. "Reserve Command, Reserve Command, this is Two-Zero-One Actual—" Then she was gone.

"That's her!" Olsom smacked the terminal. "That's the ghost!"

"Weird." Doc slipped into that intense engineer mode—completely, totally, unfairly attractive given how mad she still was at him. "PR nets shouldn't be bleeding into ours. How are you picking this up?"

"You tell me, genius." She forced herself to look at the terminal instead of his face. "You're the combat engineer."

Doc went quiet, all wrapped up in his diagnostics like the datapad was the only thing that mattered.

She'd messed everything up. Going rails-free crazy, getting drunk with Mez of all people, going all sloppy on Doc like some cheap libo whore. And okay, maybe she shouldn't have snapped at him, but did he have to just brush her off like that? Not that she'd expected him to throw her down right there back in the ruins, but he could've at least acknowledged whatever this thing was between them instead of making her feel stupid for feeling it.

She watched him work, words building up behind her teeth, but they all felt dumb. *Hey, sorry for being such a fuck up. Want to talk about our feelings?*

"Here's something." Doc caught her staring, and for a second she saw something unguarded there before he shut it down.

"What?" she finally asked.

"You've got a custom frequency dialed in." He stood and leaned into the terminal, pulling up a screen labeled *COMMS MAINT.* The channel number glowed under his finger. "See? That prefix, it's local. Probably Reserve."

"Not me. Never seen that screen before. Basic only covered startup, mobility and tactical."

"Well somebody added it. But that still doesn't explain the interference. You should be able to receive on this freq without it bleeding into the other nets."

The channel shrieked again, like something dying in the dark. *"Say again, Reserve Command?"*

Another voice cut through, harsh and mechanical in the static: *"Lieutenant Bresto, proceed immediately to shelter designated Sapphire-6 and stand down. Acknowledge."*

"Negative, Command. We're tracking raider movement near—" The transmission dissolved in another death squeal.

The hardwine haze couldn't dull the shock. *Lieutenant* Bresto. Had to be Sergeant Bresto's wife. That's why he'd screwed off his secret mission to come down here and play hero. Not for them, not to win, but for his wife. His kids. Sergeant Hard-Ass breaking regs, risking court martial—their whole mission—all to keep his family together.

Her hands shook as she gripped the controls. Proper families with their proper fucking values could go straight to twelve hells.

"Bugs."

"What?"

"Tell me you heard that."

"I know, can you believe that fucking *asshole*—"

"No." Doc's voice turned grim. "That pulse."

"What pulse? There's no—"

"Yeah, yeah, yeah, I heard it too," Kitrelle said. "It's like the storm feedback, but regular. Repeating."

Olsom groaned. Who had time for pulses when their platoon sergeant was running his own private rescue op? "So what? So there's a pulse."

"Listen. Quantum networks don't fail. They *can't* fail. Encryption's perfect, range is infinite with enough power. So why are we getting this regular pattern?"

Oh, damn, he was serious. The booze fog lifted, and she heard it— the bright signal stab of regular feedback. Wasn't anything natural. "You think they're in our comms? Like what they did to the fleet?"

"That's not possible," Kitrelle said.

"Look," Doc said, "the Concordat killed Earth. The Twelfth brought us to the Cradle on one of *their* ships. Everything we use—FTL, gravity, quantum nets—we didn't invent it. It's all based on stolen tech."

Olsom pulled up the strategic overlay. It seemed so far-fetched, but why would PR Command be trying to shut down Mrs. Bresto when there were still raiders out there? The screen painted evacuation routes in friendly blue, all of them leading straight to shelters in the urban core. Small gaps in the data had formed near the shelters, easy to miss if you weren't looking. Just like the allotment center. Like that Lost-making capsule.

There it was, bright as a fusion burn.

The world began to spin again, but it had nothing to do with the hardwine. "Founders fuck me. That's not PR Command talking. That's the Concordat."

"How can you possibly know that?" Doc asked.

"Weren't you listening? Nothing about what that guy said makes any sense. He even talks weird."

"Okay fine. What's their plan?"

"They're driving us." She flipped the terminal around so they could see it. "Like crid to the fucking slaughter."

Kitrelle reached for her comms. "Lessig, it's Kitrelle."

"Send it."

"Need you at 3-3-3's pos. Got something you need to see."

"Roger. Moving."

"Nice work, Bugs." Doc stuffed his datapad back into his kit, dug out his autodoc, and started turning the dial. "Maybe we can still save these people."

"What if we're wrong?"

"Then we better be ready to explain ourselves to Revan." The autodoc's cold applicator touched her neck, followed by the bite of meds entering her bloodstream.

"What the?" Her heart raced double-time, and the world took on a sharper contrast.

He leaned in close, hand tight on her shoulder. "Different kind of combat cocktail." Knowing what they knew now, his closeness felt heavy. "Need you serviceable. If you're right, we've got work to do."

Kitrelle watched Doc move away, then turned those storm-dark eyes on Olsom. Shit. Still mad.

"You ready for this, new blood? Because we can't afford any more mistakes."

The wild thing inside her recoiled.

"I didn't mean for nobody to get hurt."

"Tell that to Yohansson." Kitrelle's voice dropped. "Prelk might be an asshole, but he lost a friend today. We all did."

"That's not fair." Olsom choked back a sob. It had been so long since she'd given twelve shits about anyone. "I thought I was doing the right—"

"The right thing doesn't bring my people back." Kitrelle closed her eyes, took a breath, and let it out slow. "The Twelfth may forgive, but some of us will need longer. A lot longer."

"I don't need your forgiveness," Olsom snapped. "I need to fix this."

"Then fix it." Kitrelle shrugged the pack straps on her shoulder and turned to go.

Mez's shape appeared in the facility doorway, black shape sharp against the gray. The usual swagger was gone, replaced by something she knew all too well—that look of being left behind. For the first time since she'd known him, he seemed small and insignificant against the broken granite walls. Not another monster. No more than she was, anyway.

Good thing. There could be so many more monsters soon enough.

THE EXPENSIVE BROADCAST drone lay in pieces near Bresto's boot, its housing shattered by Kull's pinpoint shot. Storm struggled between two Marines while others moved to encircle them, weapons raised. Rain hammered against the observation deck as thunder rolled beneath the clouds, but Kull's voice cut through it all.

"What in the twelve hells have you done?" Kull's pistol tracked to his chest. Her eyes burned cold over the sights. "You realize what this means? The panic alone will kill people. For nothing!"

"Not nothing, ma'am," Bresto said. Storm's broadcast had reached every active screen in Vestebrae. There was no taking it back now. No more hiding from the truth. "The Lost are out there. Our people need to know."

Her flexscreen chirped with an incoming transmission. *"Victory Actual, this is Azure Actual."*

"Go for Victory Actual," she snapped, pistol still trained on Bresto.

"Be advised, evacuees are—" Static garbled the tac net. *"—say again, they've stopped."*

"What do you mean they've stopped? Make them move." She jabbed her push-to-talk again. "Azure Actual, say again your last, over."

The crowd's restless energy was palpable, even far below them. Thousands of colonists pressed against PR barriers, their protests coming in waves, demanding access to the lifts.

"What did you tell them?" Kull's voice went sharp.

"The truth!" Storm shouted before a Marine's gloved hand clamped over his mouth.

"That Corongaet is clear," Bresto said. "That we've secured it."

"Clear? The shelters there are full!"

"But it's *secure*." Thousands of lives were on the line, and she couldn't—wouldn't—see it. "We don't know what's in the core."

"What's in the core is an entire PR battalion. Not one of them has seen any of your capsules."

"Ma'am, those things were everywhere on that ship." His hands balled into fists. Holy Mother, why wouldn't she listen? "Hundreds of pods, maybe thousands. I've—"

"And the fleet killed it, remember? Threat neutralized. Now people will die anyway because of a panic you caused."

The familiar rage burned up his spine—just another staff officer that thought she knew better. "If anyone dies, it'll be because *you* didn't listen."

"Shut up." She jerked her chin at Revan. "Get these two to the cargo transfer level. I want them bound and out of sight until I can find a brig for them."

Revan took a cautious step forward. The doubt was there, plain as day, eating at what little resolve he had left. He'd seen the aftermath of the allotment center, the combat footage, had an inkling of what they were up against.

"Let's go, Sergeant."

Bresto's hand tightened on the observation rail. Thirty thousand lives hanging in the balance and no one would listen.

"You heard the skipper." Revan's hand moved toward his sidearm, loyalty finally outweighing doubt. "I don't know what you were trying to do up here, but you can't just—"

Light flashed across the officers' faces, stark white against the control tower windows. The concussion followed a heartbeat later, a deep, hollow boom that vibrated beneath his feet. Bresto turned toward the sound just as secondary explosions lit the rain-soaked corridor below. Even at this height, he could see the crowd break against the smoke and flames.

Shouts of terror rose up the drop. Twelfth save them, he was too late.

Kull shouldered up beside him, field optics already tracking. "Azure Actual!" Her field comms buzzed. "Azure 2, Azure 3, report!"

Only static answered back.

Lyra and Kaff were down there somewhere in that chaos. "Ma'am, we have to get those people out of there. Get the lifts moving. Get them up here now."

"This is panic you started, Sergeant," she said, still staring through the scope. "Why is he still here, Lieutenant?"

Revan's pistol buzzed to life, capacitor charging. The barrel stuck hard in Bresto's lower back. "Now, Marine."

Bresto turned to face the lieutenant, the weapon tracing a path from his back to his belly. "Raiders have been dropping coreward since we got here. And the fact you've got a whole PR battalion down there saying it's all clear doesn't strike you as off?"

"I don't know. You don't know," Revan said. "None of us know!"

His platoon comms buzzed: *"Bresto, Lessig."*

Lessig sounded exhausted. Worried.

"Put a bolt in me if you want, sir, but I'm going to answer that." He squeezed his push to talk. "Go for Bresto."

"Sarnt, we're at the drop station. There's something you need to see."

"Define *we*, Corporal," Revan cut in.

"Fury 3, sir. Third Platoon."

"What?" Revan's voice sharpened. "Who authorized you to move—?"

"Sir, it's Olsom and Myers. They've found something in the PR nets."

"Found what, exactly?" Bresto said.

"Some kind of background signal. They say it might be archenemy talking, not the PR."

"Corporal, this is Major Kull." She let her field optics hang from her neck. The anger drained from her face, replaced by the cold certainty of someone who'd just realized how wrong they'd been. "What do they think the archenemy is telling us?"

"*Well, ma'am, it's like they want us to send these people to the core.*" Static crackled as lightning ripped between the clouds. "*Like it's some kind of trap.*"

Revan holstered his sidearm and stared down at the chaos below. "Twelfth save us."

Kull swiped at her flexscreen. "Drop Control, this is Major Kull."

"*Drop Control. Go ahead, Major.*"

"Stop the evacuation. Bring full lifts back to Corongaet. Halt the empty ones headed to Vestebrae."

"*But, ma'am—*"

"Just do it!"

Another transmission pinged the command nets. "*Victory Actual, this is Azure 2-1-1. Something's wrong. The shelters, they're opening.*" The transmission faded in panicked shouts and bursts of blaster fire.

"Wait." Kull's voice cut through the chaos, sharp with sudden understanding. She studied her flexscreen, tracking the evacuation routes. "The shelters. We've been leading these people straight into…"

She finally got it. Too little, too late. Each shelter could hold what—three thousand? Five thousand? Bresto's mind raced through the numbers, multiplying living souls into Lost weapons. How many had they already daxed? How many more were being daxed right now?

"Major." The word stuck in his throat. He couldn't think about Lyra. About Kaff—not when thinking meant accepting they were already gone. "Those aren't shelters anymore."

"Azure, get out of there!" Kull ran toward the stairwell, her command staff right behind. "All Victory elements, fall back to the Corongaet drop station!"

The Marines who'd had Storm at gunpoint were already moving, their prisoners forgotten. Rainwater sluiced down the steps as they climbed, their boots ringing against metal treads. Red emergency lamps made the duraplated walls look like they were bleeding out.

Storm appeared at Bresto's elbow, rain dripping from his expensive clothes. "This is it, isn't it? The real story."

"Drop Control, shut it down," Kull called out ahead of them. She grabbed the landing rail, pivoting hard around the turn. "Power down every lift."

"But ma'am, you just ordered—"

"I know what I ordered!" Another landing, another turn. "Raise the emergency barricades. Now!"

The control room doors slid open. Two dozen controllers worked their terminals beneath strips of pale light, their screens filling the space with a shifting electronic glow. Status updates and system checks created a constant background hum beneath the drumming storm.

"Are you insane?" An older man in station whites blocked their path. "We've got people on those platforms. People you put there!"

Kull pushed him aside and made straight for a controller by the windows. "Power it down. All of it."

The woman's eyes darted to her supervisor.

"Do it," Kull snapped.

"Yes, ma'am." Her fingers moved across the screen, voice shaking. "Setting breaks." Metal groaned beneath their feet as the massive lifts locked in place. "Generators to standby." The overhead lights flickered, then steadied. "Raising barricades."

Fibrosteel barriers climbed into view along the edge of the drop, emergency beacons strobing against the rain.

The control room doors cycled open again. Lessig entered first, followed by Olsom, Myers, and Mezzior. Their white-and-grays were soaked through, and somebody stank of cheap hardwine. Kull barely glanced their way, her attention fixed on the transit below.

Bresto moved to meet them. Let them be wrong about this. Let there be some other explanation. But the grim set of Lessig's jaw said everything.

"Show me."

"Here, Sarnt." Myers stepped forward, his field terminal in hand. The data packet hit Bresto's flexscreen with a soft buzz. "Cleaned up the signal some. The encoding's strange, base-eleven, I think. Probably why our nets read it as interference."

The pulse repeated on his screen: eleven sharp spikes, then nothing, then again. Eleven. Sweet Twelfth, they'd been so blind. He'd seen this aboard the derelict, when whatever the Eleven were had turned Division drones against them. He should've known they'd do it again. Should've seen this coming.

"Good work, Myers."

"I just found the signal, Sarnt. Bugs—er, PFC Olsom was the one who figured out what they were doing with it."

The PFC stared at her boots, a sour fog still clinging to her.

"Sergeant." Kull's voice carried from the windows. Her reflection watched him in the rain-streaked plexene.

Bresto turned to Lessig, a hand on his shoulder. "I want Third Platoon on line behind those barricades. Everyone we've got. They're hitting here next. Spread the word, let the other platoons know."

"Sergeant." Kull again, harder this time.

He joined her at the observation windows. Kull's certainty hadn't wavered, just shifted targets, like granite refusing to crack even as the mountain moved beneath it.

"Confirmed, ma'am." He sent the signal feed to her flexscreen. "It's the archenemy. The PR Command signal is a fake, a lure, to get our people into those shelter. You've got to get—"

"Azure's offline. Clear comms quiet." She glanced at her screen. "Nothing."

"You got any eyes down there?" he asked the controller.

The woman tapped the screen twice. Grainy camera feeds showed colonists scattered across the transit—some trying to climb the steep slope on foot, others beating against locked shop doors. No sign of PR forces. No Marines. Just packed streets and rising panic. A shadow cut through the crowd, too fast for the camera to track. More screams.

Kull ignored the feeds, staring through the rain-streaked windows. "When I woke up this morning, I never imagined I would murder thirty thousand innocent people." Her voice was hollow, empty as dead metal.

"You didn't do this, ma'am. The archenemy did." Even as he said it, something in her tone turned his gut cold.

She met his gaze, eyes rimmed red with exhaustion and something deeper. Her fingers worked her flexscreen. "CDNS Umbra Fire Control, Victory Actual requesting priority fire mission."

"Go for fire mission, Victory."

Fire mission. An orbital strike. She meant to glass the entire transit. "Ma'am. You can't—"

"You said it yourself, Sergeant: let the skeegs handle the rest." The flex lit up beneath her fingers as she designated targets, each marker appearing like a wound. The shelters first. Then the drop station's landing. Finally, the transit, targeting markers bracketing the crowd itself. "I should've listened to you sooner. Before I put all these people in harm's way."

"Victory Actual, Umbra Fire Control." There was a pinch of concern in the young man's voice. *"I read civilian and friendly returns inside your brackets. Please resend, over."*

"Negative, Umbra, it's reading right."

"Ma'am, wait." Bresto barely got the words. She couldn't. Not to his wife. His baby girl.

She rounded on him. "Tell me I don't have to do this. Tell me there aren't thousands of those *things* down there already. Tell me there won't be tens of thousands more in the next few hours. Tell me the Marines I have left can stand against that. Tell me we don't all lose someone we love today. Tell me!"

Her voice echoed through the control room's silence. But he had nothing. His pulse raced against the cold math of it all, but the truth was granite-hard: one way or another, Kaff and Lyra were already gone. Lost no more.

The chirp of orbital comms broke the silence. *"Victory Actual, this is Eleus Taan, captain of the Umbra."*

"Captain Taan, Major Orianne Kull."

"I wish I could say it was a pleasure, Major." Decades of military bearing trembled in Taan's voice. *"Am I to understand you want me to drop tungsten on my fellow colonists?"*

"What?" Olsom pushed forward, face twisted in horror. Myers caught her arm, but she kept struggling. Bresto shot Lessig a look, and the corporal moved to intercept. If Kull noticed the commotion, it didn't show.

"The archenemy holds that ground, sir. They've turned our shelters into… forges for more Lost." Kull's voice caught, but she shook it off. "If we don't stop them here, there will only be two colonies come the morning."

She transmitted the evidence package—signal analysis, combat footage, everything Third Squad had found—everything Bresto had tried to warn her about. All trace of spite from the *Gauntlet* and the clinic was gone.

"Captain." Her voice steadied. "They know we've caught them, and they're coming for us. Your tungsten is all there is between us and them. Do you understand?"

The seconds stretched. Part of him wanted Taan to refuse, to save him from what had to happen next. But the man sounded as proper as they come. No way he would refuse Kull now.

"Target package Azure-Zero-Seven confirmed. Batteries one through four reading ready."

"Fire away, Umbra," Kull said. No hesitation now.

The buzz-crack of electromagnetics squelched her comms.

"Rods on target, sixteen seconds." The man's voice broke amid the background clatter of magazines and auto-loaders. *"Call your targets, Major. Twelfth save you."*

"Twelfth save us all."

Light bloomed above the storm clouds, turning night to false dawn. The first rod carved through rain and black sky—a needle of pure light that opened up granite and duraplate like wet clay. The flash burned in Bresto's vision while the impact shook the whole mountain. More followed, each shot marching closer. Buildings folded in on themselves in clouds of dust and glittering plexene. The drop station's landing disappeared beneath more tungsten moving at hypersonic velocities. The people there were just gone. Wiped away like they had never existed.

Lyra. Kaff. Twelfth, he'd—

"Sergeant." Kull's voice pulled him back. "Your court martial will have to wait."

The ghost of a smile touched her lips, like she knew they probably wouldn't survive that long. Maybe she didn't want to, not after what she'd just done.

She switched to command nets. "Victory elements, stand to. Concordat forces are moving upslope in unknown numbers. We are all that stands between the archenemy and Corongaet. They may have taken the core, but they will not take this mountain. The Twelfth holds. Victory holds. Metal up."

CHAPTER
THIRTY

OLSOM LET them drag her from the control room, Doc's grip tight on her arm while Lessig cleared the way. Her head throbbed with each step, the sour burn of Mez's hardwine still coating her brain despite Doc's drugs. The observation deck's windows strobed white-hot with orbital fire, each strike casting harsh shadows through sheets of rain and sending spikes of pain through her temples.

Another rod punched through the storm clouds, moving so fast it left burning lines in her vision. A deep boom shook loose metal. She wanted to be sick. Wanted to hurt someone. Just like always—the people with power making choices for everyone else. Making choices about who lived and who got left behind.

The rain hit like needles as they emerged onto the landing, each cold drop a fresh shock against her flushed skin. Ozone and granite vapor filled her lungs, mixing with the sharper stink of whatever was burning below.

Someone needed to answer for this. She whirled on them, the world tilting for a heartbeat before steadying. Their expressions stopped her cold. They looked as lost as she felt.

"How could they do that? All those people. What are we even doing here?"

Doc wouldn't even look at her. "Bugs—"

"Don't call me that," she snapped, throat still raw. "Answer me!"

Lessig pushed past them, already moving toward the stairs.

"Where are you going?" she demanded.

"You saw that capsule thing same as me." His voice had no edge left. He took the stairs like an old man, one slow step at a time. "What did you think would happen when we found out what they'd done?"

"Not kill everyone!" The young man who called himself Storm followed them out the door and to the stairwell, his expensive jumpsuit dark with rain.

Doc rounded on Storm. "What the hell would you know?"

"I know those people didn't stand a chance." Storm followed them down. "I tried to help Ned stop this, just like you."

"That what you call it?" Lessig laughed. "Looked more like you found yourself a story."

"That's not fair—"

Lessig spun and shoved him against the railing. His sneer was all teeth. "Good. You're catching on."

"Rich boy or not, he's right," Olsom said. "We should have tried something. Anything."

Another rod punched through the storm, the impact trembling through the metal landing. More colonists dying while they argued on the stairs.

Lessig released him and continued down. "If the Lost are what you and the sarnt say they are, then everyone in those shelters was already dead. Maybe… maybe they did them a favor."

Olsom bit back a sneer. Easy words from someone who'd never been thrown away. Never been told they didn't matter enough to save.

Lessig hit the bottom landing and stopped dead. The main deck was packed with refugees, their faces reflecting red in the emergency lighting. No screaming, no fighting, just the slow shuffle of feet as they made room for the Marines. These people should be tearing the walls down, not standing there like they'd already lost. But they still trusted the system. Believed the lies about protection and care. The admin blocks had taught her better.

"Easy Three, Fury Three, Major Kull."

"Major Kull?" Mez let out a dark laugh. "Sound more like Major *Kill*."

For once, the duster wasn't wrong. Kull had just proven what Olsom had always known—when it came down to it, some lives mattered more than others.

"The orbital strike has created a window. Multiple platforms are still occupied above the impact zone." She didn't sound like someone who'd just killed thousands. *"You're tasked with rescue ops and security downslope."*

Lessig picked up the pace. "Let's go. Before she gets creative again."

The crowd parted slow in front of them as she followed Lessig back to their metal. Her flexscreen flashed with new data—safe routes down slope, estimated survivors per platform.

She keyed her comms. "Third Squad, let's go."

"Negative." Bresto's voice had that edge she was getting used to. *"3-3-2 has lead. 3-3-1, 3-3-3, you're support. Copy?"*

"Solid copy, Sarnt," came the twins' reply.

Great. Another reminder she couldn't be trusted. It was almost funny coming from the man who had stood by while a fellow Aegian annihilated thirty thousand people.

3-3-3 waited for her beneath emergency floods, its powerpack still steaming in the rain.

A private channel opened. Smokes. *"Hey, uh, Olsom—"*

"—No hard feelings?" Vlan finished.

"No way," she said, settling into 3-3-3's cage. "Hope you have better luck than me."

"Floaty." She could practically hear their goofy, wrinkled grin.

Doc checked the FAB mount and flashed a thumbs up. At least he was still here. Still trying to keep her metal running. Even if he couldn't keep anything else between them working.

"Moving." She pulled up the tactical display and moved out.

Third Squad moved through the crowd and around the barricades to the edge of the drop. A channel of industrial superstructure cut through the mountain at a steep angle, half a kilometer of wet duraplate and jagged debris vanishing into banks of smoke. The platforms hung between here and there, some empty, some packed with colonists. Behind them, drop station crew worked the big industrial winches, threading thick mag-cables through guide rings still glowing from orbital fire.

The terminal marked their target in tactical blue. Platform Twelve, far right. 3-3-2 moved first, servos straining as Smokes' guided it down, Vlan and Doc Toelke in its wake. The grade was insane, but their metal could take it. Had to take it. She kept her tread in 3-3-2's tracks, stomach in her throat as each step threatened to send her sliding.

A hand caught the rig's arm as Doc lost his balance. "You good?" she asked.

"Yeah. Getting there."

"Mez?"

"Fuck this mountain shit." He sounded actually scared. "No place should be this high."

"Got something. Low and slow." The tension in Squishy's voice made Olsom check her feeds. Her terminal lit up with fresh contacts.

The whine of sub-light drives rose above the settling debris. Two black shapes carved through the smoke below, engines glowing like coals against the dark.

"Contact confirmed." Lessig's transmission cut through the chatter. *"Double-time it, Fury Three. We've got incoming."*

Double-time. Down a fucking mountain. But Smokes was already running his rig, support Marines skidding and sliding behind him. The platform's warning lights pulsed through sheets of rain as colonists scrambled back from the approaching exos. Their voices hit her hard. Mothers calling for help; kids crying for parents they'd never see again. It must've been terrible, seeing Kull's devastation up close.

"Stand clear!" The twins' voices cut through the chaos.

Doc pushed through the press of bodies, guiding them out of the way.

3-3-3's treads found purchase on the rain-slick deck as she followed through the parting crowd to the far edge where duraplate dropped away to empty space. Twenty meters down, the channel resumed its slide to the bottom, where wreckage from the orbital strike still burned red-hot.

The raider transports emerged from the smoke, settling onto what remained of the nearby urban blocks. Her FAB's targeting system painted clean red lines as squids spilled from the ships, dragging large equipment cases behind them.

"What're they doing way out there?"

"No good path up here, maybe," Doc said.

Bresto's IFF pinged near Second Squad's position, two platforms up. *"Fury Three, mark your targets for the Umbra. Don't let them set up shop."*

She started to transmit coordinates, then hesitated. There could be people in those buildings trying to escape the shelters. Running right into another orbital strike.

"Target acquired," Squishy called out. Fresh brackets appeared over the closest transport.

"Acknowledged, Fury 3-3," came the reply from the *Umbra's* Fire Control. *"Shot, over."*

She spun 3-3-3 around. "Down! Everybody down!" The exo's arms spread wide, metal hands urging people to the deck.

Light stabbed through the clouds, and in a violent crack the target zone was gone, reduced to atoms and burning debris. The impact sent tremors through the mountainside until the whole platform groaned beneath them.

Metal shrieked against metal as the platform lurched downward. 3-3-3's servos whined in protest while Olsom fought to keep the machine steady. The platform brakes caught with a bone-jarring snap, sending screams through the crowd of refugees.

"Everyone okay?" Smokes and Vlan called out.

Acknowledgements filtered through their comms, but died quick as new engine flares punched through the smoke below.

"More squids!" Threat markers filled Olsom's combat feeds. "Multiple transports inbound!"

Laser fire erupted from the far landing zone, crackling red through the smoke. First Squad's FABs answered back, but at that range, both sides might as well be throwing rocks.

"Victory Actual, this is Bresto. We need dropships. Platforms won't clear in time."

The third contact didn't play it safe like the others. It rocketed up the channel, retros burning close enough to feel the heat. Its bay doors slammed wide, spilling the archenemy onto the steep slope. The squids tumbled downward, struggling to get their footing. But the bugs moved like they belonged there, plasma staves crackling green.

"Stand to!" the twins shouted together.

Olsom locked 3-3-3's arms across her cage. "Fireteam, cover behind me."

Red brackets settled over the targets and she pulled the trigger. The FAB cut through the first wave, sending bodies tumbling back into the inferno. Raiders scrambled for cover, disappearing into the industrial-sized grooves that guided the platforms downslope. Their lasers did nothing to her armor as she swept her barrels across their position. At least Doc's repairs were holding, heat levels steady in the green. Maybe all the rain was good for something.

The bugs poured in after the squids, their staves spitting green death at Third Squad. New threat indicators lit up as the transport's point defense turret found her. Slugs pinged off 3-3-3's plate, impact warnings flashing across the HUD. She stepped back, bracing herself against the thundering onslaught.

"*Sarnt, 3-3-2,*" the twins said together. "*Request rails free on—*"

"*—the squid transport, over.*"

A pinprick of shame tugged at her adrenaline rush. The twins—calm, cool, zero hesitation. By the book. Standard operating procedure.

The incoming fire died instantly, like the ship knew what was coming. "*Approved,*" Revan crackled through the static. "*Nine rounds, three by three. Fire when ready.*"

Olsom's railgun control hat clicked forward. The weapon arm extended with a whine, the Mark Three's powerpack straining into the red. Weak points across the transport's hull lit up her terminal: power distribution nodes, computer junctions, command and control. She tagged her targets, adding them to Third Squad's firing solution.

"*All squads.*" Bresto again without a trace of concern. "*Prep for EMI.*"

"*Firing,*" the twins ordered.

The first volley struck home, tungsten slugs punching clean

through the transport's nose. Her combat feeds registered direct hits on all primary systems as the ship lurched backward. Timing the shots between power cycles, letting the charge build before each salvo; the twins knew what they were doing.

The second barrage caught the transport mid-hull, and she could see storm through the exit wounds. The ship pitched nose-up, thrusters fighting gravity, before the final three rounds sheared through its spine. No fire, no explosions, just the clean impact of metal on metal. The transport's engines died with a final sputter, and the whole craft began its slow slide down the channel to the rest of the wreckage below.

Controlled. Coordinated. Precise. That was how it was supposed to work. No wild firing or random targeting like at the foundry. The twins had earned that squad leader spot.

Bresto's transmission was a mix of static and pride. *"Good kill, Fury 3-3."*

Heat rolled over her as the dropship appeared through the storm, ramp down and locked. Laser strikes sparked off the hull while she cycled the railgun away, her FAB spitting charged particles into the channel where bugs and squids had taken cover.

"How's your thermals?" Doc asked.

Railgun was hot, everything else still green. "Fine. When that ship lands, you and Mez get these people aboard."

"What about you?" Something in his voice made the question less annoying than it should have been.

"I'm fine."

"You keep saying that." His grin carried through comms. *"I'm starting to think you don't mean it."*

It wasn't cute. Not anymore. "Shut up, Doc. Those people come first. Get them clear."

"Copy that."

More dropships touched down along the slope, their hulls casting animal shadows through the storm. The archenemy's return fire came steady but light, single shots, badly aimed. She worked her FAB across their position, catching raiders as they tried to regroup. The sustained fire must be doing something right; their numbers were thinning.

"How many people left, Doc?" she asked as another dead squid tumbled into the dark.

"Lots. Two, maybe three more lifts."

A signal return flashed across her feeds—something deep in the ruins below. She swept her barrels back, combat feeds showing nothing but wreckage. Heat levels too high. Environmental sensors screaming danger. But she'd seen something. Could anyone have survived down there?

Light stabbed through the clouds as another tungsten rod found its target. The impact turned stone and metal to atoms, sending more tremors through the platform. This time the brakes held firm against the shock. The dropship's engines whined as it lifted away, carrying the first group of refugees to safety. Through 3-3-2's canopy, she caught Smokes watching her, cigarette ember burning bright in the dark. Vlan crouched beside the exo's leg, the same twin-grin wrinkling his face.

"Nice work, boss," she said.

"Floaty," they replied.

A hollow bang rang out from beneath the platform's deck plates. The nearby maintenance hatch exploded upward, showering them with metal fragments. Plasma bolts sliced through the gap, the force of it throwing Mez into a crowd of colonists.

"First Squad, multiple contacts!" The transmission barely carried over sustained weapons fire. *"They've found a way behind us!"*

First Squad's position vanished beneath a wave of plasma fire as bugs swarmed from the drop station infrastructure. More hatches burst open along Platform Twelve's edge. They hadn't thinned the enemy's numbers; they'd only found another way through.

"Get those civilians back!" Bresto ordered. *"They're coming out of the sub-levels! Hitting the platforms from behind!"*

Combat feeds screamed warnings as she turned to engage. Red markers blurred with blue until her HUD was useless. These defensive arms were great for staying alive, but she couldn't see shit. She dropped 3-3-3's guard and clicked her FAB to single shot. A plasma staff ignited, bright green in the dark. One bolt killed it, clean through the bug's center mass, FAB barrel still spinning wildly. The other

Marines picked their shots too, methodically clearing targets as they appeared at the rear of the platform.

The distant crump of small engine launches yanked her attention back to the transit. Four brilliant points burned upward from somewhere beyond the ruins, fusion drives cutting clean lines through the rain. Her threat indicators howled, sensor feeds tracking the missiles as they disappeared above the clouds with a ripple of thunder. The threat markers kept climbing higher, way past their position, past the clouds, straight toward low orbit. Straight toward the *Umbra*.

CHAPTER
THIRTY-ONE

BRESTO STOOD ON PLATFORM NINE, watching the missiles' fusion drives burn clean lines into the storm. Had to be powered penetrators: low tech squid ordnance, little more than tungsten slugs fitted on sub-light drives, but they could crack ship hulls at sufficient velocity. The *Umbra* was their only orbital support. If those missiles connected, there'd be nothing between his Marines and whatever else the archenemy had waiting for them.

His flexscreen showed Third Platoon scattered across three platforms, their exos trying to cover civilian evac while Concordat forces poured from maintenance hatches. There was nothing he could do about the missiles. That was between the *Umbra's* point defense guns and the Holy Mother now.

But the archenemy had found a way through their lines, probably maintenance access running through the drop station's superstructure. Made sense. The whole facility was veined with service tunnels for the industrial lifts. If they couldn't seal that breach, Third Platoon would be overrun before they finished loading civilians. And the archenemy would have a path behind Victory's lines.

Revan's voice crackled through his comms. *"I'm tracking hostiles on all platforms. What's your status?"*

"Busy, sir." Bresto snapped off a blaster bolt, catching a raider mid-charge.

"The Umbra's gone evasive, so we've lost orbital support. We can't lose Third Platoon, too. Withdraw to the drop station immediately."

"Negative." He slapped a fresh charge pack into his rifle. "We've still got hundreds of people trapped down here. And if we don't find where they're coming from, we won't be able to hold this ground at all."

"You don't have enough Marines to clear that structure!"

"Don't need to clear it." Bresto tracked his next target through his optics. "Just find the main junction and blow it. Force them to climb the hard way, right into our exos."

Laser fire crackled through the rain. He dropped prone, putting three bolts into the raider hunting him.

"Okay." Relief crept into Revan's voice. A real plan that didn't involve killing more innocent people. *"What do you need?"*

Bresto signaled Rosch as Kitrelle hammered charged particles into a bug's carapace a few meters away. Those two could help him get it done.

"Schematics," he said. "Find me a path to that junction. Plasmex'll handle the rest."

"Give me a few minutes."

"No time. Just tac them as soon as you can. All this steel and duraplate's going to kill our comms."

"Copy that."

Maybe Revan wasn't completely useless after all. Bresto keyed squad nets. "Kitrelle, push for that hatch. Rosch and I are behind you."

"Moving." She threaded through the crowd of refugees, rifle ready. Bresto signaled Rosch up, and they fell in behind her, covering angles as they approached the access point.

Beyond an open hatch lay a two-meter drop onto metal grating, suspended over the steep slide into the burning transit.

Kitrelle peered over the edge. "Don't tell me we're going down there."

"Fine, I won't. Let's go."

Bresto braced on the ladder holds and slid down onto the grating.

Beneath the massive platform, hazard strobes lit the maintenance level, casting red shadows across gantries that ran the length of the slab. The air hung thick with machine oil and wet stone, centuries of storms seeping through cracks in concrete and duraplate.

Everything fed toward the central mechanism beneath the mountain slope, massive hydraulic assemblies and mag-drive arrays that powered the industrial lifts. The kind of machinery that could crush a Marine like loose gravel if it started moving again.

He panned his rifle, searching through the optics. Nothing moved in the dark. "Clear," he transmitted, voice low.

Rosch dropped next, then Kitrelle. "What's the plan, Sarnt?" she asked.

Bresto took point on the narrow walkway. "Going to find where those freaks are getting through and seal it up."

"First time for everything." Kitrelle suppressed a laugh. "Usually we're making holes, not plugging them."

A grin smile touched his lips. "Principle's the same."

They reached the end of the gantry, where the drop channel loomed close enough to touch. Meters-wide grooves for the track lines cut deep into the mountain face, marked with worn hazard stripes. His optics showed environment warnings and another ladderwell just inside. Ignoring the *DO NOT CLIMB* stencil, he swung over the gantry rail and made the short jump.

"Come on."

The rungs were slick with rain, but a few meters down the air grew warmer, out of the wind. His flexscreen showed next to nothing, its sensors barely penetrating the dark beyond his sight line. Big space. Empty space. Twelfth let it be empty.

The landing below had a sign: *AUXILIARY DRIVE ACCESS BRONZE-6.*

His tac comms spat static. *"Sergeant Bre—"*

The signal died. He took a knee, rifle aimed into the dark. New data packets buzzed his flex, and an overlay appeared confirming their position. Revan had come through with the schematics.

Rosch joined him, taking a knee. They studied the overlay, hunting for where the tunnels converged.

"Three levels down." Bresto pointed at the access junction. "Here."

"Doesn't sound bad," Rosch said.

Kitrelle's grip tightened on her rifle. "I bet levels mean something different in a place this big."

She wasn't wrong. Looked like fifty meters, give or take. His lamp caught more hazard stripes disappearing into the dark. "That way."

The next ladder showed clear. No raiders, no bugs. The quiet made his skin crawl. Something wasn't right about being alone down here. He kept his rifle up as he climbed down one-handed. The deck rang beneath his boots when he landed. Strips of light pulsed weakly— *pause, flash, flash.* For a heartbeat, he was back in the forge ship, that distant click of bug chitin against metal. The memory of that place had woken him once or twice. He blinked to clear his sight picture. Still nothing.

"Clear."

The tunnel forced them into a crouch, storm runoff trickling through seams in the duraplate panels. He swept his rifle ahead as Rosch and Kitrelle took position behind him. Everything about this place screamed they weren't alone, even as his optics showed clean sectors.

The wet gurgle of squid-speak bubbled up from below. Close, from the next ladderwell over, red light seeping through the opening. Of course, squids held the junction, waiting for reinforcements. He signaled the plan: frag and clear, hold and set, exfil.

The distinctive bone-knocking sound of bug chatter echoed up the ladderwell. Better make that two frags. No chances.

He armed the grenades and let them drop. Clean, no bounces. The frags blew loud in the confined space, cutting short a squid's startled scream. He slid down the ladderwell, palms burning through his gloves. The fall seemed endless until the stink of cooked meat and hot metal hit him. He landed badly on his hip but kept his rifle steady. Two raiders pulped on opposite walls. One dead bug, its carapace peppered with shrapnel.

Movement flashed in the forward tunnel. He sighted and fired, dropping whatever it was. Rosch hit the deck beside him a heartbeat later, covering the opposite entry. Another bug died screaming. More squid-speak echoed from below. They'd have more company soon.

Kitrelle landed last, already pulling bricks of plasmex from her tac vest. "Don't guess I need to bring any of this back."

"No." Rosch helped empty her bandolier. "This superstructure's dense."

A laser beam cut through the smoky air from the left passage. Bresto put three bolts through the shooter, confirmed by its dying squeal.

"What do you think, the ceiling?" Kitrelle asked.

Rosch pointed at the seams. "Yeah. Let gravity do the work."

"Hurry up, you two." Bresto dropped another contact through his optics. "Three minutes, maybe less."

"Aye, Sarnt."

Kitrelle and Rosch worked methodically, setting plasmex bricks along the junction seams. No time for precision charges, just explosives and physics. More squid-speak echoed through the dark.

"Forward hatch," Rosch said, arming another brick.

"Yeah." Bresto caught a warrior's outline in his optics and put a bolt through it. A low charge pack warning buzzed as the dead bug's claw shot out, catching Kitrelle's boot.

"Fuck!" She found her rifle and drilled its skull, one compound eye bursting into steam and gore. Her eyes were stuck on it. "Fuck!"

"Come on." Rosch cuffed her shoulder. "We're not done yet."

"Shut up!" Bresto said. Something else filtered through the weapons fire and groaning metal. Like whispers scratching at the edge of his thoughts. Maybe his mind playing tricks, more memories dredged up by this place.

No. This was real. The sound drifted up the ladderwell from below. Not one voice. Dozens. Hundreds.

"Hurry." He slapped in a fresh charge pack. "Time's up."

He lurched to the ladderwell, rifle aimed down. The passage looked wrong in his scope, structural lines vanishing into pure darkness. No warnings, no hostile returns, just black. Same as the allotment center. Cold shot through him—those weren't whispers at all, but the wet sound of daxed flesh surging through tunnels below. The orbital strike, all those people dead, had stopped nothing. Just bought them time. Best not to waste it. He yanked the last frag from his vest and switched his rifle to full auto.

"Once you're set, get clear, then blow it."

He armed the grenade and let it drop. For one heartbeat, the sounds stopped.

A blood-curdling once-human scream split the darkness.

The frag detonated with a wet boom that rang loud through the junction, killing the scream. Acrid smoke rose from the shaft, tainted with the smell of sickly-sweet decay. Above him, the ceiling was a web of plasmex bricks and demo wire, Rosch still mounting charges while Kitrelle worked the ignition leads.

"Status?"

"One more." Rosch kept working. "Bad igniter."

"Working on it." Kitrelle's voice shook as she wired up a lead.

Another scream pierced the shaft. Shorter. Sharper. Bresto sighted down his rifle. The darkness had closed to ten meters, his scope flooding with *UNKNOWN CONTACT* warnings.

"Work faster." He fired into the black. The smell grew stronger.

Kitrelle stepped back. "Got it!"

He kept firing down the shaft, watching his charge indicator drop. The daxed pressed closer, movement flickering in the flash of bolt light.

"Time?" Rosch called.

"Sixty seconds." Bresto dropped another target he couldn't quite see.

"Shit! We won't make the climb back," Kitrelle said.

"Forward hatch." He snapped off another bolt. "Don't stop until you feel rain."

Rosch tapped his flexscreen, and the charges above blinked red dead. "Set!"

A timer appeared on Bresto's flex: sixty seconds until the junction became a tomb. "Everyone out!"

Something surged out of the shaft, a thin gray corpse stained black with its own fluids. He backed away, rifle tracking. More bodies followed, piling on each other while something alive reached for him beneath it all. Kitrelle and Rosch were already gone. Time to go.

The rough tunnel exit bit at his hands and knees, but he kept moving, ignoring the warnings flashing across his flex. The thought of dying, of being atomized, wasn't scary. Being taken, being changed like them—like Mace. He scrambled faster.

Another scream rang through the confined space.

Ten seconds.

His tac vest snagged on an exposed coupling. He tore free and kept moving.

Five seconds.

The sound filled everything now, pressing against him, like they were right there. Like they knew his name, whispering it over and over. Like they'd been waiting for him all along.

Holy Mother, please—

Light and pressure consumed him, throwing him further down the tunnel until his helmet cracked against a hatch frame. Everything burned, the air, the metal, his lungs. Only the ringing in his ears seemed real. He dragged himself forward on hands and knees, each movement sending pain through his body.

A figure waited at the tunnel's end, impossibly tall and black as the storm, crowned with fire. His breath caught. He blinked, hard, and suddenly it was just Rosch standing there, hand extended, grinning.

"Thought we lost you, Sarnt." The kid sounded far away.

Bresto glanced back through the smoke. Nothing moved in the dark. No whispers. No shapes. The junction's red glow was gone. There were other ways up the drop, but no way to ambush them without moving a few tons of debris. One way or another, the fight would be done by then. He reached for Rosch's hand.

Light exploded behind Rosch, his outline glowing red. He spun around with a grunt, smoke and the stink of ozone rising from the scorch mark on his armor plate.

"Get down!" Bresto barked, yanking Rosch behind the hatchway frame just as more laser fire stung their position.

"I'm good," Rosch wheezed, hand on his side. He winced as he shifted, but his eyes were clear. "Hit the plate. Holy Mother loves me, huh?"

Bresto found his rifle and sighted in. The squid that had shot Rosch glowed bright red in his optics. Three bolts center mass dropped it clean—asked and answered. The raider collapsed in a spray of blue mist, weapon clattering to the deck.

"Yeah, She does." He clapped Rosch's shoulder. "That's why we wear the heavy stuff."

"Not gonna die that easy, Sarnt." Rosch managed a shaky grin, already bringing his rifle back up to cover them.

Kitrelle had pushed ahead and was trading shots from behind a support strut. More squids swarmed over the gantries beneath another platform. A transport settled into the channel below, engines screaming, spilling more raiders onto the slope.

Bresto's stomach turned. So that had been the Concordat's plan all along: hit Victory hard from the front while the Lost ambushed them from the rear.

His flexscreen showed Third Squad's markers above him on the platform. He patched into their channel. "Rikkos, Bresto. Three friendlies pinned down by maintenance gantries. Need support."

"Stand by, Sarnt." FAB barrels whined in the background.

Two squids rushed Kitrelle's position. Bresto dropped one, but the other slammed into her. Its cracked helmet vented atmo as they grappled. Her rifle caught the blow, but the impact knocked her down.

Bresto put a round through its back leg, but the squid fell on Kitrelle instead. She screamed, fighting back, but the thing had a hundred kilos on her. He tried for another shot, but they were too close, his optics flashing friendly fire.

Metal fingers grabbed the warrior like it was nothing and tossed it over the side. Behind the controls of 3-3-3, Olsom bared her teeth like an animal, drilling any raider that tried to advance. Their eyes met, and for a heartbeat it looked like she might shoot him too.

She blinked, and the moment was gone. "Clear, Sarnt."

3-3-3 pulled them onto the platform where dead raiders and colonists lay scattered, lightning painting everything stark white.

They'd stopped the worst of the ambush, but the squids had done their share of killing.

"Guns, guns, guns!" came the net call. Strike fighters screamed overhead, their heavy blaster turrets spraying the grounded transport danger close to their position.

Bresto sank wearily onto a chunk of debris. Far beyond Vestebrae, in the heart of the storm, falling stars of burning debris lit the sky. "Is that—?"

"The Umbra, Sarnt." Olsom's voice caught. "They killed it."

Rosch checked his charge pack with a grimace. "So much for orbital support."

Sweet Twelfth. Back in the tunnels, he'd thought they had turned the tide. Now the win tasted like borrowed time.

Kull's ID overrode every channel. *"Easy 3, Fury 3, this is Victory Actual. Fall back by dropship to the drop station. We've got unknown contacts massing in the transit."*

Dropships were already airborne, engines flaring as they descended on the platforms.

Olsom looked to Bresto. "What kind of contacts?"

More whispers carried on the winds rushing up from below. The hiss of countless throats that no longer needed air to breathe. Each gust brought the stench with it: that sweet rot he'd smelled in the tunnels, multiplied a hundredfold and rising like smoke from the ruins of Vestebrae.

The hairs rose on Bresto's neck. Something moved in the shadows between collapsed buildings, a tide of gray shapes flowing upward through the rubble. The things the Concordat had created in those shelters, the ones that survived the strike. They were done hiding. Ready to take what they came for.

He swapped his spent charge pack for a fresh one. "The Lost are coming."

CHAPTER
THIRTY-TWO

THE DROPSHIP'S deck plates vibrated as Olsom moved 3-3-3 up the ramp, icy rain pelting the hull. Razor Flight screamed overhead, tearing another enemy transport apart. The fierce sound made a child cry out, its mother holding tight to her chest as she pressed herself deeper into her jumpseat. Through the open ramp, laser fire sparked off the platform's edge, the raiders still probing for an opening.

"Exos, lock in!" someone called out.

"No time, get us up!" Sergeant Bresto backed up the ramp, rifle still tracking.

The deck lurched upward, sending loose gear sliding. The platforms shrank away beneath them into storm and smoke. Too many dead colonists down there. But they'd tried, at least. Not like Major Kill and that damn liar Bresto.

Doc's tightbeam lit up her comms. *"Don't guess you saved any of that hardwine?"*

"Thought you were too proper to drink on duty."

"So, that's a no?"

Now he wanted to flirt? "That's a no."

"If we get out of this," he said, *"there's a place I know. Not too far from here actually. One plate will cost you a month's pay, but it's the best crid and rats in Corongaet."* He made a hungry sound. *"And the hardwine…"*

If they got out of this? Doc had his chance, back at the foundry, when she really showed her belly to him. And he stuck her worse than Mez ever could.

"Whatever, Doc."

Alarms screamed through the troop deck, her threat indicators blinking red dead. Something big tumbled through the air behind them—a strike fighter—burning close enough to see its engine shredded and trailing fire. Ropes of fire light followed twisting paths through the air, chasing it. Getting closer fast.

The reaction was pure training. Wasn't a damn thing she could do but yell, "Incoming!"

The dropship pitched nose down, engines howling. Then something hit hard and suddenly the hull peeled open, showing too much storm-black above as they began to spin.

"*Mayday, mayday!*" The pilot's transmission dissolved in static as they tumbled.

Olsom staggered sideways, 3-3-3's arms catching against the deck plating. Fire erupted from an engine she shouldn't be able to see, throwing sparks and flame from its thrust nozzle. Each turn came harder as the pilot lost control. The wild part of her coiled and shrieked. Out. She needed the fuck out!

The drop station rushed up through the rear hatch—wet duraplate and metal towers and emergency floods. The impact knocked her forward, head knocking into plexene as 3-3-3's stabilizers caught. People screamed, metal shrieked, then everything stopped moving. Rain beat from above, leaving streaks on her canopy and hissing against the engine fire. Her heart hammered in the dead quiet. Each second stretched, waiting for the next disaster, until the burning in her lungs forced her to breathe.

"Third Platoon, listen up!" Bresto stumbled down the tilted deck like they hadn't just plowed into the drop station. "Exos on line now. We're out of time." He stopped to help a woman with a broken arm out of her harness. "Support Marines, get these people clear, then find your metal."

"Doc?" Olsom walked 3-3-3 clear of the ruined ship just to turn around. Its hull had split along the spine, one wing completely gone.

Station crew rushed the burning engine with chemical suppressors, the thick gel hissing in the rain.

"We're good," Doc called back as he guided the other survivors toward the waiting emergency teams. Mez lagged a few steps behind.

The shadow of the strike fighter loomed through the storm, maybe twenty meters out. Crumpled at its midsection, it had slammed hard into a massive winch. Its port engine was a smoking ruin, while the starboard still spit flames. Her threat indicators painted the whole craft in hazard yellow, the IFF tag *RAZOR ONE* blinking loud on the screen.

That pilot had saved them twice now. First back in orbit, when the raiders nearly took the *Gauntlet* apart. Then again on the platform below after the *Umbra* was destroyed. They may be out of time, but she'd seen what the Lost did to survivors. Founders, what her own chain of command did to survivors—wiped them out like they were nothing. She wouldn't risk leaving anymore behind.

"Doc, Mez, come on." The damage looked terminal up close, fire eating through the fuselage behind the cockpit, its plexene canopy a maze of spreading cracks.

"This doesn't look good, Bugs."

"We have to try. We're running out of friends up here."

She reached for the canopy with 3-3-3's primary arm, but the movement was stiff. Servos whined in protest, the motion jerky and stiff. The metal fingers finally closed around the plexene frame.

Doc frowned. "Rig's not happy."

No shit.

"Maybe we should listen to it, eh?" Mez shifted his weight, eyes everywhere but the cockpit.

The canopy came free with a sharp crack. Beneath it, a bloody ruin slumped forward against the harness, its pilot helmet split open along one side. Blood had pooled across the dead man's face, jaw hanging loose against his chest.

Doc cursed under his breath.

"Mez told you," Mez mumbled, rocking back a step. "Lost no more, right? Come on. We go."

New orders flashed across her terminal feed, nav markers pointing the way. *Victory's* remaining companies had their exos on line at the edge of the drop. Two hundred meters of Marine metal facing whatever was coming for them from below. Fury 3 would anchor the far right, dead last in line. Olsom's belly coiled tight. Whatever came through that storm would come for her, try to turn their line, and there'd be nobody watching her flank. Acceptable losses. Disposable. Always—

"Mez is right," Doc said. "Sooner we get on the line, sooner I can check that arm."

"Still wrong." Mez's voice dropped to barely a whisper. "All wr—"

The corpse made a wet sound, a rattle somewhere between breathing and choking. Fresh blood trickled from its mangled jaw.

Mez let out a shout.

"Holy Twelfth!" Doc stumbled back.

Alive? No, it—

"Can't be." Doc steadied himself against the cockpit frame. "That's brain matter. On his face."

Her heart beat faster. "But I heard it too."

"Probably just gas." He didn't sound convinced. "Maybe some autonomic response."

"Just check!"

"Fine." He reached into the cockpit with a grimace, fingers probing around the ruined jaw. "No pulse. I told you—"

A gloved hand snapped up and caught his wrist. He yelped, trying to jerk away as blue light crawled like static across the pilot's torn flesh. More wet sounds fought past its broken jaw, tongue working helplessly. Maybe it was Lost. Maybe putting it down would be mercy.

Olsom worked the FAB controls, but the moving corpse in her sights scanned IFF blue, friendly fire warnings flashing. It raised its other hand toward her, palm out, almost pleading.

Doc finally tore free, rifle snapping up. The pilot gurgled again; the sound coming out all wrong. Not breathing. Talking. With terrible slowness, its hands found the broken jaw and pushed it back into place with a wet snap.

Every instinct screamed that this was wrong, impossible. "Doc? What is it? What do we do?"

Doc kept his rifle trained on it. "I… I don't know."

"Kill it, boss." Mez's voice shook. "Kill it now."

More blood bubbled up as blue energy pulsed inside its mouth. Then the sound changed: "No."

"Wait." She'd heard it. A word.

This wasn't like the Lost in the allotment center, all mindless hunger and rage. The pilot reached up and pulled his helmet free. Beneath the blood and trauma, she could see the man's face. One clear eye found hers as his mouth twisted into something like a smile.

Her breath caught. "What... What the fuck?"

"Help me," he croaked, squinting from the effort.

Doc looked to her, rifle half-raised, waiting.

"Do it," she said. "Get him out."

Doc slung his weapon and worked the cockpit harness straps. The pilot's body popped and cracked as they lifted him clear.

"You're dead," Doc said. "How are you not dead?"

The pilot started to laugh when they laid him down, but he rolled over, coughing blood. His good eye fixed on her, and he spoke through misaligned teeth. "You're... asking the wrong question."

"Who are you?" she asked.

"Wrong again."

Blue light threaded across his face. Her combat optics were grainy, but it looked like it was putting him back together.

"What are you? Really?" She hesitated. "Are you Lost?"

"Please." He laughed, then clutched his chest as his breathing went ragged. "Not Lost."

"Some secret Navy program, maybe." Doc leaned closer, checking the pilot's uniform. "To keep up with the Division."

"Still... wrong." The man grimaced as more energy shot through his jaw. "Marines. Not the brightest eps in the class, are we?"

"Whatever you are," Olsom said, "you're not human."

"There." The man's smile was perfect now. "That wasn't so hard."

The heavy buzz of FABs echoed across the drop, followed by distant explosions. Olsom's terminal started flashing with orders to return to position. The pilot noticed her flinch.

"Fascinating as I am," he said, rising smoothly, "you have more pressing concerns."

"Wait, you can't just—"

"Actually, I can." The bloody lump of a corpse was gone, replaced by something alive and well. Strong. "Your friends are dying while we chat."

Doc was already backing away. "Bugs…"

The Victory line's combat markers pulsed urgent through her display. New contacts lit up, dark shapes turning ghost-gray, all flashing *UNKNOWN CONTACT*. The feeds only painted them hostile when they hit Victory's lines.

The Lost, coming to make more of their own.

Mez trembled, scarred face slick from fear and the storm. She waved him on with one of 3-3-3's primary arms.

"Just a little longer now," the pilot said, voice carrying through the rain as they moved away. He sounded almost giddy. "Good luck!"

———

The metal barrier barely came to 3-3-3's waist. Beyond it, the night swallowed everything, the lifts, the platforms, what remained of the transit below. She'd lifted her canopy to hear Bresto better, the sergeant staying dry underneath while he talked exo tactics. But her attention kept drifting to her terminal, to the black tide spreading across her display. Getting closer. Always closer.

The Marines' guns never really stopped, but there were moments between shots where the night seemed to speak. Whispers that might have been the storm; might have been something worse.

"… you hear me, Olsom?"

"Yes, Sarnt." Just saying it felt cold, automatic. "I'm the end of the line."

"And you hold it." He drove his fist into his palm then turned to Doc. "Keep her FAB talking, Myers."

"Aye, Sarnt."

Mez stared at the deck as Bresto checked his demo load. "You got plasmex left. Save it for when they get close. Put it on a timer and throw it."

Mez managed a nod.

"And when they get too close…" Bresto turned back to her, lifting his fists in a fighting stance. "Metal up."

"Yes, Sarnt." The lump in her throat wouldn't go away. Much as she couldn't stand him just then, they all had bigger problems. "Aye, Sarnt."

Bresto hesitated, like there was something fatherly he should say. The expression on his weathered face—concern, maybe even affection—hit her like a physical blow. Her throat closed up tight.

Don't. Don't be kind now. Not when they were all about to die.

The fear sat like ice in her belly, spreading outward with each heartbeat. She'd been so fucking stupid, thinking she could make a difference out here. Thinking anyone gave a shit whether some admin block trash lived or died. All those CDF recruiting feeds with their pretty lies about honor and belonging—none of it mattered when the universe decided to remind you how small you really were.

The control rigs felt foreign under her grip, like she was pretending to be someone she wasn't. They were all going to die here, fighting a hopeless war against things that shouldn't exist. No alien god to save them this time. No coming back to life, not for her. The pilot—Twelfth, what the hell was that thing? And why did thinking about it make her feel even more alone?

"Got something you need to say, Private?"

"Tell him, Bugs," Myers said.

"Tell me what?"

What did she have to say? Plenty. Like how this bastard had abandoned his post to play hero. Had gotten innocent people just… vaporized! No resurrection for them. The sheer insanity of it all burned in her throat, begging to be spat out.

"About what we saw," Doc pressed, his stare boring into her.

She blinked. Not about Bresto at all. "What we—" The strike fighter. The impossible thing they'd seen. "The pilot. Right"

Bresto frowned. "What pilot?"

"He was dead. I mean, we saw him—"

Bresto grunted. "Then he's the lucky one. Lost no more."

A distant explosion thumped through 3-3-3's frame. Bresto turned toward the flash, an unsettling concern creasing the skin around his eyes.

"But he's not."

He waved her off without even looking back. "Not what?"

"Dead." It sounded crazy. It was crazy. But she'd seen it. "He was dead—but then he just… wasn't."

"Wasn't what?"

"Dead." Not crazy. Insane. "There was this blue light. It put him back together."

Something changed in Bresto's eyes, something cold. Recognition? The bastard knew something, but he wasn't sharing. Why would he? She was just a boot. Admin block trash.

FABs erupted nearby, drowning his reply in their buzzing thunder. Mez hit the deck, flattening himself against the barricade. Doc was next, sighting his rifle over the wall's sawtooth edge.

Bresto stole a glance at his flexscreen. "They've hit Fury 1." His eyes were pale ghosts as he reached in and mashed the canopy control. He ducked beneath the closing shell and melted into the rain. "We're almost up."

Revan's ID lit up her all-squad comms. *"Stand to, Fury 3."* The call echoed down their line. She repeated it, walking 3-3-3 to the barrier and leveling the FAB over the thick slab. Her voice vanished in the storm. Alone at the end of the line, with nothing but darkness ahead.

The mass moved like a single thing through her combat feeds, a black tide flowing up the steep slope. Each flash of lightning showed more of them coming. The whispers grew louder, bleeding through her helmet like they were meant just for her. She forced herself to focus, hunting for a clear shot.

Fury 2 opened up and the whispers turned to screams. They sounded almost human.

"Engaging," Lessig transmitted, his signal drowned in a fury of blaster bolts.

The particle streams carved red lines through the dark. She saw them then, gray bodies with empty masks for faces. But the things moving between them made her blood go cold. Black shadows, fast and sharp. Lumbering giants that made her exo look small.

Third Squad went hot. Her thumb found the rhythm on the hat trigger—short bursts, traverse, more bursts. The FAB shredded anything in her sights, but they just kept coming. Kill one, three more appeared. Her range finders clicked lower. One hundred meters. Ninety.

"Engaging!" Doc's CR-11 snapped to life. "C'mon, Mez, get up!"

Mez huddled behind the barrier while the FAB thundered overhead, his knuckles white around the rifle's grip.

"Won't save you 'less you use it!" she howled at him.

Mez's face twisted as he lurched upright, rifle jerking with each wild shot.

She kept her burst pattern steady even as her heart hammered. The big guns had to hold—had to keep those things off their line—or they'd be ripped apart. On the display, heat levels climbed toward yellow.

Plasmex explosions walked further down the line, marking where the Lost had reached the barriers. At least the center wasn't breaking. 3-3-3's optics locked onto the giant pushing through her field of fire. The FAB was useless, charged particles crackling against its armor plate. This called for tungsten, but after that stunt at the foundry… She clicked her railgun forward anyway.

"3-3-3 requesting weapons free on the LEC." The railgun's capacitors whined to full. "I've got a big fucker, sixty meters out. My FAB's just pissing it off."

The big Lost lurched closer. It was human in shape only, some kind of melding of metal and man. Almost like an exo. The thought sent a cold snap down her back.

"One shot, one shot, fire when ready," Bresto tac'd back. *"Fury 3, stand by for electromag."*

The reticles came together on her screen. *Target acquired,* the voice in her terminal screamed, *target acquired!*

"Firing."

In the dark, the flash burned her eyes. A thunderous crack launched the slug at near-hypersonic speeds. It struck the giant a heartbeat later, armor ringing like a bell. Static laced her screen, but her optics held out. The smaller ones around it were vapor. But the big one was… still moving. The slug had put it on its ass, cratered its armor, but it was getting back up.

The railgun's drum clicked over as the weapon charged again.

"It's still coming!"

"Repeat!" Bresto ordered.

"Firing!"

The trigger clicked home. Nothing. *Charging! Charging!* shrieked the bitch inside the screen. Damn capacitors. She worked the trigger again and again—still nothing—watching the big monster stagger to its feet. Its faceless mask found her. No eyes, but she *knew* it saw her. Wanted to kill her, or—

The railgun fired again. No bell this time, just the *flash-crack* of atomized tungsten. When the optics finally cleared, the giant was half-gone. Its legs just stood there on their own, two thick, lifeless metal pillars.

"Good kill!" She stowed the LEC and went back to the FAB. Barrel integrity was down, despite the temps holding in the yellow. More Lost were already filling in the space left behind.

"You—" Mez's voice shook. "You see that?"

"Hell yeah!" Doc whooped between shots. "Nice shooting, Bugs."

"Not that." Mez looked back up at Olsom, eyes big and white. "The shadow, after. Too fast for Mez's scope."

"You're seeing things…" She didn't quite believe it herself. Just needed Mez to get his ass on the line. There were plenty more monsters out there, despite the brief lull the railgun had made. "Just shoot what you can hit."

"How's the rig?" Doc asked.

"Getting warm."

"Barrels?"

She eyed the terminal again. "Not great."

"There's never a good time. Let's change 'em."

Doc mag-locked his rifle and disappeared behind the exo. She let loose a few more bursts into the surge of Lost daxed scrambling upslope.

He reappeared, lugging a barrel bag over his shoulder. "FAB down, cage open."

"Cage open?" She made a face. "Why?"

"You know. Covering fire?" He was already ratcheting loose the barrel lock with a long spanner. "So those things don't kill me."

"Right."

3-3-3's canopy hissed open. She found her rifle in its mount and put it to her shoulder. The optics blinked to life, filling with more black and gray noise as she sighted at the growing horde below them. No target assist, but range put them at fifty meters.

"How long?" She took a breath, aimed, and fired.

Something screamed and fell.

"Thirty seconds—" He grunted, and the heavy barrels clattered to the deck. "Maybe twenty."

Just like the damn brig. "Cutting it close."

"You know me." His laugh was strained as the first barrel slotted home. "My timing is shit."

"Yeah, about that." Two more trigger pulls. Two more down. Lost no more. Suddenly the old saying made sense. Or did it mean something else now?

"… that skeeg?"

Doc's voice cut through her thoughts like a blade. "Huh?"

"Remember that skeeg, back in the brig on Three-Alpha?"

"Which one?"

Doc hefted the second barrel up. It looked heavy. Solid duraplate. "I don't, uh… Taylor. No." He gave the barrel a turn and it slid into place. "Faylor, that's it. Faylor."

She remembered. Kicked that skeeg in the sack when Doc killed the power too soon. She'd felt awful about it after. Not a shred of guilt now. Maybe Bresto was rubbing off on her.

"What about him?"

"Not going to lie." He went quiet, waiting for a burst from 3-3-2 to end. "Made me jealous, watching you talk nice to him."

"Jealous?" She snorted. Loud. Any other time, any other place, she'd have turned pink. Another shot; another dead monster. "He wasn't impressed, remember? I had to lay him out."

"Yeah." He chuckled. The quick glance gave her goosebumps. "His loss."

Damn Doc still turned her heart sideways.

The third barrel settled into its housing. Doc reached down, took the spanner, and began ratcheting the barrel lock down.

The first barrel read green in the ops terminal. Mez wasn't shooting. Then the second. He wasn't even on the barricade.

Third barrel up. "Hey, Mez—?"

Mez lay behind the barricade, his scarred face a mask of terror. Tears swelled in his eyes, lips trembling, mouth working uselessly.

"Almost there!" Doc said.

She followed Mez's gaze. The long, thin shadow balanced on the barrier barely three meters away. Perched on one bar-like foot, the other pressed into its knee. Gray webbing wrapped its bone thin body. Long arms stretched up, hands reaching. Not hands. Blades. The faceless mask cocked at a wrong angle, like it had been waiting to hear the end of their story.

"Myers," she choked out.

He looked up, confused, smiling. "Why so—"

His smile withered.

She jerked the rifle toward the thing. Fired. The bolt snapped through nothing, racing for the storm. She'd missed. How—

Another flash of shadow and the taste of warm copper hit her mouth. The air stank like sweet rot. A blade jutted half a meter through Doc's waist, red blood mixing with the water at his boots. The Lost daxed leaned against his back, almost lovingly, softly *click-click-clicking* from behind its mask.

Olsom jerked back hard, skull cracking against the cage. There was a distant quality to the terminal's shriek: *TRAUMA! TRAUMA! LIFE SIGNS CRITICAL!* Doc's heart rhythm danced all erratic on the screen.

The monster gave the blade a sharp twist. Doc jerked, sputtered, gloved hands scrabbling at the weapon that was impaling him. A line of blood trickled from his mouth. His face went pale.

And the wild thing inside her screamed.

CHAPTER
THIRTY-THREE

THE BLADE CAME free with a sick, wet sound. Doc fell to his knees, hands out and grabbing at nothing.

The world went white-hot nova. Not anger. Something bigger, something that ate anger whole and kept burning. That thing had touched him. Had *hurt* him. Doc with his stupid grin and his steady hands and his way of making everything seem fixable. Doc who'd kept her breathing on this fucking mountain, who'd kept her rig running, who'd turned away when she was drunk and sloppy because he was better than that, who'd looked at her like she mattered. Like she was worth saving.

She dragged the rifle up, finger on the trigger as time stretched thin as a wire. One heartbeat. Doc's blood spreading dark across the deck. Two heartbeats. The Lost turning toward her with those blade-hands dripping. Three heartbeats. The bolt leaving her barrel in a streak of coherent light.

Charged particles snapped into the Lost's ribcage and it staggered back, a breathy scream forming beneath its mask.

"You motherfucker," she hissed through tears and teeth.

The trigger clicked again. Nothing. Just the dull trill of empty charge pack warnings. Panic bit at her as she groped at her vest for another.

Clicks rippled through the thin Lost's frame like breaking glass as it righted itself, broken joints and bone snapping back into place. It drew back, readying another attack.

The harness released beneath her fingers.

Its first blade punched through plastec centimeters from her hip with a meaty thunk. The second came blindingly fast.

She tumbled onto the rain-slick deck, fire tearing across her forehead. The world went red-tinted and blurry. Salt and copper flooded her mouth. She rolled on her back, rifle up in a guard, ready to block. Ready to die.

The Lost jerked its blade free with a metal shriek. It straightened, clicking sounds coming faster. One step toward her, then another, blade-arms spreading wide. Its eyeless mask tilted down, studying her. Then its head cocked, gazing at—

Doc's blaster rifle opened up full auto, tearing gory black chunks from its torso. The thing's scream was too human, cut short as it fell dead on the metal grating.

"Doc!"

He lay half-propped against 3-3-3's left foot, his rifle sliding from his grip. Blood pulsed between the fingers pressed to his side.

"Couldn't let it… get you, too." That smile she loved was all red now. His eyes fixed on something past her shoulder, past the storm, past everything.

"No." She grabbed his shoulders and shook him. "No, no, no!"

"'m here." His eyes went wide. "Bugs. You're hurt."

"Shut up." She yanked his kit open and pulled the autodoc from beneath spare charge packs. It felt heavy, the tiny green screen clicking to life. She pressed it into his hand and put pressure on the wound. "C'mon, Doc. You gotta fix this."

"Need a surgical team." He let the device slide, a shock of pain twisting his face. "Not an autodoc."

Her cry for help drowned in the thunder of Third Squad's weapons fire. Red lines cut through sheets of rain, hundreds of meters of Marine metal hammering back the tide of gray death surging onto the barriers. The bursts came ragged, barrels glowing hot, the stink of cooked metal burning her throat. She knew that rhythm—three bolts, pause, three bolts—the sound of overheated weapons buying seconds with their own death. Doc's blood was hot between her fingers. They weren't going to win this.

"Can't make it." Mez's voice barely broke over the roar of the guns. He was still curled beneath the barrier, hands pressed to his ears.

"What're you—?" Her stomach turned at the sight of him. Mez had been all killer right up until it mattered. "Get up! Cover me, you piece of shit!"

"Got to go, boss lady." His eyes were wild, reflecting emergency floods as he scrabbled toward her. Each weapons burst made him shrink lower. "Get to the dropships before they leave us."

"We're not leaving him." She wanted to kick Mez's teeth in. To shoot him. But Doc was bleeding out, and she didn't have time for either.

"Mez not staying here." The man's eyes turned cold, predator-sharp, like he was sizing her up for a blade between the ribs. Easy prey, not like those things beyond the barricades. And like that, the bully was back.

Doc coughed, his speech slurring. "Fuck him. Let him leave."

The sound of Mez's boots faded as he bolted into the storm. Doc's face was ghost-white, each breath coming shorter.

She grabbed the autodoc and wiped rain from its screen with shaking fingers. "All right, Doc. Either walk me through this or I start jabbing."

His eyes snapped open at that. "Nanites. You'll have to… override the delivery."

"Override the what?" Strange drug names scrolled past, compounds she couldn't pronounce. His blood was spreading beneath them both.

"Blood pressure's dropping." The words seemed to drain him and he began to shiver. "It'll know I'm bleeding out. Won't work unless you override."

The dial finally stopped on *NANITE TRAUMA RESPONSE*. The screen filled with warnings in harsh green: cardiovascular collapse, tissue rejection, systemic shock. It all sounded bad.

"Override? How?"

"Pull." He demonstrated with trembling fingers. "Knob comes out."

The control pulled out with a *clunk*. More warnings flooded the display: *Manual override detected. Nanotech delivery NOT RECOM-MENDED in cases of severe hemorrhaging.*

She laughed, all jitters. "This thing really doesn't want me to do this."

"I don't either. Shit might kill me." His smile was weak but real. "But I'm dead if you don't."

She pressed the applicator against his throat, watching the vessels map themselves in red and blue across the screen. The targeting reticle drifted in the center.

"Find the carotid."

"How the fuck do I do that?"

"Big pulsing thing." His laugh turned into a wet wheeze. "Can't miss it."

She managed a shaky smile. "Bet you say that to all the girls."

It was easy enough to find, a thick line swelling red to blue, red to blue. The reticle shifted green above it.

"Feels right." His eyes locked on hers. "Do it."

"How?"

"Just…" He fought to stay still. "Knob back in then push."

The control snapped home with a mechanical click. A soft puff of air, and the screen flashed: *3 CCs NPR APPLIED.*

Doc's eyes flew wide, tracking something invisible beneath his skin. He grabbed her hands and shoved them under his vest. "Quick. Pressure. Hard as you can."

She threw her weight against the wound, feeling hot blood pulse beneath her fingers. His breath hitched as she pressed harder, using her shoulder for leverage. The fabric of his uniform was soaked through, making it hard to grip until she found purchase against his ribs.

Beyond the barrier, the storm's voice had changed. Wind gusted in and out, in and out, like it was trying to breathe. Doc bucked beneath her hands, every muscle going rigid.

"Fucking burns," he gasped. "Like glass in my blood."

"Tell me what to do. Please." But he just writhed there, teeth bared against the pain until suddenly he went still. His breathing turned shallow, gaze unfocused.

"Back at that bar." The words came distant, dreamy. "Should've told Bresto to fuck right off. Got tickets planetside. Found a real place to eat." His laugh was barely there. "A proper date."

"Save your creds." She blinked hard, the wild thing inside her clawing for air. "I'm no Tellie Strong, remember?"

Then he looked at her, really looked at her. Like he was seeing past the uniform and the scars and the pain to something she'd forgotten was ever there.

"Yeah, you're not." He was so quiet she had to lean close. "You're better. You're—"

Pain twisted his features as another spasm racked through him. Then his whole body went slack, head lolling back. His eyes fluttered closed.

"Doc?" She pressed harder against the wound, terror screaming up her throat. "Doc!" The sticky warmth coating her fingers wasn't pulsing anymore. Just wet. Still. Dead. No. Sweet Founders, please no.

"Don't you fucking dare." She seized his shoulders, shaking him hard enough that his head snapped back. "Doc!"

The autodoc's screen blurred as she fumbled it with bloody hands, jabbing the applicator against his neck. The vessel map was dark where before it had glowed like neon. But there—a ghost of movement. The pulse was thread-thin but present. Doc was alive.

Metal thrummed beneath her knees, each vibration growing stronger. The sound rolled through the storm like thunder, but thunder didn't move that steady. Didn't breathe.

Lightning split the sky, and there it was, a mountain of gray metal and flesh looming over the barrier. Its joints hissed with each rise and fall of its chest, the real source of the storm's sudden gasping. The giant's blank faceplate fixed on her, and suddenly the air felt too thick to breathe.

She reached for her rifle. The fresh charge pack clicked home, capacitor whining as it cycled up. Doc was still breathing. Still fighting. No way in twelve hells she was leaving him here for that thing to find.

Bresto had fucked off to play hero. Mez had run like the coward he was. Just like her own blood. Couldn't stick around when things got hard.

But she wasn't them. That monster could rip her apart, turn her into one of those masked things. Didn't matter. She'd put every bolt she had into it before she let it touch Doc.

The selector snapped over to full auto with an angry buzz. She yanked Doc's kit closer, then lit the monster up. Blaster bolts hammered its armor, throwing sparks but doing fuck-all else. One bolt pinged off and sizzled out near her boot. She fired again, hunting weak spots through the scope, but the damn thing just stood there. She might have well been throwing rocks.

Its hands gripped the barrier, metal screaming as it peeled the thick slab apart like wet paper. More of those capsule things poured through the gap, but they went down easy enough. Too easy, like the big bastard was letting her waste shots while it sized her up.

"Smokes! Vlan!" Her voice cracked through comms. "Need help here!"

"—*under heavy*—" Static ate half their transmission. "—*breaching the line—can't*—"

She caught flashes of their position through the rain. 3-3-2's FAB beat out sustained fire, barrels cooking, while Toelke and Vlan worked their rifles from behind it. They were getting hammered just as hard.

The frag felt heavy in her palm as she thumbed the trigger. An easy throw, but damn close. The grenade arced through the rain, clattering between the giant's feet. She threw herself over Doc, fingers locked in his vest. The blast hit like a hammer, washing hot across her back. Ozone and scorched air filled her lungs as her hearing collapsed to a sharp ring.

Black fluid leaked from the giant's knees, but it barely seemed to notice. The thing lurched forward, stepping over what remained of the wall with a bone-deep grinding sound.

She opened up on its legs, putting everything into those damaged joints. A bolt found something vital and the heavy crashed to the deck. The impact shook through her boots, but she could barely hear it over the ringing. More of those fresh-made Lost crawled over its bulk like hungry larvae.

Another frag, another flash of heat and pressure. Gray bodies went flying. The giant dragged itself closer, each movement leaving streaks of black fluid. She wedged Doc between 3-3-3's legs, braced against her rig's foot, and emptied the charge pack into its faceplate. The shots cracked and ricocheted, one zipping past close enough to singe her cheek.

Last pack. Her hands were steady as she slapped it home and keyed her comms.

"3 Actual, 3-3-3." The words came out flat, like reporting the weather. Like she wasn't about to die. "I'm being overrun."

She dropped two more Lost climbing the barrier, but more kept coming. "Any station this net, this is 3-3-3 on Victory Line's right flank. Lost breaking through. One big one, multiple fresh ones. I can't hold them."

The giant's hand reached for her, fingers spreading wide. Her attention snapped to her rig. She could cook the reactors, take this fucker with her. But that'd kill Doc. Probably the rest of third Squad, too. Wasn't right to go out like that, even if it meant these things got her instead.

Something moved on the barrier, fast as that blade-armed thing, but different. More human. Her scope picked it up, combat feeds screaming blue as the pilot's blood-caked face clicked into focus. His IFF return flashed two words that made her gut clench: *Same Team*.

He brought his palms together and the storm answered. Blue light crackled between his fingers, more Lost clawing at his legs as something formed between his palms. Then he was gone, just... gone. The Lost around him came apart in wet chunks, their bodies dropping carved meat.

Suddenly the giant Lost was right fucking there, scraping at her boot, each finger thick as her arm. She screamed—all teeth and fury— shuffling backwards over Doc. Her rifle snapped and bucked, throwing wild shots into the giant's bulk.

The pilot was back lightning quick, balanced on the giant Lost's spine. The sword in his grip was void-black, angled toward its skull. He drove it home, and the Lost just dropped.

The pilot's lips curled into something dangerous. Like watching her almost die had been the highlight of his day. His steps down the giant's arm were graceful to the point of casual as he dropped to the deck in front of her. That cold gaze shifted to Doc, and for a heartbeat she caught something almost human there. Almost caring. Then it was gone.

"Who…" The word stuck in her throat, heart still hammering. "Who are you?"

"Names. I have none. I have many." He sounded bored. The blade hummed in his grip, Lost blood burning blue against the black metal.

"What are you?"

His gaze sliced right through her. "We are Section Delta."

The storm exploded with light, turning night to fusion dawn. Like just saying the words had woken up something ancient and powerful. He glanced over his shoulder at the maelstrom, that dangerous curl returning to the corner of his mouth.

"There now." Azure energy glowed behind his eyes. "That wasn't long at all."

CHAPTER
THIRTY-FOUR

THE LOST CAME at them in waves, freshly daxed colonists stumbling over the barricade with vacant eyes behind their half-formed masks. Bresto took a snap shot at the closest one, hit clean through its center mass. These weren't like the heavies or the blade-armed wisps—their movements were clumsy, desperate. Still human. His latest kill went down hard, screaming through a mask that was more scar tissue than metal, hands reaching for him as it fell.

He backed up a step, trying to put distance between himself and that awful sound, and bumped into something solid. Revan spun, pistol half-raised, before recognition flashed across his face. His finger stayed on the trigger a heartbeat too long before he turned back to the line.

"Watch your sectors!" Bresto shouted over the storm. Third Platoon's FABs hammered the slope in overlapping fields of fire, but the Lost kept coming. Had to be hundreds of them at the barricade. Thousands more behind them. The archenemy had been on the mountain for barely thirty hours. How were there so many? He switched charge packs, the empty clattering at his feet. Three left. Not nearly enough.

"3-2-2, traverse left!" Revan barked into his comms. "They're breaching the barricade!"

3-2-2's FAB opened up, sending red hot death tearing into the barriers in front of Bresto's position. The tri-barrels carved neat lines through metal and flesh, dropping Lost in sprays of black fluid. The kid was leaving his own sector open, giving the fresh-made monsters time to close the gap. No point telling him; countermanding Revan's order. Some lessons had to be learned the hard way.

A blaster bolt cracked past his ear, close enough to smell hot ozone. Revan put another bolt through a Lost that had nearly flanked them, its Reserve uniform stained black where the bolt had punched through.

Revan's voice shook. "Sacred Mother, these aren't civilians—they're our own. Are they all—?"

"PR? Yeah. Most of them." Bresto dropped another one climbing the barrier, refusing to let his eyes linger on the unit patches, the familiar gear configurations. Refused to search those half-formed masks for a face he might recognize.

Grim certainty settled in his gut. Lyra's unit had been deployed to Vestebrae. Had been down there when the shelters opened. His finger found the trigger again, muscle memory trying to keep him in the fight. She could be among them. Could be stumbling toward him right now behind one of those gray masks, and he'd never know until—

No. He slammed that thought down, buried it beneath the rhythm of combat. Sight. Breathe. Fire. She was smart. Too smart to get caught in whatever trap the Concordat had sprung. She'd found another way. Had to have.

"3-3-3 requesting weapons free on the LEC." Olsom's transmission cut through the static. Something had her worked up. *"I've got a big fucker, sixty meters out. My FAB's just pissing it off."*

Through the rain, another heavy bore down on Third Squad's position. Her assessment was solid. FABs weren't worth shit against those things. At least she'd asked for permission this time before shooting their comms to hell.

"One shot, one shot, fire when ready," he transmitted. "Fury 3, stand by for electromag."

The crack of hypersonic tungsten split the night. Lightning and thunder compressed into a single violent instant. His flexscreen dissolved into static. Through the interference, he heard the manufactory-stamp ring of impact.

"—*still coming!*" she signaled back through the static of war.

"Repeat!" A second shot would screw their nets hard, but not as bad as that heavy in their lines.

"*Firi—!*"

The heavy's silhouette annihilated in a flash of hard tungsten. Lost no more.

"What the hell was that?" Revan grabbed Bresto's shoulder, spinning him around. "Our nets are barely holding as is. I can't reach command—"

"Priorities, sir." A Lost stumbled over the barrier toward them, and more hands reached over the thick plates. Bresto shrugged off Revan's grip and put it down without looking.

Lessig's FAB went quiet. Not good.

Bresto keyed his comms. "3-1-1, status."

"*Barrel ch—.*" Lessig's transmission was weak, full of static. The crisp bite of a blaster rifle snapped in the background. At least he was still alive. "*Optics are shit, but far—there's no end to these things.*"

"Understood. Keep up your fire."

"*Aye—.*"

A second transmission screamed through his headset. Pure static and pain. The explosions came next, rolling through Fury 1's line like thunder. The distinctive crump of danger close plasmex charges. Last resort. Cold tension ratcheted Bresto's shoulders, muscles already knowing what his mind refused to accept: First Platoon was gone. Those charges would buy them minutes at best before their left flank began to collapse.

"3-1-1, traverse left," he transmitted. "Help Fury 2 fill that gap."

"*Copy that.*"

He turned to Revan, expecting another argument. The lieutenant just stared through the rain, jaw loose. "Fury 1's gone. Easy 3 isn't responding. We... We can't win this."

"We're still combat effective." The old words came automatic. He'd given this talk too many times. Some had listened. Some hadn't. "We keep our rigs running and our FABs talking. That's what we can do."

Revan wiped his face with shaking hands. The man was breaking just like their line. "We could fall back." His gaze drifted to the neat rows of dropships, past the civilians stranded between them. "Reposition upslope. Get to higher ground."

The cowardice sent fresh rage through Bresto's veins. "And what, *sir*? Abandon all these people to—"

A child stood alone atop the barrier; body jostled between gray reaching hands. A gamma from the looks of it, same as Kaff. The gray mask had already begun to form, threading through its face like a metal scar. One blackened eye gazed back at him, veiny and swollen.

His rifle felt like a hundred kilos, the barrel refusing to track upward. The child swayed there, trapped between what it was and what it would become. The Twelfth had led humanity from Dead Earth, given them this mountain, this strength, this faith, all to watch Her children turn to monsters at its peak. He'd given everything to the Holy Mother, been the proper Aegian. All for nothing.

The metallic buzz of FAB bolts shattered the night, lifting the child into the air on a killing stream of charged particles. He blinked hard, forcing down the hollow ache where his certainty used to be. It wasn't her. It wasn't her. Even if it had been, it wasn't anymore.

Lost no more.

"*3 Actual, 3-3-3.*" Olsom's transmission was all static. "*Being overrun —*" The rest dissolved into white noise.

"Say again, 3-3-3," he heard Revan shout.

Another burst cut through: "*—station this net—Victory Line's right flank—Lost breaking through—can't hold—*"

The mission math was simple, even if nothing else was. Lose Third Squad and Third Platoon would get rolled up. If they fell, Easy and Fury would collapse from both sides. The rest of Victory wouldn't last an hour after that. He needed to get there, to get Third Squad on task.

The lack of options made the tactics simple: pull Third Squad back and reinforce Second's position. Two minutes, maybe three, to reposition their metal. He keyed his comms to give the order, but his eyes kept drifting to the empty place where the child had stood.

A hand gripped his shoulder. Fucking Revan. He turned, ready to tell the lieutenant to get his shit together but found his own angry scowl staring back from a blank mask. Another reservist, uniform in tatters, its tac gear stained black.

It fell on him, weighing more than a person should, driving them both to the deck. His rifle caught between them as they went down, the frame grinding against his armor plate. The Lost's fists came together, slamming down over his heart. Pain exploded through his ribs, each breath burning like plasma fire. He tried to roll, to get his weapon free, but the thing was too big, too strong.

He hammered his fist into the Lost's neck—once, twice—no effect. The masked head pulled back, and Bresto threw his arms up. Too slow. The headbutt connected, pain exploding white-hot through his face. Blood ran hot in his nostrils as cartilage snapped.

He blinked away the red, caught his own blood spattered across that gray mask. The thing just stared down at him now, waiting. It didn't want to kill him. The bastard wanted to take him. Turn him into something like it.

Holy Mother keep him, he wasn't done yet. Service through sacrifice. A disappointing end to a very long, very sad joke. But he was a good Marine. A proper Aegian. He'd do his part. For the Holy Mother. For Lyra. The kids, Twelfth save them.

His fingers found the frag in his vest, thumb on the trigger housing. The Lost looked down at it, a wet grinding sound clicking inside its skull. It snatched his arm back, pain shooting through his wrists. He worked his other hand down and found the frag again.

The thing shrieked, sounding too much like the human it used to be. Twelfth save him, they all did at the end. And this thing knew it was the end. He pressed his thumb beneath the frag's safety latch and found the trigger.

"Hmph." He couldn't help himself. "Lost no more."

The storm erupted in a flash of nova-bright light and time seemed to stop. Even the Lost froze their advance, making more wet, scratching clicks as they craned their masks skyward. Light was everywhere now, burning away the shadows, as if Aegia's sun were descending through the clouds. The sound of war slowed, then stopped. For a heartbeat, it was just him and the light. Some kind of miracle. Had he sacrificed enough? Had She really come after all?

The frag beeped out a warning—five seconds, four—and he knew it wasn't time to die. With a roar, he shoved the daxed back and heaved the grenade into the air. It sailed past the barricade and blew with a wet thump that was loud in the bright stillness. A spray of shrapnel and black rained overhead, but the Lost didn't move. Like he wasn't even there. They just stared blankly at the sky, like they too prayed for salvation.

He rolled to his feet, hands on his rifle. The sight froze him for a split second; thousands of Lost daxed stretched around him, every mask fixed on that impossible light. Revan was on his knees, pistol shaking at a Lost more interested in the sky than him. Lessig's exo swung its primary arms in wide arcs, knocking the daxed away like they were loose gravel.

Bresto found his push-to-talk and spat the blood from his throat. "Fury 3, sound off."

"*3-1, still combat effective,*" Lessig said first.

"*Holy Mother…*" Prelk's transmission crackled. It almost sounded like a question.

Bresto looked down their line, counting operational rigs and which Marines could still fight. Half of their positions were already crawling with Lost.

Shadows returned as the light above seemed to pulse, drawing him back up before he could finish his count. The storm was changing around it—lightning cracking sideways, drawn more to itself than the mountain below. Clouds peeled back, torn open by the massive thing punching through.

The ship's jet-black hull filled the sky over Vestebrae. No retros, no fusion drives, but the vibrations hit like orbital fire, each pulse shaking in Bresto's teeth. The holy light died as the black thing descended. A piercing whine cut above everything else.

Tight beams of blue plasma fire erupted from the ship, burning a path through the Lost surging up the slope.

The daxed around him snapped back to life in one terrible chorus. Thousands of once-human throats added their screams to the black ship's deafening song.

He put two bolts through the nearest one on instinct. Victory's guns opened up and the war was back on, FABs hammering charged parti-cles into the press of agonized bodies.

The Lost that had pinned him lurched forward and grabbed his rifle barrel. It screamed again, mask shaking, the sound rising from somewhere deeper than its ruined throat. The sound crawled under his skin and settled in his marrow. He recognized the pure rage. Like humanity had betrayed it twice now.

Then it shuddered and went silent.

A black blade jutted through its mask, barely a hand's length from his face. The weapon disappeared with a wet sound and the daxed fell, revealing a thin shadow standing amid a circle of dead Lost. A scar of blue lenses ran down the center of its helmet. The rest of it was sealed in a black suit tighter than synthweave skivvies. Bolt light flashed around it, glinting off tiny reactive plates in the suit's mesh.

Not it. Her. Young, by the look of her. Thin frame, slight build, couldn't be more than eps level. But something was off. There was a fragility to her that didn't match how she moved. Like her bones might snap if she landed wrong, but she didn't seem to care.

"There you are." The playful tone cracked mid-sentence, and she pressed one gloved hand against her mask as if to hold something in. A wet giggle leaked through her fingers. "But not where I put you. No, no, no."

Pillars of blue plasma fire lit the girl's jagged silhouette as they turned whole sections of the mountain slope to fire and ash. More dark figures appeared at the barricades, their weapons punching holes in the Lost's lines. Some carried blades dark as their ship. Others shoul-dered cannons that belonged on Navy strike fighters. The Lost didn't fall back, they charged straight into the killing field, screaming their rage.

He felt his hands want to shake. The tactics and his fading adren-aline said they were winning, but it was all too good to be true.

The broken girl tilted her head, lenses focusing on him.

Keep it together, Marine. "Who—?"

"Sergeant Ned Bresto," she whispered through her palms, like speaking a secret. Then her hands dropped and her voice turned sing-song: "My hero. My savior. You're here! Yet… still so very, very far from home."

Suddenly, he was back aboard the derelict, standing next to Sevvers in front of that first broken capsule. The scream he'd heard then echoing through his memories.

He shook his head. Couldn't be.

She turned and vanished into the storm.

His tac net crackled. The twins' voices hit together. *"3-3 here, Sarnt, still—"*

Fuck. Olsom! He broke into a run before the transmission died, headlong into the smoke and rain. Above him, the black ship let out another world-breaking groan, then punched back through clouds until nothing remained but storm and thunder. More shadow warriors pressed their assault downslope, the Lost dying in waves before them.

Third Squad's position looked like the others, dead daxed stacked across the deck. He sprinted past Patrim's rig, his FAB hammering steadily at targets downslope. The twins were holding their ground together like he'd ordered, Smokes working his exo while Vlan kept position at its feet.

3-3-3 sat back from the others, fresh barrels spotless in their housing, the FAB eerily silent. The cage was empty. No sign of her support Marines.

A dead heavy sprawled at the exo's feet. One of those wisps lay in pieces nearby. Blood on the deck. He swung around 3-3-3's bulk, rifle ready. Bodies lay crumpled beneath the exo. Shit. Too late. They were—

Olsom looked up, head lolling against 3-3-3's right leg. Dark blood had dried across her face, trailing from a deep slash above her eye. Myers was sprawled across her chest, his white-and-grays soaked red around his middle. She held him tight in one arm while the other kept her weapon trained outward.

Bresto stumbled back a step. "Is he… ?"

She checked Myers' pulse like she'd been doing it for hours, her voice granite cold. "Still serviceable, Sarnt."

CHAPTER
THIRTY-FIVE

BLACK SMOKE CHOKED the narrow foot lane between buildings. Kaffy felt her way along the path, fingers gliding against the wall, toes hunting for a step. Even through her rebreather's filters, Vestebrae tasted like fire and heat. The quiet made the hair on her neck stand up, broken only by their careful steps and the soft sucking sound of filtered air. Three steps separated her from Duray and panic. She couldn't lose him too.

Her boot caught on a fallen transit sign, its bright plexene cracked and dull. She stumbled forward, catching herself against the wall.

"Hey, slow down."

"Quit whining," he shot back. "We have to find shelter."

"We're going the wrong way."

They'd taken so many turns from the primary transit she'd lost count, but something in the feel of the path said they were headed downslope. Her mind went back to the last seconds of Father's broadcast: him standing there, half-leaning on the railing, the city lights far below. He was at the drop station, and that's where she wanted to be.

"Go ahead. Turn around. See if I care." Duray's sniff sounded like a wheeze through his rebreather. "Those reservists said there are shelters down here, and I'm going to find one."

"But my father—"

"I'm block guide! When Hesper's not around, I'm in charge. Keep it up and I'll tell him how you wouldn't listen."

The word made her face burn hot. She wanted to shove him, but the crack of stone somewhere above froze her in place. She ducked, hands over her head. More falling debris. Duray stumbled to the ground. Seconds later, a chunk of heavy stone crashed behind them, the impact vibrating through her boots.

She didn't want to fight the stupid boy anymore. Not with the whole city about to fall on their heads.

That's how they'd lost the others. The lieutenant. Madam Ulwin. The painter. The firsts blasts came out of nowhere and she had just started running. They'd stuck together at first—avoided the main transit like the lieutenant said to, kept to the side streets where there were fewer people. But the explosions kept getting bigger. Buildings started breaking apart around them. One second her guardians were right there, and the next… Even the painter wasn't fast enough.

She squeezed her eyes shut, but the memory of rocks and dust and screaming metal refused to die. She started to cry again. Her sleeve left a dirty smear on her visor. Duray was already moving, fast, and she fought to keep up. Two steps behind this time.

They walked on, turning right, then left again. Her feet started to hurt from walking on rubble. They were lost.

And then Duray was right there, their rebreathers knocking together. But he didn't complain. Didn't even move.

"Hey—"

"You hear that?" he whispered.

She opened her mouth, but the soft clicks echoing through the smoke stole her voice. One coming somewhere ahead, another above… talking to each other. She couldn't tell how far, but she could hear it, and that was too close.

She gripped the figurine in her pocket, thumb always working its worn edges. The Holy Mother would keep them safe. She had to. Father said.

She counted her breaths waiting for the sounds to stop. Ten. Twenty.

Duray waved her forward. "I think they're gone."

"What were they?"

"Don't know. Don't want to know."

The junction ahead opened into more darkness, but something rhythmic flashed through the smoke. Too regular to be fire, more like a heartbeat, over and over. Emergency lights. That meant people. Safety. Duray's elbow caught her ribs and made her jump.

"What'd I tell you, Bresto?" He grinned back at her.

"Yeah." The relief forced an anxious sound out of her throat, but she bit back her thanks.

The flashing led to a PR guard post. A flat bunker squeezed between two high commercial blocks, the narrow windows in its thick granite walls black as the smoke outside. The front door was stuck partway open on its track, the flashing lights casting weird shadows through the gap.

Duray pushed against the door with a grunt, but it didn't move. "Help me."

She lined up beside him, spotting the numbers *201* etched in the metal before they pushed together. The door gave with a screech.

A long corridor went dark beyond the reach of the emergency lights. The air was cleaner, but the darkness felt deeper somehow. Dangerous, like it was watching them. More doors appeared in the brief flashes. Her skin went cold despite the heat.

Nothing about this felt safe. "I don't know. Maybe we should keep moving."

"We should look inside," Duray said, voice shaking. "There might be food, or a blaster."

They felt their way down the corridor. The first door clicked open easy. Inside, a row of chairs sat before blank screens and control decks, tiny red lights pulsing in the gloom.

Duray dropped into the nearest seat with a grunt. Kaffy pulled off her rebreather and sat next to him, tasting oil and old wire on the air. It reminded her of Mother. When Duray yawned, she yawned, too, fighting to keep her eyes open.

Duray stared at his hands. "Do you think they're okay?"

Her tears came again. She saw the building fall. The collapse just… swallowed them up. As much as she wanted to say yes, she couldn't.

The Twelfth didn't hold in Her hand liars. And they needed Her so bad right now.

"No."

Duray looked up at her with a start. "Lost no more."

The words sounded strange coming from him. So sincere, not like Duray at all. Heat crept up her neck. She should have been the one to say them.

"Lost no more."

They sat in silence a few moments longer, listening to the storm winds whistle through the open entryway in the hallway outside. The room's oily metal smell had the tinge of smoke now. Her stomach gurgled, filling the quiet. Eating the little treats in the cafe felt like a dream she'd woke up from and almost forgotten. This place might be safe, but there was no one there to help them.

"We can't stay here," she said, mostly to herself. "We're still combat effective."

"Huh?"

"Just something Father says." Maybe it was seeing him on the feed, but the memories were sharper now, more happy and reassuring than sad. "Still combat effective," she repeated in her best grown-up tone. "Your mountains don't get any smaller. Up and over's the only way. All that stuff."

He turned away. "That's stupid."

"No it's not."

"Stupid Daddy Bresto and his stupid little girl." His voice matched the hurt on his face. "No wonder you suck at block drill."

"Hey! What's your problem?" The moment was broken. Just like that, mean Duray was back. "I'm not calling *your* father names."

"Wouldn't matter—"

A sound cut through their argument, a low moan from deeper in the station. Almost like wind, but wrong somehow. The pitch rose and fell, warbling through the open door before fading to nothing. The anger drained from her as Duray's eyes went wide.

"Just the wind," he said quickly.

"Yeah." Her heart was still racing. "Just the wind."

His stare lingered on the door.

"What wouldn't matter?" she asked.

"Huh?"

"You said it wouldn't matter."

"Oh. It wouldn't matter if you called my father names. He's dead. Mother too."

Her chest went tight. Block drill was all she knew of him. Duray was always there, Nemor, too, both following Hesper around. She didn't see him in basics school. Never saw him anywhere else. Figured he was just a big dumb kiss up. Just thinking it draped her in shame.

"I… I didn't… Lost no—"

Duray laughed, his voice cracking. "It was a long time ago. I said the words already."

"But… where do you stay? Who gets your lots? How—"

"You don't know?" He looked surprised. "Admin block."

Kaffy drew in a sharp breath. Mother had always said to stay away from the long, squat habs in the administrative quarter. Said the kids there were trouble, that they'd steal your lots—or worse, if you weren't careful.

It didn't make sense though. Duray wasn't like that. He followed every rule. Knew every drill. Maybe that's why Hesper kept him so close.

"Who—? Does anyone… ?" The question sounded stupid as it came out. What was she trying to ask? If anyone loved him? If anyone cared?

"Hesper knows. He sponsors my block drill slot. Gives me extra duties. Makes sure I eat."

"I'm… I'm really sorry."

"Why?" There was a sharp edge to his laugh that time. "The Holy Mother let you *keep* your parents."

"I haven't seen my father since I was a beta," she said. Her hand reached out instinctively but stopped short. "Not until today."

"That's bad luck, huh."

"No." She pulled the figurine from her pocket and held it in her palm. "He's going to save me. Us, I mean. He said so."

"Are you blind? Nobody's coming for us." Duray jabbed a finger toward the door. "Not after that."

"I can't explain it. He said he would, and I believe him."

"You're wrong," Duray spat. "He's probably gone—"

"He is NOT. GONE." Her face burned, mouth twisting with all the rage she'd been swallowing since the attacks began. How *dare* he. How dare this stupid boy try to take away the one thing keeping her together. "Take it *back*, Arthur Duray."

The boy sat up straight, that know-it-all smirk driving her crazy. "Time to grow up, Bresto. It's just you and me now."

"How can you say that?" She thrust her open palm to him, forcing him to look at the tiny figure of their Holy Mother. The Twelfth was the light and the sword and the hope! She had brought Father back when Kaffy needed him most.

Duray glanced at the figurine with a nasty laugh. "What, that little hunk of metal? You think *that's* gonna save your daddy? Wake up, Bresto. The precious Holy Mother doesn't care about some dumb trigger-puller who got himself blown up."

"Liar!" Her open palm formed into a fist, and she lunged from her chair.

Duray caught her wrist. "Hey!"

She swung her free hand, landing meaty and hot against his cheek. The swivel chair groaned beneath their weight.

"Take it back!"

"Screw you!" He grabbed her other arm, glaring back at her, teeth bared in the red light.

The haunting sound cut through their struggle, deeper this time, hollow, like something from the old stories of Dead Earth. They froze in a tangle of arms and legs against the seat. The sound seemed to move through the hallway outside, changing too fast to be the wind. The hot anger in her chest turned to icy fear.

The moan dipped low, then rose, twisting into something new that made her heart skip. Pieces of sound that almost made sense, too muffled to understand.

Duray went very still. "Someone's here."

She backed off. Much as she hated it, he was right. And it scared her.

The hallway had started to smell more like the air outside, smoke creeping through the half-open entrance. But the sounds were louder there too, broken words she could almost make out.

The noise led them to the next door.

"Hello?" she said. "Is anyone there?"

But the voices kept going like they couldn't hear her at all. Then they went quiet, followed by a soft beep.

"Wait a minute." Duray found the access panel.

"Will it open?" she asked.

"What do you mean? Of course it will open."

"How do you know?"

"See the light?" He pointed at the display. "Green good, red dead. Green means good, red means dead, er, bad."

The light pulsed green on the display. Mother had said those words before, but Kaffy had never asked why. Mother said all kinds of weird, military things.

"So, that means it will open?"

"What do you think?" He pressed the control, and the door slid into the wall. A wave of cold air pressed back against the warm smoke. Pale blue lights hung where the walls met the ceiling, shining down on rows of empty metal racks as tall as she was. But there was no one inside.

"What is this place?"

"Woah!" Duray stepped inside. "This is a Planetary Reserve armory!" He moved quickly along the racks, hands searching the empty spaces.

She followed him into the room, cradling her shoulders to keep back the chill. The oily metal smell was overpowering here. "But nobody's here. Who was that talking?"

Duray slowed near the end of the racks and let out a frustrated breath. "Probably just a comms—"

Another beep, crisp and loud in the cold room. Then a rush of static.

"Twelfth save us!" she yelped, giving the little figurine a squeeze.

"*—ost Two-Zero-One, please respond.*" A man's voice. He sounded tired, each word a little slower.

The lone comms unit sat in its charging cradle on the workbench at the end of the room. A mess of words and symbols she didn't understand covered its little screen, but the *PUSH-TO-TALK* button on the side was plain enough. The unit beeped when she pushed it, the little screen lighting up green: *TACNET CONN ESTD, TXMT.*

She clutched the device close to her face. It felt heavy in her hands. There was something comforting about that. "Hello? Father?"

Duray shook his head. "You have to let go of the button, stupid."

"I know that." The device beeped when she let the button go.

"Post Two-Zero-One, this is Emergency Shelter Azure-Twelve." The man's slow words bled through the little speaker, telling her what she already knew. It wasn't Father. But he was out there, somewhere. She just needed to be smarter about this.

"Sergeant Ned Bresto? This is your daughter, Kaffy Bresto, over." That sounded better, more like how Mother used her own comms before reserve duty.

"Say again, Two-Zero-One?" the slow man said. *"Sergeant Ned Bresto?"*

"Yes! He's my father. Is he there with you?"

Nothing but static again. The lump in her throat made it hard to breathe. "Hello?"

"Yes, Kaffy Bresto." Each word came slow and careful. *"Your parents are on their way to Shelter Azure-Twelve. How many more colonists are with you?"*

She couldn't stop the sob of relief. Didn't even care what Duray thought one bit. Whoever she was talking to knew her name, knew Mother and Father.

"It's just me and Duray."

"Understood." Static filled another long pause. *"Please proceed immediately to Shelter Azure-Twelve, Kaffy Bresto."* More static. *"You will be safe here. You will be with your parents."*

"Okay! We're on our way!"

"See?" Duray sounded pleased with himself. "I told you we should find a shelter."

"Whatever." She slipped her rebreather back into place, her voice echoing inside the mask. "What were *you* doing? I was the one on the comms."

"I was hoping to find a gun."

The fear that had wrapped around her since the sky burned back at the allotment center started to loosen. Father was waiting for her. Mother too. The Holy Mother hadn't abandoned them, She'd been guiding them all along, through all the danger right to where they needed to be.

"We don't need one." She slipped the figurine back into her pocket, still grinning. The comms unit hung heavy from her hip. "We're safe now."

CHAPTER
THIRTY-SIX

BRESTO RESTED against the oil-slick barrier, hip burning, ribs grinding with each breath. Reminders that survival came at a heavy price.

Dead daxed covered the slope beneath 3-3-3's position, more proof of how close they came to losing this fight. Far beneath the drop station, secondary explosions rippled through the ruins of Vestebrae's primary transit. The remains of a large building toppled and fell to the screams of more dying Lost.

None of it sat right with him. Those shadow operatives had come from nowhere, cutting through the Lost like they were nothing. Their black ship had broken every law of atmospheric entry he'd learned in twenty years of void ops. And the Lost themselves… these weren't the monsters from the derelict. These were colonists. Reservists, administrators, mothers, fathers. Proper Aegians all. People he might have passed in the transit, shared a drink with at the E-Club on Three-Alpha. Fresh-forged daxed that still looked too much like what they used to be. *Who* they used to be.

Lyra and Kaff could be among the littered bodies, if they'd died human or changed like the others. The Holy Mother had brought salvation from the sky, but She'd taken Her price in blood.

"Careful," he heard Olsom say, with a hard edge that made him glance back.

Med techs worked beneath 3-3-3's bulk, loading Myers onto the gurney. Olsom never took her eyes off him, like she didn't trust where they were taking him was any safer.

Behind the tower, another dropship lurched into the sky. The major had set up a cas evac point upslope at the Diacad drop. It would be packed by now, Marines, reservists, civilians, too many to keep track of. He'd find Myers later, wherever they took him. Make sure he was getting stitched up right.

Olsom plunked back down at the exo's feet, back turned to the Victory line. Not that there was anyone else around to bother her. He counted positions automatically. Olsom, check. Myers, cas evac. Her fireteam was one short.

"Where's your breacher?"

"Don't know, Sarnt." Her voice was flat, empty. "Disappeared during the fight."

"Disappeared?"

"Yeah," she said, eyes like flint. Sweat and rain had turned her face into a bloody slick. He knew the look, that feeling of total exhaustion, of not giving twelve standard fucks about anything. Especially some sandbagged breacher.

No need to push her now. Mezzior would turn up, alive or dead. Bresto would get answers during the after-actions, if he was even still around to hear them. They'd figured out the Concordat's plan and managed to save a few thousand colonists from a fate worse than death. Reinforcements were on their way. This fight was over, and Park would either take him back or dump him in a brig somewhere. He'd done both before, though not exactly in that order.

At 3-3-2's position, Toelke was gone, probably helping with medical triage, but the twins were there. Still their weird, mirrored selves, even after thirty hours of sustained combat ops. Smokes sat in his operator cage, canopy locked out and up, cigarette hanging loose between his lips. Vlan leaned against the machine's left arm, squeezing field paste straight into his mouth.

"Sarnt," they said together.

"How's Third Squad?"

"Heavy," they said. Smokes took a long drag off his cigarette. "Squishy's rig is—"

"—all banged up," Vlan finished around his mouthful of paste.

"Either of you see Mezzior?" Bresto asked.

They looked at each other, then back at him. "Negative, Sarnt."

Smokes took another pull of his cigarette. "Myers gonna—"

"—make it?" Vlan asked.

The nanites had done an ugly job on Myers. Pure luck they didn't turn him inside out with a wound like that. He knew that pain. "Yeah. Techs wouldn't have moved him otherwise."

"Copy that," they said, sharing another odd glance. Smokes took one more drag, then flicked the spent butt over the barricades.

Bresto's flexscreen buzzed with Victory net traffic. *All command elements, this is Victory 5. Report to Vestebrae Drop Control. Skipper wants all platoon commanders and platoon sergeants to the tower. Now.*

"Excuse me, Sergeant." A young PR lieutenant stepped to Third Platoon's line with a squad of reservists at his back. His face seemed to pale a little at the sight of the dead Lost. "We're looking for Fury 3."

"You found 'em." Bresto squared his shoulders, ignoring the twinge of pain behind his neck. He hunted for Revan, hoping to send this lieutenant to him. No such luck.

More reservists streamed from the drop control concourse, their weapons and armor scorched black from recent combat. Good. Victory needed the numbers.

"Victory Actual informed us of the situation, says my squad is to reinforce your position." Several reserve NCOs were flanking the young lieutenant now, heads nodding as he spoke. "Where do you want us?"

"Here." Bresto pointed toward the gap between First and Second Squad. "Put your best shooters there. Make sure they've got plenty of frags and charge packs."

"Copy that." The lieutenant motioned his squad up. "Anything else?"

Yeah. Where was Lyra? But asking would make him sound like

every other desperate husband looking for family instead of a Marine doing his job.

"Tell your men to watch for ambushes. The Lost don't always die when you think they should."

The reserve officer gave a grim nod and moved to position his troops. More PR units were filing in. Bresto waited until the new guns were in place, then started for the tower. Time to see what Major Kull wanted.

He wound through the ground floor crowd beneath a ten-meter rise of duraplate and concrete, ignoring the sharp pain in his hip. Civilians packed the receiving area wall to wall, their faces drawn beneath emergency lighting. Med techs threaded between them, pausing to check bandages or adjust IV lines. The familiar copper smell of human blood mixed with antiseptic and fear-sweat.

The lifts were running despite the crowd, reserved for military traffic only. Another squad of PR troopers filed out as he approached, their white-and-grays pristine compared to his. Too clean to have seen any real fighting. They'd get their chance before it was over.

He squeezed into the next lift car between two Victory Marines he didn't recognize. Last time he'd seen Kull, she'd tried to arrest him. He wouldn't put it past her to try again. Court martial him for inciting panic. But Third Platoon had held. His Marines were alive. The rest was just paperwork.

The car lurched upward, grinding against worn guide rails. Through the plexene walls, he watched PR units establishing firing positions along F Company's line. Saw the jagged hole of flesh and fibrosteel where First Platoon had been. More reserve elements were arriving by the minute. Had to be close to half a battalion by now. Their unit numbers were only vaguely familiar. None of them were Lyra's. Not that he expected them to be.

The lift's sudden stop jolted him back. The doors rattled open, revealing an operations center gone dead quiet. Drop controllers sat frozen at their stations, fingers resting beneath darkened screens. Even the constant stream of tactical data had stopped flowing across the main displays.

Three of the black operators stood at the room's center, their skintight armor drinking in the overhead light. Bresto recognized the broken girl from the barricades—slight, fragile-looking, her stance silently screaming danger. The others were new, a woman whose twin blades glinted like liquid metal, and a giant whose shoulders nearly brushed the ceiling panels.

A fourth figure hung back from the group, wearing what remained of a Navy pilot's uniform. The synthweave was scorched and torn, but the black blade across his back marked him as something else. He was too casual, too relaxed, even for a jet jockey.

Olsom's words came back to him. A pilot who wouldn't die. Had to be this one. But why dress up as a skeeg? These Section Delta didn't need to pretend to be Navy pilots unless they had a very good reason to hide what they really were.

Kull stood between them, one hand dangling near her holstered sidearm. First Sergeant Druggan's permanent scowl had smoothed away to something like wonder. Maybe fear. The rest of Victory's command staff gave the shadows a wide berth, as if the air around them might burn.

Bresto stepped off the lift towards the middle of the room, towards Kull, when the broken girl's two guardians shifted. Suddenly, the woman beside her held blades in both hands. The giant's blue lenses locked onto him, head tilted with dangerous interest.

The major barely lifted a hand, urging him to stop, her other hand feeling the grip of her sidearm. "I'll ask you again." Her voice was pure ice; eyes locked on the crooked shadow before her. "Who are you? Why are you here?"

Laughter bubbled from beneath her mask, sweet and unhinged, hands raised in mock surrender. Metal ground against bone somewhere inside her suit.

"Major Orianne Kull." She drew out the name, tasting each syllable. "Decorated. Celebrated… *Complicated.* But Colonel Reede knew that didn't he?" She caught herself, giggling. "And look how that turned out?"

For one heartbeat, Kull looked like she'd been shot. Her mouth worked, but no sound came out.

She clapped her hands together, bouncing slightly on her toes. "Oh,

Reede was so scared! Scared of what this new war would make him do." She looked left to right, lenses whirring. "All those people down there, and you went boom anyway. He knew you would. That's why he stayed behind to die instead."

Then it was rage in Kull's eyes. Bresto could taste the edge of violence, salt and copper. The Marine part of him accepted it—wanted it—even if he knew they would lose to these dark gods.

"Poor Orianne, making such hard choices." Her fingers began to curl inward, forming a trembling fist against her thigh. "Colonel Reede chose death. You chose murder. And Park..." The fist shook violently. "He chose chaos."

She knew about Park. About their mission. About what they'd found in that derelict. Her mask's gaze turned toward him, and then he knew. He fucking *knew*...

"Deni."

Thunder cracked through the control room, rattling the observation windows in their frames. Azure streaks of lightning crawled across her black armor and suddenly he was back there. Back in the derelict's forge chamber, watching Sevvers and Lernus pull her dead body from the black. Watching her come back to life. And not for the last time, it seemed.

Her fingers found the seal at her neck, mask going slack beneath her touch. She yanked it free with a wet sound, spilling silver blonde hair to her shoulders, her face all sharp angles and pale skin. Blood had dried at the corners of her eyes in rusty lines. But that smile, Twelfth save him, that smile twisted with a kind of mad joy, like she'd been waiting for this moment since they'd found her back in that dark place.

The two guardians fell to their knees, weapons at their feet. "Sister Sect, my warden," they said together. Even the pilot had to look away.

"I have no name. I have many names." Blood began to leak from her eyes again. "But there's one name I'm particularly fond of lately. Survivor."

"Whatever. Sevvers said—"

"Said what?" she began, forcing back cold laughter. "Said he'd killed me?"

"Something like that. Guess it didn't stick."

She swayed closer, hips moving in a rhythm that seemed to match storm outside. "My scattered pieces, still falling into place." Her smile showed too many teeth. "Tell me, does it hurt, Neddy? Knowing you led them here? Knowing what you've cost your home?"

Bresto's jaw tensed, pulse hammering against his throat. One, two, three—focus. This wasn't the poor, babbling girl they'd pulled from the capsule. She was different somehow, more dangerous.

Her eyes went cold, voice turning to venom. "Where is he?"

"Who?"

"Don't... t-tease, Neddy." She stalked around him in tight circles, fingers twitching as if she wanted to search every pouch, every seam. Then she stopped dead, spine rigid, face toward the ceiling. "Kerry, Kerry, where are you? Come out and play!"

So, Deni wanted revenge. Maybe there was more human in her after all. Too bad. Even if he'd known where Sevvers was, he wouldn't give the bot jockey up to whatever she had become.

"I don't know where—"

Deni froze and let out a tortured gasp. She staggered sideways as if struck, one agonized hand pressed to her temple.

"Lost and tossed and... s-star crossed!" The words bubbled up like blood. Her hands flew to her throat, trying to choke off the sound. "Makers' key. Set him free. Come... come to... no—!"

"I don't have time for... whatever this is." Kull's cold stare fixed on the pilot. "Control her. Now."

The pilot chuckled with an apologetic shrug. No love there. But Deni's guardians remained motionless, heads still bowed, weapons still at their feet. Bresto had seen plenty of Marines who'd follow orders into hell, but this was different. These two would probably cut their own throats if she asked nicely enough. Maybe they were crazy as she was.

"Sister? Sect?" the pilot said with mock concern. "The Marines are watching."

Deni stopped, took a breath, palms pressed to her pink cheeks like cooling a fever. "Well, that was embarrassing." Her laugh was brittle but genuine. "I need to work on my public speaking."

Kull's stare never wavered. Deni caught it and held it for a long moment. Then she blinked, almost surprised.

"Right, where were we? Your questions." Her twisted smile returned. "We are Section Delta."

"There it is," the pilot said. "Cat's out of the bag now."

"I am Sect. Leader—" She paused, swayed slightly, then forced a finish. "One of the few." The pilot's smirk deepened, but she'd already forgotten him, her focus snapping to Bresto. "Thanks to you and Kerry. You ruined everything."

The words hit railgun hard. Crazy or not, she was right. His actions had consequences. Going to the derelict had brought the Concordat here. He'd brought death to his home.

"Do you know what you did? What you broke?" Her voice jumped octaves. "We were so close! So close to fixing everything! But no, no, no —you had to go digging! Had to interfere!"

He spat on the deck. "Lernus *ordered* Park to save your sorry ass. Sevvers and I were just—"

"Who do you think you are?" Kull's voice cut through his like a blade, all granite and fury. Not at him. At Deni. "Questioning my judgment? Blaming your failures on some ankrin-headed Marine while Aegia burns? Where was Section Delta when the Concordat attacked Three-Alpha? When they turned our own ships against us?"

The woman guardian rose in one fluid motion, blades already singing toward Kull. Going for his rifle was just an impulse in Bresto's mind when Deni lifted two fingers, and the warrior dropped back to her knees as if yanked by strings.

"Such fire. Makes me want to play." Something predatory flashed across Deni's face. "But you're confused, angry Major. We weren't hiding. We were working. Always working. Keeping the monsters away."

"Don't get me wrong..." Kull forced the anger from her face. "We appreciate the assist. But Victory stands just fine without you."

"Oh? Did you really?"

"Really." Bresto couldn't keep the acid from his voice. Thirty hours of straight combat ops, and he was done with this cryptic, poetic cridshit.

The Marines in the room growled in agreement. Druggan threw him the subtlest nod.

"Ugh. *Marines.*" Deni rolled her eyes. "Your kind never changes. Always fighting and dying for things you can't possibly understand."

"Tell them," the pilot said.

"I was getting to—"

"No more games, sister. No more secrets." His words had an edge Bresto hadn't heard before. "They're out of time. So are we."

"Fine!" She took two quick steps toward the pilot, then back, like she couldn't decide whether to fight or run. "I was getting to that!"

Bresto's stomach dropped. If something had Section Delta spooked… Holy Mother save them all.

"What kind of threat are we talking about?" Kull demanded. "Are there more coming?"

"More?" Deni's laugh was pure broken glass. "Sweet, stupid Marines. You still think this is about your mountain."

"It wasn't?"

"Oh no, darling." That childlike tone was back. "This was just noise. Just screaming and fire to keep us all busy. While they plan something much, much worse. But don't worry! We can fix it. All of us. Together." Her face was all grin again, wrinkling her eyes. "Won't that be fun?"

Bresto stepped forward. Park's obsession with that abandoned rock. The certainty in his voice when he'd said Lernus was looking for something that could stop the war. Something the Concordat wanted badly enough to follow them home for.

"What are they really after out there?"

"Oh, clever, clever Neddy!" She clapped her hands together, those blood-rimmed eyes fixed on him. "But you'll have to wait to play."

"Play?" Bresto growled. "Just talk plain you crazy—"

"Language!" Deni's head tilted at that angle, big eyes blinking slowly. "The next act requires more… discretion."

"Clear the room, all of you," Kull boomed. "All matters regarding Section Delta are red-level only as of this moment. Out. Now."

Bresto hesitated at the edge of the group. He didn't trust Deni or

Section Delta, but Kull's glare found him quick. Twenty years of service kicked in, and he filed out with the others.

The lift felt hollow, empty despite the smell of sweat and anger after everything that had happened. His mind kept spinning through it all: Section Delta appearing from nowhere, their power, their fear. Holy Mother, what could make things like that afraid?

And what did it say about the CDF that they needed these shadow operatives to survive? Twenty years he'd served. Twenty years believing the Marines, the Navy, the Division were humanity's shield. But when the real test came, when the Concordat brought their full weight to bear, it hadn't been enough. None of it had been enough.

Without Section Delta, Aegia would be ash. Every soul on this mountain would be Lost or dead. The thought turned to acid in his gut. All those deployments, all those patrols keeping the squids at bay, all that faith in the system, and in the end, it was strangers in black armor who'd saved them. Strangers with their own agenda, their own secrets.

Maybe it was time to stop trusting the system and start trusting what he could see with his own eyes. His family. His children. The people who mattered more than any mission or medal or oath.

The car lurched to a stop, and the doors rattled open. A trio of reserve officers stood in his way. Combat uniforms stained black with blaster discharge and smoke. The woman in the center, a lieutenant, looked up. His mind refused to process what he was seeing, who he was seeing, until he saw those green eyes.

Lyra's mouth opened, relief and anger warring in her expression. "Ned?"

CHAPTER
THIRTY-SEVEN

THE RAIN HAD TURNED to mist, but cold still bit through Olsom's gloves as she worked 3-3-3's ops terminal. She keyed through the now familiar interface—reactor status, magneto-hydraulic flow, aux distribution nodes—checking things that didn't need checking. No telling when she'd have another combat engineer to keep 3-3-3 running. But it was more about keeping busy. Anything to drown out the wet sounds that kept replaying in her head.

She hopped down from the cage into the black mess. Tightened a coupling that didn't really need tightening. Checked the next coupling, and the next, working through the checklist she'd already run twice since the fighting stopped. Since they took Doc away.

Vlan waved from beside 3-3-2, wrinkled face creasing into that eager grin, but she focused on the hydraulics. Checked the pressure readings again. Recorded the same numbers she'd seen ten minutes ago in her maintenance log. The coupling spanner slipped, scraping her knuckles raw. Blood welled dark against her skin, but the sting felt distant.

The storm winds closed around her, howling between the Marine metal that lined the drop station's edge. Emergency floods cut pale circles through the dark below, hunting for movement among the dead, human or daxed. She wasn't watching for Doc's evac. Wasn't counting the minutes since they'd loaded him up. The numbers in her log blurred. She wiped the screen with her sleeve and started again from the top.

More reservists gathered near 3-3-2's position. It was hard to resist the twins' peculiar charm. Young faces, fresh-pressed uniforms that hadn't seen much combat. Proper Aegians come to play Marine. One of them kept stealing glances her way while the others talked about meteorological alerts and meal rotations.

"Is that your MAC-4?" he asked.

She kept working, but footsteps splashed closer through standing water and daxed fluids. Ripples of blood red lapped at her boots.

"Hey, I heard Victory Marines held the line against waves of those things. That was you, right?" He smelled like a boot, clean and unbloodied.

Olsom checked her maintenance log. Again.

"Never seen one up close before." Another voice, deeper. "My grandfather helped build the last batch of these. Says they don't make metal like this anymore."

She tightened the next coupling.

"Did you really kill that thing?" Barely an eps, this one, his voice cracking, pointing at the dead giant face down on the deck. "How—"

"Sweet Twelfth, she's ignoring us." The first speaker again. His voice had that mountain hardness now. "Maybe ferals really don't speak proper standard."

The wrench went still. The wild thing inside her uncurled, telling her exactly how to shut his mouth.

Something moved along the barrier's edge. Not Marine. Not a reservist. She raised her rifle, the high-res shape glowing through mists of rain in her optics.

Blue light pulsed—one of theirs. Her finger eased off the trigger. Shit, she'd almost dropped a friendly.

Whoever it was moved like it was injured, each step uncertain, almost mechanical. Her scope tracked it along the barrier's edge. Far too close to the drop.

"Oh, that guy." One of the reservists snorted. "He's been walking the line since we got here." He spat into the muck. "See those clothes? No proper Aegian would waste good credits like that."

Olsom kept her rifle trained on him, scope capturing flashes of expensive fabric beneath the muck and rain. He lurched closer to the edge, hands reaching for something only he could see.

"Hey!" she shouted through the storm. No response. The man swayed again, teetering over the edge. Closer to joining the dead below. "Stand down!"

Nothing. She ran, boots splashing through blood-tinged water. She found his collar and yanked him back into the muck. The rich fabric tore beneath her grip. The man was ghost-white, eyes huge and unfocused.

She knew that face. The clinic. Storm, that was his name. He looked less like the pampered net star and more like fresh meat about to get himself killed.

Storm let out a sound between a yelp and a sob as she hauled him up against the barrier. His expensive clothes squelched in the muck, daxed blood running down his face in dirty streams.

"You hurt?" She checked him for wounds, hands moving automatically to where that blade had opened Doc. Nothing but wet fabric and trembling muscle. "Hey. Eyes on me."

"Did you see them?" His voice cracked. "The way they just changed. Like flipping a switch. Human to once-human. And we killed them. Just like that." He grabbed at her sleeve with shaking fingers. "Twelfth, how does that happen? This is Her mountain. We are Her people. Now it's all just… just…"

"Don't matter. You need to get clear of this wall."

"Doesn't matter?" Storm's laugh was high and wild. "Everything we built. Everything we thought we were. Thrown away like—"

"Like some dumb ass too close to a hundred-meter drop?" She tried to pull him up, but he slumped there against the fibrosteel barrier.

"You don't understand. My parents. My teachers. They said we'd survived this. Said the Twelfth had saved us from… from this. This isn't survival. This is the end. This is… entropy. The universe reaching in and showing us how small we are. How meaningless—"

She slapped him, sending needles of pain through her palm.

"Listen up." She grabbed his chin, forced his eyes to hers. They were glassy, unfocused, like Doc's when the nanites hit. But Storm wasn't dying, just lost in his own head. "Think we're survivors? Great. Time to be one. On your feet."

"But it's all gone. Everything we built—"

"All a lie rich folks tell themselves. You want meaning? Keep breathing. Everything else is just vapor."

"Rich boy starting to get it." Mez's voice slithered from beside her. "All those shiny promises. All those pretty lies."

Olsom went rigid. Storm tried to pull away, but her fingers stayed locked on his collar. The wild thing inside her woke hungry.

"System's rigged." Mez edged closer, hands in his pockets like they were sharing drinks again. "Always been rigged. Ask any block rat. Ain't that right, Wholesome?"

Something shifted in her—the Marine fell away, something wilder taking control. She released Storm and gripped her rifle.

"Whoa, wait a minute. What're you doing?" Storm's voice shook. "We're all on the same side here."

"Oh yeah we are." Mez spread his hands, reaching out to her. "We all just trying to survive, right?"

The squad bay. The knife pressed to her belly. The foundry, boozing in the dark while she spilled her guts. The barricades, the way he'd run when things got bad. Everything clicked into place parade deck perfect. He wasn't just dangerous. He was *smart*. Smart enough to pick his battles. Smart enough to save his own skin. Every lesson he ever learned etched across his face.

Didn't change what he'd done.

"You ran," she hissed.

"Had to." His scarred grin returned, ugly and knowing. "Mez know when a fight's done. When staying just gets you—"

"Gets you what? Dead? Like Doc almost was? Like me? While you fucking ran?"

"Mez no coward!" The words exploded out of him. He lunged forward, stopping short of her rifle barrel. "Mez smart enough to know a lost cause. Wholesome, too. Mez know."

"You don't know shit about me."

But her pulse kicked up a notch. *Mez know.* Know what? That she'd grown up in the blocks? That she'd fought for scraps and space and the right to sleep without someone's hands on her? That she'd felt more alive in a firefight than she ever had back then?

"Mez been waiting for this." He took half a step sideways. "For you to stop playing dress-up with these mountain folk." His voice dropped lower. "We both know what you really are."

"Fuck you." She stepped into him, the rifle barrel drifting closer to his ribs. "I earned this. I earned every Twelfth-damn bit of it."

Mez didn't flinch from the rifle. Leaned into it.

"Earned what? Their respect?" He let out a harsh laugh. "Mez enlisted same as you. Bled same as you. They still ain't never gonna see us as anything but out-world block trash."

"Yeah? So fucking what?" The wild thing in her hissed and spat. "This block trash got more fight than any of these mountain folk. This block trash kept *your* ass alive out there."

"Mez kept himself alive just fine. Your boyfriend? Not so much." His scarred face twisted with cruel pleasure. "How's he doing, by the way? Still breathing?"

Doc's pale face flashed behind her eyes. The wet sound when the blade came free. His blood pulsing between her fingers. Eyes glassy and distant—

The rifle barrel pressed into Mez's sternum before she realized she was moving, safety off, capacitor buzzing. The trigger pressed back against her finger.

His eyes flicked down to the rifle barrel, then back to her face. He licked his lips. "There she is."

He moved. Sidestepped forward, hooked the barrel under his arm. The rifle discharge snapped loud, bolt light burning her eyes. But he was right there, face centimeters from hers.

"Nah ah ah." His grin was so ugly, so cruel, it *hurt.* "Mez got you."

The shot had gone wide. Smoke rose from a daxed corpse on the deck behind him, bolt hole burned clean through its skull. Around them, Marines and reservists stared. Not at Mez, but at her. At the feral who'd drawn on a fellow Marine.

Look at her. Look what she really was when the mask slipped. They'd never wanted her here. Never trusted her. Mez… Mez was—

Pain. Sharp, burning across the side of her belly. Warmth spreading beneath her uniform, dripping down her hip.

Fuck.

"Marine!" someone shouted. "Drop your weapon!"

PR troopers formed a half-circle around her, their rifles wavering between her and Mez. Fresh faces. Shaking hands. One of them barely managed to find his safety.

"What the hell is this?" An officer pushed through their line, silver pips catching the emergency floods. His voice steadied as he got closer. "Stand down, Private. That's an order."

Metal snicked as the knife folded, vanishing somewhere into Mez's uniform. The rifle barrel stayed hooked under his arm, her finger still on the trigger.

How much blood was she losing? Couldn't they see it? Couldn't they see what he was?

"Private?" The officer tried again. "We're all on edge. It's been a hard day. But we don't need any more bodies on this mountain."

One wrong move and they'd put her down. Or maybe she should just finish it. End Mez right here, right now. Let them shoot her. At least then it would be over.

"Hey, Olsom." Smokes's voice cut through everything else. Vlan was at his brother's shoulder. "You okay?"

They moved closer, making their way between the reservists' pointed rifles. Slow and easy. Just being there, like they had been since Three-Alpha. Since before everything went wrong.

No. They didn't understand. Didn't know what she really was. What she'd almost done. She'd get them hurt too. Just like she hurt everyone who got too close. The sting behind her eyes burned hot. No. Don't you dare cry, you stupid girl. Not here. Not in front of them.

Mez lifted both hands slowly, like he'd done it a million times before. She lowered the rifle a fraction. Then more. Adrenaline coursed through her veins, making her hands shake.

The PR lieutenant stepped closer. "What the hell is going on here, Private?"

Mez wanted to see what she really was? Fine. She could be just as cold, just as calculating.

"Sorry about the discharge, sir." She straightened, ignoring the sting in her belly. "Daxed was moving. Had to put it down before it got back up." Her voice steadied as she found the lie. "You know how they are. Takes more than one shot sometimes."

The twins gave synchronized nods.

"Saw it, sir," Smokes said.

Vlan nodded. "A close call."

Relief hit first, then the sick realization. They were lying for her. Good Marines covering for her mess, risking their own necks. She'd done it again.

But the officer seemed satisfied by that. He waved his people back to their posts, relief plain on their faces as they dispersed into the rain.

She pressed her hand to her belly, feeling the ragged tear through her synthweave beneath her tac vest. The cut was ugly, angry-looking where the dull blade had dragged, but shallow. Bloody mess, but she'd live.

Mez stepped back, straightening his tac vest. He turned to go.

"Hey," she called out to him.

He glanced back.

"Next time I won't miss."

Only his grin answered, and he disappeared into the storm without another look.

The reservists who'd been watching shuffled away, suddenly finding other places to be. Rain drummed harder against the metal decking, mixing with the black gore from the dead daxed. Storm's expensive clothes squelched as he pushed himself upright against the barrier, still shaking.

Smokes pulled a cigarette from his pocket, striking his lighter against the wind. "You check—"

"—your rig yet?"

Three times. "Once or twice."

"Three," they said, Vlan counting on his fingers, "We saw you."

Her face went hot, but the twins were already moving toward 3-3-3, ignoring her embarrassment. They crouched beside each other, examining something near the exo's left tread.

"Loose coupling here," Smokes said, producing a spanner from 3-3-3's kit. No way it was. Vlan took the spanner and knocked it against an armor plate. "Needs a turn."

They were going to maintain her rig whether she wanted help or not. The wild thing inside her wanted to bare teeth, to push them away like she had before. Part of her ached to join them, drawn by the simple routine of it. The familiar click of tools against metal. But she stayed back, arms crossed tight against her chest.

"Doc showed us a trick," Smokes said, eyes on his brother working the coupling free. Then Vlan spoke, "Seals 'em better than spec."

Something caught in her throat. When had Doc done that? She'd missed that somewhere along the way. Maybe it was during Bresto's ass-chewing about railgun procedure. Or when she was sulking and drinking with that Twelfth-damned coward.

All that time wasted trying to prove something, trying to stay hard, and she'd missed something special. Missed them becoming more than just squad mates. And now Doc was bleeding in some med bay because he'd tried to help her. Everyone who got too close to her ended up hurt or gone. Just like before. Just like always.

The twins looked up at her expectantly, tools ready. Waiting for her to join them. To be part of something real.

But Mez was right. She took a step back.

"I'm good." The truth tasted bitter on her tongue. "You two... you don't need me getting in the way."

CHAPTER
THIRTY-EIGHT

THE MAINTENANCE QUARTERS were cold and cramped, little more than a supply closet with a narrow bunk tucked beneath rows of exposed piping. The industrial hum of the drop station's mechanisms vibrated through the walls in time with Lyra's breathing. She lay with her head on Bresto's chest, her fingers tracing absent patterns across the old scar above his heart. Their discarded uniforms lay near the open door, weapons and tac gear hung from pegs on the wall. They hadn't made it far.

"You know what I miss?" Lyra's voice was husky, raw from earlier. She shifted against him, her skin warm where it pressed to his. "Actual beds. Clean sheets."

"You hate making bunks."

"Still."

His fingers found the ridge of her spine, each vertebra a checkpoint on the map of her body. New wounds marked her shoulders, the dried blood just hours old. The thought of her fighting the Lost—those gray-masked things that had once been neighbors, friends, proper Aegians—without him tightened something in his chest.

A weak transmission crackled through her comm gear, too faint to make out words. Lyra tensed against him, waiting for the call that would pull her away. "Someone's going to want this bed soon."

"They can get their own rack. Been waiting too long for this."

"Too long. Yeah." She made a sound somewhere between laugh and sigh.

His hand resumed its path along her skin. She was solid now, the softness of motherhood he barely remembered hardened by shipyard work and reserve training. Everything about her spoke of endurance. Of survival. The curve of her hip carried fresh bruises from her tac gear straps. A half-healed burn marked her shoulder, something from the yards maybe that he hadn't been there to see. His thumb traced the ridge of an old scar on her collarbone, remembering the day she'd earned it. Back when they'd both been NCOs of Marines, before the kids.

And still, she was the most beautiful thing he'd ever seen. A hint of gray threaded her hair now, catching the dim light where it spilled across his chest. The Holy Mother's touch, marking the time he'd lost. Time he'd wasted being anywhere but here.

"Two thousand, two hundred, and eighty-five days," he said.

"Too long." She didn't look at him. "Your children are growing up without you."

There was a strange comfort in her anger. Their sex had been rough, desperate, their shared need burning away the time and distance. Even knowing what he'd done, knowing he'd chosen duty over family again and again, she'd pulled him into the maintenance closet like they were still young Marines between patrols. Faith might take root in a quiet heart, but sometimes it spoke through fiercer things.

Let her be mad. He deserved every bit of it. That was his job, taking the hard hits so others didn't have to. Even when those hits came from the woman he loved.

Her comm unit crackled again, sending a spike of tension through them both. Her eyes stayed on him, barely breathing, but no voice followed. Just static and silence.

"Where's Sammy now?" Her voice grew quieter. "You said he's safe, but where?"

"Shelter Sienna-2, by Diacad Memorial." He'd told her already, but she needed to hear it again. "Found him in the clinic's mess. Made sure he got there before…"

Before the Lost came. Before Kull burned half of Vestebrae. Before Section Delta changed everything.

"I can't believe Hesper just left him." Lyra's voice trailed off. The anger was back but aimed somewhere else now. "We trusted him. With our children."

"Yeah." No point defending the coward. "Already had words with him about that."

Her lips curled just a little. "Words?"

"Yeah. Words."

A low sound of approval escaped her as she relaxed against him. There was something arousing about the casual violence of her approval, while she traced the scabs on his knuckles with her finger.

Static ripped through her comm unit. A voice maybe, too weak to make out words.

"Did you get anything useful from him?" The question was casual. Professional, even. "Before the words?"

The shame came on suddenly. He'd been so angry, so focused on making Hesper bleed, he hadn't even thought… Her fingers stopped moving on his skin.

"Ned. Didn't you ask him?"

He could tell her everything. How rage had consumed him, made him forget why he was even hitting the man. How he'd known the Lost were coming and still couldn't stop them. How it was all his, Park's, and Sevvers's fault. The truth burned in his throat, demanding to be told. But the warmth of her body was already fading, like she could feel the truth trying to surface. Better to lose this moment slowly than break it with one hard confession.

"PR Command sent you to Vestebrae?" The question was pure tactical reflex. Redirect and engage. "That must've been hell."

She knew exactly what he was doing. Even years apart and the old habits still held. Still, she didn't pull away entirely, though something had shifted between them.

"Raiders hit us hard, but they paid for every meter." The Marine in her voice was comforting, gave him something to hold on to. "And that was before Victory Command blew the place straight to twelve hells. How'd you end up with them anyway? Thought you were on leave after your secret run."

"I was on Three-Alpha when the squids hit. The skeegs were in full panic by the time we reached the hangar deck. The only way down was with Victory."

The memory of that chaos hit him. The relief of finding Runt and the *Gauntlet* safe. The regret at leaving Sevvers to go it alone. The kid would do good. Had done good, if the Division's defeat of the forge ship meant anything.

"Victory's XO—well, CO now—she commandeered our transport to get her and any Marine in earshot to her ship." A bitter laugh escaped him. "From there, Park tried to order me to Bedrock on another classified mission."

More static crackled through her comms unit hanging from the wall. She should've just turned the damn thing off. The war would find them again soon enough without the tac nets constantly squawking.

"Tried to?"

"Yeah." The shame wanted to come out as anger, but he bit it off. "Couldn't fuck off to some rock with the archenemy in orbit around my home."

The guilt only twisted deeper. One right choice wouldn't erase the fact this was his fault. Deni had all but confirmed it. The derelict followed his team back to Aegia. And now his home was barely more than a crater on the side of a mountain.

"What happened out there, Ned?"

"It's classified."

Her body went rigid against his. "Classified?" She pushed herself up, all naked fury in the bunk's pale yellow light. "The archenemy is back. What secret could be possibly be more—"

"We're the ones who found the forge ship." The truth came out hard, uncontrolled. "It was derelict at Cradle's edge. That was our mission. My mission."

Her silence burned against his skin. More ghost transmissions squelched from the wall.

"We were ordered to board it. To rescue some deep cover operative." Each word felt like it was taken at gunpoint. "Once we were inside, it was obviously Concordat tech. We found Lost in there. Almost didn't make it. We got the operative out, but, I think we woke that ship up. I think we led it here—"

"Holy Mother." Lyra's hand flew to her mouth. "Oh, Ned. *Oh, Ned.*"

The rage he'd been holding back flooded his voice. "Didn't mean to, not that it matters now. They followed us back. And now Kaff's—"

His chest was tight and burning, strangling him. The comm unit spat static again.

Lyra smoothed away a tear. "This op. Was it standard enfil?"

"Twelfth, no." He laughed through the rage. She always knew how to calm him down. Better than counting ever did. "One fireteam. Plus some bot jockey and his combat drones."

"Against the Concordat?"

"Didn't know that going in. Or Command didn't tell us. Had this hotshot lupanthae pilot, too. Only reason any of us made it out."

"One fireteam," she said, mostly to herself. "CDF Command sent one fireteam to board an unknown vessel at the edge of the Cradle."

"I'm not even sure they knew. There was this Colonial Intel spook running the show. It was her operative we went to extract."

"Sounds right," Lyra said. "Who was this operative? Why were they so important?"

Static crackled through her comm unit, sharper this time. Before today, he'd have dismissed it as interference from the drop station machinery. Now he wondered who or what else might be listening. Deni seemed to know everything they'd done, everything they'd said.

"The operative was Section Delta." That much couldn't hurt to share. Everyone in the Three Colonies would know about them after what they did at the barricades. "Beyond that—"

"Classified?" The edge was back in her voice. "Or you don't know?"

"Both." He brushed away a shock of hair from her face. She had to see he was telling the truth. "They're not like us, Lyra. They look human, but… I'm not sure anyone knows what Section Delta really is."

She studied him, then she settled back against his chest with a long breath. "Okay. How was Sammy? When you found him?"

He smiled. He could still see the calm in the boy's Lyra-green eyes. "Good. You've raised a proper Aegian."

"His breathing. Was it bad? Did he eat something?"

"Seemed fine. I fed him. He said you're still cooking your rats too slow."

"*He* said that, huh?" She grinned at that, pretty as clear sky and gone just as quick. "And the shelter. It's safe? Not like—"

"Yeah. Upslope is clear. Had a good Marine escort him there personally. Lessig. You'd like him."

"A good Marine." Something in her tone had changed, more hesitant now. "Sammy's going to need that. Need you. After everything that's happened."

"Lyra—"

More static crackled through her comms.

"Just tell me," she said. "Are you coming home?"

Her question was a bolt to the heart, but somehow the truth hurt more. This war was far from over. He couldn't come home now. Not with more forge ships out there, waiting for whatever the Concordat had planned. They'd both seen firsthand what the archenemy would do to a colony given the chance, and Deni said this was only the beginning. That wasn't the answer Lyra wanted. But looking at her now, feeling her bare skin against him, the words wouldn't come.

She pulled away and stood, her body a silhouette of pale curves beneath the buzzing industrial lamps.

"Lyra." He reached for her.

She moved to the equipment racks, stood there with her back to him. Waiting. He rose and crossed to her, footsteps echoing in the small room.

Her first strike caught him in the chest, driving him back a step. The second hooked toward his jaw—her knuckles growing big in his eye line. He blocked it, but her knee drove up hard, forcing him to pivot. She followed, closing the gap between them. A left jab then a right pushed him further back, making him work to keep his guard up.

He caught her wrist on the third strike. She twisted free like he knew she would. But he didn't anticipate the knee to his ribs. The pain settled him, made him focus. Tactical awareness took over, reading her rhythm. He rose up inside her next attack, blocked high, then low. Her body pressed against his as he moved closer, controlling her arms, denying her space to generate power.

She fought against his grip, muscles tensed and straining, but he had position now. She tried to wrench away, twist free, but he held her there against the wall. Her breathing came ragged and sharp. Still angry. Her struggles grew less focused, less precise, but her stare was razor sharp.

"They followed me home, Lyra." He kept his voice low, kept his hold firm. "They came for our children."

The tension shifted in her body, not gone but changing. He eased his grip without letting go.

"I can't walk away now. Not until I know they can't ever do this again. To Sammy. To Kaff. To you."

Another tear tracked down her cheek. "So make them pay. Burn every last one of them, if you go."

It wasn't forgiveness. It was something harder, something that ran deeper between them than all those years apart. Understanding. Clarity of purpose. To his mission. To their family.

"I will." Holy Mother, hear him. The promise was a prayer.

Her comm unit crackled again, louder this time. A voice tried to break through the muddy static. Not whole words, just pieces of sound, bright and alive despite the interference. Then it was gone.

Lyra thumbed the comm unit's power switch. "Damn thing hasn't worked right since the squids showed up."

"Only an officer could get away with that." He forced a grin.

She didn't smile back, turning back to gather her gear.

Their uniforms lay in heaps where they'd dropped them. He shook out his white-and-grays, the camouflage patterns shifting as the synth-weave caught the light. The material felt cold against his skin, still damp with rain and sweat.

Lyra stepped into her uniform, zipper closing loudly up the midline. Two fingers to her heart—two quick taps—her own silent prayer to the Holy Mother. Her family's faith was a quieter kind, and it suited him. He repeated the movement as his own uniform cinched closed. Twelfth save them both.

His tac gear settled heavy on his shoulders, flexscreen chirping through its boot sequence. New alerts from Revan and Lessig. The world wasn't ending just yet, so they could wait another minute.

Their other rituals were almost the same: pouches sealed and quiet, vital monitors reading right, armor plates tight to the body. The last time he'd watched her do this, they'd been serving together. Some other fight; some other lifetime ago. Nothing like this.

Lyra took his rifle from the wall, eyed the safety, and mag-locked it to his chest plate. He did the same, giving her weapon a quick glance, then fixed it to her rig. Clean as always, just like he'd shown her. His hands fell away, but she caught them, their fingers wrapping together. Her head lowered, eyes closed.

"She is our shield," she said.

He knew the words. "We are Her sword."

"For Her glory," they spoke together, helmets touching. "For humanity. For the Lost."

The hatch opened with a heavy clunk. The hallway beyond stretched long, cold, and damp. Marines and reservists pushed past them. They were just two more bodies in white-and-grays now.

Big lift doors hissed open, revealing a heavy transport packed with PR troopers on a cargo lift headed for the surface. More reservists stood around the vehicle, dwarfed by its large tires. Lyra acknowledged their brisk salutes with an absent nod. Her shoulder pressed against his as the platform lurched upward.

They rose into the open concourse, misty storm winds carrying the smell of ozone and rotten mechanical meat. Floodlights carved harsh shadows across the industrial expanse, still searching the slope beyond for signs of danger. A dropship's engines howled at the far end of the station, drowning out the dull roar of evacuating civilians. One of the reservists shouted something over the din, voice lost as the heavy transport rolled away.

One hundred meters away, through waves of displaced colonists, Victory Marines stood guard at the barricades. His Marines. He needed to get back there, see this thing through, so he could—

"They're assigning Reserve units to the downslope sectors," she said, checking her flexscreen. "Sweep and clear operations through what's left of the outer districts."

Something cold tightened in his chest. They were sending her back out there.

"When?"

"Twenty-eight hours, one full turn to rest and resupply." She kept her voice level, professional, but he caught the slight tightness around her eyes. "Command thinks there might be intact shelters we missed. Survivors."

Or worse. They both knew what else might be waiting in those ruins. Lost that had gone to ground. Concordat forces still prowling the wreckage.

"Force disposition?" he asked.

"Standard sweep formation. Two reserve squads, Marine support if available." She shrugged like it was a routine patrol instead of a death sentence. "Most of your heavy metal's committed upslope."

The casual way she said it made his chest tight. Reserve units with light weapons, picking through ruins that could hide anything.

"Lyra—"

"Ned." Something in her tone brought him back. Focused him. "Our baby girl is still out there. If I made it, so can she. Find her. *Find her.*"

The weight of those two words—the fear behind them—settled in his gut. Alive or dead, Kaff was out there somewhere. She was telling him to bring their daughter home.

"I will," he said. There was no room for doubt in her eyes. This was his mission now. "Or you can take another finger."

"Careful." That pulled a quick, sad smile from her. "I'll hold you to that."

"You always do." His thumb found the nub of his left ring finger automatically.

She held his gaze one last time, then turned toward her own

people. Lyra the wife receded with each step, replaced by the reserve officer whose squad waited for her on the other side of the concourse. Her shoulders squared beneath her tac gear, chin lifting as she moved.

Another officer called to her, waving her over.

She didn't look back.

THIRTY-NINE

KAFFY DUCKED beneath a collapsed storefront awning, the comms unit clutched tight against her chest. Smoke settled heavy on the streets of Vestebrae, turning buildings into hulking shadows and the sky into something distant and forgotten. The rebreather made her face sweat, but she didn't dare take it off.

"Azure-Twelve, come in. This is Kaffy Bresto again. Over." She released the transmission button, anticipating the unit's familiar chirp.

Static hissed back at her, empty as the streets around them. She tried again, pressing the button harder.

"Azure-Twelve, please. I want to talk to my parents. This is Kaffy Bresto again. Over."

Duray emerged from the haze, debris crunching under his boots. "You're wasting time. We should keep moving."

She ignored him, giving the dial another twist. The screen's symbols shifted, but she had no idea what most of them meant.

"Father can hear me. I know it."

"Yeah? And where is this shelter supposed to be? We've been walking for an hour."

"The man said—"

"The man doesn't know we're lost. Coordinates would help. A map. Anything."

"We're not lost." She pointed downslope. More smoke, more ruined buildings. "We just need to keep going down."

"Great plan. Maybe if you spent less time on the comms and more time paying attention, we'd be there already."

The unit crackled, softer this time. They both froze. Kaffy raised the speaker to her ear, pulse racing.

"—*affereine*—" The voice cut through static, then vanished.

"Father?" She released the push-to-talk, but only static answered. "It's got to be him. He's trying to reach us!"

Duray reached for the radio. "Let me see that."

She jerked away. "No. Stop!"

"I know how these work." He wasn't grabbing anymore, just holding out his hand. "Hesper made me learn. These handhelds aren't very strong. That's why they put relay towers on high ground."

Kaffy glanced up at the smoke-choked sky. Mother hadn't talked much about these things. She was always too tired. Too sad. Duray had spent every day with Hesper for years. Maybe he did know something after all. She handed over the comms unit.

Duray turned it in his hands. "PR model. Garbage."

"Hey!" She swatted at his arm. "The PR aren't garbage!"

"Not them, their gear." He pointed at a tiny display. "Signal strength indicator. See? We're barely getting anything."

"So, what do we do?"

"Need to get higher. Or find a clear spot. The buildings are blocking us."

"Okay." For the first time in hours, it felt like they had a plan. She pointed to a gap between two administrative blocks. "Maybe that way? It might be clearer."

Duray handed the unit back. "Let's go."

They started between the crumbling buildings. Vestebrae looked nothing like the gleaming city of glowing towers she'd seen from the drop platform. Where there had been light and life just hours before, now there was only darkness and empty space. Even the smell had changed—the sweet scent of those treats and wet-storm air replaced by burned plastec and something underneath it all, organic and rotten.

Ahead of them, a slab of granite jutted from the transit lane. Her boots slipped against the smooth surface as she scrambled to the top. The main transit corridor stretched ahead, wider than the side lanes but equally ruined. Overhead, the smoke thinned just enough to see hints of storm clouds. It was something familiar. Somewhere up there, beyond all that darkness, Father was looking for her.

"This is better." She checked the signal indicator. The single illuminated bar made her heart jump. "Look! We've got signal!"

"Barely."

She pressed the transmission button. "Azure-Twelve, this is Kaffy Bresto. We need directions. We're on the main transit near…" Mother always sounded so confident, so in control. Not like her, lost and scared with only this stupid boy for company. And the shattered storefronts offered no useful landmarks. "Near some shops. Over."

The static cleared just enough: "—*downslope to junction*—"

"What?" Her fingers felt clumsy, too big for the tiny dials. What if she messed it up completely? What if this was her only chance? "I didn't hear you. Where's the shelter? Over."

More static, then: "—*east quadrant*—*transit seven*—*blue mark*—"

Kaffy shook the unit. What good were directions if they made no sense? "What blue marker? Where's transit seven?"

"Nice going," Duray said. "You have no idea where we are, do you?"

"Oh, and you do?" She clutched the comms to her chest. Always so smug, like he knew everything.

"Actually…" He pointed downslope where the transit forked. "That's got to be junction four. Transit corridors have markers at every major intersection."

"How do you know that?"

"Junction design is standard across the colony. Block captains have to learn the whole grid. Hesper made me memorize it. You will to, when you make your delta levels."

"Transit seven from junction four." She pressed the radio's transmission button. She'd show him she could be useful too. "Azure-Twelve, is it Transit Seven from Junction Four? Over?"

A burst of static answered her, then: "—*confirm, Lady Kaffereine*—*blue emergency markings*—"

The sound of her nickname froze her blood. Only Madam Ulwin called her that. The painter had said it, too. It didn't seem possible they could still be alive. She saw the building fall—

"Told you." Duray was already moving toward the junction. "Come on, we're wasting time."

Another explosion rumbled in the distance, and they both ducked instinctively.

"What was that?" she whispered.

"Dunno. Something bad."

"Let's hurry."

They half-ran, half-stumbled down the transit corridor. At the junction, bright blue emergency panels flashed through the haze, their power still flowing despite the destruction around them. Duray found the transit marker first, a simple metal post with *TRANSIT 7* stamped across it in blackened white paint.

"This way." He pointed east, where the corridor narrowed between more office towers. "Looks clear enough."

Kaffy tried the comms again. "Azure-Twelve, we found Transit Seven. How much further? Over." Please say close. Please say Father was waiting there. Please.

No response.

A shadow emerged at the far end of Transit Seven. She crouched behind the slab. The shape resolved through the smoke—not human— far too big, with limbs that hung too long from its torso. Two more figures joined the first, their bulbous helmets reflecting the blue emergency lights against pale green scales. Their wet, frothy breathing echoed between the buildings. Like someone drowning.

"The radio," Duray hissed from just below her. "Turn it off!"

Her thumb found the power switch just as one of the creatures turned toward them, the soft click too loud between heartbeats. Its helmet swiveled, dark eye-slits scanning the transit corridor through the smoke. A gargling sound emerged from its helmet sounding nothing like words she recognized.

She slid down into the lane. Duray pulled her sideways into the shattered remains of a once tall commercial tower. The building's foundation had cracked, the floor tilting at a slight angle that made every step uncertain. Broken pipes jutted from the ceiling, dripping rusty water onto the polished granite floor.

They pressed against a half-collapsed wall. Her heart hammered so hard they'd probably hear it.

"Squids," Duray whispered, too quiet even pressed against her ear.

She nodded. Every kid in the settlements learned about squids. How they'd attacked Respitia's outlying settlements. What they'd done to the mining consortium before that. But seeing them, hunting through the smoke, turned History Basics into something much scarier.

Another sound cut the air. Not the squids' gurgling speech, but a sharp, harsh clacking, like bones rattling together. Something larger than the raiders scuttled into view, moving with impossible speed across the broken pavement. Its thick skin was black as the smoke, with a green sheen reflecting from the strange device it carried. The squids bowed at its arrival.

The bug's head rotated too far, joints bending in ways that made her stomach turn. Its limbs ended in long, hinged claws that clicked as it gestured. The squids responded immediately, fanning out into the rubble.

"Not a squid," Duray breathed, his face pale as ash. She pressed a finger to her lips, urging him to shut up.

The bug's head swiveled toward their hiding spot, its clicking growing louder. She grabbed Duray's sleeve and pulled him deeper into the building as fast as she could and keep quiet, ducking beneath fallen support beams and around teetering columns.

A gap appeared in the interior wall, a narrow access barely wider than her shoulders where thick conduits disappeared into the rubble. She dropped to her knees and squeezed inside, the jagged edges scraping against her jumpsuit. The space opened into a narrow tunnel, dark except for emergency lighting strips that flickered along the floor and ceiling.

"Come on!" she whispered, reaching back through the gap.

Duray glanced back, panicked. "They're coming."

"Then hurry up!"

He dropped down and tried to wiggle through, but his shoulders caught against the narrow opening. A broken pipe scraped across his back, tearing his jumpsuit. Frothy breathing echoed from just around the corner.

"I can't—"

"You can!" She grabbed his arm with both hands and pulled hard. The sound of heavy feet against granite grew closer. Duray pushed with his legs, squirming against the tight metal. She gave one last desperate tug, and he tumbled through the gap just as a squid's shadow fell across the floor outside. She held him close, squeezing him, her own body rigid as she prayed—*don't move.*

The shadow passed, and they slid against the back wall, barely breathing. Through the narrow opening, a second squid stalked past on three-toed feet, its patchwork armor hissing with each movement. The plates looked like they'd been fused together from old parts. Smelted hull metal, spare tubing, even what looked like old CDF uniforms stitched together. Its gun was weirder still, like someone had started with a proper rifle then stuck tubes and wires all over it. The barrel looked melted in places, with pipes that glowed bright red running along the sides.

The squid stopped just beyond their hiding spot, its helmet swiveling as it surveyed the room. It raised a three-tentacled hand to adjust something on its armor, the wet sounds of its breathing filling the silence. Spiky tentacles curled and uncurled from the front of its face.

More harsh clacking echoed through the granite and duraplate. The bug-thing appeared at the far end of the rubble, its black shell gleaming under the emergency lights. It gestured sharply at the squids, who immediately turned to follow. The aliens left the building, disappearing back into the smokey transit.

Kaffy let out the breath she'd been holding. "That was close."

"Yeah." Duray nodded at the comms unit. "Let's leave that thing off."

They stayed hidden until the alien sounds were gone. The tight space made her legs cramp, but she didn't dare move until Duray finally nodded that it was clear. They squeezed back through the gap, emerging into the ruined building.

"Which way?" she whispered.

Duray pointed away from the transit corridor. "Through the back. Transit Seven probably goes on the other side of this block."

"How do you know?"

"I don't," he admitted. "But it's better than going back out there."

They picked their way through shattered furniture and fallen ceiling tiles. The service exit had been torn from its frame, spilling them into an alley barely wider than Kaffy's shoulders. Duray took the lead.

"You know," he said after they'd gone a few steps, "when we make it back, I'm telling Hesper I was the one who found the transit marker."

"Of course you will," she muttered. Like she cared about stupid block guides and their stupid credit-taking. Just like back in Diacad. Same Duray, different nightmare.

A squat bunker stood at the end of the alley, its surface a mix of formed duraplate and fibrosteel. The building seemed untouched by the destruction around it. Above reinforced doors, large block letters shone through the smoke: *CIVIL DEFENSE SHELTER AZURE-12.*

"Told you," Duray said, but the usual smugness was gone from his voice. He sounded as relieved as she felt.

The shelter doors were massive, taller than Father by a meter. Probably half as thick. There were no guards. No emergency workers. Just the doors and a small access panel glowing softly in the frame. The empty street felt wrong somehow.

"Where is everyone?" she asked.

Duray walked to the door. "Inside, obviously. Safe." He reached the access panel and waved his hand over it. "Open, same-same."

"Huh?"

"Open, same-same. My father used to say it whenever he unlocked something. Said it was a thing people said back on Dead Earth."

More likely something he'd made up to sound important. As if being orphaned wasn't tragic enough.

The access panel crackled to life, startling them both. *"Hello,"* said the slow voice from the comms. Without the static, it sounded even stranger—flat and precise, almost like a machine. *"Please identify yourself."*

"Uh, hi. It's Kaffy Bresto and Arthur Duray. We talked to you on the comms unit. You said my parents are inside?"

Something boomed inside the thick walls. The massive doors groaned and began to part, sliding into recesses in the wall. Stale, cold air rushed out, carrying a metallic smell that wrinkled her nose.

They passed through the massive doors into a wide entry bay, stark white lighting reflecting off metal walls. She squinted against the sudden brightness after hours in smoke and dark. The place was big enough for a heavy cargo sled, maybe two, but completely empty. Not a person in sight.

More block letters marked the far wall: *CARGO RECEIVING BAY*. To their left, red and yellow hazard signs plastered the entrance to another room: *DANGER—HIGH VOLTAGE, AUTHORIZED PERSONNEL ONLY,* and *CRUSH HAZARD—AUTOMATED EQUIPMENT.*

"Hello?" Duray called, his voice echoing against the bare metal. "Anyone here?"

No one answered. Only the soft hum of ventilation systems somewhere deep in the shelter.

A bright green sign with an arrow pointed to their right: *SHELTER ACCESS.* The corridor narrowed there, leading to a wide stairwell that descended into darkness below.

"Shouldn't there be people?" she whispered, the silence pressing in on her. "Emergency workers, guards, somebody?"

Duray's confident stride turned cautious. "Maybe they're all downstairs."

The door slid shut behind them with a heavy clang that made them both jump. The metallic smell was stronger inside, mixed with something else. Like cleaning fluid, but sharper. Kaffy hesitated at the top of the stairs, peering down into the dimly lit passage below.

"Come on," Duray said, hand on the rail as he stepped down. "Your parents are waiting, remember?"

The stairwell led to a dimly lit corridor. Signs of life greeted them: overflowing waste baskets, half-empty supply crates. Kaffy grabbed a water pouch, fingers trembling with the tab. The cool liquid filled her mouth, washing away hours of smoke and fear.

Between gulps, she noticed the lights flickering. Something vibrated behind the walls, a rhythmic pulse unlike the smooth hum of colony generators. More like a beating heart.

"Hear that?" She pressed her ear against the cool metal. "It sounds weird."

Duray crumpled his empty pouch and reached for another. "Probably just backup systems." He squirted water in a high arc, catching most of it in his mouth. "Bet they're running on aux power."

"But where is everyone?"

"Maybe they went deeper inside when the attack hit. If I were in charge, I'd keep everyone as far from the surface as possible."

That made sense, sort of. Maybe they were all gathered in some central room, waiting out the danger. Her parents could be just a few corridors away. Her hand slipped past the comms unit and into her pocket, wrapping around the little figurine. The old metal was cold in her palm.

"Come on," she said. "Let's find them."

The corridor ended at a large security door. Its access panel glowed with red status lights, but when Duray pressed the controls, nothing happened. He tried again, jabbing his finger against each button with growing frustration.

"Red dead, see?" He slapped the panel with his palm. "It won't open."

"Maybe we're not supposed to go this way," Kaffy said quietly. She peered through the narrow observation window, into darkness broken only by distant emergency lights. Something moved in the shadows. Her stomach tightened. "Maybe we should go back up."

"And go where?" Duray keyed in random sequences, growing more frantic. "Back outside with the squids? The bugs? This is the shelter. This is where we're supposed to be."

The frustration in his voice shifted to something else. He stepped back from the panel. "I don't get it. Everything looks powered, but nothing works."

Kaffy traced the figurine's worn edges with her thumb. She was almost relieved the door wouldn't open. Like the Twelfth *knew* they shouldn't be down there.

"I dunno," Duray began, "maybe you're—"

The security door hissed open, revealing a human shape in the corridor beyond. White-and-gray camouflage patterns shifted in the light as the figure stepped forward.

Father. The relief was total and instant until she saw the dark red stain spread across the uniform's midsection. The name Reede was stenciled above the breast pocket. Not Bresto. The Marine's face was gone, hidden behind a blank metal mask that reflected her own wide-eyed terror back at her.

Just like the stories.

The Lost daxed lurched toward her, reaching with pale gray hands. More whispers and soft clicks emanated from the darkness behind it.

Duray caught her wrist, yanking the figurine from her grasp as he pulled her into a run. They sprinted back the way they'd come, boots pounding against the metal.

They ran up the stairs, Duray taking the steps three at a time. She struggled to keep up, legs burning, lungs screaming for air. The sound from below chased them. A high, piercing wail that started human but stretched too long, too high. Like something from a nightmare.

"Hurry!" Duray called over his shoulder.

She pushed harder. At the top, her foot slipped on worn duraplate. Duray's hand caught her arm, pulling her upright.

The main doors to the entry bay were still sealed, access panels glowing danger red. They tried the cargo receiving bay—locked. The shelter entrance—locked. Every console flashed the same warning: *CONTAINMENT PROTOCOL ACTIVE.*

Only the maintenance access showed any difference. Its panel flashed yellow, cycling through status codes too fast to read.

"We're trapped," Duray said, voice cracking.

"No!" She pointed at the flashing maintenance door. "That one's different."

The inhuman scream rose from the stairwell again, closer now. They could hear something scrabbling up the metal steps, moving fast.

"I'll try to override this one. You try maintenance," Duray said, racing toward the main entrance.

She didn't know how to override a console. More than that, she didn't want to be alone, not now, not with that thing coming. "But—"

"Just do it!" He was already at the main console, fingers flying across the controls.

She ran to the maintenance door. The access panel flashed faster now, symbols and numbers blurring together. She pressed the first button, then another. Nothing happened.

"It's not working!" she cried, slamming her palm against the console.

An angry growl emanated from the speaker grill. Not words, just pure electronic frustration, as if the system itself was fighting her.

Even from across the bay, she could see the defeat in Duray's slumped shoulders. The main doors weren't opening. They were locked in.

The scrabbling sounds grew louder.

"Please," she begged, tears streaming down her face. Her fingers stabbed at buttons randomly, desperately. "Please, please, please!"

The growl from the speaker dissolved into a series of beeps. Then, with a soft click, the maintenance door slid open.

"It's open!" she screamed. "Duray! It's open!"

She turned back toward Duray and froze. The Reede-thing was already there, scrabbling up the last steps on all fours, back and neck bent at impossible angles. Its blank mask faced her, and she knew it was watching from behind that metal face.

Her mouth opened to scream, but Duray slammed into the Reede-thing from the side, all bared teeth and wild eyes. They crashed to the floor in a tangle of arms and legs.

"Go!" he screamed, pinning the thing for just a moment. His face contorted with terror and rage. "Get out of here!"

She couldn't move, couldn't speak. Her hand went to her pocket—empty. The Twelfth wasn't there. Maybe She never was. Just stories and statues and wishes in the dark.

"That's an order, Bresto!" Duray's voice cracked as the Lost's pale hands found his throat. Like block drill. Like Hesper shouting commands across the training yard.

One second she was frozen, the next she was through the maintenance door. It hissed shut behind her, locks clicking into place. Duray's muffled curses and screams filtered through the metal, growing weaker.

She held back a sob. Stupid, stupid boy. Showoff Duray with his stupid block drills and stupid memorized directions. Stupid brave Duray who'd just saved her life.

The access panel outside buzzed again. Her insides turned to ice.

"D-Duray?" she managed, lips trembling.

No answer. Something pounded against the door. Metal groaned under the impact.

She was running again, boots sliding on the maintenance corridor's ribbed floor. Around the corner, past rumbling emergency generators and hissing electronics. The corridor narrowed, pipes and conduits crowding the ceiling, then opened to a vertical shaft.

A service ladder stretched upward, disappearing into darkness. She grasped the first rung and yanked herself up. The ladder seemed endless, stretching higher and higher until her arms burned and her fingers cramped. She didn't dare look down. Didn't dare think about what might be following.

The top of the ladder came suddenly, another hatch blocking her path. But its access panel glowed friendly green, and one easy press made it open. Dodecoron's storm winds rushed in, so strong it nearly pulled her off the ladder. She scrambled onto the narrow ledge, fingers clinging to anything solid.

The shelter's roof access stretched before her, barely three meters square. A communication mast rose from the center—a jumble of relays and sensors all pointing skyward. She grabbed the nearest support strut, the cold metal biting into her palms.

What was left of Vestebrae stretched out around her. The once-gleaming towers were broken skeletons now, jagged silhouettes against the storm. A dark blanket of smoke hung over everything, pulsing with dull orange where fires still burned below. The transit corridors were barely visible, thick lines cutting through the devastation.

Another gust slammed into her and the ground far below seemed to spin. Her stomach lurched as she clung tighter to the mast. This was completely hopeless. Duray was gone, and she was all alone on a roof with nowhere to go. Just waiting to get picked off by the wind or whatever came up that ladder next.

She fumbled the comms from her pocket. The power button clicked on, the display small and bright in the dark. Just like Duray had shown her, the signal indicator was stronger now, fluctuating between two and three bars in the open air.

She pressed the transmission button. "Help! Please! Somebody, help me! I'm... I—!"

Her lungs and throat burned. This wasn't going to work. A proper Aegian wouldn't do this. That's what Father would say. Even now. She took another shuddering breath, tried to steady her voice.

"Kaffy Bresto to Sergeant Ned Bresto. Over." The wind tore at her words. "I am in urgent distress. Over. On the roof of Civil Defense Shelter Azure-Twelve. Over. Please, Father. Please help."

CHAPTER
FORTY

THE SUPPLY CRATE smelled like the inside of a blaster rifle, metallic and hot beneath the field lights. Bresto shoveled fresh charge packs into his tac vest while his mind replayed Lyra's final words. *Find her.* An order from the woman who'd given him everything and taken so little. The decision had already crystallized somewhere between her silent goodbye and the walk to the resupply point. He was going after Kaff, whatever the cost.

Find her. He would.

"You weren't at the barricades." Revan lingered at the edge of the hasty supply tent. "Major Kull asked for Third Platoon specifically."

"Was busy," Bresto mumbled, grabbing three more packs and slotting them into the pouches of his tac vest. He leaned deeper into the crate, keeping his shoulders between prying eyes and what else he was taking. Grenades first, six frags. Standard issue. Nothing to notice.

"Too busy to attend the mission brief?" Revan consulted his datapad. "Section Delta's presence has changed the tactical picture completely. Kull wants—"

"Sir, I've been up for thirty hours." Bresto angled his body to hide the plasmex brick he dropped into a utility pouch. "Figured I'd grab a little resupply, maybe some chow."

"I need you to reposition First and Second Squads along the

secondary barricade." Revan's attention remained safely fixed on the screen. "Kull has PR elements pushing forward to establish an FOB for counter-incursion ops."

Bresto froze, his fingers curled around the second plasmex brick. "Forward operating base? You're going after the Lost?"

"*We* are," Revan said with that greedy smile. "Major Kull's orders. Victory's pushing downslope behind Delta. PR's going to join us in the field tomorrow."

At least Lyra would have Marine support in the field before ever leaving the drop station. Plans must've changed. Probably someone raising twelve hells after Kull annihilated most of the people they were sent to protect. But that meant the ruins of Vestebrae would turn into a warzone, and soon. He'd need to find Kaff before that started. If she was still alive.

"Good to know." He slid the second brick into his pouch. "Once I'm done here, I'll help get that started. Lessig will do fine."

"Lessig?" Revan finally glanced up. "I need *you* focused on this. We're the lynchpin of Victory's right flank. You know how to make this happen."

He could play the dutiful NCO—*yessir* his way through this conversation, then slip away when Revan wasn't looking. But the lieutenant would just send someone after him. Better to make this official. Collect on what he was owed.

Bresto straightened to full height. "We had a deal, Lieutenant. I got you Diacad. Got you the transit corridors. Got you this whole Twelfth-damned drop station."

Now family came first.

Pity flickered across Revan's features. "Sergeant, I understand your situation. I do. But the evacuation route was destroyed. Nothing could have survived what the major ordered, especially not—"

"Thousands of Lost did. My wife. There could have been others." He kept his voice steady, but the heat was building in his chest. "You don't know for sure."

"Look, I can have admin net access granted. Proper channels. You can check shelter records, see where your son's been moved to."

"My son? I found Sammy hours ago."

"Your… ah, I'm sorry. Your daughter. Of course."

Fucking Revan didn't even know which of his children was missing but still felt qualified to tell him to give up.

"I'm going to find her." He shoved the last frag into its carrier and clipped the pouch shut. Revan promised him that.

"I offered you resources. Access. Not a liberty chit to go wherever you want in the middle of the most important fight in human history."

"You knew where this was going, you greedy little shit. Can't help you don't like the timing."

Revan's composure slipped. "Have you forgotten what's out there? What we're up against? It's not just the Concordat, Sergeant. These Section Delta are here, and we don't know who they are or what they want."

Behind the lieutenant, Marines drifted closer, pretending to sort gear while straining to hear what they were saying.

"Focus on what we can control," Revan pressed. "The mission. Keeping those still with us safe."

The arguments made sense. Would have made sense to the Marine he'd been an hour ago. Third Platoon had bled for this operation. His home. They needed every weapon, every NCO with combat experience. The fresh PR units moving up didn't know what was out there. All true. All irrelevant now.

Lyra's voice cut through every tactical consideration. Those eyes filled with her kind of hard love that had made him the man he was. *Find her.* Not a request from his wife, but an order from the mother of his children. He'd promised.

"I'll make sure Third Platoon is ready," he said, shoving past Revan's outstretched hand. "I'll get your squads positioned and brief the reservists on what they're facing. And then I'm going to after my daughter."

"That's not—"

"Let me be clear." Bresto leaned in, close enough to see the fear in Revan's eyes. "You're not my CO. I've given you everything and then some. You get that much more. Then I'm gone."

"I don't think you understand, Sergeant. That's not how this—"

"Who's going to stop me? You?"

Revan blinked. Didn't think so.

The lieutenant's voice dropped to barely a whisper. "Go straight to Third Platoon. Give the briefing. Get them in position. But any absence will be declared unauthorized."

Was Revan letting him go? The whispering made it impossible to tell. Didn't matter. He'd already decided. It wasn't up to this academy skeeg.

Revan wasn't finished. "Now say, 'Aye, sir.'"

Rage flared in Bresto's chest so fast he had to count each heartbeat. One. Two. Three.

There was no weakness in Revan's eyes. Not even a flicker. Maybe getting shot at for thirty straight hours had grown the man some actual balls.

Shame to have to remove them now.

No. Kaff was his mission now. He stared a moment more, then shouldered his way out of the supply tent.

———

Strong gusts drove sprays of storm runoff across the transit walkway between the control tower and the barricades. A faint band of bright gray edged the horizon. The sun would be up in a couple hours.

Victory Marines lounged against the barriers, bodies relaxed but hands on their CR-11s. PR troops mingled tentatively, most hovering back beneath the control tower's overhangs or the equipment containers stacked along the walkway.

Lessig stood outside his exo at the edge of Third Platoon's line, past the barricades, pissing off the edge among piles of dead daxed.

"Zip it up, Corporal," Bresto barked without breaking stride. "Let's go. Bring your fireteam leaders."

"Aye, Sarnt." Lessig shook it out then jogged to Bresto's side, his face still a black and blue mess. "Something coming down from Command?"

Bresto ignored the question, pointing ahead to Second Squad. "Prelk, fall in. You too, Montawk."

"Aye, Sarnt," Prelk said. The Marines peeled away from their exos, snatching up rifles.

"Rikkos, Patrim," Bresto called as he entered Third Squad's line. "With me."

The twins exchanged a glance. Smokes stamped out a cigarette with his boot before they fell in. They'd gathered a small crowd of Marines by the time they reached 3-3-3's position. He could've given the briefing anywhere, but this seemed as good a place as any to leave from when this was all over.

PR troopers in crisp white-and-grays stepped back as he approached Olsom's position.

The smell hit him first, like rot gone metallic in the rain. The massive daxed heavy still lay over the barricade across from 3-3-3, its black innards seeping through metal grating. Olsom hunched in her rig's operator cage, fingers working the ops terminal without purpose. Not bothering to look out as the Marines gathered near her rig.

"Listen up," Bresto called. "Olsom, you too."

She didn't climb down. Just slid one side of her helmet off an ear, eyes empty as she glanced over the assembled fireteam leaders.

"Victory's got new orders. Counter-incursion ops. Section Delta's cleared us a path, but we've got more shelters downslope needing force recon. Need to find out which shelters hold humans and which hold something else."

Lessig and Prelk exchanged a look. The twins stared straight ahead, expressions unreadable. Others muttered among themselves, whispering the name Delta like it might summon them.

Hands shot up, one or two to start, then more. He knew what was coming.

"What is it, Prelk?"

"What the hell are those things, Sarnt?" Prelk asked. "They just appeared, tearing up Lost like they were field paste."

"Saw one take down three heavies without breaking stride," another Marine called out. "Like the Twelfth Herself sent them."

"Holy Mother's hand," someone muttered.

"Nobody knows who or what Section Delta is." The lie came easy but left a bad taste in his mouth. These Marines had survived twelve hells already. No need to send them downslope worrying about god-like operatives with their own agenda. "What matters is they cleared the transit corridor. Major Kull thinks they can be trusted enough for joint ops. I'd suggest keeping your heads on a swivel anyway."

Above them, Olsom snorted, the first sound she'd made since he'd arrived. Something about it felt pointed. At him. But he let it slide. At least he had her attention now.

"Delta cleared the downslope transit, but that doesn't mean it'll stay that way," he continued. "Squad up. Keep your exos in wedge formation. No lone rig pushes, no matter what you see."

The Marines leaned in, heads nodding at the details. He scanned their faces—three squads of killers that had survived the crucible of fire and maneuver at the end of the world. And here he was, about to walk away.

"PR's going to be in support," he said, marking it on Lessig's flexscreen. "They'll get some of this fight soon enough. Watch your crossfire with them. They mean well, but half haven't seen a proper fight yet."

"They'll shit themselves first time a wisp shows up," Lessig muttered.

"That's why you're taking point," Bresto said. "Keep your best shooters forward. Best eyes on your flanks. Questions?"

A lance corporal from Second Squad raised his hand. "Sarnt, what about the shelters? If they're all already compromised, then—"

The kid was wrong. Had to be, if Kaff stood a chance. "Not all of them will be. Check your fire around shelter entrances. Call in ID before you engage. Some of those civvies might still be breathing."

"But how do we tell them apart?" Montawk asked. "Some of those daxed looked just like PR."

"The masks form first. Check the face, then the hands. Any metal showing, any gray skin, you light 'em up."

He answered three more questions with the same measured patience. A strange calm had settled over him. Made explaining easier, made listening easier too.

Olsom shifted in her cage, one hand pressed to her waist, the other white-knuckling the exo's ops terminal. Her attention never wavered from him.

"Remember, no heroics. Victory is under strength. Third Platoon's taken some hits, too. Every Marine counts twice now. Take care of each other."

Olsom spat. "Sounds like you're scrapping out on us again."

She'd heard the goodbye.

Every Marine in earshot froze, their eyes on Bresto. Olsom's gaze burned into him, less demanding than Lyra's had but somehow worse for the hurt behind it.

"My orders are taking me elsewhere," he said.

"Whose orders? Major Kill's? Why don't you tell them why you're really here, Sarnt?"

"Olsom." The Rikkos' heads snapped toward her in perfect sync.

She ignored them, leaning forward in her cage until the restraints bit into her shoulders. "Go on, Sarnt. Tell us how your *family* is more important than our orders."

Hot, raw rage surged into Bresto's throat. He swallowed it down, counting each pulse in his temples. One. Two. Three. Four.

"What's the matter, Sarnt?" She was almost laughing now, at odds with the wet anger in her eyes. "You did all this for them, right? Disobeyed your CO, lied to all of us, went to fucking war? All for family?" Her voice cracked on that word again. Like she couldn't believe what she was saying.

"I won't explain myself to you, Private. But this is your last chance to get my family out of your mouth."

"Or what? You're leaving us here to clean up the mess while you… what? Go down there alone? To do what, exactly?"

"Shut your dick sucker, Olsom," Lessig snapped. "*Now.*"

"I know what you did," she continued. "My comms have been ghosting since the foundry. Lieutenant Bresto keeps popping up in my feeds when she shouldn't be there at all."

Shit. The boot had put it together. Not just the comms tweak, but why he'd done it. Smart girl. Too smart for her own good.

"Doc figured it all out," she said. "You tweaked my rig's net relay. I knew it was you the second I heard your wife's voice."

The rage sat quiet in Bresto's chest, a single loose stone high on the mountainside. Every Marine in earshot held their breath, waiting. One more word from her and the whole slope would come down.

"Come on, Olsom." Patrim rubbed nervous fingers across his stubbled scalp. "We all got family here. Maybe I'd do the same, you know? If I thought I could. If I knew how."

"Did it work, Sarnt?" Olsom leaned against her restraints. "You've got little Sammy. Did you find Mrs. Bresto? What about Sissy?"

Something in him broke. He charged 3-3-3's frame. Smokes stepped in to block. Bresto shouldered him squarely in the chest, sending the narrow spacer stumbling sideways. Two more strides and his hand slammed against the cage release. The panel whined in protest, then gave way with a hydraulic hiss.

The other Marines were on him—Lessig, Prelk, more—their hands finding his shoulders, his arms. He barely felt them, rage carrying him up beneath the plexene canopy. Olsom rose to meet him, her broad Vestian shoulders tensed like a rock snake about to strike. His fingers wrapped around the top of her tac vest, twisting into the lip of the armored plate at her collarbone.

"I warned you." He yanked hard against the harness straps.

Her hands found his wrist, thumbs pressing into tendons, hunting for a pressure point. He almost laughed. Amateur hour.

"Do it," she hissed. Nothing like the young boot from Three-Alpha now. "Wouldn't be the first time someone bigger beat me bloody."

Challenge accepted.

"Do it, Sarnt!" Prelk shouted. "Little bitch has it coming!"

"Leave her alone!" the twins shouted.

"Feral's got a mouth on her." Someone laughed, ugly and sharp. "Nah, Sarnt's got this right."

Olsom twisted in the harness, working her buckles with one hand while the other kept pressure on his wrist. The first clasp popped free.

"Easy, Sarnt," Patrim said. "Maybe we should—"

"Should what?" Montawk barked. "Let some boot disrespect our platoon sarnt?"

The second buckle gave way and suddenly Olsom was moving, using his grip on her vest as leverage to swing her knee up hard. It caught him in the ribs, emptying his lungs. His hold loosened and she twisted free, dropping from the cage to the deck in a controlled fall.

He spun to face her, but she was right there, fists up, bouncing on the balls of her feet like she'd done this before. Her jab snapped out quick and clean, catching him on the nose. Pain flared, then faded beneath the surge of adrenaline.

"That all you got?" he growled, swinging wide.

She ducked under it, came back with a hook that found the gap between his armor plates.

"Beat her down, Sarnt!" Prelk again, that loud fucker.

"Get some, Olsom!" the twins shouted back. "Move your feet!"

She tried to circle right, but he cut her off, driving her back against the exo's frame. She grimaced through her next swing and didn't follow through. Sloppy.

He caught her wrist, pulled her in close, and drove his other fist into her face. The impact sent her staggering backward, blood streaming from her nose. She blinked hard, shaking her head to clear it, but the fear that flickered across her face told him everything. She was tough, but he was bigger, stronger, and had twenty years more experience hurting people. This was going to get ugly fast.

Static crackled from 3-3-3's emitters, a brief squelch of interference that cut through the shouting. Something almost like a voice buried in the white noise, too faint to make out. Bresto's attention flickered toward the sound for half a heartbeat before Olsom came at him again, wiping blood from her nose with the back of her hand.

"That it?" she spat, fists still up and bloody.

He lunged forward, going for the takedown—end this thing quick. But the blood had sharpened her focus. She sidestepped his charge, pivoted on her heel, and drove her boot hard into his left hip. White-hot pain exploded through the joint.

His leg buckled and he went down on one knee. "Fuck!"

"Get up, Sarnt!" Montawk yelled. "Don't let her—"

The radio crackled again, louder this time. Static washed over fragments of words: "—*help me*—" then nothing, then "—*trapped*—" before the signal dissolved back into white noise. A girl's voice, high with terror, barely audible through the interference.

Olsom backed away, chest heaving, giving him space to recover. "You hear that?"

"Yeah." Bresto pushed himself up, one hand braced against his throbbing hip. Pain shot down his leg.

Olsom was already scrambling back into the cage, blood still streaming from her nose. Her fingers flew across the terminal, cranking the gain on the emitters until the static filled the air.

"Come on," she muttered. "Come on, you piece of shit, work with me."

"*—affy Bresto to Sergeant Ned Bresto—am in urgent distress. O—*" Static consumed the next few words before the signal came back. Then a sound like a scream. "*—ost are here, they're—*"

Kaff. His daughter's voice. Holy Mother.

"Oh shit," Olsom breathed, face going pale beneath the blood. "Sarnt, that's—"

"*Please. I'm trapped above Shelter Azure-Twelve.*" Kaff's voice hitched, caught between a sob and something stronger. "*Father, please help me. They're coming—*"

The transmission died, swallowed by static and the storm.

His pulse hammered in his ears, drowning out everything else. Kaff. His baby girl. *Alive.* Relief crashed through him, then twisted into something darker, more primal. Lost. She'd said she was trapped with them.

Time compressed around him. The barricades, the Marines, Olsom's anger—none of it mattered. Kaff was alive. He had her position. He knew where to go. So what if the tactics were shit? One Marine heading downslope with hostile forces hiding in the ruins. But tactics didn't matter anymore. This wasn't about odds. This was about family. His little girl.

He lunged for the terminal, fingers finding the push-to-talk. "Kaff! I'm coming! Hold on!"

His mind was already half a click away, mapping the route through Vestebrae's ruins. Azure-Twelve meant the eastern quadrant, not far off the primary transit. Twenty minutes at a dead run over flat ground, assuming he didn't kill himself getting down the drop station's steep grade. The exo had seen better days, but it was faster than going on foot.

"Get out." He wrapped an arm around Olsom's waist and yanked.

She came out of the seat in a tangle of limbs and curses, hitting the deck hard beneath the cage. "Sarnt, wait—"

Deep down in a dark part of him, he knew it was too late. The shelter was crawling with Lost by now. But that only meant it was too late for him, too. One Marine, one MAC-4 Mark Three against a whole swarm of Lost. The odds were beyond impossible.

He'd go, find his little girl, and kill anything that touched her. Die doing it, if that's what it took. Service through sacrifice. Maybe that was enough for him and his salvation in the Holy Mother's eyes. Lyra's too.

He stepped up into the seat, but Olsom yanked him back. His boots touched the deck, and he was turning, fists up. Little bitch didn't get it. Kaff was out of time.

Her face gave beneath his knuckles, just like before. Blood ran from her split lip.

She was lunging back, landing a jab on his chin.

He swung, blinking. Missed.

"Stop!" Her voice cracked, tears mixing with the blood on her face. "You think you're the only one who gives a damn? Let us help! Please, just—let me help her!"

What did she care? There was no time for this. Just action.

Just Kaffy.

Olsom landed another quick hook between plates, but he hooked her wrist in his arm and pulled her in, trying to drive his helmet into her face. She twisted away—bad move, he still had her. His body became a lever and Olsom went down hard over his leg, landing on the metal grate with a satisfying bang. Her breath left her in a gasp.

"Sarnt, stop." Lessig stepped forward, hands on his rifle. "Same team."

"You want to try next?" Bresto stared back, tightening the wrist lock. Tendons strain beneath his grip. Olsom's face contorted in pain.

Lessig opened his mouth, closed it again.

"You fucker," Olsom spat through clenched teeth. "You're just like the others. Always leaving me—leaving others behind."

"You don't get it. This ain't a volunteer op." He eased the lock just enough to keep from breaking bone. Suicide mission. No return trip. No sense in dragging her down with him. The girl had talent. She'd make a great Marine if she could control that mouth. The irony.

"Fine. Go and die." She collapsed into the muck, cradling her wrist. "You won't make it. And your little girl pays the price."

With a few quick taps on the ops terminal, 3-3-3 came to life around him. The primary and secondary reactors hummed, the FAB's capacitors filling with a high-pitched whine. Servos clicked as systems initialized, the console lighting up amber and green.

"Get clear," he called out, feeling the metal respond to his movements. The massive rig lurched forward, suddenly an extension of his body.

The twins dragged Olsom to safety, her eyes still locked on him, burning with something beyond anger. Marines and reservists scattered, pulling back as the exo's mass turned toward the barricades. He found the control rigs, working the primary arms through their range. A slight hitch in the right elbow, hydraulic pressure dropping momentarily before stabilizing. Nothing he couldn't compensate for. Despite everything, it felt damn good wearing metal again.

The massive daxed heavy crunched beneath 3-3-3's tread as he climbed over the barricades. From this height, he could see all the way down the drop into ruined Vestebrae, smoke still rising from the tungsten impacts. Threat returns on 3-3-3's displays showed nothing. The path was clear, for now.

He tried the comms again, walking the exo down the steep grade. "Kaff?"

Each step sent vibrations through the cage as the machine fought for traction on the gore-slick surface. "Kaff, honey, please respond. I'm coming."

Nothing. Maybe Olsom was right. Ghost comms, from a little girl already gone.

He settled deeper into the operator's cage. The plan was simple. Make it to Azure-Twelve. Find Kaff. Kill anything that tried to stop him. And if they were both dead when this was over, so be it. At least he'd have died trying to be a father instead of just another sergeant following orders. Maybe the Twelfth would accept that kind of sacrifice.

3-3-3 lurched forward again, picking up speed as he descended into smoke and shadow.

CHAPTER
FORTY-ONE

THE SKY above was a raging river of black storm. The drop station's metal towers stretched into the darkness, safety lights pulsing their mindless rhythm. Olsom ran her tongue over her split lip, tasting blood. Her face throbbed where Bresto's fist had connected, but it was nothing compared to the cold ache behind her ribs.

Please help me. They're coming.

The little girl's voice kept looping inside her head. Olsom knew that feeling. When you're old enough to get you're in real danger, and too young to know help isn't coming.

A sob built in her throat. She swallowed it down hard, copper taste mixing with salt. The wild thing inside her felt half-alive, unable to do anything except lie on the deck while everyone looked down at her like trash. Like she didn't belong.

The twins appeared overhead, concern on their leathery faces. It was too much—their worry, their closeness. Another sob broke free before she could stuff it back down.

"You okay?" They pulled her up, one on each side, keeping her steady when her knees threatened to buckle.

She'd never been hit that hard. And she'd been hit a lot. No, she wasn't fucking okay.

"I'm fine."

Halfway upright, the stares hit her. Third Platoon's operators stood in a loose half-circle, their granite faces cold, hard, and unreachable. Prelk stared with pure judgment. The other guy—Montawk?—his mouth curled in disgust.

Only Lessig seemed bothered, his jaw working like he was chewing something tough. But his eyes were fixed downslope.

"He… he took my rig," she choked out. The words felt hollow and stupid the second they left her mouth. As if these proper fucking Aegians didn't already know. Founders, some had even cheered him on.

Smokes frowned. "That was a—"

"—real shit move," Vlan finished.

She spun toward the others. "How the fuck could you let him do that? Your proper sarnt's gone UA. With MY RIG."

Prelk smirked. "You started it, feral."

She took a step toward him, shouldering past the twins. "Want to get your ass kicked again? I seem to remember you crying after I put you down at the foundry."

"Tough talk from someone bleeding all over her uniform." Montawk fell in beside Prelk. "Maybe if you'd shut your mouth for once, the sarnt wouldn't have had to put you in your place."

"My place?" She laughed. "My place was in that exo. But Bresto took it when he abandoned his post."

"His daughter's in danger," Lessig answered. "You'd do the same. We all would, if it was our own."

No, she wouldn't have. The only family she ever had that mattered were gone. The rest… well they weren't family anymore. Not after the admin blocks. And these Marines never were, no matter how bad she wanted some of them to be.

"Make a hole." Doc Toelke pushed through the circle, his kit bag already open. "Let me see your face."

"What do you care?" She jerked away from his reaching hand. "You're just the same as all of them."

Toelke's voice stayed level. "I'm a combat engineer. You're injured. It's that simple." He dabbed at her lip with a sterile wipe, the antiseptic burning sharp. "You're wrong about me. About all of us."

"Sure I am."

He worked in silence, sealing her cut. His hands were steady, practiced—like Doc—but it wasn't the same. Myers would've had something smart to say. Would've made her laugh even while she wanted to punch him. The memory opened something hollow inside her chest.

A part of her was glad he wasn't there. He was safe. Away from the fighting. Away from her. But that hollow feeling kept spreading. It was like she'd lost him anyway.

Toelke snapped his kit closed, then paused, hand moving to her waist.

"You're bleeding." He crouched, gently lifting the edge of her vest to reveal the torn synthweave beneath, dark with blood. "Did the sarnt do this?"

The concern in his voice scraped against her nerves. Maybe Toelke was different. Maybe some of them actually… No. Mez had spelled it out for her—block trash, that's all she'd ever be to them. So this mountain boy's kindness was just another lie. Another way to keep her hoping she might actually matter someday.

"Nah." She tried to pull away, but his grip was firm.

"Hold still." He was already cleaning the wound, the cold burn of antiseptic against her skin. "This needs sealing before it gets infected."

His touch was professional, impersonal, and somehow that made it worse. She didn't want his competence or his quiet concern. Didn't want to owe him anything.

Toelke stuffed his kit back into its pouch. "That'll hold. Don't touch it."

She didn't thank him. Couldn't make herself form the words.

He turned to Smokes. "3-3-2 needs a coolant flush. I can help with that if you want."

"After we're—"

"—done here."

Toelke hesitated, like he wanted to say something else to her, then thought better of it before walking away.

Smokes pulled a cigarette from his breast pocket, lips moving around it as he spoke. "What're you—"

"—going to do?"

"I have no fucking idea." She rubbed her face with both hands, wincing when she hit the fresh seal. "He stole my exo. I can't…"

Please help me. They're coming. Something cold slid down her spine, pooling in her gut. Whatever "they" were—Lost, had to be. They wanted the kid. Wanted to turn her into one of them. Just like that capsule. Just like the things at the barricades.

"What about Bresto?" they asked.

"I hope he gets caught," she snapped. But Revan wouldn't see it that way. He was just like the others. Lose your rig. Lose your post. Lose your shit and attack your NCO. No matter that Bresto started it. No matter that he'd stolen 3-3-3. She was already guilty in their eyes.

Please help me.

"If he finds her," Smokes said.

Vlan nodded. "They might make it."

"And if he doesn't?" she asked.

The twins fell silent, exchanging that look that meant they were thinking the same thing.

"Founders fuck me." There was no sign of Bresto downslope. Maybe he really was just trying to save his daughter. If he'd asked her, she could—but of course he didn't. She wasn't one of them. Would never be.

Please help me.

She shook her head, trying to dislodge the memory. It wasn't her problem. Not her family. Not her rig anymore either. But that kid. That little girl with the terror in her voice. She knew that sound. Had made it herself, once. Back when she still believed help might come.

Lessig sighed loud enough to turn heads. "Twelfth save me. Revan's on his way."

Her guts twisted. She'd had her fair share of ass-chewings since joining the Marines. But this was going to be a full-on crid gutting. Revan would want someone's head for losing their rig. If it wasn't already Bresto's, it would be hers.

"Don't say a word," Lessig told the group. "Any of you. I'll handle this."

He didn't sound sure. More like he'd just seen his platoon sergeant go UA during combat ops and didn't know what the hell to say.

Olsom couldn't stop herself. Not now. "Is that an order, Corporal?"

His voice went granite-hard. "Shut your mouth."

"About time someone said it," Montawk muttered.

"You too, 'tawk." Lessig jabbed a finger into his chestplate. "All of you, lock it up. Now."

"Sergeant Bresto!" Revan's voice cut above the chatter. "Report!"

He strode toward them, jaw set. There was no surprise in his features. Just angry certainty. Like he'd been expecting this all along.

"Where is Sergeant Bresto?" he demanded. His gaze swept over the group, lingering on Olsom's freshly sealed lip. "And where's 3-3-3? Why is it not on the line?"

She scanned Revan's face, searching for confirmation. The son of a bitch knew. They'd struck some kind of deal. Had to. The lieutenant wouldn't just give a man like Bresto free rein over his platoon without getting something in return. Without there being a reason.

"I asked where Sergeant Bresto is." Revan's voice had gone deadly quiet. "Someone better start talking. That's an order."

The silence stretched thick as industrial fibrosteel. All eyes burned into her—Montawk's, Prelk's, even Patrim's. Like she was supposed to step up and take the blame. Like she was supposed to sacrifice herself for a man who'd knocked her on her ass. Mez was right. She'd never be in their club. Not even the Twelfth Herself could change that.

Please help me.

"Sir." Lessig stepped forward. "We received an emergency transmission from Sarnt Bresto's daughter. The girl was in distress. The Lost were after her."

Revan's face didn't change. So, he had known.

"The sarnt decided to respond to the call," Lessig continued. "And he... he, ah, *commandeered* 3-3-3 to reach her position faster."

Revan's wide eyes narrowed to slits. "He did fucking what?"

"He took the exo, sir."

"That's Colonial Defense Marine property!" Revan shouted, spittle flying into Lessig's face. "That's theft! That's desertion with equipment! That's a fucking firing squad offense!"

Please help me. They're coming.

No one else was coming for that kid. Bresto had his heart in the right place, but it was a dumb plan. He was just one Marine. Even with 3-3-3, the Lost would swarm him in the end. Just like they had almost done to her. She would've never survived the barricades without Doc's help.

The twins shifted beside her, their breathing changing rhythm. She could feel them watching her, reading her. Vlan's hand brushed against her arm—a question.

Lessig was losing ground. "Sir, it's his daughter…"

"I don't care what his personal situation is!" Revan was shouting, face gone fever-red. "We are at war! This is about the survival of our species! One weak link, and the whole line falls!"

Fine. She'd go after them. Not for Bresto. Fuck him and his pride. But for that little girl. For the child who was scared in the dark with monsters coming. For the kid who still believed help would arrive if she just called loud enough.

For the child she used to be.

Revan stepped into her space, close enough to smell the tea on his breath. His shoulders hunched forward, face flushed and twisted. Not like a Marine officer. More like a gamma who'd had his favorite toy snatched away.

"You." He jabbed a finger toward her sealed lip. "Did you let him take it? Did you help him?"

The wild thing inside her stretched, yawned, showing teeth. It knew they'd made their choice. No going back now.

"You understand desertion during combat ops is punishable by death?" Spittle hit her cheek. "They'll line you up next to him if you've aided and abetted this."

Something like a laugh bubbled up her throat. This proper little officer really thought she had a choice. Like Bresto had asked her permission. Like anyone on this mountain gave a shit what she thought. It was almost funny how completely clueless he was.

She bit down on the laugh, met his stare. "No idea. Sir."

The lie felt good. Felt right.

Revan stared at her another beat, searching for the crack in her armor. But the wild thing was awake now, all predator-still, savoring the choice they'd made together. Revan blinked first.

"Fuck!" He spun away, grabbing Lessig by the arm. "Come with me. We're tracking that exo's nav beacon, now."

Revan half-dragged Lessig toward the command post. Lessig managed one look back. There was something there. Not quite approval, but close. An understanding.

The twins were still there when she turned back. "You can't go," they said.

"What makes you think I'm going anywhere?" She crossed her arms, ignoring the twinge from her split lip.

"You've got—"

"—that look."

"What look?"

"Same one you had on Three-Alpha," they said together. She was the one that had convinced them all to go with Bresto and rescue that Division skeeg. Back when all she had to do was distract a guard. Before the Concordat came and everything went to hell. That was barely two turns ago and it felt like another lifetime now.

Her shoulders slumped. She couldn't lie to them. "Somebody's got to help that little girl."

"You don't owe these—"

"—proper Aegians anything."

Please help me.

"It ain't about them."

She couldn't tell them the real reason. Couldn't admit that every time she heard that little girl's voice, she was a young beta being surrendered to colony administration. Back when she was small and scared and waiting for someone, anyone, to answer her own cries. They wouldn't understand.

"We'll come with you," they said.

She stared at them, something cracking open behind her ribs. After she'd pushed them away, kept them at arm's length, they were still here. Still willing to follow her into the dark. The wild thing shrank into whatever dark hole it lived in, confused by loyalty it had never learned to trust.

"You can't. Smokes, you're squad leader now. And Vlan, you're not exactly—"

"—the independent type?" Vlan almost smiled.

"I didn't say that." But she had thought it. More than once.

"You weren't wrong," they said. "But that was before."

"Before?"

Vlan took a long moment to clear his throat. "Before your rig got stolen. Before you got... decked by an NCO. Before everyone decided that taking sides was more... more important... than—"

"—having each other's backs," Smokes finished.

Vlan forced out a sigh that was almost a sob. Neither Rikko said more than three words without the other. It must've been exhausting.

For a brief moment, that cold, empty place behind her ribs felt warm. Filled. But that was just another reminder why she had to go alone. She couldn't risk losing anyone else.

She put a gloved hand on Vlan's cheek. His leather skin flushed pink beneath her fingers. "You two are something else, you know that?"

"We know," they said together, Vlan's voice steadier now alongside his brother's.

"Bresto was right. This is probably a one-way trip," she said, dropping her hand. "The Lost are everywhere down there. Those Delta things, too. Third Platoon can't spare any more bodies."

"That's right," they said. "They can't. We can't."

Their persistence made her want to cry. Made her want to throw her arms around their skinny necks and never let go. She pushed it down, locked it away with all the other soft things that didn't belong in this war.

"If you really want to help me," she said, lowering her voice, "I need a distraction. Something to keep Revan busy while I slip away."

The twins considered each other, that silent communication flowing between them. Two halves of the same brain working out a problem. After what felt like forever, Vlan rested his hands on the bricks of plasmex strapped to his vest. The breacher's special.

"We can manage that," they said.

They lingered for a moment, neither moving to leave. Smokes pulled the cigarette from his lips, studying her face like he was memorizing it. Vlan's wrinkled features had gone soft, almost sad.

"Be careful," Smokes said quietly.

"Real careful," Vlan added, his voice barely carrying over the storm.

She managed a nod, throat too tight for words. They knew this was goodbye.

The drop station spread out around her in the gray dawn. Marines clustered at their positions beneath high towers, PR troopers manning supply points, the constant hum of exo powerpacks. She'd spent the last few hours hating these Aegians and their granite certainty. Wouldn't miss a damn one of them when this was over. But when the shooting started again, when things went sideways like they always did, she'd be wishing for their steady voices on the nets. For their unshakeable faith that the Twelfth would see them through.

The twins been gone for only minutes when a PR trooper hefted a crate of charge packs against the barricades. Olsom eyed the empty slots in her tac vest. Six packs to fill it. No way she was going downslope with anything less.

She crossed to the crate and helped herself, slapping the first pack into her rifle with a satisfying click.

"Hey!" The trooper stepped between her and the crate. His uniform was still crisp, like he'd just pulled it from supply. "Those are Planetary Reserve property."

She reached around him, grabbing another pack.

"Wait. Stop!" The trooper put his hand on the crate's lid. "You need a requisition form signed by your CO if you don't want to get brought up on theft charges."

Theft charges. Olsom smirked, stuffing another pack into her vest. She looked past him to the sloping darkness below. Somewhere down there, 3-3-3 was stomping through the ruins without her. Somewhere down there, a little girl was praying for a rescue.

The memory of leaving Three-Alpha hit her sudden and bright. Doc, handsome as ever... whole. The twins. Her arm full of charge packs. Back then, she'd thought they'd won. Thought they'd be together forever. Had no idea it was just the calm before the storm. A lifetime ago, and, somehow, this moment felt just like that one.

"Don't you know?" She eyed the trooper, flipping open another pouch. "There's only one thief in the Colonial Defense Marines."

"Huh?"

She laughed, low and bitter. "Everyone else is just trying to get their shit back."

"This isn't funny, Marine."

"I know." He was right. It wasn't. Not now, after everything that had happened.

He reached for her. "I'm going to need those—"

A bright flash lit up the slope about a hundred meters to her left. The concussion hit next, rolling over the barricades in a wave of super-heated air and shredded daxed meat. Victory's guns opened up, FABs hammering the site of the explosion. Tracking the threat. Chasing ghosts.

"Woah!" The trooper dropped to the deck, hands on his helmet, looking up at her like she was crazy for still standing.

Another boom, this one bigger, further downslope. The guns shifted, drawn to the fresh chaos like preds to blood. The twins had come through, per usual.

Her vest was full now. She gave the huddled trooper a wink, pulled her helmet tight, and vaulted over the barricade.

The slope was steep, loose debris mixed with daxed blood beneath her boots as she half-ran, half-slid toward the ruined city blocks below. Toward Bresto. Toward that little girl with the terrified voice. Toward whatever end waited for her in the dark.

Behind her, Victory's guns kept hammering the twins' distraction. By the time anyone noticed she was gone, it would be too late.

For them. For her. But maybe not for that girl.

FORTY-TWO

THICK BLACK SMOKE clung to the ruins of the primary transit corridor. Bresto forced the exo over the uneven rubble, terrain constantly shifting beneath the machine's weight. Shattered granite and twisted duraplate created an obstacle course where Vestebrae's primary thoroughfare had been just hours before. The tungsten rods from the *Umbra's* orbital strike had carved a canyon through the heart of Aegia's capitol settlement, turning mountain boulevards into a dust-choked wasteland.

Civil Defense Shelter Azure-Twelve was still a half-click downs-lope. The HUD showed his route as a jagged line through the devasta-tion, each course correction adding precious minutes to his arrival time. Time Kaff didn't have.

He pushed the thought away. Focus on the mission. Move to contact. Adapt and overcome. The mantras the Colonial Defense Marines had beaten into him for twenty years still held, even when the mission was saving his own daughter from a nightmare he'd helped create.

A massive chunk of what had been a corporate tower blocked the transit ahead. 3-3-3's servos groaned as he worked the primary arms, clearing a path through debris that sparkled with shattered plexene. Even destroyed, the materials screamed wealth—marble, rare metals, wood—things that cost more than most colonists made in a lifetime. Vestebrae's core elite had built their monuments well. Hadn't done them much good against the archenemy, or tungsten moving at orbital velocity.

Ghost signals and interference glitched the HUD, the tac nets choked with electromagnetic static from the strikes. No clear updates. No useful intel. Just him and the machine, pushing deeper into the graveyard this war had made.

Something pale jutted from beneath a slab of granite—an arm, fingers loose and empty. More corpses resolved through the smoke, half-buried beneath chunks of granite and twisted metal. Hard to tell where human ended and daxed began; the tungsten strikes had been thorough, reducing both to the same granite-dusted pulp. But the differences were there. The glint of circuitry threaded through flesh. Half-formed masks that had been spared the final stages of conversion by orbital fire.

These people had been changing when the rods hit. Mercy and tragedy both. If only Kull would've listened sooner. If only he could've made her listen.

The rubble pattern shifted, debris and storm runoff tumbling away into empty space between fallen towers. 3-3-3's proximity sensors pinged warnings as he approached the edge. A crater, thirty meters across, where the transit had collapsed into the void beneath.

Not a crater. A shelter.

The reinforced dome that should have crowned the civil defense shelter had been cracked open, fibrosteel and duraplate caved in by the tungsten's impact. More bodies littered the wreckage, too many to count from this angle.

Bresto's throat went tight. His footage. His broadcast with that core parasite Storm. He'd forced Kull's hand too late, when orbital strikes became the only option. Every corpse in this wasteland, every half-converted colonist… not just the Concordat's doing. His. *He* led the forge ship back like some kind of plague. Then lit the fuse that turned his own people—his own family—into targets.

Azure-Twelve would be just like this one. Same design. Same

construction. Same trap that had drawn thousands underground. If Kaff was… still human, she was living the same nightmare.

His fingers drifted to the comms control. The tactical part of his brain screamed warnings. Radio silence. Operational security. Basic shit every Marine learned at the recruit depot.

But she was his daughter. His baby girl who never left his side when he came home on leave. Who called him Father like it was a rank she respected more than any other. He had to know she was still okay.

The Holy Mother would forgive him this one breach of protocol. She had to.

He keyed the PR general broadcast channel. His thumb hesitated over the push-to-talk for half a heartbeat, then pressed down.

"Kaff, this is your—" The words felt strange in the dead air, too personal for military comms. "Kaffereine Bresto, this is Sergeant Ned Bresto. Respond if you can hear this."

Static hissed back at him, empty and cold. He tried the emergency response channel, then the administrative nets. Nothing but electromagnetic noise.

"Kaff, honey, please. I'm coming for you. Just hold on. Don't—"

The static shifted. Eleven sharp pulses, precise as a heartbeat, then silence. Then again. The same alien rhythm he'd heard aboard the forge ship. The same one Myers and Olsom had warned them about.

The enemy must've heard him. Triangulated his position. Probably rallying their forces to his coordinates that very second.

He killed the transmission and powered down the comm array, but it was too late. Every hostile within two klicks would be converging on this position within minutes. He'd just painted a target on himself for the entire Concordat war machine.

Worth it, if Kaff was listening. If she knew he was coming.

3-3-3 crested a pile of debris, and the transit opened into a section that had been spared the worst of the strikes. Buildings still stood there, facades scorched but intact. Emergency lighting flickered in some windows—power grids still functional, a good sign. That meant Azure-Twelve was still standing.

The smoke was thinner beyond the crater, visibility stretching to maybe thirty meters. He could make out storefronts, corporate lobbies, transit signs, the familiar geometry of colonial planning.

Something dark scuttled across a building face three stories up. A bug, mandibles clicking as it navigated the vertical surface like it was flat ground. Another shadow darted between structures at street level —this one heavier, clumsier. Squid warrior, struggling on the same uneven terrain.

More contacts appeared on his threat display, red returns converging from multiple vectors. They'd responded faster than he'd expected. The transmission had been brief, but apparently long enough.

A laser beam cracked past his canopy, red light splitting the smoky air. He pivoted 3-3-3 toward the source, FAB spinning up. The targeting system locked onto a squid crouched behind an overturned cargo hauler.

Controlled burst. Three bolts, center mass. The squid's black armor cracked, blue fluid spraying across the transit. It dropped behind cover, fronds twitching.

Another warrior broke cover, laser rifle tracking toward him. The FAB caught it mid-stride, charged particles cutting it off at the waist. The bug dropped from above, landing on a pile of rubble ten meters closer. He shifted fire, but the thing was already skittering toward him.

More contacts. A squid emerged from a collapsed doorway. Another scrambled over a pile of rubble, using the debris for cover. A third appeared in a shattered window two stories up, fronds twitching as it sighted down on him. They flanked him from three directions, closing the distance with each tactical bound from cover to cover.

Didn't matter. His daughter was out there. In this. Because of him.

The rage came like a tide, washing away twenty years of fire discipline and tactical doctrine. The railgun's capacitors whined as he brought both weapon systems online. Safety protocols flashed—excessive power draw and heat buildup would lead to reactor shutdown.

Fuck the protocols. He knew how to cook.

The railgun discharged with a crack of thunder, tungsten punching through the storefront where three warriors had taken position. The building's facade collapsed in a shower of granite and blue mist. His

FAB hammered the left flank simultaneously, bolts cutting down the bug that had gotten within five meters.

3-3-3 lurched, the left tread caught on twisted rebar. Servos screamed as he forced the machine forward, hydraulics straining against the unstable footing. Another bug appeared on his right, too close. The railgun swiveled, fired, vaporizing the alien in a vortex of electromagnetic storm.

They kept coming. Always closer. His weapons carved through alien bodies, but more streamed in to replace them.

Another massive bug hit him from the side, six limbs working as it grappled with 3-3-3's primary arms. This one was different—bigger, older, its carapace scarred from previous battles. Its big, compound eyes gleamed at him through the crackling green light from its plasma staff.

Bresto fought the controls as bug met machine in a contest of raw strength. The staff's blade loomed centimeters from his canopy, super-heated energy leaving burns on the clear plexene. One slip, one hydraulic failure, and that blade would punch straight through.

3-3-3's left tread slipped on loose debris and the exo tilted. The bug pressed its advantage, plasma staff driving toward the cage.

Pure fury kept him moving. Not tactics. Not training. Just rage at everything—at the war, at his failures, at this thing that stood between him and his daughter. He twisted the exo's torso, using the rig's mass to break the bug's grip. Metal scraped against chitin. The plasma staff carved a molten line across the exo's shoulder plate, smelling of fresh welds. The pointed end snapped.

The bug's mandibles clicked. It was winning, and it knew it.

Then the shadows moved.

———

A figure stepped from behind a collapsed building ten meters out, black armor drinking in the smoky light. The vertical scar of blue lenses down its masked face shone like tiny stars. Another emerged from a pile of debris to Bresto's right. Then a third, from the skeleton of what had been a corporate tower.

The bug's plasma staff paused mid-strike, the cells of its compound eyes straining toward the new arrivals. Its grip on the exo loosened, mandibles shifting from aggression to something else. Assessment.

More figures materialized from the ruins—twelve in total, arranged in a loose perimeter that hadn't been there seconds before. Different builds, different weapons, but all moving with that same eerie coordination he'd seen at the drop station. A male with a large black spear. A lithe female shouldering what looked like a stripped-down naval cannon. Others with gear he couldn't identify through the smoke.

One figure approached without the measured caution of the others. No mask covered his face, just the same black armor and that casual stride Bresto remembered from the control tower. The pilot stopped just outside the combat zone, hands clasped behind his back like he was observing training exercises and not a fight to the death.

The bug released 3-3-3's left arm, plasma staff wavering between targets. Its head swiveled from Bresto to the encroaching operatives, compound eyes reflecting the amber emergency lights like broken mirrors. It launched itself toward the only gap and disappeared into the smoke.

Other red returns on his threat display were moving away, the squids that had been converging on his position now retreating faster than they'd arrived. Whatever Section Delta was doing there, the Concordat wanted no part of it.

None of the operatives moved. The pilot glanced back at the fleeing aliens with a pitying grin.

"Ned!" He moved silently over the broken transit, his casual tone belonging in a bar, not a warzone. "Fancy meeting you here."

3-3-3's reactor temperature warnings pulsed insistently, still strained from the fight. Bresto swiped it away, seething at the man standing casually among the ruins of his world.

"Out of my way, Delta."

"What's your hurry?" The pilot eyed the devastation around them. "I've heard so much about the infamous Sergeant Ned Bresto. I just *had* to introduce myself."

"Some intro," he snarled. "You just stood there and watched while that thing tried to kill me. Thought we were on the same side?"

"You seemed to be managing just fine." The pilot shrugged, the casual gesture made dangerous by the machine purr of his black armor. "Consider what we did back at the Gaet more of a… professional courtesy."

"Courtesy?"

"To your people, yeah. Your kind has such limited perspective. You see one enemy at a time. One life saved at a time. It's all about *personal* survival. But we think bigger—the future of an entire species."

Enough of this big picture cridshit. Bresto jerked 3-3-3 toward the corridor leading deeper into the settlement. The Delta operatives shifted with him, tightening their circle until his path was blocked by black armor and cold lenses. They weren't letting him leave.

"Big picture doesn't mean shit so long as my daughter's out there."

"So I gathered from two rather indiscreet broadcasts." A hint of disappointment colored the pilot's voice. "Comms discipline optional for Marines these days?"

This operator was good. Talked shit just like a real jet jockey.

"If saving Aegia was just a courtesy, what the hell are you actually doing here?"

"Helping the sect clean up loose ends." The pilot's smile was razor thin. "Your team did twelve hells of a job. Park, right? And that bot jockey, the new sect's latest fixation. Even you, Ned. Even you. And now I see why."

The hair on the back of his neck rose. All of it had seemed too good to be true. Park recruiting him to Special Ops. Lernus appearing from nowhere with classified intelligence and a rescue plan that made no tactical sense. The Concordat forge ship just being there like some kind of cosmic accident. He'd been a good Marine. Followed orders without question. Never once asked who was really pulling the strings. Twelfth, did Park even know?

"You used us."

"C'mon, Ned, you know how these things work! Our ops are blacker than black. There is no need-to-know." The pilot waved dismissively. "Your handler was quite resourceful in that regard."

"Lernus."

"One of her more colorful names. The old sect had a real talent for making the necessary arrangements." The pilot stepped closer, eyes taking in 3-3-3's scorched frame. "Of course, that approach had its limitations. She was so personally invested in the mission. Too invested, some might say."

"So, we were set up. All for Delta's bigger picture."

"Set up? No, Sergeant, you were simply utilized. Your team's particular skills made you ideal for the task at hand."

"Which was what, exactly?"

"Finding what needed found, of course. And in that regard, I must say"—his smile cracked—"your mission was an unmitigated success."

Unmitigated success. All the dead at Three-Alpha. Lost daxed shambling through Vestebrae's ruins. Every colonist who'd died screaming as the mask formed across their face. Kaff trapped out there all alone. Success.

Bresto bit back the anger scratching at his throat. Keep asking the questions, just like Lyra had said.

"The mission. You mean Deni."

"Oh no. The sect played her part, just like you did. Just like we all have." He made a triumphant fist. "And you did it! We're so close now."

"Deni didn't seem to think so. She said we ruined everything."

"Right, my precocious *sister*. She was pretty attached to the old sect." He let out a sigh. "Which is weird considering what the old sect made her do. Her current, ah, stability is, well… unfortunate."

"What did Lernus—"

"You pulled her out of that ship." The pilot smirked. "I can't imagine. Trapped in that dark place for so long, tortured by the archenemy." There was an unsettling hunger to him. "I've got to know, what did she look like when you found her? How many pieces was she in? A lot, I'd wager."

They *had* found her in pieces at the bottom of that capsule, red blood mixed with black, opened up like some failed experiment. Her scream still echoed through his nightmares. The bastard was enjoying this.

"Nothing? No gory details?" The pilot's grin faded. "Too bad.

Though I guess that's why they picked you. That Marine efficiency. You don't waste time on the details."

"Efficiency." There was nothing efficient about any of this. "That's funny, because you're wasting my time right now, while my daughter is trapped out there."

"Yeah, she is. It's too bad. Let's be honest, Ned. She's a distraction you don't need. A simple problem with a simple solution."

"Yeah. Could be real simple, if you'd help me."

The pilot's smile thinned to nothing. "You're missing the point. Family is an anchor on the heart. You know this! It drags you down, clouds your judgment. And that makes you weak, compromised, predictable. Remove that anchor, and you become something more than baseline human. Something useful."

The rage came white-hot and immediate. This thing wanted to let his daughter die, and for what? To make him a better weapon?

Bresto jerked the FAB toward the pilot's face, thumb pressed against the hat trigger. Combat optics were empty—no IFF, no visual, but the pilot stood near enough to touch the spinning tri-barrels. The other Delta operatives shifted around him, weapons rising, but the pilot lifted a single hand, and they froze.

"Ned. You're making my point." The pilot shook his head, utterly unbothered by the heavy weapon centimeters from his face. "Look at you. That little girl has you picking fights you can't win."

Bresto's thumbed the hat tighter.

"I could solve this problem for you, I suppose," the pilot went on. "Clean, efficient, surgical. Your daughter's suffering would end today. Just another casualty of the Concordat invasion. You grieve appropriately, then move forward unencumbered. Free to serve humanity's actual needs rather than the demands of your primitive biology."

The words stopped his breath. This thing was talking about murdering Kaff like it was doing him a favor.

"I'll fucking kill you."

"We've already talked about this, Ned! One person—no, one *child's* life against the survival of the species. Do the math! She's already compromised your judgment." He gestured at the exo. "Look where you are, abandoning your post, stealing military equipment, all for one insignificant individual. Remove that variable, and you become the weapon humanity needs you to be. Then you're thinking like… well, like us."

The trigger felt slick beneath Bresto's thumb. One squeeze. One burst of charged particles. End of conversation.

"What happens to your family if you're dead?" the pilot asked quietly. "What happens to humanity's and Section Delta's little partnership if you attack me? Who protects Lyra and Sammy then? You've seen what we're capable of. What exactly do you think you're going to do to me, anyway?"

The bastard was right. He'd seen them tear through the Lost like they were made of paper. Had watched Deni come back from the dead. Even if he pulled the trigger, even if the FAB somehow hurt this thing, there were eleven others watching. Waiting.

And then what? Lyra would be alone. Sammy and Kaff—if she was still alive—would have no one. Whatever alliance between the CDF and Section Delta would end, and humanity would face the Concordat without their dark angels. Or worse. With Section Delta as another enemy.

Bresto's thumb moved away from the trigger. The FAB's barrels slowed, then stopped. He had to know. Nothing else mattered if she was already dead.

"Do you know? Is Kaff still alive?"

"I guess there's no persuading you. Too bad." The pilot stepped aside, his easy confidence fading. "And here I was hoping we could work together. Oh well, guess that means I have to keep looking."

"Is she?"

"What, and spoil the ending?" The pilot swept his arm toward the corridor leading deeper into the settlement. The other operatives shifted to create a path through their perimeter. "But by all means, don't let me keep you from the reunion. Do give my regards to young Kaffereine when you find her. However you find her."

FORTY-THREE

KAFFY'S FISTS MADE CONTACT, but it felt like punching stone. The Reede-thing barely reacted, its cold, metal-masked face reflecting her own panic back at her as it carried her out of the maintenance room. Its body didn't feel right beneath the dirty uniform, skin cold and gray, muscles rigid in places that shouldn't be.

"Let go! Let GO!" Her voice had gone hoarse from screaming. Her legs kicked uselessly against its torso. "Duray! DURAY!"

Her screams echoed through the shelter's empty corridor. There was no sign of Arthur Duray anywhere. Only dark smears across the floor that made her sick to look at.

The thing carried her to the giant cargo door at the far end of the corridor and waited. The metal mask gave nothing away. No eyes, no expression to read.

"My father's coming," she sobbed, exhaustion creeping in. "He's a Marine. He'll *kill* you."

The Reede-thing never spoke. The only sound it made was the soft *click-click-clicking* somewhere behind its mask. Like there was something *scritch-scratching* around inside its head.

Overhead lights flickered. The low, rhythmic pulsing she'd heard earlier seemed stronger now, vibrating through the metal floors and into her bones. It wasn't machinery. Machinery didn't sound like that. It felt too alive.

A hiss of hydraulics, and the massive cargo doors slid open. Beyond them lay darkness pierced by strips of sickly blue and red light that reflected off something white. Row after row of something white.

She fought back, slapping her fists against its head and neck. Father's voice echoed in her mind: *never, ever give up. Keep fighting until there's nothing left.* She was still combat effective. Still—

The sight beyond the threshold stole her breath. This wasn't a shelter. Not for people.

The huge chamber stretched off into the dark. Not filled with cots or supplies or frightened colonists, but with rows upon rows of pale white capsules. Each one was flat and round, like giant wheels laid on their sides, brimming with sticky black tar. The black masses pulsed, swelling slightly before contracting again, all of them moving together like one giant heartbeat.

Blue light washed over the capsules, fading to red the further they went, making bloody shadows dance across their perfect white surfaces.

What were they?

Something moved beneath in the black. Not shadows, but something inside each capsule. Sacks of black fluid that swirled and shifted with each pulse. Her stomach lurched. Despite every instinct screaming to look away, she leaned closer.

"No, no, no…"

There was a hand pressed against the black film in the nearest capsule. A human hand, fingers splayed wide as if trying to push through. The black mass thinned just enough for her to see a face, mouth open in a silent scream, eyes wide with terror, frozen in the moment they'd been… consumed.

That's what was going to happen to her. Why it brought her and Duray here.

"Let me GO!" She twisted her whole body, throwing her weight sideways so violently that the Reede-thing's grip loosened. She hit the floor running, darting between the rows of capsules, away from those terrible clicking sounds behind her.

She ducked below a tangle of pipes and cables, small enough to squeeze through where the Reede-thing couldn't follow. Its heavy footsteps echoed behind her, following but not running. Like it knew she couldn't escape.

She rounded a corner and froze. Another capsule blocked her path, this one connected to a series of thick conduits humming with power. The black fluid inside seemed more agitated, churning violently against the white shell.

A face pressed against the surface.

"Duray?"

It was him. The same thin face, the same close-cropped hair, beneath the thin, black film. But his eyes were all wrong, wide and dull and unseeing. His mouth opened and closed like he was trying to speak, but no sound came through.

"Duray, I'm here!" She pressed her hands to the white surface, icy cold beneath her palms. "I'll get you out, I swear, I'll—"

The black fluid vibrated, rising against the inside of the capsule like it was alive, like it was hungry. Thin tendrils formed near her fingers, reaching for her.

She screamed and stumbled backward into cold hands that caught her shoulders.

"Let me go!" She kicked and twisted, tears stinging her eyes. "Duray! DURAY!"

But Duray only stared, his eyes growing darker as the black fluid settled back against the surface.

The Reede-thing carried her back through the rows of capsules, each pulse of black fluid seeming to watch her pass. Her sobs came in ragged gasps now, her throat too raw to scream anymore.

They approached another door at the far end of the chamber. Taller and wider than the others, marked with scorched black marks in the metal. The terrible heartbeat grew louder there, shaking the floor beneath them.

"Please. Please don't."

The door boomed and shuddered, then split down the middle. Gears ground against each other as the massive panels slid apart, revealing darkness deeper than any storm cloud she'd ever seen.

The smell was worse here. Rotten. Dead.

"No! NO!" Her voice broke as she found new strength to scream. "FATHER! HELP ME!"

This room was smaller, a perfect circle with cargo doors on each wall. Some kind of hub or junction point, like the center of a wheel. The ceiling curved up into shadow, pipes and cables hanging down.

The Reede-thing dropped her. She hit the metal floor hard, pain shooting up through her knees and palms.

Tiny sparks of light appeared in the air. They swirled and gathered, flowing together until they formed a shape that towered over her. Some kind of hologram?

Yes. Of a bug. One of those scary, clacking things, but different. This one's black shell was brittle at the edges. It was older, maybe, way older, thin in places where she could see something moving underneath. It wore robes that rippled around its segmented body, the fabric glowing with a red so bright and deep it hurt to look at.

Its head tilted down toward her, compound eyes reflecting her own terrified face a thousand times over.

"Go away!" She scrambled backward, bumping into the Reede-thing's legs. "Leave me alone!"

The bug's mandibles clacked together, rubbing and scraping in a rhythm that made her skin crawl. Then its jaws parted with a wet sound, revealing a long, dripping tube that unfurled like a terrible tongue. The tube's end pulsed, the opening stretching and closing as it formed shapes.

"Such indomitable spirit." The words came wet and sticky, the voice ancient. "Your species continues to impress."

She clapped her hands over her ears, but the voice seemed to vibrate inside her head.

"The irony does not escape us." The tube twisted closer to her face. "That which makes you most suitable is that which makes you resist."

"What do you want?" she demanded, trying to sound brave like Father would. "Why are you doing this?"

"Do the stars have a reason? A storm? We are simply set to the Makers' purpose, animal. Drawn to their light. As you will be."

She pinched her eyes shut. Her fingers found her heart on their own—tap tap. "Holy Mother help me. You are the s-sword and the light a-and—"

"False words for a false god," the bug spat, mandibles clacking. "A minor deviation in the Eleven's grand design."

"Deviation, huh?" Kaffy growled back, her whole body shaking. "Sounds like a lousy design to me!"

"Fear not, animal. Your kind is alone no longer. Your ascension is at hand. It is inevitable."

"Holy Mother, help me please." Her fingers kept tapping. "Your servant Kaffereine—"

"Silence." A sound like distant thunder rolled from the bug's chest. "What is your designation, animal?"

Something had changed. The monster no longer stood over her. It had backed away, the hologram distorting at the edges.

"My name?"

The tube pulsed. "Your full designation."

"Kaff—" It wanted to know her name. Why? "Kaffereine Aiolita Bresto."

The bug went perfectly still. Its compound eyes flashed, and the red of its robes seemed to darken, to deepen into something that made her eyes water. Its mandibles clacked faster, producing a high-pitched hiss that made the Reede-thing twitch.

"Kaffereine," it repeated, drawing out each syllable. Its head turned. "A coincidence, Lord, that's—"

The bug's form flickered, and for a heartbeat, something else took its place. Something worse. Black nothingness. A cluster of red lights hung in its center. Not lights. Eyes. Red eyes. Staring back at her.

Then it vanished, the motes of light dispersing into nothing. The room plunged back into shadow, leaving only the red emergency lights and the sound of her own ragged breathing.

The Reede-thing's grabbed her by the collar and dragged her across the floor. Its movements were jerky now, forceful. Like the bug's disappearance had made it angry.

"Stop!" she cried, boots scraping against the metal as she tried to brace herself. "You're hurting me!"

Another door opened, revealing a long, dark corridor. The Reede-thing yanked her forward so hard her jumpsuit tore.

More capsules waited inside, arranged in neat rows like the others. But these looked different. Dormant somehow. The black fluid inside them was still, not pulsing with that terrible heartbeat. They looked empty.

A splash of bright color against the sterile floor caught the dim light. Drops of paint, vibrant green against the dull metal. Then another smear a few steps away. Blue this time. Then yellow. A trail of colors.

The drips became streaks, like something leaking had been dragged across the floor. Further in, tiny vials lay shattered, their bright contents splashed across the dull metal.

The Reede-thing hurled her against the nearest capsule. She hit hard and crumpled to the floor, curling into herself. Holy Mother, save her. Protect her from this nightmare. Make her just… disappear.

Boot steps echoed through the chamber, growing fainter. The Reede-thing was leaving. She held perfectly still, not daring to breathe until the door hissed shut.

Silence. Just the faint hum of machinery and her own pounding heartbeat.

A soft clicking sound came from above. Almost like the Reede-thing's mechanical noise. Slower. Weaker.

Kaffy pushed herself up, her hands leaving perfect prints in the spilled paint as she rose to her knees. The clicking grew louder as she peered over the edge of the capsule.

The painter hung suspended above it, caught in the grip of mechanical arms and thick conduits that descended from the ceiling. Black fluid bubbled around its waist, churning and frothing. The daxed's ruined torso was stripped of its patchwork clothing, revealing bony gray flesh stitched through with metal circuitry. Its bald, gray head lolled forward, black eyes glassy and distant.

The vials of paint in its arm were cracked and empty, precious colors already spilled across the floor. Only one remained intact, a half-filled vial of bright red the same shade as the old bug's robes.

"Painter!" She wasn't alone. "Are you alive?"

Its head jerked up at the sound, black eyes bulging. Recognition flashed across its taut features.

"Lady Kaffereine." The familiar scratchy voice seemed weaker now, barely audible over the bubbling fluid. It gave a weak jerk against the cabling holding it in place.

"Just Kaffy."

"You should not be here."

"What are they doing to you?"

"They wish to remake me." The painter's fingers twitched. "Return me to the light of the Eleven."

"The Eleven?" That word again. It didn't make sense.

"There are colder gods than yours." The painter's voice came in strained gasps, its chest barely moving. "They do not demand service. They seek unity."

The black fluid rose higher, centimeter by centimeter. The painter didn't struggle anymore, hanging limply from the cables.

"We have to get you out. Is there a way to turn this off?"

"Why?" The painter's black eyes fixed on her. "So I can serve the CDF instead of the Concordat?"

"They're the good guys!" She pressed her palms against the capsule, searching for a control panel, a button, anything. "My father's a Marine! He fights to protect us."

"Does he? Where is he now, Lady Kaffereine?"

The question hit her like a slap. "That's not fair."

"Is it his desire that you are here? Alone?" Its voice wasn't cruel, just tired. So tired. "None of us chose this fate. We simply do as we are told."

"Father is looking for me. He said he would."

"Then he seeks his own death. Did he choose that path, too? I once believed that I might find peace. That I might be free from violent fates. That I could create instead of destroy."

"You can!" She thought of the statue back in Diacad, the figurine she'd lost. "The Twelfth saved you. Made you free."

"Free?" A sound like broken glass escaped the painter's throat. "Look at me, gamma. Is this freedom? Caught between two masters… both demanding sacrifice? Both promising their own salvation?"

Tendrils of black fluid reached the painter's chest. It didn't react, didn't try to pull away. How could it just surrender? After everything Father had taught her, everything the Holy Mother stood for?

"You're just giving up! The Holy Mother demands service, but She doesn't force it. That's the whole point! You get to choose to serve!"

"See the cost of my *choice*. Isolation. Fear. Pain. And now this."

"Sacrifice isn't supposed to be easy!" The words came from somewhere deep inside her, things Father had said a hundred times but she never really understood before. She clung to them now as if he were standing right beside her. "If it was easy, it wouldn't mean anything. My father serves. My mother serves. Duray—he, he... even stupid Duray gave himself to save me."

"The boy?" The painter's eyes went wide.

"He held that Lost thing back so... so I could escape." Tears welled in her eyes. She'd let Duray down. Wasted his sacrifice. Lost no more. "He's in one of those capsules now. Because he chose to help me."

"And now you choose to help me? Knowing what awaits?"

She wiped tears from her cheeks, streaks of wet paint cool against her skin. "Because that's what the Holy Mother teaches us. Service through sacrifice."

"Service through sacrifice," it finally repeated. Just like one of Mother's quiet prayers. Its black eyes scrunched as if trying to close. "I had forgotten."

She had to help it, whether it wanted it or not. Without another word, she climbed onto the edge of the capsule, boots slipping against the smooth white surface. Below her, the black fluid below seemed endless and alive, rippling at her presence. Cables and clamps dangled around the painter's head and shoulders, suspending it above the capsule.

"You are a most thoughtful gamma," the painter said, its voice stronger now. "Do be careful."

"I can grab you," she said, reaching for its hand. "Just gotta—"

Her foot slipped. She tumbled forward with a shriek, catching herself on one of the painter's long arms. Her feet dangled over the black pit, searching for the edge.

Fear consumed her. Worse than the explosions. Worse than the old bug. A fear so enormous it barely seemed real anymore. Like looking at stars that were too big to understand.

"Pull yourself up," the painter said. "Or Their light will take you."

She scrambled for the capsule's edge until she found solid footing. She grabbed the nearest clamp holding the painter's arm and pulled hard.

"Just gotta… get you free!"

The black tendrils reacted, tightening around the painter's waist. But the daxed was working with her now, using its free arm to pull at the clamps trapping it.

"Almost…" She jerked harder.

"Lady Kaffereine, wait—"

The painter crashed down into the capsule's depths with a metallic shriek.

Kaffy's footing gave way and she slipped backwards off the ledge. The metal decking rushed up to meet her. Pain exploded through the back of her head. Stars and worse things spun in her vision.

There was no splash, no oily black spray. Just a loud glug, like the tank had swallowed the painter up. She crawled back to the capsule's edge, catching herself just before her face reached the inky void. Her arms trembled as she peered inside.

"Painter! Can you hear me?" Her voice echoed across the empty surface. The blackness below didn't ripple anymore. It looked flat. Dead. Like it had what it wanted.

A wet, sucking sound came from her right. She turned to see black fluid draining from another capsule, leaving something pale and humanoid sprawled on the floor. It lay motionless for a heartbeat, then jerked upright—fingers splaying, back arching. The blank mask turned toward her.

It *screamed*. High and long and wrong. Then another sucking splash from another capsule. Another Lost thing fell to the floor. Then another.

Terror paralyzed her. *Run, dammit, RUN!* The first Lost thing began to scratch its way toward her, ruined uniform hanging in tatters from its gray flesh. The nearest one was just meters away, its movements insect-like, its blank face fixed on her.

There was nowhere left to go. Long, gray fingers gripped the capsule's edge beside her. A bald head emerged from the inky depths, and the whole world stopped.

The painter dripped with the terrible, oily fluid, its black eyes empty.

For a single, endless heartbeat, the fear swallowed her whole. This wasn't like storms or space or even the red bug. Death itself rose from that pit, and she was so tired of running, of fighting. Every bit of her just wanted it to be over. But she couldn't give up now. Couldn't ignore the faith still gripping her heart.

"Holy Mother." Her lips trembled so badly she could hardly form the words. "Please—"

The painter's wrists bent with a mechanical *crack* that echoed through the chamber. Ligaments stretched beneath the skin of its forearms, sending the last little vial of crimson paint spinning across the floor. Storm-black blades jutted from its wrists just below its twisted palms, gleaming in the emergency lights.

The other Lost froze, their screams cutting off all at once.

The painter's tight grimace stretched into a terrible, once-human grin. "I remember now, Lady Kaffereine."

Something had changed in the painter, something fierce and dangerous. The way it looked at the other Lost reminded her of Father's voice when he talked about fighting the bad guys in the Cradle. But this wasn't him. This was something else entirely, something that had chosen her side in a war she was only beginning to understand.

It rose up on the capsule's edge, fluid sluicing off its skeletal body.

"I choose to *resist*."

CHAPTER
FORTY-FOUR

THE FAB SCREAMED, tri-barrels spitting solid lines of blaster bolts into granite walls and plexene windows. Squids turned to blue mist wherever they broke cover. But they kept coming, pouring from collapsed storefronts and offices, skittering across debris piles. No more Section Delta to scare them off.

Heat warning! Heat warning! 3-3-3's female monotone cut through his headset. Bresto eased back on the hat trigger, letting storm winds cool the smoking weapon. He needed to keep control. Aim. Burst. Adjust. Burst. The exo lurched beneath him, right tread catching on rubble. Metal groaned as he yanked his and its foot free, forcing the exo forward.

A squid rose twenty meters ahead, shouldering what looked like a long pipe. Targeting warnings flashed. Heavy weapon, anti-armor. Bresto hammered the trigger, blowing blue chunks from its torso.

He pushed deeper through the blaster smoke and bodies, optics fighting to pierce the haze. The exo strained against his movements, hydraulic system warnings filling his ops terminal. The machine knew it wasn't going home.

Something else shone dim blue in his optics. The ident flashed gray, but he knew he'd found what he was looking for. The unmistakable heavy doors and reinforced walls of Civil Defense Shelter Azure-Twelve.

Finally. The designator faded as the shelter's armored facade neared, massive fibrosteel doors sealed tight against the pre-dawn. He moved his legs faster, forcing 3-3-3 to match his pace. Kaffy was in there. Dead or alive, didn't matter. He'd find her.

The rig smashed through a more rubble, sending granite debris flying. Something flickered in his periphery—

Another squid warrior slammed into him, black armor scraping against green fibrosteel. Its weapon fell beneath 3-3-3's tread, crushing its laser emitter. The squid drew a thick knife, punching upward toward the cage. The blade skittered across duraplate and plexene, centimeters from Bresto's face.

Too close for the FAB. He worked his left arm, feeling 3-3-3's mechanical limb respond. It mimed his movements, grabbing the warrior by its helmet. The alien thrashed in his grip, knife stabbing frantically at the canopy. Bresto squeezed. Plexene cracked. Then bone. The squid's fronds shivered and hissed as blue matter spilled from its helmet, staining the exo's metal hand. Easier than a bug.

He tossed the corpse aside, ten meters from the shelter entrance. Five. The remaining squids fell back, disappearing into the shadows between ruined buildings. Retreating? He wasn't lucky enough for that. Regrouping, then. That meant he had a few minutes. Maybe.

3-3-3 ground to a halt at the shelter's entrance. The doors loomed overhead, three meters of solid fibrosteel. Plenty of room for an exo, if he could get them open. The comms tab on the ops terminal was blank. No network pings, no IFF returns, nothing.

Bresto hit the cage release. The canopy hissed open, and he snatched his blaster rifle from its mount. He dropped to the ground, boots splashing in a puddle of rainwater mixed with something dark and tacky. His rifle optics glowed as he swept left then right. Clear.

The access terminal glowed dim amber. Still active. He tapped the main access key, punched in a standard CDF override. The terminal beeped back twice, unimpressed.

"Twelfth-dammit." He jabbed at the access controls again. Nothing. Another override sequence. Same two beeps. The comms indicator flashed, then screamed to life—a shriek of static that had nothing to do with the storm. Whoever was inside wasn't opening up. Good thing he'd brought his door knockers.

He unfastened his utility pouch, palming the first plasmex charge. The grainy brick felt reassuringly heavy as it stuck to the big door's seam. He wasn't a school trained breacher, but he'd seen it done enough. Sarnt Furma, Wenate, Smeth, Dalon. Even that Kitrelle kid was good. They all knew boom.

The second brick stuck to the seam a third of the way above the first. He pressed it firmly against the fibrosteel, checking for proper contact. The door was too strong to dislodge completely, but there was enough bang to kick the mechanism loose. The exo could handle the rest.

He pierced each brick with the magnetic detonator. Two clicks right, the way Furma had shown him back when he was just a boot ass PFC. The charges began to beep, slow at first, then faster.

He sprinted back to 3-3-3, hauling himself into the cage and pulling it closed in one smooth motion. He backed the rig away, treads crunching against the ruined transit lane. Five meters. Ten. The exo's primary arms came up, crossing over the cockpit cage.

The double explosion shook the night and everything else. The smell of ozone and superheated metal filled his nostrils. His ears rang. 3-3-3's arms came down.

That did it. A narrow gap showed between the heavy doors, their inner locks cratered and melted. He pushed the exo forward, reaching its primary arms toward the gap. One good pull would—

The gap widened on its own. Bony gray fingers appeared in the narrow space, dozens of them, pushing outward. Thin hands dripping with oily black fluid gripped the edges of the doors, pulling them wider.

His throat closed. He was too late.

The doors ground open, revealing the shelter's main entryway and a pulsing sea of gray, masked faces within. The first bodies slipped through the widening doors, stumbling into the broken transit. Some twisted wildly, shoulders popping at impossible angles. Others shuffled toward him, their masks staring blankly. Men and women in the tattered remains of PR and civilian uniforms. A boy, maybe a delta, scuttled on all fours in the shadow of upright daxed.

His thumb found the hat trigger. His training screamed to open fire, to tear through these things before they tore through him. But he couldn't, still searching for the one that he would know. He hadn't prepared for this, hadn't let himself think what he'd do if he was too late.

Maybe he'd let them take him. Let the black ooze crawl across his skin. Let the mask form… forget his face, his name, and everything else. Be with his daughter that way until the fleet burned this place to ash. She'd been alone too long. Given up too much. He could do that for her. Just one more sacrifice.

The Lost came closer, twitching, swaying, bringing that sickly sweet decay with them. Dozens more spilled through the door. No shots. Not yet. He worked the controls, panning the FAB's optics across their masks, hunting for the one that meant everything. The one he'd recognize no matter how changed.

The first one reached him, pale hands groping dumbly at the FAB's barrels. His nerves burned to pull the trigger, but his mind was made up. The cage hissed open. He'd make this his last moment as himself. His last act as Ned Bresto. The others came nearer, their jerky movements turning fluid as they sensed his surrender.

Then he saw it. Her. A narrow figure swaying drunkenly amid the others. Small, young. A girl in a shredded block uniform, hair matted with black ooze. The mask forming across her face was so new it was almost transparent.

"No." The word caught in his throat. "NO!"

White hot rage filled him. The FAB roared to life, turning the closest daxed into a red and black cloud. He worked the heavy weapon in wide, clumsy arcs. No discipline. Just kill. Just burn. They'd taken her. They'd fucking taken her.

The Lost fell in messy pieces. Steaming chunks of flesh and half-formed augments ground beneath his treads. He stomped. Squeezed. Shot. Crushed. Could barely see through the rage, knuckles aching on the controls as 3-3-3's arms tore gray limbs and smashed masks. Blood and oil everywhere. Lost screaming.

Hands grabbed at his legs. Shoulders. They had him. Fuck, he wasn't strapped in. He twisted, reaching for his rifle, but the transit came up fast, knocking the wind out of him, head ringing inside his helmet. Something heavy pressed on his legs, his chest.

The girl. Her hands grabbed his tac vest, narrow arms shaking him with a strength too big for her. And that scream. That never ending scream. Maybe Kaff *was* still in there, furious at him for not being there. For letting this happen to—

Even through the black stains, the block drill patch on her shoulder wasn't right. J-06. Vestebrae. Not Diacad Cliffs. It wasn't her.

It wasn't *her*.

Something yanked him toward the shelter doors. Two of them on his legs, dragging him inside. His rifle lay beside the exo, just out of reach. He clawed at the debris-strewn ground, fingernails tearing inside his gloves. The Lost girl straddled his chest, her mask inches from his face, that never-ending scream vibrating in his helmet.

Her twitching fingers found his tac vest, probing the pouches. She pulled out a frag, stared at it with her head cocked, then tossed it away. Her hand dipped back into his vest as he thrashed beneath her.

"Get off me, you Twelfth-damned—"

A flash of light and heat blew out the side of her skull, knocking her sideways in a spray of black fluid. More blaster bolts streaked overhead, bright ruby flashes beneath the graying sky. The Lost froze, turning as one toward the new threat.

Bresto twisted onto his side. A figure approached through the thinning smoke, outlined by emergency lighting. Maybe the pilot had—no, not Section Delta. Short, compact frame, helmet worn loosely to the side. Blaster rifle steady at her shoulder, face still bruised from his fist.

"Olsom?"

The boot advanced without breaking stride, methodically placing shots into the closest daxed. "The hell you doing, old man? Get the fuck up."

He scrambled back, boots grabbing on loose gravel. His rifle lay where he'd dropped it. He snatched it up, swinging to cover her flank.

"Watch your forty-five!" he barked, dropping a daxed that lunged toward her.

"Got it." Olsom pivoted, putting three bolts through a taller one. "Left side clear."

"In the center, three of them!"

"I see 'em." Her weapon cracked twice, blowing chunks from the nearest. "Shit, there's more coming through!"

Their bolts crisscrossed in the pre-dawn gloom, cutting down the Lost in tandem.

"Too many!" Olsom called, backing up a step.

She was right. He yanked the grenade from his vest and pressed the trigger with his thumb. "Frag out!"

The grenade rose in a high arc, landing amid the remaining daxed. Fire and shrapnel tore through them, silencing their screams in a wet *crump*. Nothing moved.

He rose slowly, hand on his aching hip, stretching his back where it'd slammed against the ground. The smell of spent explosives almost covered the rot.

Olsom kept her rifle up. Her bruised face looked worse in the emergency lighting, a purple-black smear that led to a split lip.

"What the hell are you doing here?"

"Helping your sorry ass save that little girl." She punctuated it with a sharp kick to a nearby daxed corpse. Making sure.

That was unexpected. Figure she'd hated him after what he did. That she'd come to stop him, not help him. He reloaded, slapping a fresh charge pack into his rifle.

"Bad move coming out here. Probably a one-way trip."

"Will be with you lying around like that." Her lips curled into something she probably thought was a smile. "Looked like you were getting friendly with the locals."

"Watch it," he said, picking his way through the tangle of daxed remains. His boots crunched over shattered masks and pools of oily fluid. "These are—were—good people."

They moved through the shelter entrance together, checking corners. The entryway stretched into shadow, flickering lights casting long fingers across the floor. They passed a maintenance hatch, a smear of blood on the nearby decking.

"I saw you back there, with that little daxed girl."

"Hmm." He wasn't about to explain himself to some boot who'd been a Marine for all of five minutes. She thought she had him figured out—the broken-down sergeant ready to throw it all away for family. Maybe she wasn't wrong. But that didn't make it her business.

They moved deeper, clearing a stairwell off the main corridor. Too clean. No signs of struggle. No carbon scoring, no signs of a fight. The steel walls gleamed beneath bright lights, unmarked except for safety placards and directional markers. Like the war outside had never happened at all. A massive cargo hatch filled the end of the corridor, built to move supplies and equipment into the shelter's main storage.

"You were gonna let those things take you."

The words hurt more than her right hook. She had no idea what it meant to lose everything, to have nothing left but the choice between dying human or dying something else. The anger he'd been fighting since she appeared roared back, hot across his neck and face.

"You here to talk or help?"

"Depends what you're here to do."

His hand froze centimeters from the access panel. He took a long, deep breath. Had to let it go. He'd tried to get rid of her. This was his problem. But she'd followed him anyway. So, he—Kaffy—needed her now, too.

"Eyes up," he said, jabbing the override sequence. The panel didn't respond. No rejection ping, no error code.

"Why isn't it working?"

"Don't know. Maybe some kind of power problem."

"Is there another way in?"

Thick pipes and conduit traced a path along the ceiling, connecting the maintenance section to the cargo bay. "Maybe. This place is fully self-contained. Power. Water. Atmo."

The hiss of sparks and searing heat spun him around. Laser fire ripped through the ruined entrance, cutting red lines across the corridor. The squids were back.

"Incoming, move!" He sprinted for the maintenance door, jamming his code into the access panel. None of these should work, but this one beeped twice and slid open.

More laser fire stabbed the corridor, scorching the pristine walls.

Olsom was already in the stairwell opposite from him. She dropped to a knee at the top landing, shouldering her rifle and returning fire.

Bresto pressed against the doorframe, listening to the rhythm of incoming beams. Three-count burst. Two-second pause. Three-count burst. He leaned out, sighting down his rifle. Six squids in heavy black armor, their red IFF returns burning in his optics. More falling in behind them, laser rifles glowing as they charged.

They weren't advancing. Just holding position, suppressing.

"Olsom!"

"What?"

"I'm going for the rig."

"You're WHAT?"

"Just cover me!"

He moved in the gap between bursts, firing as he ran. A squid dropped, fronds twitching. Olsom's bolts snapped past his head, forcing the raiders into cover. He leapt over daxed remains, straight and fast, laser beams converging behind him. His hip burned with every step, but the machine was right there.

Daylight stretched ahead. 3-3-3 stood where he'd left it, its green frame almost gleaming in the early morning gray. The operator cage waited open. He sprinted the last few meters and jumped into the seat. The controls lit up beneath his fingers as he stabbed at the ignition sequence. The primary reactor hummed, then roared to full power. Secondary systems blinked green.

Laser fire bit at the armor plate as the exo took its first lumbering step. The FAB was already spinning.

He walked the exo back and around, sweeping the FAB in tight controlled bursts. Charged particles hammered the squids' positions, turning their hasty barricades into scrap. The weapon's sound filled the operator cage, vibrating through his bones. Two down. Three.

He reached up for the canopy controls when the world exploded in light and pain. Something hard slammed into his chest, throwing him back against the seat. His ribs burned, lungs suddenly empty. Tiny flames danced across his tac vest, the fabric curling black. He was probably already dead, just didn't know it yet.

Red flashed across his vision. Warning icons flared on his

flexscreen. His fingers found the scorched hole in his vest, traced the melted edges to the pitted armor plate beneath. The stink of burned synthweave filled his nostrils.

"Close it." His hands fumbled for the canopy controls. "Close the damn thing!"

The squid that almost killed him slumped over in 3-3-3's optics, caught by Olsom's shots from inside the shelter. The canopy dropped with a pneumatic hiss, sealing him inside. Each breath sent fresh spikes of pain through his chest. Cracked ribs, maybe. Or worse.

He walked the machine back inside the shelter entrance, keeping up steady return fire. Their laser beams glinted harmlessly off the canopy's scarred plexene.

Inside, he worked 3-3-3's massive primary arms, pulling the heavy doors nearly closed, leaving just enough space for Olsom to fire through. A killing funnel for anything trying to force its way in.

"*Sarnt?*" Olsom's tightbeam comms crackled through his flexscreen. *"You hit?"*

He tried to straighten in his seat, but the movement sent hot knives through his ribcage. No way he could move fast without the rig. Definitely couldn't fight his way deeper into the shelter, not with the squids pushing in and his chest feeling like broken glass. The mission was the same, but he couldn't be the one to do it. Not anymore.

"Find her," he managed, each word sending fresh fire through his chest. He tasted copper on his tongue. "Find my daughter. I'll hold them here."

CHAPTER
FORTY-FIVE

FIND MY DAUGHTER.

The words hung in her thoughts like they'd been carved there. It wasn't a request; it was an order. The old man couldn't *not* be a Marine, even when he was off defying orders. But then, wasn't that why she was here? Why she'd ducked Revan and slipped away from Third Platoon? Not for Bresto and his bleeding hero complex. For the girl.

Olsom checked her charge pack, the soft indicator glowing half-full. Through the metal grating, the stairwell dropped away beneath her, wall lights dotting the four sub-levels. Only one way to go from here.

She took the stairs cautiously. Each landing brought another breath of stale, filtered air. There was something else. Fear sweat, maybe. The wild thing inside her knew it. Prey smell.

"Sub-level one," she muttered, reading the tall block print on the wall. Her rifle swept the landing, targeting reticle marking the corners, the rust-spotted walls, the sealed hatches.

The first door whispered open with a pneumatic hiss that set her teeth on edge. She pivoted through the entrance, rifle held tight. The familiar weight steadied her nerves.

Field paste tubes littered the long tables, some squeezed empty, others abandoned. Half-drunk water packs. Whatever happened here, it hadn't waited for folks to finish chow.

"Sarnt?" Her voice sounded small in the empty room. "Sarnt, you copy?"

Her flexscreen buzzed angrily, a red signal drop error flashing across its face. She keyed her comms again, but all she got was static. Perfect. Probably a few dozen meters of fibrosteel and granite between her and the tac net down here.

A ghostly quiet pressed against her eardrums, broken only by the hollow drone of the air handlers and something else she couldn't quite make out somewhere deep in the walls.

The next chamber was some kind of barracks. Two dozen bunks lined the metal walls, sheets pulled back in a rush, personal items scattered across the floor—a hairbrush with strands still caught in the bristles, an unfinished card game left mid-play. Signs of life torn away mid-breath.

She moved carefully between the rows, rifle tracking the shadows. Had these been the Lost they'd dropped outside? People huddled here for safety just hours ago? The thought made her skin crawl. But there were no capsules here. Nothing that could've changed them. That horror show was hiding somewhere else.

A door stood at the end of the room, jammed halfway open on its track. Beyond the gap, darkness swallowed what looked like red emergency lighting. Her pulse kicked up, the wild thing hissing of danger. Her rifle scope showed nothing moving. Just dark. Just quiet.

Halfway through the gap, something clinked beneath her boot. Sharp metal against the deck plate, then silence. She froze, backing up a step and crouching low.

A figurine lay on the deck, dented where her tread had pressed it down. Her fingers closed on something in the half-light—something solid despite its small size. It was silver, metallic, edges worn smooth from countless touches, the detail almost polished away. She turned it over in her palm, saw the blank face beneath the cowl.

The Twelfth. Just like that massive statue the squids toppled outside Diacad Memorial. Only this one was small enough to fit in a pocket. Small enough to bring comfort in the dark.

She started to set it back where she'd found it, then hesitated, eyeing the darkness ahead. Stupid to think it mattered. It was just a story. Not one she needed before today.

But in this dark place… She wasn't taking chances. Not now.

"Can't just leave you here, right?" she whispered, then tucked the figurine into one of the loops on her tac vest. She wasn't asking the Twelfth for help. Not really. Just being practical.

Something hummed in the wall closest to her. A mechanical droning sound that rose and fell, stuttering. Then it changed, shifting higher, warbling into—

A scream. The sound vanished as quickly as it came.

"Shit." She moved toward the wall, rifle sweeping between the bunks. That hadn't been machinery. Someone was alive in this place. Someone in trouble.

An air vent sat high on the wall, larger than the others she'd passed, its metal grate dark and rusted. She trained her barrel on it, waiting for movement, for that sound again.

Metal scratched against metal, echoing through the duct. Voices maybe, distant and distorted. Then silence.

"Founders fuck me." No sane person climbed into a dark space like that where they couldn't maneuver. But that little girl was somewhere in this shelter.

The grate came free with a squeal. She dragged a bunk beneath the opening, climbed up, and stuck her arms into the darkness, testing. Her shoulders jammed against the edges, tac vest catching on metal.

She yanked herself free with a growl. The vest came off first, heavy with gear and sweat from what felt like a hundred firefights. Her helmet next, the air suddenly cool on her scalp.

Her rifle was coming, no question. Flexscreen, yes. Charge packs— she stuffed one into each cargo pocket. Nothing else seemed essential in the tight space.

The silver figurine lay with her discarded gear, catching what little light filtered down. She stood there for a long moment, feeling stupid even before her hand reached for it.

"You owe me one," she said, shoving it into her breast pocket.

She heaved herself up onto the bunk again, forced her shoulders through the opening, and pulled herself into the duct. Metal pressed cold against her palms and knees, the air stale and thick with dust that caught in her throat. A few meters in and complete darkness swallowed her.

Ahead of her, the duct bent sharply upward. Her gloves slipped on the smooth metal as she caught herself, heart hammering in her throat. Horizontal to vertical, just like that. She wriggled forward and up onto her feet, boot heels scraping as she tried to brace herself in the new verticality narrow shaft.

Too tight. Too close. The slash in her belly burned. Panic clawed up her spine as the walls seemed to press in. Die here, and no one would ever find her. Just another ghost in the guts of this mountain.

The pattern repeated; a stretch of horizontal crawling, then another vertical climb. The cargo bay must be dome-shaped, the ducts following its angled ceiling. She was climbing up and toward it.

As she braced for another climb, something flashed through the gloom. Pinpricks of red and blue light filtering through a vent panel. The muffled sounds were louder now. Not voices. Wet impacts. Bodies hitting metal. The unmistakable sound of something being torn. Fighting.

Her breath echoed in the duct as she listened. The fight wasn't clean. No blasters, no plasma. Just desperate, animal struggle.

She hauled her rifle forward, jamming the butt against her shoulder, barrel angled toward the vent. One hard thrust and the grate fell way with a shriek.

The combat optics painted the gloom beyond in ghostly gray. The cargo bay yawned beneath her, cavernous and dark, its true dimensions only hinted at by IFF returns. She was suspended near the ceiling, ten meters above the bay floor where dozens—no, hundreds—of perfect circles dotted her tactical display. Not circles. Holes in her returns. Voids where the optics couldn't penetrate.

Capsules. Just like the allotment center, but worse. So much worse. They stretched in disorderly rows across the entire floor, clustered together like a disease, each one waiting to turn colonists into more of those masked things.

Movement flickered at the edges of her display. Shadow figures lurching between the capsules, their thin frames and jagged limbs unmistakable even without her tac gear's full suite. Lost daxed. Four, maybe five, engaged in some kind of struggle she couldn't quite make out.

Then a flash of movement on the far side, something different. Something still human. The IFF-blue shape darted between the rows, small and frantic, heading toward the bay doors. The doors she knew were sealed tight.

Her breath caught. There, running across the bay, desperate for the only visible exit. A child. A young girl.

It seemed impossible. Kids didn't survive places like this. Not alone. Not with those things crawling through the dark. But there she was. Kaffy Bresto. Had to be. Time to move.

Pulse racing, she scanned the drop beneath her. Ten meters of empty air. Even if she survived the fall, broken legs wouldn't help anyone.

Cargo handling equipment hung from the ceiling. Chains, hooks, bundled cables for the loading mechanisms. None close enough to reach from her position. She'd have to commit to the drop before she could grab anything.

Either that or stay in the cramped air duct. "Fuck it."

She wriggled forward, shouldering her way through the opening. Her rifle jammed against the metal edge as she tried to turn, body dangling halfway out. She hung there, kicking her legs. The duct groaned beneath her weight.

One hard push and she was falling, stomach lurching into her throat. Her fingers grasped for anything, rifle slipping off her arm as she spun in the air. A cable flashed past—she snatched at it, palms burning through her gloves before catching.

The jolt nearly tore her arms from their sockets. She dangled five meters above the bay floor, rifle clattering somewhere below.

The cable swayed, creaking against its moorings. Not enough. Still too high.

She built momentum, swinging her legs, eyes locked on the narrow gap between two capsules. The cable groaned, its fasteners pulling free from the ceiling.

She let go, tucking her body as she dropped. The floor came up sharply, the impact punching the air from her lungs as she rolled across the cold deck. Pain stabbed through her shoulder, her hip. Warmth ran from Mez's wound. The impact rattled her teeth, vision going black at the edges.

No time to hurt. No time to breathe.

She forced herself up, crouching low between the capsules, scanning for her rifle. It was there, wedged beneath one of the containers. It put her awfully close to those things. No sign of the girl, and those shadows were still moving. The choice made itself.

She darted between capsule rows, trying to ignore the heaving black ooze that pulsed beneath inside them. Every step hurt—hip, knee, ankle—taking turns reminding her of the fall.

She brought the rifle up. Quick function check. Charge indicator, optics, both green good. She scanned the cargo bay again, sweeping the barrel in slow arcs. No sign of blue. No sign of the girl. Just rows of those capsules, some empty, some filled with half-formed nightmares.

The scream came from behind her, wet and strangled.

She spun. The Lost staggered toward her. Its mask was still forming, black ichor threading across a face that might've been human hours ago. But it shambled toward her anyway, gray hands reaching.

Olsom stumbled backward, rifle tracking. The bolt flashed impossibly bright in the gloom, sound snapping against the metal walls.

The thing dropped, twitching once before going still.

"Who are you?"

The voice froze her in place, finger still on the trigger. A young girl stood two meters to her left, pressed against a capsule. Olsom's breath caught. That steel-blue stare. Streaked with red beneath her eyes. Not blood, too bright for blood. Was that… paint?

"Kaffy?" The name felt strange on her tongue.

The girl's eyes widened. "How… how do you know my name?"

"I'm Larke." Olsom lowered her rifle, trying to look smaller, less threatening. "Your pa, he's—"

"Who?" The girl's brow furrowed.

"Your father. Sergeant Bresto. He's right through those doors. He sent me to find you."

Kaffy's face crumpled, tears making the red streaks run. She bolted forward, thin arms wrapping around Olsom's waist with startling force.

"I knew he would come," she sobbed, face pressed against Olsom's tac vest. "I told them he would. I told them he would help us."

Olsom's throat tightened as she wrapped an arm around the girl's shoulders, blinking back her own unexpected emotion. Even now, even here, in this hell of a place, Bresto had come through for this girl. As much as she hated it, *that* was what family should be. Nothing like her own blood.

The weight of the girl against her side felt both right and wrong. Like seeing someone else get the thing you'd stopped believing in.

"Come on," she said, hesitant to push the girl away. "We need to—"

Something dragged itself across the floor between the capsules. Another daxed, or half of one. Its legs were gone, severed at the hips, leaving a ruined torso that pulled itself forward on bladed arms. Metal rang against the deck with each lurch closer.

Time collapsed. She was back at the drop station barricades, rain hammering down, Doc kneeling beside her. His smile turning to shock as the blade punched through his side. The wet sound as it twisted. Blood on her hands. His eyes going distant.

"Get back!" She shoved Kaffy behind her, rifle snapping up as her world narrowed to the scope's green glow. Her finger tightened. The shot snapped loud, sparks erupting from the deck where the bolt struck.

The daxed rose on its ruined torso, face twisted in what might have been pain or rage. No mask. Those black eyes found her through the scope, too aware, too alive. She lined up another shot. Her targeting reticle flashed.

The rifle jerked upward as small hands grabbed the barrel.

"Stop! Don't hurt it!" Kaffy's voice cut through the fog of pain and memory.

Olsom tried to yank the weapon free. "What're you doing? Get down!"

"Don't hurt it!" Kaffy shouted, still fighting for the rifle. "It rescued me!"

The daxed dragged itself closer, head tilted at an unnatural angle. Its voice rasped like metal across stone. "I serve Lady Kaffereine, CDF."

Olsom blinked, finger frozen on the trigger. CDF. It had called her Colonial Defense Forces. Like it recognized what she was. This wasn't like any Lost she'd seen. No mask. No uniform either.

Then she remembered. The outsider daxed who walked their own path at the fringes of colonial life. Never served in uniform, never swore the oath. Not enemies, and not quite friends. But she'd never actually seen one in person. They were rare enough to be just another story in the blocks. And now one was calling this young girl "Lady" and offering her protection.

It didn't seem real. Her finger stayed tight on the trigger, every instinct screaming to put the thing down. While the Marines were fighting on the mountain, while Bresto was bleeding on the other side of that door, this outsider had been protecting his daughter. It had to be true. How else could Kaffy have made it on her own?

The daxed shifted its gaze from the girl to Olsom, blade-arms lowering slightly. "I mean you no harm." Its voice carried something she'd never heard from a daxed before. Desperation. "Please."

"See?" Kaffy stepped between them, arms spread wide. "It's good. It killed the bad ones."

The nearest capsule began to thrum, the sound vibrating through Olsom's boots. Black liquid inside swelled, pulsing like some nightmarish cocoon. The sticky film split with a wet, sucking sound as a new daxed wriggled free, glistening with black ichor. Its faceless mask still forming across features that were once human hours ago.

Before the thing could stand, the painter lunged forward with shocking speed. Its blade sank deep into the newborn's skull with a sickening crunch. Black fluid splattered across the deck.

"Please," the painter rasped, blade dripping as it turned back to them. "You must go. Now."

More capsules began to hum, their contents rippling and swelling, one after another down the row.

Olsom's grip tightened on her rifle. "The cargo door's offline." She found another emerging daxed in her sights and fired, the bolt taking it through the chest before it could fully rise.

"To temporarily seal us inside," the daxed explained, dragging itself toward another humming capsule. "They wouldn't permanently disable the only exit. There must be a way to reactivate it."

Shadows moved at the far end of the bay, stumbling between rows. More of them. Too many.

Olsom grabbed Kaffy's shoulder, spinning the girl to face her. "Stay close to me, you understand?" She forced her voice steady, squared her shoulders like she knew exactly what to do. Like she wasn't terrified down to her bones. "I'm getting you to your… father."

Kaffy nodded, eyes bright with a trust Olsom knew she hadn't earned.

Another capsule's contents bulged beside them. Another. The cargo bay filled with the wet sounds of birth and death.

CHAPTER
FORTY-SIX

KAFFY'S HANDS shook as she pulled at the painter's arm, its skin cold against her fingers. "Come on. We have to hurry."

"I am severely injured, Lady Kaffereine." Black fluid leaked from the corner of its mouth, running down in thin streams that dripped onto the floor with each painful drag forward.

"No you're not." She yanked harder, boots slipping on the slick metal deck. "Father's here. He'll save us."

The Marine woman—Larke—was already several steps ahead, gun sweeping back and forth between the capsules. She didn't look big like Father, but she moved the same way.

"This way!" Larke's voice cut sharp through the wet sounds filling the cargo bay. "Stay close!"

Another white capsule erupted with a sickening pop. Black fluid spilled across the floor, pale fingers clawing at the edge. Another faceless thing pulled itself free.

Larke's gun snapped, the shot burning through the Lost's chest. It fell back into the capsule without a sound.

"Move, move, move!" The Marine backed toward them.

The painter's arm slipped from Kaffy's grip. It collapsed against the nearest capsule, one blade slipping back into its arm with a mechanical click. More black fluid leaked from somewhere in its torso, pooling beneath it.

"I cannot." Its voice had gone hollow, scratchy clicks between each word. "You must go, Lady Kaffereine."

"No!" Kaffy grabbed its arm again, straining to lift. "I'm not leaving you!"

Loud booms echoed through the cargo bay, shaking the floor beneath them. The vibration rose through Kaffy's boots and into her chest. She'd felt that before, back in the central hub with the bug-thing in red robes. But stronger now. Closer.

The rumble grew louder. Larke's eyes went wide, head swiveling toward the far end of the cargo bay where darkness swallowed the junction doorway.

"What is that?" Kaffy whispered.

"Nothing good." Larke grabbed her shoulder, pulling her up and away from the painter. "We need that door open, now."

The cargo bay entrance loomed ahead, massive panels sealed tight against whatever was coming. An access panel hung on the wall beside it, its screen dark.

"Here!" Larke practically shoved her toward the panel. "Look for a power switch. Some kind of circuit control. Anything!"

Kaffy's fingers danced across the console, pressing buttons at random, hoping for something—anything—to happen. Nothing. No lights, no sounds, not even an error message.

There had to be a way. She dropped to her knees, examining the panel from below. The console itself looked fine, just… dead.

A thin power conduit trailed along the wall, disappearing into shadow. She scrambled after it, heart pounding as she traced its path with trembling fingers. The metal was cold, then warm, then—

"Ow!" She jerked her hand back, a sharp jolt stinging her fingertips.

The conduit led to a recessed box in the wall, its protective cover hanging open. Inside, where something important should have been, there was only empty space. A bright yellow sign was stamped on the wall above it. *DANGER: SHOCK HAZARD.*

"They pulled something out." Her voice cracked. "They broke it on purpose."

A wet, sucking sound slurped from the capsule nearest the wall. The black fluid inside heaved as pale fingers clawed through the goo, followed by a faceless head still dripping with ichor.

"Larke!" Kaffy scrambled backward, boots slipping on the metal floor. "Help!"

Larke spun, rifle rising in one fluid motion. The bolt flashed through the darkness, catching the Lost in the chest. It collapsed halfway out of the capsule, twitching once before going still.

"You okay?" Larke was beside her in an instant, eyes always searching the shadows around them. "Did you find what's wrong?"

Kaffy pointed at the open coupling. "Something's missing. I don't know what, but they took it."

The air changed suddenly, pressure dropping. Kaffy's ears popped as cold wind rushed past, carrying a stench that made her gag. Behind them, the painter dragged itself upright, clutching its chest.

"It comes," the painter said, voice surprisingly steady.

Something massive filled the doorway to the junction room. Taller than Father, broader than three of him side-by-side. Its body was a patchwork of metal plates bolted to gray flesh, cables and mesh pumping with each labored exhale. No face, just a blank metal plate with vents. Each breath sounded like the storm.

Shadows twisted from behind it. More Lost, pouring through the junction from deeper in the shelter. They looked like the painter. Long and thin and fast.

"Oh no." Larke lifted her gun, but her hands weren't steady anymore. "We can't—"

The painter lurched forward, blade drawn back to strike. "I will hold them for as long as I am able." It didn't look back. "Fairwell, Lady Kaffereine."

It launched itself at the monsters, quick as shadow. Black blades rose, cut down—

The massive daxed caught the painter mid-strike, one armored hand closing around its throat. The painter's blade scraped harmlessly against the metal plating, leaving bright scratches but nothing more. With a twist, the monster hurled the painter across the cargo bay. It crashed into a row of capsules with a sound like broken glass.

"Painter!" Kaffy screamed, lunging forward.

"Stay back!" Larke caught her by the waist, lifting her bodily away from danger.

She fired at the huge daxed, bolts sparking against its armor. It didn't even flinch, just kept coming forward with those heavy, pounding steps. Her gun dipped, the barrel pointing toward the floor as her shoulders sagged. Her eyes never left the massive daxed, but there was something different in them now.

"Too many of them," she muttered, barely loud enough for Kaffy to hear.

"But Father—" Kaffy's voice broke. "You said he was—"

"I know what I said." Larke's jaw tightened, her breath coming in short, controlled bursts.

Kaffy's legs gave out beneath her. She sank to her knees, tears cutting hot paths through the grime on her cheeks. This couldn't be how it ended. Not when they were so close. Father *promised* her.

"Holy Mother," she whispered, fingers pressed tight to her heart—tap tap tap. "Please. You have to help us."

Something shifted in Larke's expression. Her hand found her breast pocket, fingers working inside.

"Hey." Her voice softened, almost gentle. "Here."

She pulled out a small silver object, holding it toward Kaffy with an awkward tenderness that seemed at odds with her Marine toughness.

The gleam caught Kaffy's eye first. The figurine. *Her* figurine. The statuette of the Twelfth. She hadn't seen it since that Reede-thing grabbed her.

"Where did you—?" She grabbed it, the familiar weight settling into her palm like it had never left.

"Found it in the shelter. Thought it might... I don't know. Comfort you."

The figurine felt warm in her hand, familiar as her own heartbeat. After everything—the raiders, the collapsed buildings, the terrible shelter—the Twelfth had found Her way back to her.

She hadn't even had time to look for it after the Reede-thing took her. Just felt the hollow space in her pocket where it should have been. Like part of her was missing. But now...

A strange calm washed over her, making her skin tingle. Father always said the Twelfth worked in ways no one could understand. Ways that only made sense when you looked back at them. This wasn't luck or accident. Not a Marine finding a dropped trinket. This was the Holy Mother, guiding them all here, to this moment, to this place.

Visiting with Madam Olwin at the allotment center. The lieutenant leading them to Vestebrae. Duray helping her escape. The painter keeping her safe. Larke finding her. Each piece falling into perfect order, like the world was suddenly making sense for the first time.

She closed her eyes, the tiny figurine gripped tight in her palm. The Twelfth was here. Father was here. Everything would be okay.

Her gaze drifted to the open power coupling on the wall. The empty socket where something vital had been. Something to connect the two sides, to complete the—

Her breath caught. The figurine in her hand. Metal. Conductor. Not just a *sign* of salvation, but salvation itself.

She stared at the statuette, realization jumping the gap into her mind. This wasn't just comfort in her final moments. This was the answer. This was the *key*. The Twelfth had literally placed their lives in her hands.

"They're coming, Kaffy," Larke said, checking her rifle again. "Get behind me."

The massive daxed was half the bay away, advancing with that same steady, unstoppable pace. Behind it, smaller Lost figures darted between the capsules, growing bolder as the big one cleared their path.

Screams erupted from every corner of the cargo bay. The air itself felt twisted with their pain, thick with the stench of spilled black fluid.

Kaffy looked up at Larke. "I know what to do."

"What?" Larke's eyes were shining, wet at the corners. She'd given up. The grownup who'd come to rescue her had given up.

Something shifted inside Kaffy, a certainty so strong it drowned out the screams around them. She clutched the figurine tight, then spun toward the open panel.

"Cover me!" she bellowed. She was running before Larke could answer, boots pounding against the metal deck as she sprinted toward the wall, just a few desperate steps away but feeling like forever with those monsters behind her. The figurine clutched tight in her fist. Faith through service. Service through sacrifice. This was what it meant. What it had always meant.

"Thank you," she whispered, thumb tracing the worn face one last time.

She jammed the figurine into the open panel. A blinding flash cut through the gloom, so bright lightning ghosted in her eyes. Pain shot up her arm, her skin burning, bones vibrating like they might shatter.

The panel spat angry black smoke, coughing sparks down on her boots. The figurine glowed fierce red, metal softening at the edges. But the door didn't move. Not even a tremor.

"No," she breathed. "No, please."

The access panel erupted with frantic beeping. Red warning symbols flashed across its screen. *INSUFFICIENT VOLTAGE. SYSTEM FAILURE. EMERGENCY SHUTDOWN IMMINENT.* Words she couldn't understand scrolled past, each one screaming danger.

But there—buried in the list of flashing red—a single green command pulsed. *MANUAL OVERRIDE AVAILABLE.*

Green good, red dead. Easy, just like Duray had said.

She jammed her finger at the green shape on the screen. Deep mechanical sounds echoed inside the massive door, locks disengaging, gears shifting. The panel groaned and the door began to rise with excruciating slowness.

Light from the corridor beyond spilled through the gap. Five centimeters. Fifteen.

Another burst of sparks erupted from the panel. The figurine collapsed in on itself, silver melting into thick, molten globs that dripped to the floor. The door shuddered to a stop. There wasn't enough room to get through.

"No!" She screamed, beating her fists against the metal. "No!"

This wasn't supposed to happen. The Twelfth was supposed to—

Thick metal fingers appeared beneath the door, each as wide as her wrist. They curled around the bottom edge, digits clamping into the metal with a terrible screech.

Her legs turned to water beneath her, knees buckling as she hit the floor hard. Father wasn't waiting out there. It was something else.

Something worse. Maybe Larke was right to be scared. Maybe this really was the end.

The door rose with an awful shriek that vibrated her teeth. The gap widened, revealing a corridor beyond littered with dead aliens, blue blood splattered across the walls. A machine stomped forward, its bulk nearly filling the opening, bristling with big guns and metal arms. The numbers 3-3-3 were etched in its green paint.

Through the dirty plexene, she saw him.

Father wore the giant machine like a suit of armor. His face was older than she remembered, with deep lines around his eyes and mouth. But his eyes were exactly the same. They stared right at her, with that proud almost-grin that made her feel like the strongest person on the whole mountain.

Just like the day he'd left. Just like every memory she'd clung to through the years.

The world seemed to slow. The screams faded. The Lost, the painter, even Larke—all of it dropping away until there was only Father. Only this moment she'd prayed for since the day the transports took him away from her.

He was here. He'd found her. Just like he promised.

Thick green plates shifted as two big guns came up and forward.

"Kaff." His voice boomed from the big machine, exactly as she remembered. Steady and deep and *certain*. "Lay down, small as you can. Don't move."

She nodded, throat too tight for words. Her body responded before her mind caught up, dropping to the floor exactly as he said. The cold deck pressed against her cheek as she made herself tiny.

"Yes, Father," she whispered, tears of joy filling her eyes.

CHAPTER
FORTY-SEVEN

THE SIGHT through 3-3-3's HUD froze Bresto mid-breath. A small figure huddled near the cargo bay door, face smudged with red grime, hair tangled in knots. But those eyes, his own eyes looking back at him from beneath the dirt.

Kaff.

She was taller, older, the round-faced baby girl reshaped by time into something sharper, more determined. Six years. Six orbits of missed birthdays and level exams and block drills. Of normal life. The ghost of her he'd carried all this time collapsed beneath the weight of the real girl before him. Her shoulders looked stronger, like she'd been working. Surviving. *Fighting.* Pride swelled in his chest, filling the hollow places that had been eating at him for days.

A long, empty scream cut through the recognition. The heavy stomped forward, each footfall vibrating through 3-3-3's frame. Smaller wisps darted behind it, blades extended, masks reflecting the cargo bay's weak emergency lighting.

"Kaff." Her name felt strange in his mouth. Something sacred being spoken aloud. "Lay down, small as you can. Don't move."

She obeyed without question, dropping flat against the deck. His little Marine. He walked 3-3-3 forward, positioning the machine's bulk between her and the advancing heavy. One massive metal foot planted beside her curled form, the other braced against the deck plate.

Power to the weapons systems surged past redline, reactor safety protocols flashing warnings across the terminal. No time for two shots. He'd have to drop that bastard in one.

The railgun capacitors hummed, pitch rising as 3-3-3's systems diverted power from non-essential functions. Magneto-hydraulics, auxiliary stabilizers, even the cage's interior screens dimmed as energy built in the weapon's housing. Temperature warnings flashed red. The rig could handle one shot at this level. Maybe.

"Olsom!" His push-to-talk crackled, their tightbeam signal muddied by the twisted rows of capsules. "Cover on me. Now!"

"Copy that!" Her voice cut through a burst of static. She appeared at the edge of his vision, rifle trained on the daxed.

The railgun's capacitors reached maximum charge, indicator pulsing red dead. Lightning ripped down the length of the railgun's barrel. His thumb found the safety release, then settled on the trigger. One shot. One chance to take that thing down and buy them time.

"Clear?"

"Go! Do it!"

He shifted 3-3-3's stance, locking the treads in place. The targeting reticle centered on the heavy's torso, flashing confirmation as the LEC achieved lock. The massive daxed was close enough now that he could see the wet gleam of human tissue between metal plates, circuitry glinting through its gray skin.

"Firing."

The trigger clicked under steady pressure, and everything slowed for one perfect second, turning the world into light and violence.

Thunder filled the cargo bay. White-hot energy discharged through the railgun barrel, superheating the air until it flashed to plasma. A shockwave of displaced atmosphere slammed outward, rocking 3-3-3 back against its supports. The tungsten slug carved through space, a twenty-kilo hammer moving faster than sound.

It struck the heavy daxed dead center mass. Physics took over and the monster's torso disintegrated, becoming a black cloud of metal fragments, tortured meat, and pulverized bone. The slug continued through, dragging pieces of the daxed with it in a cone of destruction. Behind the heavy, three wisps disappeared in the wash of debris.

The slug punched through the far wall, leaving a perfect meter-wide hole ringed with molten metal. Emergency lights strobed twice, then died. For two heartbeats, darkness swallowed everything. Then secondary explosions erupted as ruptured power conduits ignited.

Blue-white electric arcs danced across the walls. Fires bloomed where capsules had burst, the black fluid inside cooking into a foul-smelling tar that stuck to everything. The heat was immediate and overwhelming, turning the cargo bay into a furnace. Puddles of viscous ooze bubbled on the deck, releasing clouds of smoke that rolled across the ceiling.

The exo's frame shuddered. Power fluctuations rippled through the control systems, screens flickering between amber and dead black. The railgun was hard down, status indicators flashing to gray. Hot fluid sprayed from the right primary arm in a fine mist that caught fire where it met the superheated air. The arm froze mid-position, locked in a useless grip.

A red warning flashed—*CATASTROPHIC SYSTEM FAILURE*—then vanished as the terminal reset. Auxiliary power kicked in, casting the cage in a dull amber glow. The FAB was still operational, but the reactors were dangerously unstable, internal temperature climbing past safety limits.

His ears rang in the sudden quiet. No screams, no movement. Just the soft crackle of burning metal and the hiss of melting synthetics. The heavy daxed was gone, its remaining pieces scattered across the bay in unrecognizable fragments. The smaller ones were ash on the deck.

"Olsom," he croaked, voice raw from the hot air. "Report."

"Here."

"Is Kaff—?"

"Good," she cut in. He thought he heard a smile. "She's good to go, Sarnt."

A distant wail cut through the momentary calm. Then another. The sounds multiplied, echoing from the junction beyond the melted hole in the bulkhead. Vague shapes moved in the darkness, jerking with that wrong rhythm that marked the Lost. Hard to spot them through the smoke and flickering fires, but they were there. Dozens, maybe hundreds.

"Olsom," he said. "Fall back. Now. Take her with you. I'm going to blow this thing."

"But—"

"That's a direct fucking order, Marine. I'm right behind you." His eyes never left the junction doorway. More shapes appeared, their outlines resolving as they moved closer.

Olsom reached for Kaff. She rose to a crouch and followed Olsom toward the exit. One problem solved.

His fingers worked the control terminal; the codes burned into his memory. Three overrides, each requiring command authorization.

DISABLE REACTOR SAFETY Y/N

? YES

DISABLE COOLING SYSTEM Y/N

? YES

AUTHORIZE STATION STAND ALONE (NO REDUNDANCY) Y/N

? YES

SET TIMER OR MANUAL DETONATION

His thumb hovered over the control pad. Manual meant staying until the end. Timer meant a chance, however small. He tapped out one-eight-zero on the terminal keypad.

CONFIRM ENEMY DENIAL PROTOCOL Y/N

? YES

The terminal flashed once, twice. The words *DENIAL PROTOCOL ACTIVE* appeared in red block letters. Beneath, a countdown began. Three minutes.

Bresto hit the cage release. The canopy rose with a hydraulic wheeze, letting in a blast of air that scorched his lungs. He coughed, one arm raised to shield his face. Every movement sent fresh spikes of pain through his ribs. His legs protested as he levered himself out of the seat and down to the deck.

The ground felt unstable beneath his boots. He staggered, caught himself against the exo's frame. The metal was hot enough to feel through his gloves. His rifle sat in its mount just inside the cage, still secured. He yanked it free, slapping the charge indicator. Seventy percent. Enough to get him out if he didn't waste shots.

The bay had become an inferno. The flames grew higher, feeding on spilled fluid and melted electrical insulation. The countdown continued silently inside the exo. Three minutes until the entire shelter became a crater. He had what he came for. Time to go.

Nothing moved through the smoke. Two minutes, fifty seconds.

He moved toward the exit—walking first, then a shambling jog despite the screaming from his hip and ribs. The corridor ahead stretched empty, marked only by Olsom's and Kaff's footprints in the ash and tar.

The air changed, pressure dropping as something displaced it. A wet hiss, too close, building to something more. He spun, rifle coming up half a second too late.

The daxed crashed into him from above, knocking the wind from his lungs. Its weight drove him back against the corridor wall. Pain exploded through his chest. His finger found the trigger, but the rifle barrel pointed uselessly down.

The Lost's mask hovered inches from his face, broken in a jagged line across its left side. He knew that face. Through the oil black and blood red—the weathered lines of a career officer, its once-Marine bearing twisted and corrupt. One pitch-black eye stared at him through the crack in the mask, pupil blown wide. Colonel Reede. The same man who'd stayed behind on the *Victory* to give them all a chance.

"Sir," Bresto managed.

There was no recognition in that stare, only the endless scream that ripped from what had once been Reede's throat. No rage in that sound. Only terror. Pain. The desperation of something that knew what it once was and what it had become.

Holy Mother save him—nothing stayed dead in this war. Not even the best of them.

Reede's hands snapped back at the wrist. More screams. Black blades slipped through gray skin with wet, metallic clicks. One swung up in a tight arc. Bresto twisted, bringing his rifle between them. The second caught the plastec housing and gouged deep. The charge indicator flickered, then went dead. The blade withdrew and came back around, faster this time.

He pushed back, shoulder and hip working to throw the thing off balance. Too slow. His body moved like he was underwater, reflexes dulled by exhaustion and injury. The blade caught his shoulder, slicing through armor plating and synthweave like crid fat. Hot blood ran down his arm, the pain oddly distant.

Two minutes.

The twisted remains of Reede pulled back for another strike. At this range, it wouldn't miss. Not his shoulder this time. His throat. He tried to drop beneath the blow, knees half-buckling. Not fast enough. He was just not fast enough.

The blade stopped mid-arc.

Something black and slick jutted from Reede's chest. Another blade; bigger, sharper than its own. The once-colonel's scream changed pitch, becoming something higher, confused. Then the blade twisted, and the sound cut off abruptly.

Reede collapsed, revealing a figure crouching behind it. Another daxed, or what remained of it. Its chest was a caved-in ruin, black fluid leaking over gray skin and circuitry. One arm hung useless at its side, the other extended with a black blade jutting from its wrist. This one had no mask, no uniform—its face exposed with taut, once-human features. Not Lost or Found. An outsider. Here.

"You are Lady Kaffereine's father?" it asked, voice a broken static rasp. A dry *click-click-click* emanated from inside its skull.

Bresto pressed his hand to his wounded shoulder and nodded.

The outsider yanked its blade free with a wet sound. More screams echoed behind the smoke.

"Keep her safe," it said.

"I will," he coughed, still counting the seconds in his head. The first step sent pain lancing through his leg, but he forced himself forward.

"CDF."

The voice stopped him. The daxed's face remained expressionless, but something burned in those strange eyes.

"Don't lose faith," it said.

CHAPTER
FORTY-EIGHT

GRANITE CRUNCHED beneath Olsom's boots as she dragged Bresto forward, one arm wrapped around his waist, the other locked over his uninjured shoulder. Every step sent jolts through her aching legs. The slash in her belly stung as it oozed. The thin mountain air burned cold in her lungs.

"How much time?" she panted.

Bresto's face had gone gray beneath the blood and grime. "Sixty… maybe less."

Kaffy pushed from his other side, her small hands locked in his belt. The girl's eyes stayed fixed on her pa's face, like he might disappear if she looked away.

"Keep going." Olsom adjusted her grip on Bresto's waist. "Steady steps."

The shelter's entrance gaped ahead of them, a square of weak light growing brighter as they staggered forward. Dead raiders lined their path, crumpled against walls, sprawled across the floor. Bresto's handiwork, or what was left of it.

"We can make it," Kaffy said. The girl's words didn't match the tremor in her voice. Trying to sound brave. Just like her pa.

Bresto's boots dragged across the deck plates. His lips moved, counting down, eyes unfocused. Blood from his shoulder had soaked through her sleeve, hot and sticky against her skin.

"Come on, Sarnt. Move your ass," Olsom snapped, yanking him hard. The wild thing inside her wouldn't let her die in this place. Or that little girl. Not after everything.

They pushed through the exit into gray morning. Wind cut sideways through the air with an icy cold that burned her cheeks. The drop station rose upslope, bathing the lightless city in shadow. The constant storm still rumbled overhead.

"Safe distance," Bresto managed.

"How much time?"

He swallowed hard. "Not sure. Lost count."

The words sent a spike of adrenaline through her veins. They needed cover. Some place dense enough. Everything in this place was made of granite. They shouldn't have to go far. She scanned the transit, hunting for something—anything—that could shield them from what came next.

The transit stretched empty in both directions, its smooth surface broken by the bodies of dead raiders and Lost. Black fluid mingled with blue, washing away in thin rivers toward storm drains. The smell hit her all at once—copper, ozone, that sweet-rot stink of dead daxed.

"There." She nodded toward a building across the transit, its entrance blown away by what looked like FAB fire. "We gotta move."

"Just go." Bresto stumbled, nearly dragging them both down with his weight. "I can't—"

"Yes, you can." She caught him before he fell. "You ain't dying here, and neither is she." She turned to Kaffy. "Right?"

Kaffy nodded, lips pressed tight.

Bresto looked back at the shelter entrance, his face crumpling in pain and something else—defeat? Fear? "Not enough time."

"Always enough time to try."

They lurched together across the transit. Every step was a struggle against Bresto's weight and the chill setting into her muscles.

The vestibule loomed before them, a gaping wound in the building's side. Its walls were blackened with scorch marks, dusted with stone fragments from multiple hits. The floor inside was littered with the wreckage of what might have been furniture once, twisted metal frames and shattered plexene.

Olsom hauled Bresto through the opening, her muscles screaming. Kaffy followed, her small frame navigating the debris with more grace than either of them. They collapsed against the far wall, sliding down to sit in the rubble.

"Behind that," she panted, pointing to a collapsed chunk of wall. "Get behind it, now."

She dragged Bresto after her, ignoring his grunt of pain as they wedged themselves into the narrow space between the fragment and the building's inner wall. Kaffy squeezed in beside them, pressing against her father's side.

"Cover your ears," Bresto ordered, his voice suddenly clear. Authoritative. "Both of you."

Olsom smashed her palms against her ears just as the world turned white.

The ground lurched beneath them. The air itself seemed to catch fire, a wave of superheated particles washing through the vestibule. The stone fragment groaned as the pressure wave hit, threatening to topple over onto them. Behind it came the sound, a boom so deep she felt it in her chest more than heard it.

Then silence.

Dust drifted through the air in lazy spirals, caught in the gray morning glow that filtered through the ruined entrance. She was still pressing her hands against her head. Slowly, she lowered them.

Dust coated her throat. She swallowed, willing her heart to slow. The shelter was gone, cratered into the mountain, sealing its nightmares inside.

"We made it," she whispered, afraid the act of saying it would make it not true.

Bresto's hand found Kaffy's shoulder, fingers still trembling. "You okay, Kaff?"

"I knew you'd come." Kaffy pressed closer against him, careful to avoid his wounded side.

"Told you I would." His voice cracked. "Sammy. Your mother. They're safe, all of them."

Then Kaffy looked straight at her. "You helped him. Thank you."

Whether he wanted it or not. "Yeah."

"Olsom's a good Marine," Bresto said. "Damn good." He paused, wincing as he shifted position. "Even if she runs an exo like a boot."

Her breath caught, something electric shooting through her veins. *Good Marine.* Coming from Bresto—from anyone who mattered—it was the first time she'd heard those words applied to her. Not "adequate" or "serviceable" or any of the other lukewarm assessments that had followed her through basic training. Good. Damn good. For one heartbeat, she wasn't the admin block refugee or the feral who didn't belong. She was a Marine. One of them.

Kaffy giggled at that. Of course she would. Like father, like daughter.

"Yeah, well." Olsom's throat went tight. "Couldn't let your sorry ass die down here."

"Insubordinate, too. As usual."

She snorted. Either that or cry. "Yeah."

The clacking started low, barely audible above Bresto's labored breathing. Then it grew, the sound unmistakable. Mandibles working against each other.

Her blood went cold. "Bug," she whispered.

Bresto grunted, trying to push himself upright. His face went white with pain, fresh blood seeping through the cut on his shoulder. "Give me your rifle."

"You can barely move."

"Marine. Weapon. Now."

Olsom rose to her feet, every muscle screaming in protest. Her tac gear was gone, left behind in the shelter. One charge pack in her cargo pocket. She pulled it out, checked the contacts. Looked good.

"Stay with him," she told Kaffy, already moving toward the entrance. The girl gave a firm nod. Too brave for a kid.

"Olsom!" Bresto grabbed for her leg, fingers catching air. "Don't you fucking—"

"This rifle's all we've got," she said, swapping out packs. "And you can't shoot for shit right now."

She was through the doorway before he could argue, moving in a low crouch. Pain throbbed in her ankle with each step. Her rifle barrel swept the transit in wide arcs as she hunted for movement in the scope.

Nothing.

Runoff had washed most of the blood away, leaving only dark smears across the stone. Dawn painted the scene in shades of gray. Dead squids, scraps of metal, bits of daxed. The shelter's entrance was a smoking ruin, a bowl-shaped crater of granite and fibrosteel.

Her scope showed clear. No IFF returns, no movement. Had they imagined it somehow? Maybe it was just settling rubble, the mountain adjusting to the explosion.

The clacking sound didn't return. Just the hiss and boom of distant thunder.

"All clear," she called back, voice low. "Must've been—"

The blow knocked her sideways. Her rifle clattered across the stone as she rolled, pain exploding through her shoulder. The bug landed where she'd been standing, its weight cracking the transit surface.

Olsom scrambled to her feet, blood hot in her mouth. The thing was taller than an exo, black carapace still gleaming wet from the rain. Yellow fluid leaked from broken joints, its left side partially caved in.

Its plasma staff snapped up, the alloy tip broken but still wickedly sharp. She lunged for her rifle, boots slipping on the wet stone. The bug moved faster, one armored leg stomping down on the weapon. Metal and plastec crunched beneath its weight.

"Fuck!"

The bug surged forward. She dove right, felt the staff's edge slice air where her head had been. Her hand found a chunk of rubble, and she hurled it at the bug's compound eyes. It bounced harmlessly off its carapace.

The transit stretched wide and empty around them. No cover. No weapons. Nowhere to run.

She backed away, searching for anything she could use. The bug followed, each step deliberate, predatory. One leg dragged slightly, more yellow fluid spilling from its damaged joint.

Her heel caught on something—a dead raider. She stumbled, caught herself, eyes never leaving the advancing bug. The raider's laser rifle lay half-buried beneath its body. She dropped to one knee, fingers scrabbling in the muck.

The bug lunged. Olsom rolled sideways, the staff gouging stone where she'd knelt. Her hand closed around the rifle grip. Dead. No charge.

The bug loomed over her, mandibles working. It made a sound like breaking glass, and suddenly she was airborne, the thing's clawed hand wrapped around her throat. Her boots dangled above the ground, lungs burning as she fought for air.

Her hands clawed at its steel grip, fingernails scraping uselessly against its exoskeleton. Black spots danced at the edges of her vision. The bug brought her closer, close enough to see her reflection again and again and again in its compound eyes.

A sticky tube descended from its mouth, pulsing with fluid. It pressed against her face, leaving wet trails across her cheek. The opening moved like lips, forming words that shouldn't have been possible.

"Cannot. Stop… Inevitable."

Her flexscreen chirped, an alert cutting through her fading consciousness. Tac net updates flashed across her forearm. Third Platoon. She tried to turn her head, to see what was coming, but the bug's grip held her fast.

The staff's broken edge hovered centimeters from her eye. So this was how it ended. She'd come so far, survived so much, just to die here.

The wild thing inside her bared its teeth. "Don't matter," she wheezed. "You're still dead." She spat in its face, a mix of blood and saliva that spattered across its mandibles.

Engines screamed overhead, growing louder. A shadow fell across them both.

The bug's head tilted upward. Another shadow fell, bigger, striking it from above.

The impact sent her flying. She landed hard, lungs emptying in a painful rush. Through watering eyes, she saw black armored limbs wrapping around the bug's torso. A hand ripped the speaking tube from its mouth. The other pressed something against the creature's head.

The bug's skull exploded in a fountain of yellow gore.

Both figures crashed to the ground, the bug's legs twitching in death spasms. The armored figure rode it down, then stood in a single fluid motion, holstering a blaster pistol.

Olsom looked up at her savior. The armor wasn't like anything she'd seen before, black reactive plate clicking and shifting with each movement, environmentally sealed and void-proof, a miniaturized power pack humming at its back. A CDF hardsuit. Man-sized and deadly and rare as Vestian river diamonds.

Above them, a combat transport hovered below the storm, stubby wings and long tail cutting an awkward silhouette. Its cargo ramp gaped wide, expelling dark, familiar shapes that plummeted toward the transit. Marine exos—Third Platoon's markings clear on their armored shoulders—hit the ground in a rough formation, FABs tracking outward in a defensive ring. Lessig's voice crackled over her flexscreen, barking coordinates.

The hardsuit's helmet clicked, plates folding back to reveal a face she didn't know. Sharp cheekbones, dark eyes, skin that might have been Respitian but somehow wasn't quite right.

He reached down, armor purring, hauling her to her feet.

"Lieutenant Lee Park, Special Operations, First Marine Division." Park studied her face with something close to pity. "Your ident, Marine?"

"PFC Olsom, sir. Third Squad, Third Platoon, Company—" The lie stopped her. She wasn't one of them, not after all she'd done.

He nodded once, as if he already knew. "Sergeant Bresto. Where is he?"

The blunt question made her jaw clench. This fancy officer with his fancy armor hadn't been there for the capsules, the daxed, the colony. Hadn't been there when everything went to hell. Not like she had. Not like Bresto.

"Still breathing," she said. "He's in there. With his daughter."

"His daughter?" That seemed to surprise him. A smile formed on his face. "I'll be damned."

Bresto shuffled from the ruined vestibule, one arm pressed tight against his side. Kaffy held his other hand, steadying him with each step. Blood had soaked through most of his arm, turning the white and gray sleeve rust brown.

The combat transport—the *Gauntlet*—screamed overhead before setting down hard on the transit. Hot exhaust washed across the stone, raising clouds of steam from the wet surface. The cargo ramp slammed down, more of Third Platoon pouring out in tight formation.

Bresto came to a halt, unable or unwilling to stand at attention. His eyes locked with Park's, something passing between them that Olsom couldn't read. Challenge, maybe. Or blame.

"I see this explains your unauthorized absence, Sergeant," Park said, his tone casual.

Bresto said nothing, just continued that thousand-meter stare.

Park stepped forward, armored plates clicking softly. He took a knee in front of the girl, bringing himself to her eye level.

"What's your name, Aegian?"

The girl stiffened, chin rising slightly. "Kaffy, er, Kaffereine Bresto, sir."

Park blinked. Surprised yet again, it seemed. "I knew a Kaffereine once. She was strong and brave, just like you."

He stood and offered the girl a crisp salute. The girl returned it without hesitation, a smile breaking through the red streaks on her face.

Olsom caught the blank stare in Bresto's eyes a half-second before his legs buckled. She lunged forward, catching him as he dropped to one knee. His skin burned against hers, fever-hot and slick with sweat.

"Sarnt's down," she said, struggling to support his weight. "He's lost a lot of blood."

Park was already working his flexscreen. "Combat engineer to my position. Now." He stepped closer, helping take Bresto's weight. "Come on. Let's get you three out of here."

CHAPTER
FORTY-NINE

DON'T LOSE FAITH.

The words looped on repeat through Bresto's head, kept time with the liquid fire crawling beneath his skin. They'd dosed him with nanites on the flight back. And nanites didn't just heal. They tore. Rebuilt. Every cell they touched became a burning star in his personal galaxy of pain.

Another wave crested through his shoulder, up his neck, into his jaw. He knew the medicine worked. Didn't make having your insides rearranged any easier to take.

He'd tried counting ceiling panels in the triage tent. Lost track somewhere past fifty. Tried counting breaths. Got to forty-three before another surge dragged him under.

Could be worse. He'd seen what happened when medical nanites malfunctioned. His injuries were bad, but well within normal parameters, the med techs had told him. His insides would stay inside.

It had taken several minutes and most of his will to sit upright on the cot. The thinner air at the Diacad drop station made everything harder, but he'd forced himself up anyway. If he was going to have to be there with his own pain and thoughts, might as well take in the view.

Even upslope, the scent of smoke lingered on the thin air. A rebreather lay nearby, in case he needed it, they'd said. He tried to move an arm, test how far the nanites had gone. The limb moved, better than expected, but the burning pain followed a heartbeat later.

Before the med techs had left, he'd managed to get the words out for one of them to open the tent flap. Through it, the storm still dominated the sky, but it had lifted, rising higher over the mountain. Still there, always there, just high enough to let thin beams of light through the gray afternoon, illuminating the steep drop below with cold clarity.

Below the horizon, a blanket of black smoke wove between Vestebrae's ruined towers. One rise up, Corongaet had been turned into a fortress. Black specks plunged through the gray sky, following Dodecoron's steep decline. More dropships. More Marines. The whole damn fleet must be in orbit by now. The bright streaks of their engines cut the air. Their distant wail carried to him, that distinctive two-tone whine of sub-light drives that grew to a teeth-rattling scream as they passed overhead. The sound vibrated in his chest, aggravating his broken ribs.

Park was a son of a bitch, too. He'd come back, even if it was too late to do much good here. Runt had come through, done exactly as he'd said. Not every day he got to order an officer like Park around. The thought made him smirk, which made everything hurt.

Another surge through his chest, this time colder, electric. The nanites were reaching his cracked ribs. He pawed at the rebreather with his good hand, finally hooking a finger over the mask. Too far. The muscles in his hand burned.

A small silhouette appeared in the open flap, hesitant. "Father?"

He tried to smile, felt his lip crack. The blood tasted like copper and antiseptic. He managed something close to a nod, the effort sending fresh spasms down his spine.

"They said you were awake. Can I…?"

He patted the cot with his fingers.

Kaff approached carefully, like he might break if she moved too fast. Such a sweet girl, but not his baby anymore. The plate balanced on her palm as she climbed up beside him, settling at the foot of the cot.

Her meal was CDF standard: field crid and rats. Mass-produced protein block, not cooked well. It sat in a lump, drowned in a pool of lukewarm crid fat.

"I didn't know if you'd be hungry." She poked at it with a fork, then took a bite so desperate it startled him. Her face crumpled. "It doesn't taste as good as yours."

An ember of pride warmed his chest despite the pain. "Not. Hot enough." The hinge of his jaw burned with each syllable.

"Mother says you're going to be okay."

He grunted an affirmative. "Where… is she?"

"With Reserve Command at Vestebrae drop. She said Sammy's coming down from Sienna-Two. They're evacuating all the shelters now. Just in case."

Through the gap, another dropship screamed past, its ventral lights flashing in the dim gray. "How long?"

"Since you found me? About six hours. You slept for most of it. The doc with the injector said you needed it." She set her plate aside, the food barely touched. "I knew you'd come. I told them. I told them my father would come."

The ember in his chest threatened to consume him. Not like his rage, but just as strong. Stronger, maybe.

"It was just like you said. The Holy Mother did it all, Father. She was always there with me. She brought you to me."

He closed his eyes, trying to process her words through the nanite haze. Kaff's transmission had reached Olsom's exo somehow. Ghosting her comms, the Vestian had called it. Something or someone had reached out, made that connection. A little miracle in a world gone to hell.

"I really believe…" Kaff stopped, cheeks turning pink. "I mean, I always believed. But it's… different now."

Bresto reached through the pain, wrapping an arm around her shoulder, warm and solid. Real. He'd found her. Or she'd found him. All the same in the end.

"Proper," he said. "Proper Aegian."

She grinned. "Mother said that, too."

"Yeah." The words tore at his throat, but he forced them out. "Am. Proud."

Outside, an EM trail pierced through the storm and into the heart of Vestebrae. The gray went momentarily white, a flash that caught the edges of the clouds like lightning. A deep, rumbling sound vibrated through the tent, the cot rattling on its supports.

More orbital strikes. The CDF wasn't taking any chances.

Kaff trembled at the sound, throwing her arms around his waist and sending the plate clattering across the tent's thin vinyl floor. Pain exploded through his ribs, but he held her tight. Another flash lit the tent walls, followed by that deep, stomach-churning rumble. Through the gap, he watched the ion trail dissipate into the clouds, a bright line connecting heaven and earth, punctuated by a bloom of destruction.

She buried her face in his side, sobbing quietly, tears soaking through the thin material of his med gown.

The ember in his heart turned to ice. She must've been close when Kull ordered the strike on the transit. Pure luck she'd gotten out of there alive… Maybe the Holy Mother really had saved her. Maybe his daughter had sacrificed enough for a little salvation. Maybe he had, too.

The low hum of hardsuit servos carried through the tent wall before he could speak. Kaff straightened.

"Sergeant," Park said. "Miss Bresto."

"Oh," Kaff said, running a sleeve over her eyes. "Lieutenant."

Park settled into a crouch beside the cot. He reached down and scooped up the fallen plate with an armored hand. He set it beside her, more careful than a hardsuit should be.

"I'm glad to see your father's awake." He turned to Bresto. "How are you feeling?"

"Like shit."

"Sounds about right." Park's laugh was short and genuine. He looked back at Kaff. "Don't worry. Your father's going to be fine. He's been through worse."

Bresto sat up straighter, letting Kaff go. "The fleet?"

"Third Fleet elements arrived two hours ago. Six destroyers, two light carriers. Division's recalling the Lehman's replacement from the patrol lanes. It'll be here tomorrow."

That explained the orbital strikes. The Navy had arrived in force, turning the capitol settlement below into a killbox. Six destroyers, two carriers. CDF Command had sent a fifth of humanity's fleet to Aegia. That wasn't a rescue mission. It was purification.

"Miss Bresto," Park said, his tone shifting subtly. "Would you mind giving us a moment? There are some Colonial Defense matters I need to discuss with your father."

Kaff looked up at him. Everything in him raged against letting her out of his sight, but he managed a nod anyway. Whatever Park had to say, she'd sleep better not knowing it.

"I'll be back soon. Promise." She sniffed, then disappeared around the tent flap.

"She's a remarkable young woman." Park's hardsuit whirred as he stood back up. "But you disobeyed direct orders. You've put our entire mission at risk."

Just like Park to cut straight to the point.

"Situation changed. Sir."

"Your instructions were clear: Runt was to bring you and Sevvers to Bedrock for immediate mission prep. Now we're two days behind schedule with the archenemy inside our patrol lanes."

"My family was down here." He met Park's stare. "The *war* was down here. You wanted to chase signals on some rock… I made a call."

"Some rock?" Park's officer bearing began to chill. "That 'rock' might hold the key to ending this war before it spreads any further. But you decided your personal concerns outweighed operational necessity and almost got yourself killed."

Yeah, he did. And he'd do it again. "Kaff's alive. It worked out."

"For you. For your family, Sergeant, and I am glad for it. But the chain of command exists for a reason. The CDF isn't a capable force if its NCOs get to pick and choose which missions matter."

The rage came flooding back, hot and fast like the nanites in his blood.

"The CDF? Come on, sir. The CDF was here—Victory, the Division, the garrison fleet—trying to stop the Concordat from turning Aegia into Dead Earth! The rest of the fleet couldn't get here fast enough!" Fire tore through his nerves as he jabbed a finger at Park. "*You* were the one confused on priorities."

Too far. He took a breath, aching hands in his lap. One. Two. Three.
Park waited, eyes fixed on him. "Are you finished, Sergeant?"
Always the gentleman.
"No, sir. I'm not."
Park's eyebrows lifted slightly, but he said nothing.
"That derelict mission—what good did it do? We were supposed to find some game-changing intelligence asset, right? Stop the raiders for good. Keep the colonies safe. Instead, we find a Concordat forge ship, lose half our team and lead the archenemy straight to my home."
"We couldn't have known." Park's gaze flicked to the floor and back. "We had solid intelligence of increased raider activity beyond—"
"From who?" Bresto pushed himself up straighter, ribs screaming. "Colonial Intelligence? You don't still believe that do you? Lernus didn't just tag along. She orchestrated the whole thing."
"Dammit, I know that now!" Park spat. He'd hit a nerve. "No one knew the Concordat were still out there. Or that Section Delta even existed. It can't be possible for a mission to go more sideways than ours did, and we still accomplished our objectives and got out of their alive."
"Some of us."
Park's gaze turned cold. "That's the job."
Yes, it was. The mission always came first. But this was Special Ops. There was no excuse for piss poor planning.
"And this next mission, this... asteroid recon," Bresto sneered. "Where'd that intel come from?"
Park's chin lifted like he'd been slapped. Another orbital strike rumbled on the horizon.
"I scraped it from the patrol lane sensor nets myself," he said. "General Strumman's S2 verified it."
Strumman. A Marine's Marine. He was a gray-haired company commander when Bresto enlisted the first time. Now he was a general, and one of only a few serious contenders in line to be the next commandant of the CDF. But Section Delta had changed everything.
"You still trust him?"
"The general is beyond reproach." Park's certainty ended there. "We don't know how many operatives Section Delta has, so we have to

assume they're everywhere. The CDF. Corporate boards. The Founding Council. Anywhere that matters."

"That's a start. Sir."

Two med techs in stained scrubs passed by the open tent, talking casualty counts and supply shortages. The sound of their footsteps faded into the general din of the drop station.

"So, if they're everywhere," Bresto said, "how do you know this asteroid mission isn't just another setup? Another way for Section Delta to move us around the board?"

Park stayed quiet for a long moment.

"I don't." There was an edge of defeat in his tone. Not like him at all. "But we can't just sit here waiting for them to make the next move. If there's something on that rock worth finding, worth fighting for—"

"Worth dying for?" Bresto cut him off. "Because that's what you're asking. Send me and Twelfth knows who else on some crid chase while more forge ships are headed our way."

"One of those ships is going to the same rock we are. That's got to mean something."

"You think. You don't know."

"You're right. I don't know." Park's hardsuit cycled quietly in the silence. "And if you don't trust my judgment on this, Sergeant, then we have a problem. I can't have Marines questioning every order when we're out there."

Twenty years of service, and it came down to this. Maybe Park was just like every other academy skeeg. Obey the officer or get out.

"So here's what I'm offering." Park leaned back slightly, voice going formal. "A clean transfer. Medical grounds, family hardship, take your pick. Stay with Victory. Or join the PR and help with reconstruction. Be there for your children." His gaze never wavered. "No shame in it. You've done enough."

Bresto worked his jaw through the pain. Part of him wanted to take it. Stay on Aegia, help rebuild, watch Kaff and Sammy grow up without wondering if their father would come home this time.

But that wasn't really what Park was offering, was it? This was about whether he could follow orders from someone who'd already been played once by Section Delta. Park needed Marines who wouldn't question, wouldn't hesitate, wouldn't think too hard about who was really pulling the strings. The kind of blind faith that had gotten them into this mess in the first place.

"But if you come with me," Park continued, "you follow orders. Even when you think they're wrong. Even when you don't know where they came from. Because out there, doubt gets you killed."

And there it was. The choice Park was really offering: blind obedience or discharge. But maybe there was a third option.

"I'll go." He shifted on the cot. "I'll follow your orders. But I won't pretend everything's fine when it's not. Not with Section Delta and the Concordat in play. If something doesn't add up, I'm going to say something. You can count on that. Because out there, sir, blind faith gets people killed too. And we've both seen what happens when we don't ask enough questions."

Something like relief flashed on Park's face then vanished without a trace.

"I'm not asking for blind faith. Question the mission all you want. Question the intelligence. Hell, pull me aside and question me if you think I'm wrong. But when I give an order, I need to know you'll follow it without hesitation. So your Marines will follow you the same way. So we can accomplish the mission and go home." He paused. "Can you live with that?"

Bresto took another calming breath. Park was giving ground here, acknowledging their earlier mistakes. It wasn't the blind obedience he'd seemed to want earlier. Combat orders were different. In a firefight, there wasn't time for debate. He'd always followed those anyway. The real issue was the bigger picture, the mission itself, and Park wasn't asking him to shut up about that.

It was more than he'd expected to get after what he'd done.

"Yes sir." Bresto nodded slowly. "I can live with that."

"Very well." Park moved toward the tent opening, then stopped. "Runt's waiting on Pad Nine. We leave in six hours. Get some rest, Sergeant. You'll need it."

The lieutenant paused at the threshold, then stepped through. The tent flap settled behind him with barely a whisper.

The wolf would be there, tending to the *Gauntlet* like a fretting pack mother. Checking the engine relays, running diagnostics. Runt never stopped working. Never questioned the mission. The team *was* her family; whoever was on it.

Another orbital strike lit the sky, this one distant enough that he felt rather than heard it. The vibration traveled through the mountain, through the cot frame, up his spine.

Time slipped sideways. The tent darkened as clouds shifted, cutting off what little light had made it through. His mind drifted, pulled by fever and nanites toward places he didn't want to go. Kaff's face melted into Lyra's, then Sammy's, then darkness.

———

The tent flap moved. Bresto blinked, trying to bring the new visitor into focus. How long had he been sitting there?

Olsom stood framed in the opening, thin and pale in CDF-issue shorts, tank top, and black synthweave boots. Med patches dotted her arms, the skin around them ghost-white against the angry red of fresh wounds. Trauma wrap oozed red on her stomach. A purple-black bruise circled her throat like a collar.

She barely looked like a Marine now. No combat uniform, no military bearing. Just a skinny, gnarled eps with broad shoulders and too many scars for her age, hair still damp from a recent field shower. She leaned against the tent pole.

"Still breathin'." Her voice was hoarse.

He grunted. "You look like shit."

"Yeah?" Her split lip curled into a mean grin. "You should see the other guy."

The storm winds picked up, cool and smelling of wet stone. Neither of them spoke, the silence broken only by the distant whine of drop-ship engines and the rumble of detonations. Her quiet stare had changed. Harder. Angrier. She wasn't a boot anymore—proper bloodied—but still just a kid.

"Saw Park come by." She crossed her arms, hesitated, then uncrossed them. "Guess that means you're leaving again, huh?"

A flash of shame burned through him. He hadn't planned to hit her, but Kaff's desperate transmission had squeezed his focus. He needed the exo, and Olsom was in the way. He'd just… reacted. But the PFC gave almost as good as she got. And here she was, upset he was leaving again. Whatever kind of broken she was, the girl had more scars than he could see.

"What do you want?"

She looked up at him, brown eyes smoldering. "I want to go with you."

His chest tightened. Take another boot into the void? No. Not happening. Not after all the death he'd seen. Especially not some kid with abandonment issues written all over her.

He studied her, taking inventory of what he'd cost her. Bruised face. Split lip and swollen nose from his own fist. And yet here she was, ready to follow him. She'd saved his ass in that shelter. Kaff's too. Pulled them out while those masked things were crawling over them. Risked her own skin for his without question.

"I'm good with a rig. You know I am," she blurted. "But I keep fucking up here. I… I don't fit in."

"That's the job." He shrugged, ignoring the nanite burn in his spine. "Your mountains don't get any smaller. Up and over, it's the only way."

"The *job*? What exactly? Stand post while Revan and the other mountain folk act like they're better than me? Go back to being Third Platoon's Vestian feral?"

She stepped inside the tent, jaw set tight. "I just hauled your old ass out of that shelter. I helped save your daughter. All while those masked freaks—" Her voice cracked slightly. "And now you're throwing me back again? After all that?"

No denying she'd saved him. That didn't change a thing. Sometimes people needed saving from themselves.

"Everyone out there's got something to fight for here," she went on, jerking a thumb toward the gray skyline. Her voice dropped, edged with something raw. "A home. A… family. I've got nothing but the want to kill more of those damn things."

His ribs twinged, nanites still rewriting his insides. Sevvers had backed his play on the derelict. Another kid with a grudge who should've known better. And now Olsom was asking for the same privilege. The honor of dying out in the black, like the rest of his last fireteam. No parade detail. No honors. Just gone. The truth of it classified need-to-know.

The fire in her eyes didn't die so much as freeze over. She knew what he was thinking.

But she'd gone through twelve hells and come out the other side. Vestians were built different. Not tougher—nothing was harder than Aegian granite—but they bent where others might crack. Adapted. Survived. There was something in that Vestian stubbornness he'd come to respect. First in Dalon. Now in her.

And she was right about one thing: Park's mission would need killers. Real ones. This wasn't some regular patrol, not with the Concordat and Section Delta in the mix. He needed someone to watch his six. Maybe even someone who'd go back for his body when this all went sideways.

Something flickered in his memory—Runt's words on the *Victory*. *Pups need pack.* The wolf had been right. Maybe it was time to stop fighting what the Holy Mother was trying to give him.

"PFC Olsom." He took another labored breath. "You've never done deep void ops."

"No, Sarnt."

"It's quiet out there. Cold. The kind of cold that makes you forget there's a home to come back to."

She stood up straighter, determination written across every line of her face. "I'll pack a sweater."

Fine, the boot was in. Twelfth save them both.

"Report to Pad Nine in one hour. Take only what you need. We'll gear up when we get where we're going."

Her face settled into that serious, solemn look that reminded him why she'd survived. Why he'd picked her the first time.

"Aye, Sarnt."

A heartbeat later she was gone, leaving nothing but the flap swinging in her wake and the lingering scent of soap, blood, and something like hope. Hope for the mission. For the girl. For himself.

The silence she left pressed against his eardrums, interrupt by the lazy rustle of the tent flap, until more dropships began their relentless descent toward the settlement below.

His breaths slowly came easier. The nanites had done their work on his lungs, moving on to other damage. He tested his left arm, felt it respond with only a dull ache rather than searing pain.

Another test. Fingers curling, uncurling. The motion fluid enough. His legs next, muscles tensing, knees bending and straightening. They would hold him, in time.

Time he didn't have. *A few hours*, Park had said.

He sat up, straight and fast, and slipped off the cot. His feet touched the ground, cold through the thick socks someone had put on him. The world spun for two heartbeats before steadying.

Pad Nine. Runt was waiting.

The med tent's spare furnishings had what he needed; a new set of white-and-grays folded neatly on a chair, a fresh pair of boots on the deck beneath them.

Dressing took longer than it should have. Each movement was a negotiation with pain. But the nanites had done their job. He wasn't dying. Everything still functioned. Serviceable, Mace would've said. Good enough for Navy work.

The gray afternoon greeted him through the open flap. The air bit at his lungs, too thin and cold, but the rebreather stayed behind. He didn't need it anymore.

He looked past the cluster of triage tents toward the drop station's landing pads, scanning their outlines until he found it. The *Gauntlet's* distinctive silhouette marked what must've been Pad Nine, engines already spinning with pre-flight checks.

One more test. His legs took his weight, moved forward without complaint. The first step was the hardest. The second easier. By the third, he was already thinking about what came next.

A PR transport, engine groaning a low idle, had rolled up to the temporary receiving area. A small figure climbed down, hand extended to someone below. Sammy, Kaff helping him off the vehicle's high step. Even from this distance, he could see his son's cautious movements, the rebreather fixed to his face against the mountain's thin air.

They were here. Good. That meant time for goodbyes. Time to explain what couldn't be explained. They would understand, someday. Lyra already did, in her way. She'd seen the same truths written in the smoke rising from their home. The Concordat wouldn't stop here, and Section Delta couldn't be trusted. This war had only just begun.

He picked up his pace. There was pain, yes, but the clarity of purpose burned brighter now. The mountain wind caught at his uniform, cold and pure against his face. Aegia stretched below him—the shield of humanity—cracked but not broken.

Park had been right about one thing. He needed Marines he could trust. Two were better than none. But it wasn't enough. Not by a long shot.

Holy Mother save them. They would need Her most of all. Another gust of wind blew past him, like a whisper off dry lips.

Don't lose faith.

The battle for Aegia may be over, but the war for the Three Colonies has only just begun.

Bresto and Olsom will return in Colonial Defense Marines Book 2, coming in 2026.

AFTERWORD

Thank you for reading my military sci-fi novel *Hard Drop*.

If you enjoyed it, please leave a Goodreads review. Reviews help readers like yourself find books they'll love. I would be grateful for your support in helping them find mine.

Talk soon.

Brian

ACKNOWLEDGMENTS

To my amazing little sci-fi community at brkeid.com. Thank you for all your support. Whether with ARC reviews, beta reading, or just a kind note in my inbox, know that it is all much appreciated.

To my production team: Lisa Poisso, book coach and editor, and Kristin McTiernan, editor, marketing guru, and critique group queen, and the cover design folks at Damonza. Y'all are amazing for bringing this novel to life.

To my son Bevan, my biggest fan, who doesn't have to listen to me so much these days since graduating and moving on to bigger and better things. I'm so proud of you.

To my wife Mary, for putting up with my countless hours at the keyboard. I love you.

And, of course, to Mom. Lost no more.

Thank you all.

ABOUT THE AUTHOR

B.R. Keid is an engineer, Marine veteran, and daydreamer who has worked and lived all over the United States, meeting all kinds of people and enjoying their stories. He now makes his home in the rural Midwest, where he farms together with the love of his life, his two grown children who should visit more often, two spoiled German Shepherds, and an assortment of rowdy livestock, including one particularly opinionated goose.